PERSONAL INJURIES

ALSO BY SCOTT TUROW

The Laws of Our Fathers (1996)

Pleading Guilty (1993)

The Burden of Proof (1990)

Presumed Innocent (1987)

One L (1977)

Published by Warner Books

PERSONAL INJURIES

SCOTT TUROW

WARNER
VISION
BOOKS

A Time Warner Company

WARNER BOOKS EDITION

Copyright © 1999 by Scott Turow
All rights reserved. No part of this book may be reproduced in any form or by any electronic or mechanical means, including information storage and retrieval systems, without permission in writing from the publisher, except by a reviewer who may quote brief passages in a review.

A portion of the book appeared, in slightly different form, in Playboy magazine.

A signed first edition of this book has been privately printed by The Franklin Library.

Lyrics from "Yesterday," by John Lennon and Paul McCartney, are quoted with the permission of Sony/ATV Music Publishing. Copyright © 1965 (renewed) Sony/ATV Songs LLC. All rights reserved.

Lyrics from "A Bushel and a Peck," by Frank Loesser, are quoted with the permission of the Hal Leonard Corp. Copyright © 1950 (renewed) FRANK MUSIC CORP. All rights reserved.

This edition is published by arrangement with Farrar, Straus and Giroux

Warner Vision is a registered trademark of Warner Books, Inc.

Cover design by Diane Luger and Rachel McClain
Cover photo by Geoff Spear

Warner Books, Inc.
1271 Avenue of the Americas
New York, NY 10020

Visit our Web site at
www.twbookmark.com

 A Time Warner Company

Printed in the United States of America

First International Paperback Printing: September 2000
First Warner Books Printing: December 2000

10 9 8 7 6 5 4 3 2 1

FOR GAIL HOCHMAN

PAM WINDS INDIA INTERNAL PRINTING 2000

10 9 8 7 6 5 4 3 2 1

Welcome, thou kind deceiver!
Thou best of thieves; who with an easy key
Dost open life, and unperceived by us,
Even steal us from ourselves.

JOHN DRYDEN, All for Love

THE BEGINNING

THE BEGINNING

the contrary, most of them felt, with good reason, that

CHAPTER 1

HE KNEW IT WAS WRONG, AND THAT HE
was going to get caught. He said he knew this day was
coming.

He knew they had been stupid, he told me—worse,
greedy. He said he knew he should have stopped. But somehow, each time he thought they'd quit, he'd ask himself
how once more could make it any worse. Now he knew
he was in trouble.

I recognized the tune. Over twenty-some years, the folks
sitting in that leather club chair in front of my desk have
found only a few old standards in the jukebox. I Didn't
Do It. The Other One Did It. Why Are They Picking on
Me. His selection, I'm Sorry, made the easiest listening.
But they all wanted to hear the same song from me: Maybe
I Can Get You Out of This. I said it usually, although I
knew it would often prove untrue. But it's a complicated
business being somebody's only hope.

This is a lawyer's story, the kind attorneys like to hear
and tell. About a case. About a client. His name was Robert

Feaver. Everyone knew him as Robbie, although he was getting old for that kind of thing, forty-three, he'd said, when I asked his age. The time was 1992, the second week in September. The pundits had finally stopped predicting that Ross Perot was going to be the next President of the United States, and the terms "dot" and "com" had not yet been introduced to one another. I recall the period precisely because the week before I had returned to Virginia to lay my father to rest. His passing, which over the years I'd assumed I would take as being in the natural order of things, had instead imbued all my waking moments with the remote quality of dreams, so that even my hand, when I considered it, seemed disconnected from my body.

Robbie Feaver's troubles were more immediate. Last night, three Special Agents of the Internal Revenue Service's Criminal Intelligence Division had visited him at home—one to talk and two to listen. They were, as you would expect, rumpled men in inexpensive sport coats, grave but polite. They had handed him a grand jury subpoena for all of his law partnership's financial records and tried to ask Robbie questions about his income tax returns. Wisely, he had refused to reply.

He could suit himself, responded the one agent who spoke. But they wanted to tell him a couple things. Good news and bad. Bad first.

They knew. They knew what Robbie and his law partner, Morton Dinnerstein, had been up to. They knew that for several years the two had occasionally deposited a check they received when they won or settled one of their personal injury cases in a secret account at River National Bank, where the firm transacted no other business. They knew that out of the River National account Dinnerstein and Robbie had paid the usual shares of what they'd earned—two thirds to the clients, one ninth to the referring attorneys, odd amounts to experts or court reporters.

Everyone had received his due. Except the IRS. They knew that for years now, Feaver and his partner had been writing checks to cash to draw down the balance of the account, never paying a dime in tax.

You guys are cold-cocked, the agent added. Robbie laughed now, very briefly, repeating the words.

I didn't ask how Robbie and his partner could have ever believed a scheme so simpleminded would work. I was long accustomed to the dumb ways people get themselves in trouble. Besides, the fact was that their scam had operated smoothly for years. A checking account that paid no interest was unlikely to come to the Service's attention. It was, frankly, noteworthy that it had, a development that would inevitably be traced to freak coincidence, or, if things were spicier, betrayal.

Feaver had heard out the agents in his living room. He was perched on a camelback sofa smartly upholstered in bleached silk, trying to contain himself. To smile. Stay slick. He opened his mouth to speak but was interrupted by the unexpected sensation of a single cold rill of his own sweat tracking the length of his side until it was absorbed in the elastic waistband of his boxers.

And the good news? he asked on second effort.

They were getting to that, the agent said. The good news was that Robbie had an opportunity. Maybe there was something he could do for himself. Something that a person with his family situation ought to consider.

The agent then walked across the marble foyer and opened the front door. The United States Attorney, Stan Sennett, was standing on Robbie's doorstep. Feaver recognized him from TV, a short man, slender, kempt with a compulsive orderliness. A few gnats zagged madly under the light above the careful part in Sennett's head. He greeted Feaver with his in-court expression, humorless as a hatchet blade.

Robbie had never practiced a day of criminal law, but he knew what it meant that the United States Attorney was standing in person on his front stoop late at night. It meant the biggest gun was pointed straight at him. It meant they wanted to make him an example. It meant he'd never get away.

In his terror, Robbie Feaver found a single useful thought.

I want a lawyer, he said.

He was entitled, Sennett finally responded. But perhaps Robbie should listen to him first. As soon as Sennett set a polished brogan across the threshold, Robbie repeated himself.

I can't promise the deal will be the same tomorrow, Sennett told him.

Lawyer, Feaver said again.

The agents took over then, offering advice. If he was going to an attorney, find a good one, someone who'd been around. Talk to that lawyer—and no one else. Not Mom. Not the wife. And certainly not his law partner, Dinnerstein. The U.S. Attorney passed one agent his card, and the agent handed it to Feaver. Sennett would be waiting for Feaver's lawyer's call. About to step down into the darkness, the prosecutor asked over his shoulder whether Robbie had anyone in mind.

Interesting choice, Sennett told Feaver with a shallow smile when he heard my name.

"I'm not a rat," Robbie Feaver said now. "That's the play, right, George? They want me to dime somebody out."

I asked if he had any idea who.

"Well, it better not be Mort. My partner? Never. There's nothing to say about Mort."

Feaver and Dinnerstein were lifelong friends, he told me, next-door neighbors as boys growing up in the Jewish enclave of Warren Park, here in DuSable, roommates through college and law school. But their secret account was joint, both men had made deposits and written the checks to cash, and neither had reported the income. There was enough damaging paper that it seemed unlikely the IRS was going to need anyone's assistance to install either one of them in the trophy case.

I asked if there might be something else the government wanted Robbie to tell them about Mort, or any other person, but Feaver hitched a shoulder limply, looking lost.

I did not know Robbie Feaver well. When he'd called this morning, he'd reminded me that we'd met several times in the lobby of the LeSueur Building where we each had our law offices, and of the committee work he'd done for the Kindle County Bar Association a couple of years ago during my term as president. My memories of him were vague and not necessarily pleasant. Measured according to the remaining reflexes of a proper Southern upbringing, he was the kind of fellow who'd be described simply as 'too much.' Too good-looking in the sense that he was too well aware of it. Too much stiff, dark hair that reflected too much fussing. He was tanned in every season and spent too much money on his clothes—high-styled Italian suits and snazzy foulards—accompanied by too much jewelry. He spoke too loudly, and too eagerly to strangers in the elevator. In fact, in any setting, he talked too much—one of those people who went one up on Descartes: I speak, therefore I am. But I now saw one apparent virtue: he could have told you all of that. Diminished by fear, he maintained an air of candor, at least about himself. As clients went, therefore, he seemed, on first impression, better than average.

When I asked what the agent had meant about his family, he sagged a bit.

"Sick wife," he said, "sick mother." Waging a running war against the medical establishment, Feaver, like many personal injury attorneys, had absorbed the lexicon of physicians. His mother was in a nursing home. "CVA," he said, meaning a stroke. His wife, Lorraine, was worse. She had been diagnosed nearly two years ago with amyotrophic lateral sclerosis—ALS, or more commonly Lou Gehrig's disease—and was on a certain downward course toward total paralysis and, eventually, death.

"She's got a year maybe before things get really hairy, no one knows for sure." He was stoical but his black eyes did not rise from the carpet. "I mean, I can't leave her. Not practically. There's nobody else to take care of her."

That was the agent's point. Feaver would talk or be in the penitentiary when his wife reached the point of total helplessness or passed. The dark shroud of that prospect fell over us both.

In the resulting silence, I picked up Sennett's card, which Feaver had laid on my desk. Without it, I might have questioned whether Robbie had identified the right man on his doorstep. The United States Attorney, with ninety-two assistants and several hundred cases to supervise, would ordinarily have no direct role in a straightforward tax case, even one against a successful personal injury lawyer. Whatever Stan Sennett had come to Robbie's house to say last night must have been a mouthful.

"What did it mean," Feaver asked, "when Sennett said that George Mason would be an interesting choice? Does he hate your guts or think you're a pushover?"

It was complicated, I responded. I believed in some moods Stan would say I was a close friend.

"Well, that's good, then, isn't it?" Feaver asked.

When it came to Stan Sennett, I never knew the answer. Sometimes friends, I told Feaver. Always rivals.

CHAPTER 2

IN THE FASHION OF MOST HIGH-RANKING bureaucrats, the United States Attorney's personal office was vast. The shag carpeting was tattered at places into little raveled strands, and the drapes of greenish raw silk had covered the wall of windows on the north since sometime in the fifties. But the space could be measured by the acre. There was a bathroom, with a shower, and a hideaway study. In the corners of the principal space, a sturdy government-issue conference table stood on one side, while across the room various endangered species, seized by Fish and Wildlife inspectors from a rogue taxidermist, were displayed in a long row of mahogany cases. A bald eagle and a spotted snake adjoined something that looked like a marmoset. Behind a desk the size of a tomb, Stan Sennett, one of those dark, driven little men who turn up so often in the law, rose to greet me.

"Hey there, Georgie," he said. I attributed this rare mood of impressive good cheer to Stan's eagerness to talk about Feaver.

"Blue stuff," I told his secretary when she offered coffee. We loitered a minute over personal details. Stan showed off the photos of his only child, Asha, a three-year-old girl, dark and gorgeous, whom Stan and his second wife, Nora Flinn, had adopted after years of futile fertility treatments and in vitro. I recounted the leisurely progress of my two sons through their higher educations, and bragged for a second about my wife, Patrice, an architect who had just won an international design competition to build a spectacular art museum in Bangkok. Stan, who'd been stationed in Thailand in 1966, told me a few funny stories about the country.

In his most relaxed moments, Stan Sennett could be a delight, a stylish wit, an amusing collector of arcane facts, and a canny observer of the fur-licking and hissing in local political circles. The rest of the time, you had to deal with a more complicated package—a thousand-megahertz mind, and a potful of seething emotions liable to scald anybody nearby before Stan managed to slam down the lid.

He had graduated first in our class at Easton Law School. At the bar, it is possible to travel forever in the slipstream of law school success; but Stan had bypassed the riches or policy pinnacles in Washington that usually reward his kind of legal intellect. He was a prosecutor. After clerking for Chief Justice Burger, he had returned to Kindle County to join the Prosecuting Attorney's Office, rising on indisputable merit until he became Raymond Horgan's Chief Deputy. In the early eighties, when his first marriage dissolved, he joined the U.S. Justice Department. He went first to San Diego, then D.C., and had just returned to California when President Bush named him U.S. Attorney here. He had established relations with local law enforcement agencies and no political ambitions. He therefore had figured to make it through his four-year term, which would end next year, uncompromised by the cabals and rivalries that had broken out after the death of our legendary Mayor and County Executive, Augustine Bolcarro.

Like most persons, I was wary of Stan's lethal side, but we had always been companions in the law. As students, we shared our learning: he informed me of the deeper implications of the cases we studied; I was, so far as I know, the first person to tell him that a gentleman did not tuck his necktie into his trousers. In practice, we had been ongoing opponents since he became a deputy P.A. while I was in my first legal job with the State Defenders. At all times, we were tied together by a mutual admiration that bordered on envy. My casual, highborn manner, a false front in my eyes and thus always something of a burden, represented an ideal, I think, to Sennett, for whom sincerity and charm were mutually exclusive. I was impressed, first, by Stan's abilities, but even more by his committed sense of high purpose.

Some in the defense bar, like my friend Sandy Stern, could not abide Sennett's sanctimony or his ham-handed methods, such as his late-night intrusion on Feaver. But Stan was the first U.S. Attorney in my quarter of a century here who was fearlessly independent. He'd begun a long-overdue era of zero tolerance for the scams and dirty dealing that were forever viewed as a perk of local office, and he took on the mighty commercial interests, like Moreland Insurance, the largest private employer in Kindle County, whom Stan had nonetheless prosecuted for fraud. Sennett's agenda, in short, had been to let the light of the law into the crabbed corners of Kindle County, and, as his friend, I often found myself applauding behind the mask of horror I was required to wear as a defense lawyer.

Eventually, he turned to my new client.

"Odd fellow, I take it," Stan said with a calculating glimpse my way. We both knew that, even dressed up in Armani, Robbie Feaver was your basic Kindle County hustler, complete with South End accent and too much cologne. "No, he must be peculiar. Because what they did with that account over at River National was pretty strange. The partnership of Feaver & Dinnerstein hasn't reported an annual income of less than one mil for a decade. Four's been more the average. I hope you knew that, George, when you set your retainer." A sweet little smile zipped by, the proper revenge of a man who's lived his life within the confines of a government salary. "Odd to be chiseling forty K on taxes when you're showing numbers like that, isn't it?"

I dipped a shoulder. The explanation would never make sense to anyone but them, yet over the years I had learned that it was only the poor whose desire for money was bounded by pure reason.

"And here's something stranger, George. They'll go months sometimes without a hit on this account, then boom, it's ten, fifteen thousand in cash inside a week. And in the meantime, George, they both bang their ATMs on a regular basis. So why this sudden appetite for currency?" Stan asked. "And where's it going?"

Offshore. Drugs. The usual. Not to mention more eternal vices not banned by the federal criminal code.

"Something on the side?" asked Stan, when I suggested that alternative. "And how. Your fellow needs an odometer on his zipper." He rolled his eyes, as if he no longer recalled that it was a weakness for one of the secretaries at the P.A.'s Office that had ended his first marriage. I mentioned the sick wife and Sennett chuckled archly. Robbie Feaver, he said, had been enshrined long before in the Hall of Fame down on Grand Avenue, the strip of high-end watering holes often referred to as the Street of Dreams.

"But Mort's a solid family man," he said. "And your guy sees more beds than a hotel maid. He's not paying any tootsie's rent. So that's not where the money's going. Wanna know my theory, George? I think it's the cash they're hiding. Not the income."

Sennett unbent a paper clip and twirled it between his fingers. Behind the huge desk, he was smug as a fat house cat. Here was the Essential Stan, the dark narrow boy always in a heat to reestablish himself as the smartest person he knew. He had been born Constantine Nicholas Sennatakis and was raised in back of the family restaurant. 'You've been there,' he'd told me dryly when we met in law school. 'Menu pages coated in plastic and one of the relatives chained to the cash register.' During his induction as U.S. Attorney, he had misted over recounting his parents' struggles. But for the most part, all that ethnic opera, all that carrying on, was self-consciously left behind. Stan's public persona was as the sort of man who barely snapped his fingers when music played; in private, with friends and colleagues, he was apt to take on the droll pose of a grumpy initiate soiled by knowing it all. Yet to me, although it was shrewdly disguised, Stan remained full of teeming immigrant striving. His entire world was often at stake in a case, as if he had an inescapable obligation to rise and prosper at every opportunity. As a result, he suffered his losses far more intensely than he savored his many achievements. But he clearly knew he was winning now.

"Aren't you going to ask how I stumbled over these fellas and their private cash machine?" I would have, had I thought he'd answer. But apparently Stan was having too much fun today to indulge his usual secretiveness. "Our friends at Moreland Insurance," said Sennett. "They got our whiskers twitching."

I might have thought of that. Stan's fabled prosecution of Moreland for a series of fraudulent sales practices with which the company had gallivanted through the eighties concluded with the insurer sentenced to a staggering fine— more than $30 million—and also to a period of probation during which they were obliged to cooperate with the U.S. Attorney in correcting any wrongdoing they knew of. I was not surprised to find that Moreland had taken the opportunity to tattle not only on themselves but also on their natural enemies, plaintiffs' lawyers.

In almost every personal injury suit, the real defendant is an insurance company. You may sue the neighbor whose tree fell on your house, but it's his insurance company who'll pay the damages and hire the defense attorneys, and which often feels antagonized by the lawyer on the other side. I realized that, in all likelihood, it was one of the checks Moreland had issued over the years to Feaver & Dinnerstein that had been trailed to the partners' secret bank account. Unfortunately, though, Moreland's records had revealed more than that.

"Your guy's a tough opponent," Stan said. "Somehow, every time Moreland has a big case against these fellas, the company just can't win a ruling. By now they've learned to settle. Especially since any lawsuit where your guy is looking at a six-figure fee always ends up in front of one of a handful of judges. And guess what? We crawled through the records in the courthouse and it turns out the pattern holds for other companies. Whenever Feaver & Dinnerstein has a big payday coming, it's the same deal: bad rulings, big settlements. And the same four distinguished jurists on their cases, George—even though there are nineteen judges sitting in the Common Law Claims Division, all of whom are supposed to be assigned to matters at random." Sennett issued a stiff look. "Know now where I'm thinking the cash is going, George?"

I knew. Rumors of funny business had lingered like some untraceable foundation odor in the Kindle County courthouses since I'd arrived here for law school. But no one had ever proved it. The judges who took were said to be carefully insulated. There were bagmen and code words.

And the lawyers who paid told no tales. It was, by report, a small faction, a secret society whose alliances were fierce and ancient, going back decades to high schools, churches, to the Prosecuting Attorney's Office in its bad old days, to union halls, or, even, mob connects. And always the bonds were fired in the overheated politics of the Party.

These grumpy suspicions were often repeated by the losers in Kindle County's courtrooms. But in my more innocent moments, I liked to discount them, believing that cronyism, not cash, explained the obvious favoritism I, like every other lawyer, had witnessed on occasion over the years. For my client's sake, I was skeptical now.

"I'll tell you what clinches it for me," Stan replied. "Morton Dinnerstein's uncle is Brendan Tuohey." Sennett took a beat to let the portent of the name gather. "Brendan's older sister is Mort Dinnerstein's mother. She raised Brendan after their mom kicked the bucket. Devoted to her, he is. And to her son. Looks to me like Tuohey's given nephew Morty a real helping hand."

As Stan expected, he'd caught me by surprise. When I'd arrived in Kindle County in the late 1960s, a Tuohey marrying a Dinnerstein was still thought of as miscegenation. More to the point, Brendan Tuohey now was the Presiding Judge of the Common Law Claims Division, where all personal injury cases were heard. A former cop and ex-deputy Prosecuting Attorney, Brendan was celebrated for his intricate political connections, his general Celtic amity, and his occasional bare-knuckles meanness. In most quarters, among reporters, for example, he was renowned as able and tough but fair. Tuohey's name was the one most often mentioned when people speculated about who would eventually replace old Judge Mumphrey and wield the vast powers of the Chief of the entire Kindle County Superior Court. I'd had my ears scratched by Brendan during my year as Bar President. But both Stan and I could recall

Tuohey's tenure long ago in the Felony Division, when there were persistent rumors that he was often visited in chambers by Toots Nuccio, a reputed fixer.

I asked, mildly, if Stan thought it was fair to condemn Robbie Feaver because of his partner's relatives, but by now Sennett had lost patience with my temporizing.

"Just do your job, George. And I'll do mine. Talk to your guy. There's something there. We can both see that. If he gets religion, we'll cut him a break. If he sees no evil and speaks no evil, he's going to the penitentiary for evasion. For as long as I can send him. And with these kinds of dollars, we're talking several years. He's got his chance now. If he doesn't take it, don't come groveling in six months, strumming your lyre about the poor wife and her miserable condition."

Stan set his chin against his chest and eyed me gravely, having become the Stan Sennett few people liked, or could even deal with. Behind him, out the window, a boom swung on an immense construction crane a block away, carrying a beam and some daredevil ironworker riding on it. In this town, they were all American Indians, who, reputedly, knew no fear. I envied them that. Somehow my father's death had sharpened my lifelong concern about my lack of daring.

In the meantime, Stan took my silence for crusty disdain. It was one of the occasional rewards of our friendship that he was vulnerable to my opinion of him, perhaps because he knew so much of it was favorable.

"Did I offend you?" he asked.

No more than usual, I assured him.

He rumpled his lips and stood. I thought he was going to show me out. Stan was famous for that, for abruptly announcing a meeting was over. But instead he perched on his long mahogany desk's front corner. I remembered yet again that I had always wanted to ask how he got to four-thirty in the afternoon with his white shirt unwrinkled. But the moment, as usual, wasn't right.

"Listen," he said. "I want to tell you a story. Do you mind? This is a real chest-thumper, so get ready. Did you ever hear the one about when I knew I was going to be a prosecutor?"

I didn't believe I had.

"Well, I don't tell it often. But I'm going to tell it now. It has to do with my father's brother, Petros, Peter the kids called him. Uncle Peter was the black sheep. He ran a newspaper stand instead of a restaurant." That was meant to be a joke, and Stan briefly permitted himself a less constricted smile. "You want to talk about hard work—I listen to young lawyers around here pull all-nighters and complain about hard work—that, my friend, *that* was hard work. Up at 4 a.m. Standing in this little corner shack in the worst kind of weather. Bitter cold. Rain, sleet. Always there. Handing out papers and collecting nickels. He did that twenty years. Finally, near the age of forty, Petros was ready to make his move. Guys he knew had a gas station down here on Duhaney and Plum. Right in Center City. Place was a gold mine. And they were getting out. And Petros bought it. He took every nickel he had, all that he'd saved from twenty years of humping. And then of course it turned out there were a few things Uncle Peter didn't know. Like the fact that the corner, the whole damn block actually, was scheduled for condemnation under the new Center City Plan, which was announced only two or three days after Uncle Peter closed. I mean, it was a flat-out no-good, dirty Kindle County fraud. And every drachma the guy had was gone.

"I was only a kid, but hell, I'd read my civics book. I said to him, Uncle Petros, why don't you go to court, sue? And he looked at me and he laughed. He said, 'A poor man like me? I can't afford to buy a judge.' Not 'I can't afford a lawyer.' Although he couldn't. But he realized that anybody who knew in advance what the Center City Plan provided couldn't be beaten in the Kindle County Superior Courthouse.

"And I decided then I was going to be a prosecutor. Not just an attorney. A prosecutor. I knew suddenly it was the most important thing I could do, to make sure that the Petroses of the universe stopped getting screwed. I'd catch the corrupt judges and the lawyers who paid them, and all the other bad guys who made the world so lousy and unfair. That's what I told myself when I was thirteen years old."

Sennett paused to regather himself, absently fingering the braiding carved beneath the lip of the desk. This was Stan at his best and he knew he was impressive.

"Now, this crap has gone on too long in this county. Too many good people have looked the other way, hoping to persuade themselves it's not true. But it is. Or telling themselves that it's better than the bad old days. Which is no kind of excuse." Somewhere in there, as he had bent closer for emphasis, my heart had squirmed. But it was ardor that energized him, not any kind of rebuke. "And so I've been watching. And waiting. And now I've got my chance. Augie Bolcarro is dead and this stuff is going to die with him. Hear this carefully, because I'll get that son of a bitch Tuohey and his whole nasty cohort, or flame out trying. I'm not going to send a couple of low-level schmoes to the joint and let Tuohey become head of the court in a year and do it all again, on a bigger scale, which is how it's always gone around here.

"And I know how people talk about me. And I know what they think. But it's not for the greater glory of Stan Sennett. You know the saying? 'If you shoot at the king, you better kill the king'?"

A paraphrase, I told him, of Machiavelli. Stan tossed that around a second, not certain he liked the comparison.

"Well, if I shoot at Tuohey and miss—*if* I miss, George—I'll have to leave town when I step down from this job. I know that. No law firm in its right mind will go near me. Because neither I nor they will be able to set foot in state court.

"But I'm going to do it anyway. Because I'm not going to have this go on unchallenged. Not on my watch. You will forgive me, George. You will please forgive me. But it's what I owe my Uncle Petros and all the other people of this county and this district. George," he said, "it's what's goddamned right."

CHAPTER 3

"HOW THIS STARTED," ROBBIE FEAVER SAID, "is not what you think. Morty and I didn't go to Brendan and say, Take care of us. We didn't have anything to take care of, not to start with. Mort and I had been bumping along on workmen's comp and slip-and-fall cases. Then about ten years ago, even before Brendan was appointed Presiding Judge over there, we got our first real chance to score. It was a bad-baby case. Doc with a forceps treated the kid's head like a walnut. And it's the usual warfare. I got a demand of 2.2 million, which brings in the umbrella insurer, so they're underwriting the defense. And they know I'm not Peter Neucriss. They're making us spend money like there's a tree in the backyard. I've got to get medical experts. Not one. Four. O.B. Anesthesia. Pedes. Neurology. And courtroom blowups. We've got $125,000 in expenses, way more than we can afford. We're into the bank for the money, Mort and me, with seconds on both our houses."

I had heard the story several times now. This rendition was for Sennett's benefit, a proffer, an off-the-record session in which Stan had the chance to evaluate Robbie for himself. It was a week after I'd visited Stan in his office and we sat amid the plummy brocades of a room in the Dulcimer House hotel, booked in the name of Petros Corporation. Sennett had brought along a bland-seeming fellow named Jim, slightly moonfaced but pleasant, whom I marked as an FBI agent, even before Stan introduced him, because he wore a tie on Sunday afternoon. They leaned forward intently on their fancy medallion-backed armchairs as Robbie held forth beside me on the sofa.

"The judge we're assigned is Homer Guerfoyle. Now, Homer, I don't know if you remember Homer. He's long gone. But he was a plain, old-fashioned Kindle County alley cat, a ward-heeling son of a bootlegger, so crooked that when they buried him they had to screw him in the ground. But when he finally maneuvers his way onto the bench, all the sudden he thinks he's a peer of the realm. I'm not kidding. It always felt like he'd prefer 'Your Lordship' to 'Your Honor.' His wife had died and he hooked up with some socialite a few years older than him. He grew a fussy little mustache and started going to the opera and walking down the street in the summer in a straw boater.

"Now, on the other side of my case is Carter Franch, a real white-shoe number, Groton and Yale, and Guerfoyle treats him like an icon. Exactly the man Homer would like to be. He just about sits up and begs whenever he hears Franch's malarkey.

"So one day Mort and I, we have breakfast with Brendan, and we start drying our eyes on his sleeve, about this trial coming up, what a great case it is and how we're gonna get manhandled and end up homeless. We're just young pups sharing our troubles with Morty's wise old uncle. 'Well, I know Homer for years,' says Brendan. 'He used to run precincts for us in the Boylan organization. Homer's all right. I'm sure he'll give you boys a fair trial.'

"Nice that *he* thinks so," said Robbie. Feaver looked up and we all offered the homage of humoring smiles to induce him to continue. "Our case goes in pretty good. No bumps. Right before we put on our final expert, who'll testify about what constitutes reasonable care in a forceps delivery, I call the doc, the defendant, as an adverse witness, just to establish a couple things about the procedure. Last thing, I ask the usual jackpot question, 'Would you do it again?' 'Not given the result,' he says. Fair enough. We finish up, and before the defense begins, both sides make the standard motions for a directed verdict, and, strike me dead, Guerfoyle grants mine. Robbie wins liability by TKO! The doc's to blame, Homer says, he admitted he didn't employ reasonable care when he said he wouldn't use the forceps again. Even I hadn't suggested anything like that. Franch just about pulls his heart out of his chest, but since the only issue now is damages, he has no choice but to settle. 1.4 mil. So it's nearly 500,000 for Morty and me.

"Two days later, I'm before Guerfoyle on a motion in another case, and he takes me back to his chambers for a second. 'Say, that's a wonderful result, Mr. Feaver.' Yadda yadda yadda. And I've got no more brains than a tree stump. I don't get it. I really don't. I'm like, Thanks, Judge, thanks so much, I really appreciate it, we worked that file hard. 'Well, I'll be seeing you, Mr. Feaver.'

"Next weekend, Brendan's guy, Kosic, gets Morty in the corner at some family shindig and it's like, 'What'd you boys do to piss off Homer Guerfoyle? We have a lot of respect for Homer. I made sure he knows you're Brendan's nephew. It embarrasses us when you guys don't show respect.' Monday, Mort and I are back in the office staring at each other. *No comprende.* 'Piss off'? 'Respect'?

"Guess what happens next? I come in with the dismissal order on the settlement and Guerfoyle won't sign. He says he's been pondering the case. On his own again. He's been thinking maybe he should have let the jury decide whether the doc had admitted liability. Even Franch is astonished, because at trial the judge was acting like he was deaf when Franch had argued exactly the same point. So we set the case over for more briefing. And as I'm leaving, the bailiff, a pretty good sod by the name of Ray Zahn, is just shaking his head at me.

"So like two goofs from East Bumblefuck, Mort and I put all the pieces together. Gee, Mort, do you think he wants money? Yeah, Rob, I think he wants some money. Somebody had to finance Homer's new lifestyle, right?

"We sit on that for about a day. Finally, Morty comes back to me and says, No. That's it: No. No way. Nohow. He didn't sleep. He hurled three times. He broke out in a rash. Prison would be a relief compared to this.

"That's Morty. Nerves of spaghetti. The guy fainted dead away the first time he went to court. Which puts the load on Robbie. But you tell me, what was I supposed to do? And don't quote the sayings of Confucius. Tell me real-world. Was I supposed to walk away from a fee of four hundred ninety–some thousand dollars and just go home and start packing? Was I supposed to tell this family, that's got this gorked-out kid, Sorry for these false hopes, that million bucks we said you got, we must have been on LSD? How many hours do you think it would be before they got themselves a lawyer whose word they could trust? You think I should have called the FBI, right then? What the hell's that mean for Morty's uncle? And what about us? In this town, nobody likes a beefer.

"So, Morty or not, there's only one answer. And it's like tipping in Europe. How much is enough? And where do you get it? It's comical, really. Where's that college course in bribery when you really need it? So I go to the bank and cash a check for nine thousand, because over ten thousand they report it to the feds. And I put it in an envelope with our new brief and I take it over to the bailiff, Ray. And man, my mouth's so dry I couldn't lick a stamp. What the hell do I say if I've read this wrong? 'Oops, that was my bank deposit'? I've put so much tape on this envelope he'll have to open it with a hand grenade, and I say, 'Please be sure Judge Guerfoyle gets this, tell him I'm sorry for the miscommunication.'

"I go to a status call in another courtroom, and as I'm coming out the bailiff, Ray Zahn, is waiting for me in the corridor, and there's one damn serious look in his eye. He strolls me a hundred feet and, honest to God, you can hear my socks squish. Finally, he throws his arm over my shoulder and whispers, 'Next time, don't forget somethin for me.' And then he hands me an order Homer's signed, accepting the settlement and dismissing the case." A decade later, Feaver tossed about his elaborate hairdo, which overflowed his collar in indigo waves, the relief still live in his memory.

"So that was it. I spun Morty a yarn about how Guerfoyle had seemed to realize that we'd turn him over on appeal and had backed off. Then I went and bowed down before Brendan's honor guard, his two sidekicks, Rollo Kosic and Sig Milacki. As I'm leaving, Sig says, 'You ever got a special case like this, gimme a call.' So I just kind of kept on from there."

He shrugged at the inevitability of the bad-acting that followed and looked around again to see how he'd been received. I suggested he go down for coffee. Sennett was rolling his eyes before Robbie got out the door.

"That's a fairy tale about Mort," he said.

I nearly batted my lashes in my efforts to feign surprise, but naturally I'd given my client a good shaking in private. Nonetheless Feaver swore that for a decade Dinnerstein had remained unknowing, which was just the way that Brendan Tuohey, as a doting uncle, liked it. Through the partnership, Mort received half the windfall derived from the corruption Tuohey engineered, but bore none of the risk. Robbie alone delivered the payoffs to the judges.

Feaver claimed Mort was even misled about the nature of the secret bank account at River National. There are people in many occupations—nurses, funeral parlor directors, cops—who often are in a position to recommend an attorney to someone who's had a serious injury. Ethical rules forbid the attorney from sharing the legal fees he or she then earns with non-lawyers, but the nurse or the cop who'd handed out Robbie's card might well ask anyway, and Robbie was not the first personal injury practitioner to decide it was better to pay than have anybody forget his phone number. That was where Robbie told Mort the cash they were generating from the River National account was going (as indeed some portion of it was). Bar Admissions and Discipline, the agency that licenses attorneys, might go after Mort for aiding in these shenanigans if they ever learned about them, but Robbie's explanation protected Dinnerstein against criminal prosecution, at least in our state. Even the tax violations did not meet prosecution guidelines, since Robbie had, in his version, led Mort to believe that the income they weren't reporting was fully offset by these unsavory business expenses. It was all too convenient for Stan.

"He's covering his partner, George, and it's dumb. No matter what kind of deal we cut, when I get the evidence he's lying about this, your guy catches the express for the cooler."

I knew Morton Dinnerstein about as well as I knew Feaver, which is to say not very well at all, only from idle meetings around the LeSueur Building. According to my limited understanding he was the scholar in the duo, the one to turn out appellate briefs and motions and manage the files, while Robbie played show dog in court. It was the kind of arrangement that succeeded in many offices. I was nowhere as certain as Stan that Feaver was risking the penitentiary for his pal. Mort was a somewhat otherworldly creature, with a kinky mass of thinning blondish hair that sprang up in small unruly patches like crabgrass. He suffered from a noticeable limp, and his soft manner was characterized by a mild stammer and persistent blinking that introduced itself in his lengthy pauses as he was searching for words. Mort's guilelessness, and the lifelong symbiosis between the two men, made it seem possible that Feaver was telling the truth. I argued the point with Sennett at length, to little effect.

The other shortcoming in Robbie's account from Sennett's perspective was that Feaver had never dealt directly with Brendan Tuohey. Robbie recognized that the silent arrangements brokered for him with several judges occurred under the gravitational force of Tuohey's influence. The story—no better than a rumor to Feaver—was that Brendan got 'rent,' a rake-off on what the judges received from Robbie and a few other attorneys. The money was passed to the two retainers who acted as a sterile barrier between Brendan and anything corrupt: Rollo Kosic, whom Tuohey had installed as his Chief Bailiff, and Sig Milacki, a cop who'd once been Brendan's partner on the street. To get to Brendan, Sennett would need them, or some other witness Feaver might ensnare.

"Believe me, Stan," Feaver told him when he returned, "no matter how much you think you hate Brendan, you can get in line behind me. I've known Brendan my whole life and I've got my share of stories. I love Morty, but you think I *like* the way Brendan's made me the water boy on this thing? Except for the fact that he's got people who'd cut my tongue out and use it for a necktie, I'd love to give him to you. Only I can't. Brendan's twitchy as a cat and twice as careful. Catching him? Good luck."

Sennett appeared to relish the challenge. His eyes lit briefly with the remarkable energy that he inevitably deployed against any serious opponent. Then he beckoned Robbie to go on providing the details he could. Over the years Robbie had made 'drops' to many judges and he retained vivid recall of each occasion and of the envelopes of cash quietly passed in men's rooms and cafeterias and taverns to assorted bagmen and, much more rarely, to the judges themselves. Despite Stan's suspicion that Feaver was protecting Mort, or his disappointment that Robbie could not take him straight to Tuohey, it was easy to see that he was excited, even as he attempted to maintain his familiar veneer of tense restraint.

"Is there any reason you couldn't keep making drops?" Sennett asked Feaver near the end of the session. "If we leave you out there in practice, everything looking the same as it always has, would you be willing to wear a wire against all these folks and record the payoffs?"

That was the question we'd known was coming. It was the big chip Feaver could put on the table to keep himself out of the pen. But hearing the proposition aloud, Robbie grabbed his long chin and his black eyes took on an inward look. I could sense him recycling the strong emotions of the last few evenings, which we'd spent together, when he'd vented about Sennett and his terror tactics, and anguished over the cruel dilemmas confronting him. And then, as I'd learned was his nature, he let go of all that. Instead, he hiked himself forward on the sofa to face the United States Attorney and the Supervising Special Agent dispatched from D.C. He did not bother with rancor. He simply told them the hard truth, much as they'd forced it on him.

"What other choice do I have?"

CHAPTER 4

EVERY SUCCESSFUL NEGOTIATION IS SUS-
ceptible to Tolstoy's observation about unhappy families:
they end up in the same place, but each one gets there its
own way. For his part, Feaver set simple goals in bar-
gaining with the government. Unlike most lawyers I'd represented, he seemed resigned about the loss of his law
license. It was inevitable anyway for someone who admitted bribing judges, and by now practice had made him rich.
Instead, he hoped to maintain his bundle in the face of the
forfeitures and fines the government could exact. More important, he wanted no part of the penitentiary, not so much
for his own sake, he said, but so he could attend to his
wife during her inevitable decline.

On his side, Sennett's foremost requirement was that
Robbie go about his bad business wired for sound, and
agree to testify later. For that reason Stan also insisted on
a conviction, knowing it would enhance Feaver's credibility before a jury if he'd pled guilty to what he was ac-
cusing others of doing. Finally, Feaver's role as government

operative had to remain an absolute secret, particularly from Dinnerstein, who might spill the beans to his uncle.

After days of haggling, we made a deal that required Robbie to plead to one count of defrauding the public by bribing various judges. Assuming Robbie delivered on what he'd proffered, the government would depart from the federal sentencing guidelines and agree to probation with a $250,000 fine.

Everyone felt reasonably satisfied with these arrangements—except the Department of Justice, more specifically UCORC, the Undercover Operations Review Committee, which controlled all clandestine operations directed at public officials. UCORC had been established in the wake of ABSCAM, the FBI sting aimed at the Capitol, to calm Congress's newfound agitation about the perils to innocent citizens posed by undercover operations. The innocent citizens whom UCORC was concerned about now were the people on the other side of the cases Robbie would be fixing. UCORC said flatly that the government could take no part in depriving the opposing parties and their lawyers of an honest day in court.

Sennett flew to D.C. to butt heads several times. Eventually, UCORC agreed the problem could be resolved if Feaver were to fix only sham cases. The idea was that just as FBI agents had played Arab sheikhs in ABSCAM, they could act the part of the defense lawyers and parties in fictitious lawsuits Feaver would file. All of that make-believe, however, would entail a far more elaborate and expensive operation than Sennett had envisioned. Many weeks passed while Stan did combat within the Department to wring the approvals for his budgetary and manpower requests. It was late October by then, and naturally, at that point UCORC said no again.

The difficulty, they now realized, was that Robbie Feaver was an acknowledged felon. The government could hardly allow him to keep practicing law on the honor system. If he got into any of the mischief that could be expected of a crooked P.I. lawyer, it would be blamed on them. More pertinently, Sennett's plan offered no safeguards to keep Robbie from continuing to secretly pay off on the real cases on which he'd still be working in order to maintain his cover.

In essence, UCORC demanded that Feaver practice under police watch. Robbie chafed, but in the end he agreed that an FBI agent could be planted in his office to pose as the new paralegal Mort and he had already agreed to hire to enable Feaver to spend more time with his wife. To account for the fact that the paralegal would be virtually welded to his side, Sennett suggested that a female agent be assigned, someone who could pretend to be the latest of Robbie's many office liaisons. Late in November the woman proposed for the role, known as Evon Miller, flew in so we could all meet face-to-face.

At Sennett's direction, we each arrived separately at a room in the Dulcimer House. Jim, the agent who'd attended Robbie's proffer, was sitting with Stan when I got there. Jim had become a fixture and I'd realized by now that UCORC had designated him to run the operation. The new agent came up last. She spoke the code word 'Petros' and the door parted to reveal a woman in her thirties of medium height with a sturdy athletic build and agreeable looks. The first impression was of a pert, pug-nosed girl-next-door with a sincere, unassuming style. She wore jeans and a polo shirt, and a trace of eye makeup beneath her narrow wire-framed glasses; her brass-colored hair was pulled back in a ponytail. Yet even there on the threshold, she was noticeably ill at ease. Her brow was pinched and she advanced flat-footed into the room, shaking hands without meeting anyone's eye. Attempting his usual gallantry,

Feaver fetched her a juice from the minibar, which she accepted with a polite smile.

"So, Evon——" Robbie pronounced the name as we all had, as if it was a variant on 'Yvonne,' but she shook her head.

"Evon," she said. "Like 'I'll get even.' My mom meant it to be said the other way, but no one ever did."

I caught Sennett's quick grin, a fox in the brush. 'Evon Miller' was a nom de guerre, invented for her, along with her driver's license and social security card, at FBI headquarters in D.C. Robbie did not realize that she was, in the parlance, 'telling her myth.'

"That's just like me," Robbie told her eagerly, "my last name. People get confused all the time. Mine's like 'Do me a favor.'"

She managed a lukewarm grin, but did not seem fully persuaded they had much in common. Feaver plowed on, intent on winning her over.

"Which reminds me," he said. "I ask people all the time when I meet them: Which do you like better? Even numbers or odd?" From her narrow look, I could see she recognized it as a bar line. Clearly, she'd been warned about Robbie and had no use for his flirting. "I like even numbers," he added, with a futile little smile at his pun. She nodded rather than say anything else and moved to the other side of the room, before Sennett hailed us to our seats so we could talk over the necessary arrangements to be sure no one in Feaver's office questioned Evon or the fictitious cases.

"Did you say she was a Bureau agent or a prison guard?" Feaver asked afterwards. To my eye, she'd been no worse than correct. Robbie, I suspected, was upset by the reality of being watched twelve hours a day in his own office. The truth, though, was that none of us—Robbie, me, even Stan—knew anything about Evon Miller's true identity, any more than we did about Jim or the other undercover agents, the so-called UCAs, who eventually came to work on the case. Project Petros, as the operation was now labeled, ran strictly on the rule of need-to-know, meaning that all players, whether the agents or Robbie or Sennett, were supposed to receive only the limited information required to act their parts. That would minimize the chance that critical secrets would slip out and bring down the entire façade.

The only facts we eventually gleaned about Evon Miller's true background came to us in a roundabout way, largely because Stan had initial reservations about her. He'd found her more tentative than he'd hoped, and was also afraid her low-key style might give her away, since she appeared an unlikely match for someone as flashy as Robbie. Privately, Feaver found that concern entertaining; he said he was not known as 'especially picky.' In any event, Jim, who'd been given control over the agents by UCORC, stuck by his choice. He was impressed by her personal history, which made him believe she had the resilience to handle the rigors of life undercover.

"Apparently, she competed in the Olympics," Sennett explained to me one morning. He tipped a shoulder, knowing no more than that. We were in Warz Park, where Stan ran several miles at 6 a.m. Stan's mania for secrecy was so intense that he had not yet even informed anybody in his office about Feaver. Thus, to avoid questions, we often met here. I'd bought a snappy running suit and followed him once or twice around the tarred oval before we would appear to happen upon one another on a bench. We had gotten together today so that I could hand over documents— the final, signed copy of Robbie's plea agreement and his acknowledgment that he'd reviewed the lengthy written protocol for the undercover operation UCORC had generated—both of which were hidden in the folds of the morning's newspaper. By now it was past Thanksgiving, and winter, like an infection, was beginning to breed in the wind.

As Stan casually picked up the paper, he told me the little about Evon Miller he'd learned. In confidence, Jim had let loose this lone detail about the Olympics in order to reassure Stan. Sennett's motives for telling me, again as a supposed secret, were more pointed.

"Make sure your guy knows she's tougher than she looks," he said. "Don't let him think he can roll over her or outfox her. He plays games, we'll know." A smile tempted me, as it often did confronting Stan's prosecutorial macho, but that riled him. I was jogging in place to keep warm, and Stan stood up from the bench and showed me the newspaper where the signed documents were concealed.

"I have all my cookies on the line here, George. Every IOU and benny. There's nothing left in the favor bank. Don't let him mess with me. And not just for my sake. For his. He screws around, and the way D.C. wrote the guidelines, we have to roll it up and land on him with both feet. Make sure he understands."

I assured him Robbie recognized that if Stan caught him lying he was certain to end up in prison. But Stan laid a finger on my chest for emphasis.

"I'm telling you this as a friend," he said and repeated himself once more before he took off again down the path in the lifting darkness: "We'll know."

AS I SAID, THIS IS A LAWYER'S STORY. I mean that not only because it is an account of the law's fateful impact but also in the sense that I tell it, as attorneys often do, for those who cannot speak for themselves. I witnessed many of the events of Project Petros firsthand, inasmuch as Robbie always insisted, as he had from the moment Sennett appeared on his doorstep, that I be present whenever

Stan was. My memories are enhanced by the hundreds of hours of conversations I have had over the years with the participants, and also by the kind of historical detritus the law often leaves behind: tapes and transcripts and volumes of FBI case reports, called 302s.

Yet, left at that, the tale would be incomplete. The law's truth never ends strictly with the evidence. It depends as well on what attorneys call 'inference' and what less-restricted souls refer to as 'imagination.' Much of Robbie's day-to-day activity was observed only by the agent code-named Evon Miller, and for the sake of a full account, I have freely imagined her perspectives. Whether she would agree with everything I attribute to her, I cannot say. She has told me what she may, but much of her version is for-ever locked away behind FBI regulations. My surmises, my conjecture and inference—my imagining—would never pass muster in a courtroom. But I regard them as the only avenue to the whole truth that the law—and a story—al-ways demand.

As for my own role, I hope not to appear like those old warriors whose glory only seems to grow over the years. There was nothing heroic about my part in Petros. The un-comfortable truth is that as soon as I heard what Stan Sen-nett had in mind that first day in his office, I wanted no part of representing Robbie Feaver.

As a lawyer, I lived by a solemn watchword: Never of-fend a judge. I laughed at all their jokes. When they ruled against me, even stupidly, I said thank you. I solemnly re-frained from any discussion about the ability or tempera-ment of anyone on the bench, living or dead. I have rarely seen a judge who did not bear grudges—it is one of the perks of unquestioned power—and I knew the grudges formed against the person who represented Robbie Feaver would last. Not because all our judges were corrupt. On the contrary, most of them felt, with good reason, that they'd been lifting their skirts high for years to avoid the muddy playing fields of Kindle County. Now they'd be soiled nonetheless. The newspapers would print editorial cartoons representing the courthouse as a cash register; drunks at ball games and bars would make crude jokes whenever a judge took a $20 bill out of his pocket. Having traded the bounty of private practice for the esteem of the bench, they would feel swindled in life's bazaar. And the first person they'd pick on was me, who, unlike Stan or Robbie, would be seen as having chosen to participate for the grubby motive of a fee.

So as I wandered down Marshall Avenue, returning that mid-September day from Stan's office, I was trying to figure how I could get out of the case. I could ask for a staggering retainer. Or claim that I'd been suddenly called for a trial that would consume all my time. But I knew I wasn't going through with any of it.

In the simplest terms, I couldn't stand to draw so dismal a contrast between myself and Sennett, who'd just given me his valorous speech about his Uncle Petros. I never fully understood my lifelong contest with Stan, but I always felt I was running behind. Part of it was that I'd chosen the lucre of private practice, while he lived the more chaste life of a public servant; part was because, as a defense lawyer, I circumvented and thwarted and apologized, while he, as a prosecutor, smote hard blows for what he believed was good and just. Yet now, in the wake of my father's death, I realized there was a way in which I'd always compared myself to Stan in fear.

At the age of twenty-two, with my degree from Charlottesville, I'd become a hand on an ore freighter, which had brought me in time to Kindle County. Ostensibly I'd joined the Merchant Marine to avoid Vietnam. But I was really fleeing my parents' hermetic world in southern Virginia, escaping from my mother's relentless social preten-

sions and, even more, from my father's call to the invio-
lable credos of a Southern gentleman. A lawyer before me,
my father adhered to what he regarded as the right things—
Christ and country, family, duty, and the law. He found late
in life, as he watched less able and principled colleagues
promoted to the spots on the bench which he craved, that
his unwavering virtue marked him in many eyes, probably
including his son's, as a bit of a fool.

In the raw democracy of Kindle County, where honor
was not a matter of social attainment, I'd felt free to live
a life of reasonable adult accommodations. But with my
father gone, I suddenly feared I'd cast away too many
things he had exalted. I was a decent man, but seldom
brave. That was why Sennett for the moment seemed so
formidable. Like my father, he was a person of rigor, of
standards, a purist, who believed powerfully—and uncom-
promisingly—in the wide gulf between evil and good. As a
boy, Stan had briefly been a seminarian preparing to enter
the priesthood of the Greek Orthodox Church, and I always
sensed that in his mind—as in my dad's—law and God were
not far apart. Yet, unlike my father, Stan had the fiber to
recognize that in this world good things do not happen by
accident. I realized now that a piece of me had always seen
Stan as the man I might have been were I more determined
to be a loyal son.

So I knew I'd have no peace with myself if I turned
away from Robbie Feaver. I remembered the lines from
Frost about the road not taken. And then, like the poet,
turned to follow Robbie and Sennett down that unfamiliar
path.

JANUARY 1993

CHAPTER 5

THE LESUEUR BUILDING, WHERE ROBBIE and I both made our law offices, had been erected just before the economic collapse of the 1920s. It stands on a part of Center City called the Point, a jut of midwestern limestone that the river Kindle in its swift course somehow chose over the eons to avoid rather than wear through. The building commemorates the French missionary explorer, Père Guy LaSueur, whose family name was perpetually misspelled by the unlettered settlers who followed him two centuries later to this part of the Middle West.

The LeSueur was built in the era of Deco. Waif-like naiads modestly shield their nakedness behind the leafy adornments embossed at the center of the elaborate brass grilles that decorate the elevators, the air vents, and much of the lobby. A cupola of stained glass, the design of Louis Tiffany himself, rises over the seven-story center atrium and lures frequent tour groups who often obstruct the tenants racing to work. For the most part it is law, not art, which preoccupies the denizens. More than half the space in the building has always been leased by attorneys, inasmuch as the LeSueur stands at a favored location, the center of a triangle formed by Federal Square at one point, the state criminal courts on the second, and on the third, the architectural recycling bin that is the Kindle County Superior Court Law and Equity Department.

Late in November, a lawyer named James McManis leased a vacant suite in the lower-rent region of the LeSueur's eighth floor. McManis, who appeared to be near fifty, was making a late start in private practice. For many years, he explained to various lawyers in the building to whom he eagerly introduced himself, he had been an associate general counsel for Moreland Insurance, situated in their South-Central Regional Office in Atlanta, in charge of personal injury claims. McManis told a complicated story about leaving Moreland so his wife could tend to her elderly mother in Greenwood County, and said his move had been supported by Moreland's General Counsel, who had agreed to jump-start McManis's practice by hiring him to conduct the defense of various personal injury claims brought in Kindle County against Moreland's insureds. Listening to McManis's tale, one could not avoid the impression that it had been sanitized a bit, and that McManis was actually one more middle-aged expendable cut adrift in another of the ruthless corporate downsizings familiar to recession America.

Jim McManis quickly assembled a staff. Every few days, there was a new employee—a secretary, an investigator, a receptionist, a law clerk, a paralegal—each of whom was offhandedly introduced to the adjoining tenants. All, of course, were FBI agents hailing from locales far from Kindle County. Given the fact that not long into January, The Law Offices of James McManis had four separate matters against Feaver & Dinnerstein, it was not unusual that Robbie and his paralegal, Evon Miller, made occasional visits downstairs. So did I. My cover, employed with the greatest reluctance, was that I was the referring attorney on these cases, the lawyer who'd put the plaintiffs in touch with Feaver and who would be entitled to a piece of Robbie's fee in exchange for working with him on the lawsuits. McManis had also joined the Kindle County Bar Association's Task Force on Civility in the Courts, chaired by Stan Sennett. Thus Sennett, too, became a frequent visitor to Mc-Manis's.

Each of us came to Jim's office—referred to by the agents within as 'the off-site'—at least once a week, far more often in the early days. We approached at prearranged intervals, always equipped with a briefcase or an envelope as a prop. Arriving in the reception area, richly paneled in red oak, I felt as if I were watching TV from inside the set. Everyone was playing a role, but until the steel-lined doors to the conference room were secured, all maintained a convincing atmosphere of earnest busyness, phones bleating, printers groaning, the various 'employees' dashing back and forth. What each of them was actually up to was not shared with me, but in one of the early meetings a door was left ajar on a wall-length cabinet in the conference room, where I noticed a full bank of electrical equipment, stuff with blinking lights and digital readouts.

As for the so-called Evon Miller, she was the first to respond to an ad for a paralegal Feaver & Dinnerstein placed in *The Lawyers Bulletin* in early January. She was interviewed the next day by Mort, Robbie, and the office manager, Eileen Ruben. For the interview she wore a trim blue suit, a ruffled white blouse, and a doubled strand of costume pearls she'd probably worn four times since getting them for college graduation. Her glasses were gone now in favor of contacts, and to give her the jazzier look Sennett preferred, she'd also had a makeover at Elizabeth Arden on Michigan Avenue in Chicago, at Bureau expense

It included bleaching her hair bright blond and trimming it into a high-styled do buzzed down to fuzz on one side as it slid toward her ear.

On the first day after 'Evon Miller' was hired, Robbie strutted her around the harshly lit corridors of the firm. He explained the layout, introduced other employees with maladroit quips, and unapologetically boasted about the lavish decorations. Gaudy contemporary pieces—resin figures, neon sculptures, huge clocks—were clustered on the silky peach-colored paper covering the walls. The conference room was dominated by the longest table she had ever seen outside a museum, an oval of pinkish granite surrounded by Italian-designed armchairs, its polished surface glazed with the oblique light from the large windows on the LeSueur's thirty-fifth floor. Feaver referred to the room as 'the Palace.'

"See, we lay it on thick for the play," he said. "Know what I mean?"

She didn't.

"My first legal job, I worked for Peter Neucriss. You've heard of Peter, right? Everybody's heard of Peter—the Master of Disaster, that's what the papers call him. *Peter* can be understated. We're Feaver and Dinnerstein. Who are they? The arrogant docs who come here for their depos, our clients, who are mostly little people from the apartments and bungalows, they all want to know one thing: Are these guys successful? Do they win? So it's gotta show. You drive a Mercedes, you wear Zegna, and your office looks like Robin Leach should be coming through the door any second. I told Mort, when we started—think Beverly Hills."

Beverly Hills, Evon thought. Feaver brought to mind the brassy city types she began encountering in town as a child when two ski resorts cropped up like pimples on the clear face of adjacent mountains. Dark, gabby men, stuck on themselves, operators like Feaver, with his guy's-guy air and a style that made you wonder if, like a slug, he would leave a grease track behind. But she'd been an agent for ten years now and had dealt with her share of bottom feeders and flippers. As an FOA in Boston—a first-office agent, a rookie—she'd worked with dopers, and everybody knew those people were the worst. Her job here, she told herself, was to keep an eye out, to make sure this boy did his stuff, stayed straight as six o'clock, and didn't get bushwhacked in the process. Beyond that, she figured, it did not really matter if the bugger had ringworm or an attitude. Roger, wilco, over and out.

They were in Feaver's office now. His secretary, Bonita, a pretty, smooth-skinned Latina with torrents of cosmetics-ravaged hair and eye shadow applied like finger paint, had come in to greet her. Feaver continued in the role of new employer, detailing a paralegal's duties. She'd schedule deps, issue subpoenas and interrogatories, handle court filings, even meet with clients to gather info and hold hands.

"And here's another thing," Feaver was saying, "you and Bonnie work this out, but I don't read the mail. For fifteen years, I got holes in my stomach from the mail, then I turned forty and said life's too short. Because one thing is surer than gravity: there is only bad news in the mail. No lie.

"First, there're always motions. Bane of my existence. On the other side of every case we have, there's a defense firm getting paid by the hour. So it's money in their pocket to file every brain-damaged, not-a-chance-in-hell motion they can think of. Motion to dismiss. Motion for summary judgment. Motion to reconsider prior motion. Motion to declare Puerto Rico a state. You can't believe this. And we're on a contingency. Nobody pays me to answer this dreck. And if I win ten motions, but lose the eleventh, the whole case still craters."

Feaver went on describing the disasters he could encounter in his in box every morning. There were letters from clients who'd been romanced by other attorneys and were discharging them, often after years of work; urgent alerts from trial lawyers' organizations about antiplaintiff legislation which the insurance lobby had inspired. And, of course, never the checks that defense lawyers owed on resolved cases.

"Only bad news," he concluded. Bonita stood near Feaver's glass-topped desk, chuckling indulgently, then departed, closing the door at her boss's request. The whirring sounds of the office, the phones and the machines and the urgent voices, were closed off now and Evon felt a sudden quickening. She had not been alone with him before. He chucked his chin toward her in a familiar way.

"So what's your real name?" he asked quietly.

She stood a second without moving. "Evon."

"Oh, come on. I feel like we're at a costume party. You know *my* name."

"My name is Evon Miller, Mr. Feaver."

He asked where she was really from, whether she was married. She gave him back her myth, without expression.

"Christ," he said.

Feaver's office was large, with a leather sofa and a desk and tables in contemporary stylings of glass and wood. The floor was covered by an immense Oriental rug, a wine-red Bokhara at the center of which she was standing. She tightened her jaw and spoke to him in a low hardened voice. They were not playing charades, she said. She repeated what had been drilled into her: Never give it up. Never. Not for one second. That way you don't worry about being overheard or caught out.

"You get used to breaking cover," she said, "and you'll mess up sure as sunrise when the pressure's on."

"Oh, don't you worry about me handling a role," he told

her. "I'm a pro." He pointed to the credenza behind him where a picture of his wife sat. The photo showed Lorraine as she'd been before disease had plundered her. Within the broad silver frame, Rainey, as she was sometimes called, remained an extraordinary raven-haired beauty, with eyes almost the color of an amethyst and a lengthy pointed jaw, an irregular element that somehow elevated her looks from the merely cute or pleasant. But it was a photograph beside it he had meant to point out, a glossy close-up of him, in greasepaint and a pirate's costume, apparently engaged in song. 'Bar Show, 1990' was engraved on a phony gold plaque below it. "Look, we're gonna spend a lot of time together," he said. "I'm just trying to find out a little about you. The way I figure," he said, "they couldn't just uproot you, if you didn't want to go. So you don't have kids. Right?"

She was never adept with people and somehow he had seen that; he knew she'd have no smooth way to stop him.

"No," he said. "No kids. And I figure you're single, too. Single person would be the first one they'd ask. They wouldn't expect somebody married to spend the next year away from home. Divorcee or never took the plunge? That's where I'm stuck."

"That's enough," she said.

"Relax," he answered. He was having a good time, leaning back in the chrome-armed leather reclining chair behind his desk. "I already know about the Olympics."

That finally ignited her, finding that even now, undercover, that single damnable detail was being paraded miles before her like a banner on a standard. Just that fast, she was leaning over his desk, ignoring a furtive quiver of his eyes which she immediately suspected was a brief effort to look down her blouse.

"Listen, mister, the 302s—the reports I read?—they said that some of these guys have got real mean friends. Isn't that what you told us? So you better act like your life is at stake, bud, because as far as I can tell, it is."

He shrunk his lips and turned a cheek, his beard so dense that, even clean-shaven, it seemed to turn his skin blue. The man was furry as a bear. A few renegade chest hairs peeked over his collar.

"What about a wire?" he asked. "George says you may be wired."

I had told him, actually, that the government was unlikely to do that. On hours of tape, there were bound to be a hundred idle remarks that could prove embarrassing to both Robbie and Evon on cross-examination. And there were complicated issues of attorney-client privilege with an open mike in a law office. Yet there was always the chance, in the brittle bureaucracy of D.C. where the practical often mattered little compared to camouflaging behinds, that UCORC might have insisted on taping in order to have unchallenged proof that they had kept Feaver in line.

"Are you going to answer me?" Feaver asked, as she turned for the door.

"No."

"Which means you're wired," Feaver said.

"If I were you, brother, I'd assume I was." I'd told him as much, since Evon was obliged to report any act of dishonesty that might bear on Robbie's future credibility as a government witness.

"I *knew* you were wired." He was so pleased with himself he actually clapped.

"Look, darn it, I'm not wired. Now stick with the cover and button it up."

"And what would you tell me, if you *were* wired?"

She'd had it. Coming around the desk, she grabbed him for a second by the shoulder.

"Listen," she said, "ordinarily I'd say, you want to kill

yourself, go ahead. But the sharp edge of the sword here is that if your life's on the line, so is mine. Now either you shape up, or I'll call this whole thing off and you can go sit in the can where you belong."

Feaver took his time. He deliberated on the hand with its bright nails which she'd removed by now, then turned his long face up to her.

"Hey"—he gave her a lopsided grin, aimed at appearing good-natured—"we're just fuckin with each other."

He had that half-right.

"We're gonna catch plenty of bad guys," he called as she retreated.

She wheeled and pointed: "I thought we already caught one."

I CALL HER EVON, because that's what she called herself. She once told me that as a teenager she'd undergone a period of religious passion, in which her complete devotion to God seemed to remove her from normal life, as if she'd acquired the power to levitate or leave her body behind. And now she felt something akin, a limitless stake in being Evon Miller. She'd burned the details into herself. Thirty-four. Mormon family. Born in Boise. Three years of college at Boise State. Married to her high school sweetheart, Dave Aard, a flight mechanic for United with whom she'd moved to Denver. Divorced since 1988. She'd collected a hundred particles of an imagined past with which to spice offhand conversations. When she talked to herself, she called herself Evon. She ate the food Evon Miller liked, she window-shopped in the stores favored by Evon, whose tastes for shorter skirts, brighter colors, bigger earrings were, blessedly, just a little more daring than hers. And at night, she was certain, she dreamed Evon Miller's dreams.

Six weeks ago, the ASAC, the Assistant Special Agent-in-Charge of the Des Moines Division, Hack Bielinger, had called her into his office. It was not really an office but a cubicle with a door. In his stubby hands he'd held a Teletype, on pulpy yellow paper. Bielinger was like a lot of the Bureau supervisors she'd had, hard to like, a guy who had moved up because he really wasn't cut out for the street and who still tended to resent the agents he oversaw who were good on the pavement. He was a small, fussy man—people always speculated that he'd fudged the height requirement—a born-again who didn't get what was wrong with bringing up Jesus at lunch.

"Got something interesting for you," he said.

Reading the Teletype, she felt as if somebody had hitched a generator to her heart. The message was from the DD, the office of the FBI's Deputy Director.

PLEASE ADVISE RE WILLINGNESS REFERENCED SA TO AC-CEPT ASSIGNMENT IN ORIGINATING UCO. K CTY DIV. TERM IN-DETERMINATE, EST. 6 MOS–2 YRS. DEEP COVER.

Bielinger wasn't smiling. In fact, he was tense. The DD wanted this, so he had to deliver. That was Bielinger. He said he'd had a call a week ago, kind of unofficial. He'd told them she'd be good.

"They need somebody who's trained as a paralegal." Bielinger shrugged. Why was a mystery to him. But it meant he must have asked, Why her? What's so special about her? The men in the Bureau always had the same reactions: chicks these days get first lick on every lollipop.

The agent who was going to run the op had flown out to meet her. He said to call him Jim, no last name, everything on this deal was strictly need-to-know. But she liked him. Smart. Sober. Quiet. Somewhere on the sunny side of fifty. He was good-looking, despite some chunkiness as he steamed into his middle years, with big glasses and a full head of graying hair that dropped in a boyish sweep over his forehead. He didn't say where he was from, but she figured D.C. He had an HQ finish, and knew all the right names. From the breadth at his shoulders, the way he filled up his shirts, she could see he'd been a jock at some point in his life. She took that as a bond. He had that contained aura of well-being, an aspect of sporting success she'd observed in so many others, especially men, but which somehow had never settled in her.

"It's hard," he said about what he was proposing. "I was under almost a year once." He described the case. He had worked on Wall Street. He was supposed to be a bad guy who ran the back office operations at a big brokerage house, a quiet, sullen suit who manipulated the box count and fenced stolen securities. It was a big sting. They rolled up three LCN—La Cosa Nostra—capos. One more nail in the Gambinos' coffin. "I'm proud of what we did. And on Friday night other agents will always treat you like a hero, especially if you're paying for the beer." A droll grin lit up and passed, a momentary indulgence subject to quick discipline. "But it was hard. And lonely. And dangerous, People's lives depend on whether you get made, and so you're paranoid every minute, every hour. It wears." He repeated that. It wears.

She tried to take that in respectfully, but she told him what she knew she was going to before they started: she was ready. He wanted to know why.

"Forty-four caliber adrenal glands?" she answered. He'd probably already read that in her personnel jacket: first hand raised to help out on a bust, weekends, evenings, even with the local cops; still addicted to the instant of unthinking reaction she first experienced on the playing field.

"Must be something besides that," the man whom she now knew as McManis had said. "You're gonna be putting yourself through a lot." They were in a drab little conference room in the Des Moines Division, his quiet way somehow a contrast to the phones and commotion just beyond. His eyes, pale gray, didn't leave her. In the Bureau, they were always trying to get inside your head. When she'd taken the qualifying test after college, there was a psychological portion and one question still reared up at her at times out of the murky turbulence of nightmares. 'If your mother and father were both drowning, which one would you save?' Someday, she'd have to find out the right answer.

She shrugged off his scrutiny now. It was tough to name any grand motive. She wanted it. Who knew why? But his response had rung something inside her.

"My bet," he said, "is you'll find out."

CHAPTER 6

IN HIS INITIAL DEBRIEFINGS, ROBBIE HAD confirmed what the government had already detected, namely, that at any one time there were only a few judges in Common Law Claims with whom he could 'talk.' This seemed peculiar to Sennett, since Tuohey had veto power over all assignments to his division. Robbie regarded it as characteristic of Brendan, who had an exquisite instinct for avoiding being exposed. Tuohey wanted Common Law Claims to be known for its cadre of highly capable and unhesitatingly honest judges. Their reputations would armor him with an aura of integrity, while the few exceptions could be passed off as the typical Party debris inevitable with an elected judiciary.

Of the dozen judges to whom Feaver had passed money over the years, most were gone now, retired or transferred to other divisions. If Petros ran perfectly, Robbie would try to secure evidence against them as part of the endgame. But to start, the focus would be on the four judges currently sitting in Common Law Claims with whom Feaver was still doing business. With them, there would be a chance to stage bribes, which, when recorded, would provide the government with the best opportunity to leverage those judges against Tuohey.

When the names of the four judges emerged from Robbie, I'd been shocked about two, because I knew both men. Sherm Crowthers had been one of the best defense lawyers in this city when I entered practice, a ferocious, angry advocate who, if not always liked, was deeply admired both for his abilities and for the obstacles he'd surmounted as a black man. Hearing Sherm's name had sunk my heart.

Silvio Malatesta, the other judge I knew on Robbie's list, inspired simple disbelief. Malatesta was a donnish, bespectacled Magoo, who never seemed to leave the universe of his own head, through which various elevated legal notions were always tracing like shooting stars. It was amazing to me that he even experienced the material appetites that led to corruption.

As for the other two names, I probably would have guessed them on my own, if I ever had the gumption to speak such slanders aloud. Gillian Sullivan was a lush who'd been coming on the bench loaded in the afternoons for at least a decade and about whom we'd received constant complaints during my term as Bar President. Wandering through her alcoholic wilderness, Sullivan probably thought little about right or wrong. Barnett Skolnick, the last, was the brother of the late Knuckles Skolnick, a former intimate of the departed County Executive, Augustine Bolcarro. Barney was the kind of old-time Party flunky who in my mind was typecast for envelopes of cash.

The threshold problem Stan faced in mounting these prosecutions was that except in the case of Skolnick, who might be tempted to take money from Robbie directly, all the others dealt strictly through intermediaries—a clerk, a relative, a paramour. In the ideal, Sennett would tape several payoffs to these bagmen, confront them, make a deal, and get them to record the delivery of money to the judges. But these go-betweens had each been chosen because they'd demonstrated the loyalty of Gunga Din, and it was far from a sure thing that any of them could be turned. If not, Petros might yield nothing but the convictions of a number of small-timers.

To counter this, Sennett initially hoped to design the 'contrived cases,' these imaginary plaintiff's lawsuits, so that the judges would be called upon to make a series of far-fetched rulings in Robbie's behalf. That way, even if the bagman didn't roll, Stan could still go forward against the judge by calling a bevy of expert witnesses to testify that no honest jurist could possibly have made these decisions. But Feaver adamantly insisted that approach would never succeed.

"You guys still don't get the play," Feaver told Sennett. "We got judges making ninety grand and lawyers making millions. Figure how you like, say it's a tip, or tribute, or insurance for next time, but I got cases I oughta win, and I wanna make sure the judge doesn't get confused. Maybe I get a little help when things can go either way. But if I walk in with some mangy dog and ask the judge to act like it's Lassie—which in ten years, I swear to God in heaven I have never done—if I do, the best I get is that the judge won't talk to me again. Worst case, Brendan gets hinky and sends somebody to knife me, and the only thing left to do in The Law Offices of James McManis is run the vacuum and kill the lights. This may be a little mind-blowing to you guys, but everybody over there realizes you're out here. They do something ridiculous, they know damn well that one of you"—the word 'assholes' was halfway to Robbie's lips when he managed to stifle it; he took a second to improve his posture and pulled on his shirt cuffs so that an inch of white emerged over his dangling i.d. bracelet—"the Judicial Commission, or the Bar Association, or you guys, one of you is gonna be humping them from behind."

Thus each complaint—a summary of the facts the plaintiff said entitled him to damages for his injury—had to be constructed so it fell in that borderland where victory for Robbie was reasonable, but not required. In the first suit filed, Robbie's firm supposedly represented Peter Petros. Peter had indisputedly become drunk as a lord at a Hands basketball game. In the course of an obscene tirade at the referees, he had fallen over the balcony railing. His survival was accountable only to his state of inebriate relaxation and the fact that he had hit the canopy of a hot dog cart, before bouncing to the concrete stadium floor. Petros sued the fictitious railing manufacturer, Standard Railing, claiming that because of the inherent danger of balcony seating, Standard was automatically liable for not building a product that prevented Peter's injuries. In behalf of Standard, The Law Offices of James McManis immediately filed a motion to dismiss, contending that even if everything Peter said was true, under the law he had no case. The legal arguments had been designed so that the decision on the motion was a toss-up.

On January 12, Evon went with the other paralegal, Suzy Kraizek, and filed the complaint at the Kindle County Courthouse, a normal procedure. It was the next step, getting the case to what Robbie referred to as a 'good' judge, which represented the first deviation. To do that, Robbie left a phone message at the office of Sig Milacki. Milacki, Brendan's old partner from the Police Force, was now assigned as the police liaison to the sheriff's deputies who acted as courthouse security. Robbie simply asked for a case number on a new matter, *Petros v. Standard Railing*. What happened then had never been spelled out to Feaver, and he had no reason to ask. Over the years, though, it had become apparent that Milacki passed the message to Rollo Kosic, Chief Bailiff to the Presiding Judge, who somehow overrode the court's computerized system for random case assignments. When Evon returned to the courthouse on Monday to pick up a file copy of the *Petros* complaint, Judge Silvio Malatesta, one of Robbie's unholy foursome, had been assigned.

We met again in McManis's office, where the government personnel began preparing to ensnare Malatesta and, before him, his bagman, an ill-tempered docket clerk named Walter Wunsch. According to the well-ingrained custom that ruled these matters with the firmness of religious practice, Robbie would not deliver a payoff to Walter until the end of the case. But both Stan and McManis wanted to get a recording earlier. McManis thought Robbie should have experience wearing a wire in a less pressured situation than passing money; Stan was eager to develop live evidence, since UCORC had him on a standing thirty-day review, which meant they could fold the entire Project whenever they were unsatisfied with its progress. Robbie agreed that in the ordinary course he might pay a visit to Walter when he filed his response to McManis's motion to dismiss, just to make sure that Malatesta recognized the merits of plaintiff's position. With that, arrangements began for Robbie to go out wired for the first time as soon as the motion and response were filed, in about two weeks.

After the meeting, Robbie and I went up to my office. I left to speak to my secretary for a moment, and when I returned, I found Robbie in a reflective pose in front of the large old windows, taking in my view of the Center City skyline. The new steel-shelled structures, sleek as airliners, mingled with the buildings of the twenties, which were usually topped off by some impression of bygone architectural styles—Gothic spires, Italianate cupolas, or even one that had a glimmering helmet of cerulean tile, an allusion to a Middle Eastern mosque. To the west, the river's waters were smoke-colored and mysterious under the wintry midwestern sky. The bleak season had started; these days it seemed like living under a pot lid.

I asked Robbie if the arrangements for the recording had sounded okay.

"I suppose," he answered. I thought it was the fear of detection that had made him subdued. But as it turned out, his concern was elsewhere. "I'm going over the bridge," he told me when he looked back my way.

Up until now, I had largely seen all of this in my own terms. My job was to keep Robbie out of prison and I was delighted with my apparent success. Despite that, Robbie faced many losses: His practice. And the money that came with it. Not to mention his reputation. But now he was going to make his first real break with everything he had. If all went well with the wire, he would betray Walter Wunsch in a fashion that every friend and acquaintance would deem unpardonable. The community he'd always belonged to would be left behind. The man who had said on the first day he came to see me that he was not a rat had undoubtedly stood at the window staring not so much at the city but at what he saw of himself.

UNDER THE PROTOCOL for Petros specified by UCORC, Evon had to accompany Feaver to every professional engagement—depositions, meetings, court calls, even his wooing of prospective clients—in order to keep an eye on him. Robbie's day often started early, with courtroom appearances in distant counties. Therefore, after Evon's initial few days, the scenario called for Feaver to pick her up each morning. Coming into the office together would also help foster the impression of a romance.

An FBI deep-cover team had settled her in South River in a former auto parts warehouse the size of a fortress. Her building, like many in South River, had been recently refurbished into an intriguing warren of condos and apartments, with few common corridors. The deep-cover team had chosen the apartment building because it was the biggest along Feaver's route to and from the office. Large was better, more anonymous. Living undercover, she was supposed to avoid making new acquaintances, since even the friendliest inquiries might trip you up. From the time Feaver dropped Evon off after 6 p.m., until the sleek white Mercedes appeared at the curb the next morning, she often felt as if she were dwelling in an isolation booth.

But there was rarely silence during the long stretches they spent in the car each day. When Feaver was not on the phone, which he could dial from a little panel above the temperature controls, he lectured her on any subject that crept into his head. By now she was in mind of a phrase of her father's—the man ran over at the mouth like he'd busted a pipe. Did he ever keep a thought to himself? Ostensibly, he was familiarizing her with the details of his practice, but he clearly felt he was entertaining. He was also quick to recognize that the car was the one place he could comfortably break cover. There had been no further problems in the office, but in the Mercedes Feaver was like a grade school bad boy who needed recess so he could behave himself in class. He was forever trying to pry details about her identity, or offering commentary about their meetings with Sennett and McManis. She'd face the window and watch the tri-cities whiz past, or close her eyes to savor the armchair luxury of the passenger seat.

The silver plate on the trunk lid identified the car as an S600—top of the line, Feaver told her several times. The creamy leather, with its pinpoint air holes, had the feel of the calfskin shoes she could never afford, and the dark walnut of the front cabin reminded her of a museum. Yet it was the quiet that impressed her most. In this thing, outside was really outside. The heavy door thudded shut with a cushioned sound reminiscent of a jewel box.

Feaver was enraptured with his Mercedes, which he had purchased only a few months before. He often spouted the staggering price, $133,000, unabashed that the car had cost more than some of the four-bedroom houses they passed in outlying developments. Secure within the elegant cabin and its fortress feel, Robbie was apt to become a random element. He zoomed around as if he were in a spaceship. On the way back from the Greenwood County Courthouse, he would pop in on his mother, who was at a nursing home along the way, or visit Sparky, a scalper who was holding tickets for a Hands game which Robbie was sending to a referring attorney. Feaver also loved to shop. He was a devotee of sales and fancy name brands and frequently made impulsive stops at the malls. Under the bright store lights he'd scrutinize the merchandise, then call his wife from the car to describe what he was bringing home, as if he were a big-game hunter.

In every venue Feaver entered with a sense of membership: he was known; there were friends of decades and tireless stories. For Robbie, all the world was in some measure a fraternity, a place for upbeat banter, tasteless jokes, and booming laughter. Arriving for a dep where he hoped to eviscerate the opposing party, he nonetheless greeted the other lawyer with cheerful enthusiasm. At the tony haberdasher where he acquired his expensive wardrobe, Robbie had his own salesman, Carlos, a Cuban refugee who welcomed him with the palms-up grip of a brother. The store was full of men like Robbie, with careful haircuts and a showboat air, guys who considered the fit of their garments in the mirror with an exacting look at odds with the carefree swagger with which they strolled down the avenue.

One day in the third week of January, apropos of nothing, Feaver cried out that they had to go see Harold, who turned out to be a client disastrously injured in a collision with a delivery truck. Evon could barely stand to look at the man. He was hunched to one side in a wheelchair; there were sores on his arms and face. Robbie, however, took Harold's hand and with barroom gusto told him he looked great. Feaver chatted away for nearly twenty minutes about highlights of the basketball season in the Mid-Ten. Afterwards, in the car, he told her he was determined to keep Harold alive. The defendants—the auto manufacturer, the state highway department, the trucking company—had dragged the case out nearly nine years in the clear hope Harold would die. If he did, a case presently worth $20 million, with comps—compensatory damages for lifetime care—might bring one-fifth of that, most of which would go to repay his medical insurer. There would be zilch for Harold's mother, a large-bellied, middle-aged woman in a shapeless dress, who had greeted them and who had cared for her son since his wife deserted him shortly after the accident.

"What about your fee?" Evon asked dryly. "That goes way down, too, doesn't it?"

"Hey," Feaver answered. "You ever meet Peter Neucriss, he'll tell you before he says hello about all the good he's doing for the world, sticking up for everybody who gets abused. Not me. The rules of this game are that we give people money to make up for their pain, and everybody who steps on the field knows how we're gonna keep score— the judges, the jury, me, the client, the folks on the other side. It's money. How much do we get, how much do they keep. Whatever people say, let me give you a fast translation: You can dress it up and make it say Mommy, but this baby's really talkin do-re-mi." He nodded firmly. "That's the play."

As always, his smugness was exasperating. Of all the people to think he'd figured everything out.

"What is 'the play' anyway?" she asked suddenly. "It's always the excuse. And I never get it. Are you saying, like 'I made the play' in sports? Or 'I have a part in a play'? Or 'I played a trick on you'?"

"Right," he said.

"Come on."

He waved a hand past his nose at the difficulty she was inviting. They were in the suburbs, a land of recently built houses with peaked roofs and few exterior graces. From the highway, she saw two little boys across the distance, smacking at a tetherball in the cold.

"Well, shit," said Feaver, unable as always to endure his own silence. "It's just The Play. It's like life, you know? There's really no point, except getting your jollies, and even that doesn't add up to anything in the end. You think any of this makes sense when you stand back from it? You think God made an ordered universe? That's the laugh with the law. We like to pretend it makes life more reasonable. Hardly."

She groaned. Which made him more insistent.

"Tell me what sense there is that Lorraine is sick like she is. Any? Why her? Why now? Why that terrible motherfucker of a disease? It doesn't add. Or take a look at our cases: forty-eight-year-old lathe operator. Machine goes down and he turns the power off on the line to fix it. The foreman comes back, figures some joker is fucking with him like they do twice a day, and throws the switch. Hand is cut in half. Off-duty fireman's at somebody's house washing the storm windows. He's gone for two minutes to get more Windex and the three-year-old climbs up on a stool to look outside, and goes right through the open window, DOA at Mount Sinai. Or Harold, for Chrissake. One minute you're a cheerful salesman on the highway, the next minute you're a meatball in a wheelchair. It's The Play. Ball hits a stone on the infield, hops over your glove, and you lose the World Series. You go home and cry. It's really chaos and darkness out there, and when we pretend it's not, it's just The Play. We're all onstage. Saying our lines. Playing at whoever we're trying to be at the moment. A lawyer. A spouse. Even though we know in the back of our heads that life is a lot more random and messed-up than we can stand to say to ourselves. Okay?" His black eyes lit on her despite the highway traffic. Something—his intensity—was frightening. "Okay?" he asked again.

"No," she said.

"Why not?"

She crossed her arms, deliberating on whether he deserved an answer.

"I believe in God," she told him.

"Me too," he said. "But He made me and this is what I think."

An exasperated sound gargled up from her involuntarily. Didn't she know? Who told her to try to argue with a lawyer?

ONE OF THOSE MORNINGS IN JANUARY, Feaver and Evon were in the 600 only a few blocks from work when they became snarled in a honking line of stalled traffic. Far ahead, heavy plumes of what appeared at first to be smoke expanded in the frigid air, swirling above the yellow blinkers atop a cordon of striped barricades and emergency vehicles. Approaching by inches, they eventually saw a covey of city sewer workers in quilted vests and construction helmets leaning on the yellow rail they'd erected around an open manhole. They were engaged in no visible labor other than shouting down to a couple of their colleagues who had descended. A young woman in a hard hat waved a red flag, sending the traffic along through a single lane. When she stopped them abreast of her, Feaver lowered his window, admitting a sudden riffle of cold.

"How come the cutest girl's always holding the flag?" he asked her. She was African-American, with a broad face and wide eyes and lovely, peaked cheekbones that plumped with an enormous grin while she flagged him on.

"How do you know her?" Evon asked as the Mercedes spurted ahead in the traffic.

He looked puzzled. "I don't."

"And you just say that to her?"

"Sure. Why not?"

"Because she might mind."

"Did it look like she minded?"

"But what's the point? Can I ask? What's the point of saying that?" Her tone was careful, hoping not to be incendiary. But she'd always wanted to ask his kind of man this question.

"She's cute," he answered. "You think it's easy to look cute in a construction helmet? I don't. You think it's an accident she looks cute? I mean, she got up in the morning. She tied that bandanna on her head, even though she'd be wearing a hard hat. She looked at her tush in her jeans. Who was she doing that for?" On the morning ride, he drove in without a topcoat, and he laid the long hand with which he'd been gesturing on his bright tie. "For me. A million guys like me. And so I say thanks. That's all."

"That's all?"

"Maybe I'll come through her intersection again someday. Maybe the light turns red. Maybe she's just getting off for lunch. I mean, I can imagine anything. But right now, it's thanks. That's all."

That was Feaver. He wasn't a mouth-breather, not the kind of jerk always hopping along on his erection as if it were a pogo stick. He had some style. But he was still on alert, a heat-seeking missile shot through the sky and waiting to lock on. He stood too close when he was speaking. His wife lay at home, dying by the inch each day, and he did not wear a wedding ring. Falling into his car each morning, Evon almost gasped at the sickly mix of sweet smells from his eau de cologne, hair spray, fancy shaving cream and body lotion. He was his own most deeply prized possession and he liked to advertise this, as if the sheer power of his vanity might overcome a woman.

When she'd met McManis the first time in Des Moines, he'd warned her.

'Our c.i.'—confidential informant, he meant, a polite term for snitch—'apparently has a big rep as a ladies' man. You're gonna have to act the part, and he's the type who might want to blend fact and fiction.' Jim had given her three rules. First, don't put up with anything that bothered her; they'd back her completely. Second, don't be offended, because she wasn't going to change him.

'And third,' McManis had said, hesitating long enough that she knew this was the important one, 'don't fall for it.'

No chance of that, she'd answered. So far, there hadn't been many problems. One time in his office, she'd gotten a sly, sidewise look as he asked, almost offhandedly, when it was Bonita was supposed to stumble upon them going at it on his leather sofa, a portion of the scenario that Evon was still hoping to skip. She'd stiff-armed him with a quick look and had heard no more about it.

But there wasn't a woman in the office who wouldn't have warned her. The female employees gathered for coffee breaks and lunches in a narrow interior area that was referred to as 'the kitchen,' a place where a male never visited for a period longer than half a minute to retrieve coffee or the brown sack containing his lunch. Setting her cover, Evon had casually mentioned how kind Robbie had been, stopping for her each morning. Oretta, one of the file clerks, had hooted.

"Girl," she said, "you get in his taxi, sooner or later

he'll be askin for the fare." Shrill, lascivious laughter from each woman reverberated off the steel cabinets. But later, as Bonita was filing, she made it a point to catch Evon in the corridor.

"You know, when I started in here, I was single, you know, we partied some." She did not use a name but glanced over her shoulder and tipped the teased-up tufts of jet hair toward Robbie's office. Bonita would not have gotten through the interview without catching Robbie's attention. She wore all her clothing a half-size too tight, her pleasing contours well displayed. "But pretty soon, I went back in to seein Hector. And you know, you've got a relationship or somethin, he'll flirt a little, but he won't push or nothin, if you really mean it. He wants you to like him. That's how he is. Like a little kid." Bonita slammed the long white file cabinet back into its recess in the wall. "And you'll like him," she said. Within the raccoonish circles of shadow, Bonita's dark eyes glimmered with the penetrating light of conviction. Then she moved off, leaving Evon with a momentary feeling akin to fright.

CHAPTER 7

THE JEALOUS RULER OF ALL THE BLINK-
ing equipment housed in the conference room cabinet was
an electronics expert detailed to Petros named Alf Klecker.
Alf was a happy pirate, burly and pie-faced, with more curly
reddish hair than I would have thought the FBI tolerated.
Klecker, as I came to learn, had spent many years in D.C.
as a 'black-bag guy,' who'd done the surreptitious break-ins
when a judge had approved installing a bug. He was
renowned in the Bureau for having remained more than
a full twenty-four hours in a janitor's closet in the U.S.
Senate Building in order to avoid being detected during
ABSCAM.

Immediately before this assignment, Alf had dwelled on
the 'black world' side of the Bureau, working what the agents
called FCI, foreign counterintelligence. He arrived on January 27 to prepare Robbie for his first recorded encounter
with Walter Wunsch, carrying a bagful of gizmos that were
only now being released for domestic use. Tape recorders,
he said, were out. And the standard radio transmitter c.i.'s

usually wore, the T-4, was dangerous these days, when any kid with a police scanner could stumble on the signal. Instead Alf had brought a device called a FoxBIte. It had been developed by a retired Bureau tech guy, who'd licensed the design to his former employers for a fortune. It was about half the size of a package of cigarettes, was less than an inch thick, and weighed only six ounces. It did not contain enough metal to set off the courthouse magnetometers and it recorded not to tape but to memory cards, which were downloaded to a computer for replay. To provide an ear on what was happening, and a backup in case the FoxBIte failed, Robbie would also wear a slightly larger transmitting unit, 'a digital frequency hopper,' as Alf called it, which would broadcast an encrypted signal across a randomized series of channels. A field playback unit, programmed to receive and record the FoxBIte's signal, would be housed in a surveillance van parked near the courthouse.

Robbie shook his head as he hefted the two units.

"I got a pen that records to a microchip," he told Klecker.

"Son," Alf said, "you let a defense lawyer loose with the kind of fidelity your microchip gets and there'll be twelve people nodding when he claims the defendant was saying 'honey,' not 'money.' No offense, George."

None taken, I replied. The five of us—Evon, Robbie, McManis, Alf, and me—filled the small conference room. The design of McManis's suite had made this the most secure meeting place, since it was not visible from reception. The furnishings were somewhat spartan, a long rectangular Parsons-style conference table surrounded by black vinyl barrel chairs on casters, a contrast to the lavish improvements left by the prior tenant. McManis's personal office and the conference room each had two walls wainscoted in the same red oak as the entry. Expensive, rosy Karastan carpeting softened sound throughout.

"This puppy gives you the highest fidelity possible," Alf

said. "You can tell what kind of heels a perp's got on his shoes. No joshin."

Klecker showed Robbie the Velcro holster which he'd secure on Feaver's inside thigh to hold the equipment. The lead for the tiny omnidirectional mike, black and smaller than the nail on my little finger, would come out the top of his zipper, hidden under the flap on his trousers. Feaver had been told to wear a dark suit for that reason. Holding the two units against his thigh, he remained dubious.

"This stuff's gonna feel like it weighs two tons."

"Robbie, all c.i.'s say that the first time they put on a body recorder," McManis told him. Both Robbie and I had taken well to McManis. Jim was the sort of level, unflappable person that FBI agents are on television. I knew he was an attorney by training; UCORC would not have let him play this role were he not. But beyond that, his background, like that of all the other UCAs, was opaque. Long after Petros was over, I learned that his father was a retired detective in Philadelphia, which, somehow, was not a surprise. I had always recognized in Jim the enviably settled air of a man content both with where he'd come from and with his own enhancements of his fundamental lot.

Jim had a soothing touch with Robbie now, reminding him of all the safeguards in place. Evon would be wearing an earpiece, lacquered under a lick on the long side of her haircut, that picked up an additional infrared signal from the FoxBIte, allowing her to listen in on the conversation with Wunsch. She'd be right outside, in case anything went wrong. Jim himself would be downstairs with Alf in the surveillance van, prepared to call the cavalry, if need be.

"It's all covered," said Jim.

"I hope so," said Feaver. He had an almost superstitious fear of Tuohey and was convinced that if he were ever caught with the recorder, he would be killed, or at least seriously harmed, before getting out of the courthouse.

"Suppose you better step outside," Klecker told Evon. He was ready for Feaver to let down his trousers so he could strap on the harness.

"Right," said Robbie. "We want her to be able to keep her mind on her work."

"Yeah, really," said Evon.

Sennett arrived while she was out there, and they reentered the conference room together as McManis was going through the final formalities with Robbie. For each recording, Feaver was required to sign a consent form. Federal law provides that before the government records anybody, there must be either an interception order, signed by a judge, or consent by one party to the conversation. UCORC's protocol also required the FoxBIte to be turned on and off via a remote which one of the agents would hold on to, ensuring that Robbie could not exercise any choice over what he recorded. McManis threw the switch now and took a seat in one of the barrel chairs, discreetly directing his voice toward the mike at Robbie's belt line.

"This is Special Agent UCN James McManis," he said. It was months before I figured out that 'UCN' stood for 'undercover name.' He gave the date and time and described the anticipated meeting between Feaver and Wunsch.

Evon and Robbie waited while Sennett repeated last-minute instructions. Make sure Walter spoke. Nods, head shakes, facial expressions—none of that would be captured by the recorder. Feaver flexed his forehead and circled his shoulders, undertaking what he purported to be relaxation techniques suggested by Stanislavsky. Finally, McManis gave a thumbs-up and we all lined up at the conference room door to shake Robbie's hand. It was still stone cold when he got to me.

THE KINDLE COUNTY Superior Court Law and Equity Department, the civil courthouse, was built in the 1950s and its architecture reflects that confused American era when, appropriately, all buildings were square. It has the proportions of an armory, half a block around and equally high, constructed in yellow brick and walled in the interior with six inches of plaster, ordered up out of Augie Bolcarro's enduring gratitude to various trade unions. To add some sense of the grandeur of the law, a classical dome, in the manner of Bulfinch, was plopped atop the building, bleeding weak light down through a central rotunda. There is also a variety of silly concrete festoonery spaced along the flat cornice, including masks of Justice and other Greek figures, and a cantilevered portico, supported by greened chains. The building has always been known as 'the Temple,' a term so timeworn that it has lost the ironic inflections with which it was spoken during the structure's first years.

True to his view of himself as a stage veteran, Feaver's jitters had largely passed once the drama was in motion. He alighted from the elevator on the eighth floor and led Evon toward the rear corridor and the office of Judge Malatesta's clerk, Walter Wunsch. Walter had been a creature of the Kindle County Courthouse since the age of nineteen, when his ward committeeman found him his first job running the elevators, a position which some patronage appointee continued to fill until two years ago, long after the cars were fully automated. These days Walter was a precinct captain himself and an alternate ward committeeman, a man of considerable political swack. According to Robbie, he'd been bagging for various judges for decades.

Walter was angular, long-nosed, and moody. By Feaver's description, Wunsch, dressed with Germanic discipline in heavy wool suits, even in the heat of summer, would stand behind his desk, his hands always in his pockets, as he offered stark opinions on all matters. As revealed by the recordings, he had a sour, piercing sense of humor that occasionally reminded me, privately, of Sennett's.

"You know how some people are always talking to you like they hate your guts?" Robbie explained to us. "Sarcastic? Making fun? That's Walter. Only he isn't kidding." Wunsch's poor humor was attributed to a hard-knocks childhood, but Robbie had few details.

Walter was in his office today, dourly contemplating the stacks of court filings on his desk, when Robbie and Evon arrived at his doorway. He looked up grudgingly.

"Hey, Walter!" cried Robbie. "How was Arizona? Good weather?" Robbie had financed a golf trip for Walter late in the fall, at the conclusion of a lengthy damage prove-up which had gone quite well for Robbie and his client.

"Too damn hot," said Walter. "Hundred six, two days. I was hugging the sides of those buildings when I walked down the street, trying to find some effing shade. I felt like a lousy cockroach."

"How about the missus? She like it?"

"You'd have to ask her. She was happy I couldn't go golfin. She seemed to like that part. I don't know how she liked the rest." He moved papers from one side of his desk to another and asked what was up.

"Reply brief." Robbie turned to Evon for the document and introduced her, light-handedly laying down Evon's cover. Attempting warmth, Walter failed. His smile, as Robbie had suggested to her, was mean. In any mood, he was not very pleasant-looking, sallow, with gravelly skin. He was goat-shouldered and potbellied, one of those narrow men on whom nature had hitched an almost comical hummock of fat. His large, ruddy nose veered off noticeably at the point and his hair was almost gone. What remained was pasted in unwashed gray strands across his crown.

"All right, lady," said Robbie. He squeezed Evon around the shoulders for Walter's benefit, well aware that she was onstage and could offer no resistance. "Why don't you give me one sec with Walter? I want to tell him an off-color story."

Evon took a seat on a wooden bench across the corridor, within range of the infrared.

"Your latest?" she heard Walter asking as soon as she was gone.

"Latest what?"

"Yeah, right," said Walter.

"I wish I got half as much as people think."

"That'd be about a tenth of what you say."

"Walter, you used to like me."

"Tunafish used to be twenty-nine cents a can. So how long will she entertain you?"

"Awhile." Robbie's voice, as it next emerged, was leaking oil. "Suck a golf ball through a garden hose, Walter."

Evon started and reflexively glanced down the hall. In Wunsch's office, there was a long pause as Walter loitered, perhaps with disconsolate thoughts of his wife.

"So whatta you got besides gardening tips?" he finally asked.

She could hear the envelope crinkling as Robbie handed over the reply brief. He asked Walter to make sure the judge read it.

"Silvio reads every word. Christ, sometimes I wonder if he thinks he's the Virgin Mary. I don't think he figured out yet there's such a thing as bullshit." With that, there was a thick thwack as the envelope landed on yet another pile of pleadings on one of the cabinets. Walter's assessment of the brief's merit was plain.

"Walter, I got a case here."

"You've always got a case. At least so far as you're concerned."

"This is a good one. Strict liability. My guy's got brain damage. Trader down at the Futures Exchange. This is a million-dollar case. If I get past this bullshit motion to dismiss. The insurer's got to step to the plate then. It's only a matter of time."

"Yeah, brain damage. That must account for why he hired you. You gonna rent that chair or were you about to leave?"

Robbie's clothing shifted, chafing the microphone, and Feaver's voice dived. Listening, Evon could feel the drama sharpen. This was the moment. He was going to set Walter up. He must have leaned over the desk.

"Watch out for this one, Wally. Make sure he sees it the right way."

"I just work here."

"Right," Robbie whispered. "Right. That's why it's always Christmas."

"You are a gardener, Feaver. Full of manure. Beat it."

"Make me happy, Walter."

"I thought that's what she's for."

Evon was across the hall as Robbie swung open the door, and the last two lines were audible, even without the earpiece. Other people might have been embarrassed, but Walter, catching sight of her, administered an insultingly direct look across his wayward nose, before turning to confront the many papers on his desk.

THE RECORDING WAS A SUCCESS. Klecker played it back for Sennett and me and several of the other undercover agents as soon as Robbie had returned. Feaver had been flawless—no sign of nerves as he'd made a subtle effort to nudge Walter into incriminating himself. Stan dispensed congratulations, but he was visibly grumpy about the ambiguousness of Wunsch's responses.

"Why does he say he just works there? Or that the judge is the Virgin Mary?"

Feaver was impatient, played out from the effort and late for a settlement meeting with an insurance adjuster. I also took it that he wanted a more wholehearted pat on the back.

"Stan," said Robbie, "it's how he talks. He's not gonna bend down to the mike and say, 'I'm a great big crook.' I was stepping on his toes as it was. But he'll take the money. Believe me."

Before Feaver departed, I took a second alone with him to reassure him about how well he'd done. Returning to the conference room, we were greeted by a round of raucous laughter. For some reason, it had come at Evon's expense. She'd pulled back against the oak cabinetry with a narrow expression, and when she caught sight of Feaver she told him at once it was time to go.

He asked what had happened as soon as they were snug in the Mercedes.

"Nothing," she answered.

He asked several more times.

"It was Alf," she said finally, "if you have to know. He was doing an impression of the look on my face when they replayed that line."

Behind his sunglasses in the strong winter light, Feaver seemed to take a moment to recall what she was talking about. The golf ball. The garden hose. As she could have predicted, he was unabashed.

"Hey, Walter believed it." He smiled. "Must be you got a strong-looking jaw."

"Strong stomach is more like it. Men are sick creatures. Why do you have to *brag*?"

"Hey, Walter hasn't heard half of what he could have from me." He started a story about a juror in that courtroom with whom he had dallied throughout the last week of a trial, but interrupted himself. "Hell," he said, "forget the juror. Walter clerked for a *judge* I've messed around with."

"A judge!"

"A woman, okay? It's a long story."

"It must be." A female cop in an optic vest hurried them through the intersection in the mounting afternoon traffic.

"Look, it's my play, okay? It gives me an edge with guys like Walter, that I'm his fantasy life. Some people, I don't know, they love to think there's something they're missing. But it's a play. Truth? I mean, this'll blow your mind but I stopped skunking around on Rainey when she got sick. I can't really explain it. I barely took a breath after we were married. But now?" He shrugged in his dark cashmere overcoat. "It seems kind of crummy. Disloyal. I'll be single soon enough anyway." His eyes were indetectable behind the shades, which was just as well. His occasional casualness with the rawest truths confounded her. But she was still unwilling to allow him to sidetrack her with shock tactics.

"You enjoyed degrading me. And don't say it was just a play."

"Oh great. Right. 'Degrading.' 'Dehumanizing.' Let's hear em all. Gloria Steinem's greatest hits. Why do women always think a guy's urges come at their expense? How do you figure he feels being dragged through life by his steed?"

"I'll send a sympathy card."

"Hey," he said, "you won't ever meet a man who likes women better than me. They're the best thing on the planet. And I don't just mean horizontal. Women hold the world together."

She peeked over to be certain he wasn't smirking. Even then, she remained unconvinced. On the pavement, a fellow was pulling his wheeling suitcase behind him. He wore a bright fleece pullover, nylon moon boots, and, despite the January weather, a pair of shorts. A skier, Evon thought, headed off for vacation. For a moment, even as she went on shaking her head about Feaver, she felt a pang for the speed and the space and the snow that would always be part of home.

"Look," Feaver said, "it's the cover. Like it or not. That's our cover. Right?"

"That's the cover," she said resignedly.

"So stop fighting it, will you? You keep telling me how I'm gonna blow this deal, then you jump about ten feet every time I give you so much as a warm smile. Relax, will you? I'm not gonna take you wrong. I've got the picture. Believe me."

"And what picture is that?"

He pouted a little bit as he fiddled with the temperature controls amidst the walnut console.

"Can I give you some advice? I mean, I acted. You know that, right? Is that in my vita or résumé or dossier, whatever you guys worked up on me?"

"You told me. The bar show."

"Please," he said. "That's retirement activity. No, high school, college, that was my dream. I wanted to be on the stage. I used to wait tables at the Kerry Room. I swept up at The Open Door. I had it *bad*. I used to get in a sweat just standing next to somebody I'd seen perform, even if they'd only walked onstage playing the butler. I wanted them to touch me and give me a little of that stuff. Obviously, that's why I love the jury trials. You know. Cause I'm such a frustrated ham." In his gloves, he tightened his grip on the wooden steering wheel, seemingly staggered by the depth of this forsaken passion. After a moment, he recalled his point.

"Now, you can tell everybody in the office your name's Evon Miller from Idaho without even a quiver, but you get sick to your stomach at the thought of maybe touching my hand. It's like you're saying, I can do a part, I can tell all these white lies, but not *that*, that's who I am. And that's amateur hour, frankly. 'An actor's work is on himself.' That's what Stanislavsky said. You can't judge or try to keep some little piece of yourself sacred. It's like taking LSD. Don't trip if you're gonna fret about whether you're coming back."

She wouldn't know about that, she replied, but smiled toward her window where a small fogged patch was withdrawing in the hot breath from the air vents. He was smooth. It sounded like a farmer's daughter joke, the way he was putting it. We have to do this to keep warm.

"Okay," he said, "so here's an actual example. Once in summer stock I worked with Shaheen Conroe. On *The Point*? On TV?" Evon had never seen the show. The actress's name meant something only because it appeared frequently on the lists of prominent and acknowledged lesbians magazines liked to compile these days.

'What a talent she is. We were doing *Oklahoma!* She's Ado Annie, the girl who can't say No, and I'm Ali Hakim, the fella she's cheatin with."

"Typecasting?"

He frowned, but otherwise ignored her. "Okay, here's the play. Shaheen never made any secret about her proclivities. She had a *wild* thing going with one of the makeup girls. Open and notorious. But we had this onstage kiss, and for that moment she couldn't wait to get after me. Every bit of her. I mean, afterwards, I was afraid to turn around and face the audience. Because for thirty seconds, she'd stopped hanging on to herself. And that's what makes her great. The letting go. That's talent."

"Wait," she said. She'd actually reached out to grab the armrest. "Wait. Let's see if I'm getting this. You're so hot that even another dyke couldn't keep her hands off you?"

The car jerked briefly when he went for the brake. "What! Not at all."

"The hell."

"You think I was calling you a lesbian?"

"Weren't you? Not that I give a hoot."

"Hey," he said, "that's your thing, that's not my thing."

"I mean, it's gotta be, doesn't it? Why else would I be making faces at such a wonderful opportunity?"

"Criminy," he answered. They had arrived at the adjuster's office. He gave her a burning look and seemed on the verge of an outburst. But instead he popped the door locks and alighted. For once he did not have much more to say.

CHAPTER 8

WHO IS PETER PETROS AND WHY DON'T I know anything about this case?

The Post-it from Dinnerstein was stuck to the complaint which Evon had left sitting in her carrel. Mort apparently saw it when he'd happened by looking for something else. They'd all known this moment was coming. Nevertheless, the note left her heart rattling around like a bell clapper as she rushed off to find Feaver.

McManis had never tired of reminding her that Dinnerstein was the most dangerous person in this case. No one was more likely to sniff out Petros, and if he did, there'd be no sure way to keep him from going straight to his Uncle Brendan. But it was hard to regard Mort, with his mild stammer and his persistent tone of apology, as a menace. As a child, Dinnerstein had contracted polio, which had left him with a distinct hitch, now worsening in middle age as tertiary effects of the disease asserted themselves. Mort was tall, actually, and well built, but he made a boyish impression. Some years ago, when they first began earning what

Robbie referred to as 'real money,' he had tried to take Mort in hand, introducing him to the salespeople at Feaver's downtown haberdashery. The suits didn't seem to fit Mort. The pants drifted below his waist, so that he had difficulty keeping his shirttails in his trousers, and he snagged the rich Italian fabrics on the corners of his desk.

They had been friends for nearly forty years now, first brought together when Feaver's father had deserted the family and his mom, Estelle, had asked Sheilah Dinnerstein next door to look out for Robbie while she was working. The men had not tired of each other yet. Robbie generally reserved his lunchtimes for Mort, and every morning, after Feaver and Evon arrived, he and Mort spent a few minutes in what was called "the business meeting." Anything but business seemed to be discussed. As Evon passed by, most of what she overheard was talk about their families. Robbie had an intense interest in the two Dinnerstein boys. Mort, on the other hand, was the only person whose inquiries about either Lorraine or Robbie's mother were answered with more than a philosophical gesture.

In their practice, Feaver claimed they'd never endured a disagreement. Mort shook like a leaf in the courtroom. Instead, he did all the things that Robbie despised—office management, the brief-writing, the interrogatories, routine deps, and, especially, the endless comforting demanded by their clients, who usually felt intensely victimized.

Mort's renowned patience was being put to the test when Evon arrived with Robbie at his door. Mort, who had won the corner office on a coin flip, had furnished it in colonial style. The credenzas and desk space were crowded with photos of his family—his wife and the two boys were all dark—and an array of sports mementos: signed basketballs, lithographs of athletic stars, a framed ticket from the Trappers' lone playoff appearance, nearly twenty years ago now. At the moment, Mort was dealing on his speakerphone with a woman who was eager to engage the firm to sue her landlord.

"My boyfriend was drunk. Hal? He came in. He said a few things. I said some things. He threw me out the window. I broke my arm. My knee is messed up something terrible." The woman was nasal, harsh, excitable. She stopped there. Mort scratched a hand through the thinning springy pile atop his head. There were prospective clients who contacted them out of the blue every day, most with nothing close to a case. A number came to reception, but more called in response to Feaver & Dinnerstein's large ad in the Yellow Pages. Robbie avoided these inquiries, directing them to Evon. In just three weeks, she'd spoken to two different people who hoped to sue some branch of the government for failing to protect them from unwanted encounters with extraterrestrials. But Mort rarely screened callers. He had a moment for everyone. In the rare instances when the complaint had some potential, he'd refer the call to younger lawyers starting out, or even, in the most isolated cases, take the matter for the firm. As the saying went, though, Mort's good deeds seldom went unpunished.

"You said you wanted to sue your landlord," he reminded the woman.

"Hey, are you a lawyer?"

Dinnerstein stared at the speaker.

"Well," he said, "there's a certificate with my name on the wall."

"No, really. Are you a lawyer? Can I sue somebody in jail?"

"You can. It wouldn't be worth much."

"Right. So are you listening? I can't sue my boyfriend, I gotta sue my landlord."

"Because your *boy*friend threw you out the window?"

"Because there weren't any screens on the window."

"Ah," said Mort. He reflected. "Would you mind terribly if I ask your weight?"

"That's none of your business."

"I understand," said Mort, "and I hope you'll forgive me, but if a plaintiff weighed more than Tinker Bell, I don't think a jury anywhere in America would believe a window screen would have offered her any protection."

The woman dawdled a bit, considering her problem.

"Yeah, but when I fell, I fell in a puddle. I heard that. My girlfriend made a lot of money cause her landlord left water standing around."

"Well, yes, if you slip on it. Not if you land in it."

"Are you really a lawyer?"

As politely as possible, Mort ended the call.

"You should have asked if she drowned in that puddle," said Robbie. "You have plenty of evidence of oxygen deprivation to the brain."

Mort shrugged off the mild assault on his good nature. What could he do? Teasing was standard between the two men, and even Mort couldn't resist chortling when Robbie reminded him of the remark about Tinker Bell. Although he was exceedingly soft-spoken, Mort had a high-pitched howling laugh and it often ricocheted through the office. Robbie and he had a thousand in-jokes Evon could never quite comprehend.

"I've been meaning to talk to you about this case," Robbie said eventually. He held out the Peter Petros complaint. From the start, Robbie had known that the contrived cases couldn't remain hidden from Dinnerstein. The partners usually agreed on the matters in which they'd invest the firm's time, and besides that, sooner or later Mort was bound to pick up a file he didn't recognize, since one of his chief functions was correcting the potential mishaps invited by Robbie's cavalier ways. McManis appeared more concerned about what might happen then than Sennett, who felt Robbie would be able to handle Mort. Nevertheless, several hours had gone into planning for this moment.

The original idea had been to parade a cast of undercover agents through the office, pretending to be new clients. But Stan in time hit on something far simpler. If and when Morty came upon the cases, there was a perfect person to blame: me. George Mason, downstairs, had become a new source of referrals. As former President of the Bar Association, Mason was a stickler about actually working on the files, an ethical requirement in order to receive a referral fee. As a result, the client interviews had taken place in my office, and Mason had even scratched out a rough draft of the complaint. That was why Mort had not been party to the usual preparations.

I was the only one who didn't regard this notion as inspired. Unlike some criminal defense lawyers who see themselves as soldiers in an endless war against the state, I had no reluctance about encouraging my clients to cooperate with the prosecution when it would help them. But that was their obligation, not mine. I had something of a heritage to protect. Although my mother had knowingly married into the bankrupt branch of an aristocratic Virginia family, she managed to plant the flag for the social distinction she prized by naming me after my most famous ancestor. George Mason is believed to be the author of the line "All men are created equal," which Jefferson subsequently borrowed, as well as of the Bill of Rights, which he conceived of with his friend Patrick Henry. The legacy of George Mason—the real one, as I think of him—has been quite a bit to drag around with me, but I'd always felt that in protecting the rights of the accused, I was maintaining allegiance to my distinguished relation and his vision. For his sake, not to mention my law practice, which depended on being known as a tireless foe of the prosecution, I didn't want my name imprinted on an elaborate governmental deception like Petros.

Sennett pressed, however: I needed an excuse for my frequent visits with Robbie and McManis, which someone in the building was bound to notice eventually. And this way, the fertilizer could be spread by Feaver, not me. Robbie could send letters to my office, mention our relationship here and there. I would merely adhere to my duty to maintain his confidences. Stan argued adeptly and I eventually sank to my ankles in the familiar bog of compromise where defense lawyers dwell.

Robbie now delivered the cover story about good old George Mason, as Mort blinked several times behind the watery refractions of his wire-framed glasses. Misshapen by daily abuse, the specs rode at a noticeable angle across his thick nose. Evon, naturally, was astonished by the élan with which Robbie lied, especially to the friend to whom he claimed total devotion, and also by the fact that Dinnerstein, despite the years, still couldn't see through him. Robbie explained away a few of Mort's lingering technical questions about the case, then squired Evon from the office where Mort appeared quite satisfied.

Evon called me at once to tell me that the plan had been sprung so that I'd be prepared if I bumped into Dinnerstein in the building. But the news left me down. From the start, I'd felt a subtle undertow emanating from Sennett, and I sensed that allowing my name to be used as a prop in the Petros stage play was only the beginning. Eventually, he'd ask me to lie actively, or to talk Robbie into some dubious stratagem, requests that would not be premised on my client's best interests but on the grand importance of Petros to the legal community, and on my friendship with Stan. He'd want me to help him do his job, at the expense of doing mine. And what was unsettling was this: given the peculiar geometry of my relationship with Stan, and my funny fugue state at the moment, even I was not completely certain how I was going to respond.

CHAPTER 9

FRIDAY AFTERNOONS AT THE FIRM, ROB-
bie and Mort opened the bar in the rosewood cabinets of
the Palace and welcomed the whole staff for a drink. It
was pleasant and democratic. Evon declined alcohol, detailing, whenever she was asked, the beliefs of the Church
of Jesus Christ of Latter-day Saints for a number of the
women who had no concept about Mormons, except the
Tabernacle Choir. It was a loose mood. There was talk
about the week and the Super Bowl on Sunday, Dallas
against Buffalo. Clinton had announced his don't-ask-don't-
tell policy for gays in the military and two of the associates were debating it. Rashul, the black kid who ran the
copying machine, knocked back several jolts from Feaver's
$90 bottle of Macallan and tried to make way with Oretta,
who had him by about thirty years.

In the old days, as daylight dwindled, Feaver would snag
one or two of the younger women and take them with him
to the Street of Dreams. Now, in the slipstream of Robbie's
well-known ways, Evon drifted behind him to his office

shortly after six, leaving everyone to think that they were heading off for an overheated evening of their own.

"Say, that's good," he said, as he was searching his desk for papers to take home in his briefcase, "the Mormon girl stuff."

The office door had remained open and Evon pushed it shut somewhat harder than she'd intended.

"Not here, Feaver. You know the rules."

He'd had several shots of single-malt scotch. Turning to face her, he perched on the arm of his desk chair with his briefcase saddled in his lap. His tie was dragged down and his shirtsleeves were rolled.

"The rules," he said. "Very militaristic." He scratched his head. "Let me ask you something I've been wondering. Did they give you any choice about this? Or was this like the Army? They ordered you to volunteer? FBI, you figure that's a hard place to buck the boss."

"I've told you before, Feaver, we aren't gonna play Twenty Questions."

"No? I was hoping on the way home, maybe you'd tell me about the Olympics."

She got the message. He was angry. The testiness with which they'd left the car after the encounter with Walter, when she'd accused him of labeling her, had festered the rest of the week, and the liquor had set it loose. They were both worn out. But she wasn't any happier than he was. She watched him without reply.

"How about a hint?" he asked. "I mean, what sport? Team event? Individual?"

"How about this instead? I'll call Sennett. And I'll tell him to roll it up, because you're so determined to goof on me we're both gonna end up dead. You can go to Marion right now and I can go home. That sounds pretty good on both ends."

"You know," he said, "I never liked tough guys. Even when they're guys."

He was a dangerous man when he was angry. The lacquer seldom rubbed off his happy-go-lucky routine, but when it did, there was no restraint. His last shot had whip-cracked across the short distance between them.

"We're done, Feaver. I'm not kidding about calling this off."

"Good. Great. Call it off. Cause I've got a couple of things I've been meaning to say anyway. I know you don't like me. Don't say it isn't so, okay? I'm sure you've got your reasons. And maybe they're pretty good. But I have some breaking news for you, Special Agent Whoever-You-Are: this is not the time of my life, either, not by any stretch. Okay? If everything turns out peachy, I end up a convict, maybe my best friend loses his law license thanks to me, and I'll never be able to walk down the streets of this city where I've lived my entire life without thinking somebody is going to put a blade in my back. And that's if all goes well. If it doesn't, then I get that all-expenses trip to Marion, where you can bet I won't ever sleep a second on my stomach. And either way, I have to put up with you, with your chip-on-the-shoulder hard-ass routine, accompanying me sixteen hours a day to every locale I visit, except the men's room, where you just hang around the door.

"So as far as I'm concerned, if you want to walk your stick-up-it rear end out of here, the only thing you're going to hear from behind is applause. But don't think I don't know an empty threat when I hear it. Yon Sennett, he's got a lean and hungry look. Like Shakespeare? Stan would call this off on your say-so about as soon as my mother becomes Pope. The only person on this food chain who's lower than me, sister, is you. And we both know your career as hotshot G-man will be over as soon as you waltz out of here. I did my six months in the Marine Reserves to stay out of Nam. I know all about can-do organizations. Can't do and you're dirt. You're stuck, just like me. So stop being such a jerk."

She felt the heat past her shoulders. All her life she'd been at the mercy of her temper. By the time she was two or three, she was regularly told she had a sore look on her face. You are scowling, young woman. Girls were not supposed to let their faces grow condensed and storm-darkened. But she did.

"Then I guess I just have to kick your butt to get you to behave," she told him.

"Yeah, right." He had a good, long laugh, the kind that would get him clocked in a barroom.

"You're going to make me prove it, right? I've taken down men twice your size. When I worked the fugitive squad in Boston, I grabbed a guy six foot six and three fifty, and I had him on the ground and cuffed when the locals got there."

"You didn't hear me the first time. Why are you always telling me how well you're hung?"

She felt herself recoil. Then she told him to stand up. She widened her stance to face him.

"I'll wrestle you, baby," he said. "Strip down to our skivvies? Little scented oil? We'll have a gas." Mocking, he beckoned her with both hands toward the desk behind which he remained perched.

"Stand up, Feaver. I mean it. This is gonna happen. Or is Mr. Man scared of a woman who's five foot four?" She closed the distance between them to a few feet and kicked off her shoes on the dark red rug.

He closed his eyes to calculate. He exhaled. Finally he stood. He removed the suit jacket he'd just put on, then hunched over and extended his arms in a grappler's pose, the watch and i.d. glittering on his hairy arms.

"Okay," he said. "Come at me, tough guy."

She had hit the rug and rolled up on one hand, hooking her legs around his right knee before he did much more than turn. For a moment, as she finished the leg whip and saw him drop heavily, she was frightened, certain his head would catch the green glazed edge of the desktop. Lord God, was she crazy? Would she ever be able to explain this? But he landed solidly on his chest. She could hear the breath come out of him with a sound a little like a leaking tire. His face rested on the corner of the plastic floor mat that sat under his desk chair.

She asked if he was all right. Instead, without reply, he stood, first getting to one knee. He brushed off his shirt. There was a smudge now under the pocket that brought the white-on-white diamonds into relief, and he scratched at it for a second. From the deliberate way he moved she took it he was in pain.

When he finally spoke, he said, "Two falls out of three." He came around the desk and pulled two chairs out of the way. He lifted the coffee table and put it on the sofa, then he stood on the blood-colored rug, his arms again held wide.

"Now we have some room," he said. "You're quick. I give you that. But I'm ready now. Come on."

"Look, I was making a point. I'm not trying to hurt you. I just don't want to be sitting here for six months getting your chick act. I want you to take me seriously. And what we're doing seriously."

"Scared?" he asked.

She looked away with irritation, and while her head was still wound in the other direction, she dove at his midsection. Even as she lunged, she knew it wasn't going to work. They'd both seen the same movies and he was ready for the sucker move. He stepped aside, grabbing her arm to avoid her, then catching her around the waist. He hoisted her off the ground, his arms locked uncomfortably close to her breasts. He was several inches taller than she was, and much stronger, more solid, than she had imagined. She rammed an elbow into one arm, and swung one foot behind his knee. In response, he dropped her suddenly to the rug and sat down on her before she could scramble away, resting his full weight on her behind. When she started to flail, he grabbed her arm and applied a half nelson.

"Okay?" he asked. "Can we cool now?"

Suddenly, Evon felt him let go, even before she heard the voice.

"Oh shit," said Eileen Ruben from the threshold. The office manager had a rattling, smoke-devastated voice and a bad blond dye job on the sad remnants of what years ago would have been called a beehive hairdo. A plastic cigarette, which had been dangling from her mouth all week as she went through yet another effort to quit, hung gummed to her lipstick as she gaped.

"We're wrestling," Robbie told her.

"What else?" asked Eileen, and with that closed the door.

He had stood up by now and was suddenly back to himself, greatly amused.

"See? It worked out. Everything for the best. We're right on plan. Monday, Eileen will be out there telling everybody how I've already got you on the rug."

He was correct about that. Right on plan. But she felt no temptation to smile. She never recovered quickly from this kind of fury.

"Now, the guy thing," he said, "would be to go out and have a cocktail, bury the hatchet. Can you handle that?"

"I don't drink." She stood up and adjusted her skirt. Her panty hose had done a virtual 360 on her waist and she headed for the ladies' to correct that. Over her shoulder, she told him, "I'm Mormon."

SHE WAS NOT A MORMON. Her father had been raised in the Church and she might have been, too, if her mother had kept her word to her in-laws. But you go along in life, her mother said, and figure what's right for you. By the time Evon's oldest sister, Merrel, had been born, her mother'd turned her back on all of it. She held no doubt by then, apparently, whom Evon's father would choose.

They were from near Kaskia, Colorado, a little Rocky Mountain town that, in effect, had been seized from slumber during Evon's lifetime, awakened by the arrival of resorts and malls and multiplexes. But in her childhood, people had dwelled in the Kaskia Valley with a sense of privacy. In her family there were seven children. She was fifth. Right around the place where you'd expect kids to begin getting lost. And she was lost, she supposed. That teeming house where nine people lived, ten after Maw-Maw, her mother's mom, came to stay, swirled about her like a storm. Her parents always existed foremost in the reports of her sisters about what they'd want or expect. Don't put your elbows on the table, Ma doesn't like it when you put your elbows on the table. A kind of secondhand childhood as she thought of it, in which she too often felt isolated and unknown, and somehow inept.

She was an odd duck, she knew that. She didn't smile at the right times, she said yes when she was supposed to say no, she always realized too late when somebody was trying to be funny. She had a rear end on her that no matter how in shape she was did not seem to sit right on her frame. She'd never been at ease with folks outside her family and was forever embarrassing herself. People called her tough or callous, but the truth was she'd just never had the feel for nuance or mood. Someone asked a question, she answered plainly. She had no idea what else to do. And as people recoiled, she always thought the same thing. No one knew *her*. She didn't match. What was inside her was not what people saw.

In that mood, the mood of a lifetime, she had returned

to her apartment. She'd hurt her shoulder somehow, thrashing around with that fool. Reconsidering the scene, she wanted to laugh, but a dark thread of shame laced through her heart. The agent was supposed to run the c.i., but Feaver seemed unmanageable. Or was she the one who was somehow out of control?

Her apartment was not bad, a one-bedroom with rented motel furniture. Jim had referred to the deep-cover team from D.C. that had set her up as 'the Movers.' It had sounded mysterious, until they arrived with a truck and uniforms from one of the national van lines. Every item she'd packed had been vetted. Anything that could trace back to who she'd been in Des Moines the previous week—every appliance with a serial number, all the prescription drugs for her allergies—had been replaced. Evon Miller was like a doll that came with brand-new accessories.

Once inside, the Movers swept for bugs, checked the angles from all windows and the thinness of the walls, then delivered a lengthy list of do's and don'ts. The team leader, Dorville, handed her a wallet with a driver's license, credit cards, social security number, even private health insurance and photos of three little girls who were supposed to be her nieces. 'Don't be thinking about a shopping spree,' Dorville had told her as he'd thumbed through the plastic. 'We pay the bills out of your check.'

In the small entry, she stood before an illuminated mirror, prodding her shoulder to see how bad the damage was. Maybe she'd find someplace this weekend for a massage. Something hopeful spurted up at the thought, an unearthed memory of the lost body pleasures of the training room and the prospect of some balm for the tedium of the weekend. Monday through Friday, she was in motion. Once Robbie dropped her off, she'd go work out at the U., and on the way home grab something she could heat up in the microwave. Somewhere during the evening, in the midst of laundry or ESPN, she'd dictate her 302s, reporting on the day's activities, and drop the microcassette into a zipped compartment in her briefcase. Tomorrow, under some pretext, she would deliver it to The Law Offices of James McManis.

But the weekends dragged. On Sundays she called her mother, or her sister Merrel, from a pay phone, a different one each week, sometimes miles from her apartment. The airport was a favored location, because she had a clear view up and down the long corridors to make a tail. Next month, when it wouldn't look so strange to an outsider, she could get together with some of the other UCAs working in McManis's make-believe law office. For now, she was alone. She was going to watch the Super Bowl by herself in a sports bar a few blocks over, where she'd drink O'Doul's. She could handle that. She had before.

She was staring at herself. Even a month along, there were times she passed a mirror and thought she was wearing a mask. All that makeup! She'd worn contacts for years on the field. But the dye job and the hairdo still made her knees buckle; she looked like she'd run into a stylist who was seasick. It was the falseness she hated. When she was eleven, dressed for church—it was Easter, she believed—she'd heard an exchange between her mother and Merrel in the hallway. Merrel had twisted up Evon's hair in a curling iron, primped her skirt. 'Doesn't she look wonderful?' Merrel asked. 'She does, she does,' Momma had responded then let the weight of worry force itself out in a sigh. 'But she's never going to be that much to write home about.' Not like Merrel, she meant, the beautiful daughter, who actually represented the county twice for Miss Colorado.

It had always been a primary discipline to look into a mirror and see what was there. There seemed a cruel putdown in the fact they'd made her go around painted and hidden. Wasn't life confusing enough? How had she allowed that?

She knew this was where she had been heading, downward to confront the raw disappointment that this assignment, once so sweetly anticipated, had now become. She winced once more, with the pain in her shoulder and the accompanying memory of that tussle with Feaver. When she opened her eyes, the light from the bar of clear bulbs hanging over the mirror seemed painfully intense. She could see the granules of powder on her cheeks, the phony color of the blush. Her own green eyes were drawn tight into little points of black that somehow seemed the tiny hiding place of truth. She knew the reason she was here now. She couldn't answer McManis in Des Moines, but tonight she knew why she'd been so eager, and why she now felt so dashed.

She was thirty-four years old. She had a life about which some people—even an ineradicable fragment of herself—believed that the best was past, summed up by a four-inch metallic disk hanging in a special plastic box on her parents' rec room shelf. She had her work. Her cases. Her cat. Her sibs and their kids. Church on Sunday and choir practice Thursday evenings. But she awoke in the middle of the night, often for long stretches, her heart stirring with nameless anxieties, her dreams just beyond the grasp of memory, while she was drilled by the knowledge that life was not turning out right. And then there was a little yellow Teletype from the Deputy Director. High voltage to her heart. Caps. Initials. FBI-speak. But she could decode the message, and she felt as if every word were set to song. Adventure. Importance. A step ahead of the boys, instead of a step behind. But the best, the very best part, the deepest secret, the sweetest note, was one only she could hear. For six months to two years. Maybe forever. Someone else. The blessing. The chance. She could be someone else.

FEBRUARY

CHAPTER 10

I'D LONG CONFESSED TO ROBBIE HOW SUR-
prised I was about Silvio Malatesta. I had worked with
Malatesta on a judicial committee while I was President of
the Kindle County Bar Association and had found him in-
telligent and honorable, if somewhat woolly-headed. Immediately before going on the bench, he had been a law
professor at Robbie's alma mater, Blackstone Law School
here in town, a Torts scholar who liked to argue the occasional unusual case in the Appellate Court. That didn't strike
me as a career path to corruption, but Robbie rarely bothered with character assessment in this area. Some took.
Most didn't. Who would, he said, was never predictable.

The story told by Walter Wunsch was that Malatesta,
like many legal scholars, longed for the bench and the
chance to make the law he'd spent years studying. Silvio
lacked political connections and had turned to the overlord
of his old neighborhood, Toots Nuccio, the legendary pol,
mobster, and fixer. Toots had Silvio on the bench within

six months. Only then did Silvio learn that his genie required more in return than a rub on his lamp.

Now and then Toots would phone with suggestions about the way matters pending before Malatesta ought to proceed. The first time the judge had told Toots he didn't think his call was proper. Toots had laughed and made reference to a local reporter who'd been blinded when some unknown assailant threw a beaker of muriatic acid in his face. He was the last person, Toots said, who'd asked a favor from him and refused to reciprocate. You get, you give, Nuccio told Malatesta. Silvio was much too frightened to do anything other than comply. In time, he'd learned to accept the envelopes that arrived after Nuccio's calls, and even worked up the nerve to ask for another favor, assignment to Common Law Claims. Now Tuohey's guys, Kosic and Sig Milacki, were the persons who stopped by with occasional guidance about the lawyers to favor. Malatesta went along in the hope he'd eventually be promoted to the Appellate Court, where he could deal more in the realm of scholarship and theory, and where the three-judge panels that decided each case reduced the prospects for venality.

Perhaps because he remained unsettled about his situation, Malatesta's behavior on the bench, according to Feaver, was often confounding. It surely was in Peter Petros's case. One morning early in February, Evon found a notice in the mail setting oral argument on McManis's motion to dismiss. Both Stan and Jim were alarmed, albeit for different reasons. Malatesta could have denied the motion without a hearing, by filing a brief written order. Sennett saw no reason for the judge to call attention to the case by holding a public session. Stan was worried that Wunsch and Malatesta were somehow onto Robbie. Feaver shrugged it off. Silvio, he said, never made sense.

McManis's concerns were more practical: he'd never been to court as a lawyer. Undoubtedly, during his years as an agent, he'd testified. But he'd never had to argue to a judge and he betrayed the first nervousness Evon had seen from him. The day of the hearing, Robbie stopped briefly in Jim's office to strap on the recording equipment and to sign the consent forms. Because the FoxBIte's batteries might run out during a lengthy wait in the courtroom, Evon would carry the remote and activate the recorder there. McManis was noticeably taciturn. Robbie assured him that the worse he looked, the better it would be under the circumstances, but McManis seemed too taut to take much comfort from the jest. He had on a blue church suit and a white shirt, and his hair, usually slightly astray, was gelled in place like a helmet.

Evon and Robbie set out for the courthouse separately from Jim. Feaver today was fully relaxed. In fact, as he was about to enter the elevator in the Temple's vast rotunda, something caught his attention and he jumped out, marching to the sundries counter across the way. He addressed the blind proprietor by name.

"Leo!" The man was elderly, close to seventy and stout. His striped cane hung from a hook beside the rear displays of cigarettes and aspirin and newspapers. He wore a starched white shirt, buttoned at the collar without a tie, but he was poorly shaven. His dark glasses for some reason had been laid next to his register and he faced forward with his still, milky eyes.

Leo and Feaver exchanged sad remarks about the Trappers, a never-ending lament now renewed with spring training imminent. As they spoke, Robbie picked up two packs of gum from one of the counter racks.

"Whatta you got there?" asked the old man.

"One pack of spearmint."

"'One'! Sounded like you took the whole damn display."

"Just one, Leo." Robbie turned to Evon and winked as

he showed her both packages. She was too appalled to speak.

Feaver again insisted that one pack was all he'd taken. Then he withdrew his alligator billfold from his pants pocket and laid a one-hundred-dollar bill in the plastic dish resting on the glass counter. There was a photo molded into the contours of the tray of a carefree young woman and the logo of Kool cigarettes. The old man picked up the bill and fingered it carefully. He rubbed at a corner a long time, rolling it between his index finger and thumb.

"What is this?"

"It's a one, Leo."

"You got yourself stuck on 'one' today. I ask you how many in a dozen, you gonna say 'one'?"

"It's a one, man."

"Uh-huh. I know you, Robbie."

"I swear to you, Leo, there's a number one right on it." His voice barely contained his laughter, he was having so much fun. "Only don't put it in the drawer with the ones. Put it underneath. In the bottom of the register. It's a special One."

"Yeah, special." The old man made a tiny tear in one corner and lifted the cash drawer. He dropped four dimes and a penny in the tray on the counter and Robbie scooped them up.

"You gotta stop doin this, Robbie."

"No, I don't, Leo. I got no reason to stop. I'll see you next week." He grabbed the old man's spotted hand to draw him forward, then kissed him squarely atop his glistening bald scalp.

As Robbie walked back toward the elevator, he explained to Evon that Leo was his father's first cousin.

"He was my dad's best friend as a kid. He went blind at thirteen from the measles, but my old man stuck by him. Even after my dad took off, my ma always gave him credit for that. 'He didn't turn his back on Leo, your father, I'll say that much, he didn't forget his cousin.' " Evon had heard Robbie's mother's voice emerging from the speakerphone in his office and her son had caught the old lady's inflection precisely. Evon had to laugh and Robbie laughed himself once she did.

"My ma used to invite Leo around. You know, I'd find them sitting there, having tea, when I got home from school, laughing like a couple of old guys in a tavern. I loved to see him. Leo can be a real card. And he told me stories about my dad. Nice stories, you know. Nice for a kid to hear. How they used to run from Evil-Eyed Flavin. Or flatten pennies on the railroad tracks. Or play ball. I'd see him sittin there with my ma, and naturally I'd think what a kid would think, you know, wishing that it was my father instead." He looked down the hallway wistfully. The elevators dinged and the smell of bacon drifted from the cafeteria. "And you know who got him this stand here?" Robbie asked.

"You?"

"Well, I mean, I asked for him. But I'm dick. I ask them to hold the elevator around here, they don't even do that. You know who I went to? You know who listened to Leo's whole sad story and arranged it with Judge Mumphrey and the committeemen and all the other heavyweights who had to have their rings kissed? Can you guess?"

She couldn't.

"Brendan Tuohey. Yeah, Brendan." He made a sound then and another sad face. With no other recourse, she suddenly tapped her watch. Robbie had forgotten. "Shit," he said and scowled, despairing momentarily over everything. In his hand, he noticed the packages of chewing gum and handed them to Evon. He tapped his jaw.

"Bridgework," he said and entered the elevator as it arrived.

* * *

LIKE THE REST OF THE TEMPLE, Judge Malatesta's courtroom had a leaden, functional air. There were straight-backed pews of yellowing birch and a matching installation of squared-off benchwork at the front for the court officers. The witness stand stood lower than the judge's bench to which it was joined. The court reporter and clerk had desks immediately before the judge, and the lawyers' podium was centered yet another yard or so ahead. Everything was square. The great seal of the state hung behind the judge, between two flags on standards. On the west wall, across from the windows, hung a gilt-framed portrait of the late County Executive Augustine Bolcarro, referred to by everyone as the Mayor.

Malatesta's call was already in progress. Lawyers bustled in and out with their briefcases and topcoats in their arms. Jim entered by himself and sat stiffly on the opposite side of the room, waiting for the case to be called. He was careful not to look in their direction, nibbling absent-mindedly on his lips now and then.

Walter, in his heavy suit, was at his crowded desk in front of the bench. He called each case and exchanged papers with the judge, receiving the ones from the concluded matter as he handed up the briefs and orders Malatesta would need next. He, too, acted as if he had not noticed them, which Evon did not take as an especially welcome sign. Sennett's fretting about the hearing had affected her. If for some reason Malatesta ruled for McManis today, the whole Project was going to be in trouble. It would be hard to explain in D.C., or anywhere else, why their fixer had failed. This was the first concrete test to see if Robbie Feaver was more than hot air.

"*Petros v. Standard Railing*, 93 CL 140," Walter finally called out lethargically, after they'd been there nearly half an hour. Evon reached into her briefcase and clicked the remote for the FoxBIte. From the birch podium, Robbie and McManis identified themselves for the court reporter, a young black woman, who took the information down without glancing up at either of them. Evon followed Robbie up, and stood, as she'd been instructed, a few feet behind him. McManis had carried several pages of inked notes on yellow foolscap to the podium with him.

At near range, Silvio Malatesta did not really look to Evon like a crook. That was not surprising. Crooks often didn't run to type. Con men all had a self-impressed air, but bank robbers, on the other hand, seemed to come from any direction, plenty of gang toughs and thugs, but often the guy next door. Public corruption cases, they said, were the same, enmeshing plenty of obvious hustlers, but, often, the seemingly trustworthy.

Malatesta fit in the latter category. He appeared pleasantly avuncular, with thinning grayish hair and heavy black-framed glasses, his small quick eyes swimming within the distortions. Even in the robe he looked slightly too thin for his clothing, his shirt gapping at the neck. He licked his lips before speaking in his mildly officious tone, a bit like a clergyman's.

"Well," he said and smiled at the lawyers. "This is a *very* interesting matter. Very interesting. The papers here are very well drawn on each side. Both parties have had the advantage of top-rate advocacy. Now, counsel for Standard Railing—McMann?"

Jim repeated his name.

"Mr. McManis makes the appealing argument that a person ought not be allowed to drink himself to the point of senselessness and then blame someone else for the mishaps that follow. Mr. Feaver counters that Standard's position is a bit of a red herring: balcony railings, he says, must be built of a sufficient height and durability to prevent a fall, whether the plaintiff stumbles because he's deliberately tripped by an usher, or gets caught up in his own feet, or keels over drunk. In Mr. Feaver's view, a railing is like a lawn mower or a pharmaceutical drug, where the manufacturer is strictly liable for any injuries that result from use of the product. The cases in other jurisdictions admittedly go in both directions."

With a sudden manifestation of his usual irritable look, Walter rose up from his desk and interrupted the judge. The bench was at eye height for him and he was on his toes, reaching over it like a window ledge to point out a paper he'd handed the judge before. Malatesta was evidently confused, and he covered the microphone for the courtroom's public address system with his palm as Walter spoke to him. He was smiling faintly when he resumed.

"Well," he said. "I had intended to hear argument, but the calendar is crowded and Mr. Wunsch reminds me that, in light of that, I signed and filed an order last night denying Mr. McManis's motion to dismiss. So no need to do again what's already done. That will be the ruling of the court, with due apology to counsel. The case will proceed." Malatesta emitted another somewhat tentative smile and directed Walter to set a date for a status. In the brief hush, the only sounds were the heat from a register below the podium and Walter's pen scratching out an order to confirm what the judge had said.

"But, Your Honor," said McManis suddenly. Robbie's head shot around. McManis was sagged over the podium with a forlorn expression. Before he could say more, Feaver thanked the judge and, as he wheeled, kicked Jim in the ankle, while he steered Evon out by the elbow. Glancing back, she saw McManis slowly gathering his papers.

Klecker had stopped the FoxBIte and removed it from Feaver by the time Jim returned to the conference room from the courthouse.

"'*But, Your Honor'?*" screamed Robbie as soon as he saw Jim. McManis was too low-key and measured to be vulnerable to ribbing very often and Robbie made the most of the opportunity. "*What* were you going to do?" Robbie shouted. "Try to talk the judge into changing his mind?"

Caught somewhere between sheepishness and amusement, McManis sat in one of the conference room barrel chairs. His tie was lowered and he appeared drained by the entire experience. It had been such a confusing moment, he finally said. After all the preparation, his instinct was to react like any other loser. McManis's brief protest in the courtroom actually amounted to good cover, which made it that much easier for Robbie to give him the business. Evon and Klecker hailed several other agents in from the hallway to listen.

"You're the *patsy*," Feaver screamed. "You're *supposed* to lose."

Both Sennett and I had arrived while Robbie was carrying on. Klecker had downloaded the recording magazine to the computer equipment in the cabinet and replayed for us the brief exchange in the courtroom. Listening, McManis shook his head and said he remained utterly lost about what Malatesta had been up to. He couldn't understand then or now why the judge would schedule a hearing only to announce he'd reached a decision last night. But Sennett, running at warp speed, saw what had happened.

"That's a snow job for the record," he answered Jim. "It's wallpaper for the derriere. This guy is really clever," he said. "There's going to be a perfect excuse for everything. The motion's a close call. So Malatesta staged the hearing to show he had so little interest in who won or who lost that he even forgot he'd already ruled. If anybody ever questions him on the case, today's transcript will be Exhibit A for the defense. We can't drop a stitch or Malatesta'll go *right* through the opening."

A second of hushed admiration for Stan's deft intelligence penetrated the still air of the conference room. For the agents, perhaps, it had never been quite as clear why Sennett was in charge. He held the floor an instant longer, the smallest man there, looking about, impressing his warnings and his discipline on each of them.

CHAPTER
11

FOR ALL HIS OVERENTHUSIASTIC OPEN-
ness about everything else, Robbie was guarded concerning Lorraine. At the start, he said next to nothing to Evon
concerning his wife, as if to emphasize that, notwithstanding his deal with the government, in this arena they
could not intrude. But after six weeks around him, Evon
had absorbed a lot about Rainey and her illness. She'd
learned bits from Mort or the staff. And coming and going
from Robbie's office, she'd overheard dozens of his cheerful phone calls with his wife, as well as more sober conversations with the legion of caretakers in Rainey's
life—doctors, physical therapists, occupational therapists,
masseuses, nurses, and the home health care aide whom
he employed twenty-four hours a day. By now he'd even
ventured isolated observations to Evon about Rainey, but
only a sentence or two, rather than his usual extended di-
gressions. Recently, he'd glumly reported on the need to
puree everything Lorraine ate. "Puree of steak, can you

imagine? Pureed muffin? She can still taste, at least." His lean face took on the longing, distant look of a man at sea.

It was something of a surprise one day in mid-February when he invited Evon in to meet Lorraine. They had been in the neighborhood, down the block, in fact, meeting a prospective client. Sarah Perlan, a short and portly woman, wanted to sue the local tennis center for the Achilles tendon she'd torn when she'd stumbled on a wayward ball. When they were done at Sarah's, Robbie had suggested a visit with Lorraine. Evon was reluctant to intrude, but he insisted Rainey wanted to meet his new paralegal.

"I guess I've talked a lot about you." His furry brows crawled up his forehead as if this phenomenon struck him as unaccountable.

From the entry, you could imagine the interior as it had once been. Something of a neat freak, Rainey Feaver had tended to the austere, and had furnished almost exclusively in white. The living room, as Robbie had once observed, was the sort of place where a three-year-old with a chocolate bar could do as much damage as a tornado.

But sickness had a design sense of its own. Outside the house, Robbie referred to it as the Disease Museum, a proving ground and display space for every device, simple or complex, that might somehow improve the life Lorraine had left. Along the handcrafted walnut railing that ran up the turret staircase dominating the foyer, an electric hoist now whirred along a grease-blackened track. Metal hospital rails had been applied to all the walls, and there were a number of electronic doorbells visible that Rainey had once used to summon help.

On the first step of the staircase, he turned to Evon. "Sure you can handle this?"

He might have thought of that before, but it was too late to turn around. The truth was that she was not good with illness. Maw-Maw, her grandmother, paralyzed after disk surgery went bad, had moved in with her parents when Evon was fifteen. Her entire existence by then was founded on physical well-being, and she was often frightened in the presence of the old woman, even sickened when a sheet or hem slipped away and she caught sight of her grandmother's legs wasted to the width of a hockey stick. She kept what distance she could. 'You know, it isn't catching,' her mother finally told her one afternoon in her customarily brutal fashion.

This encounter would be worse. Maw-Maw's decline had been long but natural. Rainey Feaver was thirty-eight years old and dying. There was really no hope. Some—a distinct minority of ALS patients—lived twenty years with the disease as it smoldered through their bodies. Stephen Hawking was by far the most famous of these slow-progressing cases. But Lorraine was 'normal'—walking one day, falling down the next, and in a wheelchair within eighteen months. Her hands had weakened to the point that she could no longer hold a pencil or lift her arms above her head. And now, two and a half years after diagnosis, she could not feed herself or swallow well. She needed assistance even to remain upright on the toilet. She could not control her salivary glands, and shortly before Evon had arrived on the scene, they had been irradiated to keep Rainey from drowning in her own spit.

There were no prizewinners for the worst disease, Robbie had told Evon. He knew this from his practice. The body could fall apart in gruesome ways not even envisioned in nightmares. But this one, 'this rotten motherfucker of a disease,' as he repeatedly called it, was perhaps the most insidious. Your body deserted you. The voluntary muscles weakened, spasmed painfully, and then stopped working at all. Even the minutest volitional reflexes eventually disappeared, blinking usually being the last to go, rendering a patient entirely inert. In the meantime, intellectual functions remained unimpaired. Rainey thought. She saw. And worst of all, Robbie said, she felt. Inside and out. Movement ended with ALS. But not pain. She suffered intensely and could not writhe or lift her hand far enough to massage the muscles knotted in misery.

The Feavers had tried every potential remedy—herbalists and homeopaths and acupuncture. They'd volunteered for experimental drugs and had been accepted for one trial, a medicine that after ninety days left Rainey on the same steady downward slide. They had even gone to see a woman with a ridiculous machine made up of old vacuum tubes and a long flashing neon wand that she waved over Rainey's torso while making a 'woo-woo' noise with her mouth. The scene, Robbie said, would have been worth a laugh, had they not been so humiliated faced with the unreasoning depths of their desperation.

The Feavers' bedroom, where Robbie still slept, was full of contraptions. Evon crept to the threshold, but went no farther inasmuch as Rainey was in the bathroom. In her absence, Robbie toured the room, pointing out various machines he'd previously described. There was something called a Hoyer lift that brought Lorraine, when she had the energy, from the large hospital bed to her wheelchair, An adjustable tray table held a speakerphone, the Easy Writer—an appliance to hold a pencil—a mechanical page turner for reading, and two remote controls for the huge theater-style TV. A glowing computer monitor sat beside the bed, along with an alphabet board on which Rainey pointed out letters when she became frustrated by her efforts to speak.

All of this, of course, had cost—monumentally. Including the caregivers' fees, the figure she'd heard Robbie repeat was more than $2 million. He would soon blow through the lifetime cap on his insurance and already had a suit pending against the company for several hundred thousand dollars in covered expenses they'd refused to pay. But in a situation with few blessings, money was one. He had money, buckets of money, a hundred times the resources of most families, whom this disease routinely brought to the verge of bankruptcy. In their case, Mort had told Evon once, Rainey simply would not live long enough for Robbie to spend everything.

The process of retrieving Lorraine from the bathroom was under way. Evon retreated while Robbie assisted the aide, a tiny Filipina named Elba. Down the hall, Evon heard them encouraging Rainey as she was restored to the chair and wheeled back.

The night before, a Sunday, Robbie had gone to a wedding. Rainey had been too fatigued to go, but having promised to take his mother, Robbie attended, ferrying the old woman back and forth from the nursing home where she lived. Rainey slept in snatches between bouts of muscle cramps and had apparently missed his return last night as well as his departure this morning. Robbie described the evening's doings now.

"Mother of all Jewish weddings. Right down to the sculpted chopped liver. Great food, bad wine. And even so, my Uncle Harry was drunk like always and got so sick he didn't notice that he'd flushed his false teeth down the john."

Much more softly, Rainey answered. Her faint mumbling speech, a wobbly ghoulish drone with a glottal hiccup at the end of every word, was growing worse every day. For this, too, Robbie envisioned mechanical aid, a computer-controlled voice simulator that could be operated so long as Rainey had any voluntary movement remaining, even flexing her brow. Evon had heard Robbie's discussions with his wife's former colleagues in the computer industry who were helping. The hardware had been purchased and stored somewhere in the house, but the Feavers held out against each of these changes as long as possible, since no matter how convenient they were, there was no way to avoid the emotional impact of the lengthening shadow of decline.

"To the nines," he answered now. "Everybody. Inez bought a three-thousand-dollar dress—where she gets three thousand for a dress is beyond me—and as soon as she walks in, there's Susan Schultz in the same thing. Then my Aunt Myrna shows up in this tight white number, a lady of what? Sixty? And through the fabric and her panty hose you can see the outline of the tattoo on her fanny. You don't pick your family, right? I took my ma out on the dance floor in her wheelchair and whirled her around a few times. She got a real bang out of it."

Evon heard Rainey's voice again.

"I wish you'd been there, too," he said more somberly.

He refused to linger on the downbeat. Whatever his private moods, with Lorraine, Robbie was determined to be the spirit of brave optimism. On the phone, Evon had often heard him counterpoint his wife's reports of deterioration by reminding her of some other physical element that seemed to be withstanding the physicians' dire predictions. Frequently, he'd turned to the computer in his office to tap out a message to her, especially when he'd heard a good joke. "E-mail," he explained to Evon, an innovation to which Lorraine had introduced him. Now his tone ascended cheerily as he announced Evon. She girded herself.

A blast of air freshener could not fully conceal the many odors that shrank the large room—excretory smells, liniments and lotions, cramped body scents, the greasy effluvium of machines. As Evon entered, Robbie was massaging Rainey's arm to alleviate a spasm. She was in her wheelchair, the HiRider, a huge impressive motor-driven affair, with elaborate padding and smaller wheels. Robbie had described the chair. It not only moved smoothly in every direction from a joystick control but rose to a standing position, so that once she was strapped in, Lorraine could even greet guests at the door. Tonight she simply sat, held upright by two belts across her waist and chest. She wore a high-fashion running suit, on which the zippers had been replaced with Velcro. From the corner of her mouth a crooked tube protruded, attached to a bottle of distilled water on an IV standard, which provided a steady drip to replace her saliva.

Even behind this obstruction, Rainey Feaver's beauty had not fully deserted her, although she looked decades older than the woman in the photo behind Robbie's desk. The muscle waste had emaciated her, and left her head canted slightly to the left, but she apparently asked her attendant for makeup every day and her dark hair retained its luster. Somewhat caved in, her face was still striking. The remarkable violet eyes of the photograph remained vivid and fully focused on Evon as she approached.

Hopelessly ill at ease, Evon did her best: She'd heard so much about Rainey. Robbie was proud of her courage.

Lorraine considered that and slowly worked her mouth around several words. Her lips had lost most of their elasticity and barely responded. Rough to be you? It made no sense, and Evon had to turn to Robbie for help.

"Lovely to meet you," Robbie translated. He explained that certain letters had grown impossible—'l's especially. He smiled at his wife and touched her hand. "She always called herself a JAP."

"Rame joke," Rainey said with protracted effort. Evon laughed with Elba and Robbie, but despite all warnings, Lorraine's acuity was jolting, a dismal register of the vast inventory of thoughts and feelings even now going unvoiced. The laughter, which had rippled through Rainey like a light current, led to a spell of coughing. This reflex, too, was weakened, and in order to clear Lorraine's air passages, little Elba bolstered Rainey and applied a cupped hand repeatedly against her back, speaking sweetly in her sharply accented voice.

When Lorraine recovered, she resumed where she had left off. The interruption was unnoted. Life was what could be grasped in the intervals. She asked Evon about work. How long? Where from? She mustered only two-word questions. Robbie hovered over the chair and mediated. Even this woman in extremis Evon answered in her undercover identity. Robbie, who had shared nothing of his own situation with Rainey, would have wanted nothing else.

"Whah rif?" asked Rainey. "N'by?" She was asking if Evon lived nearby, apparently curious about why Evon was here in the dwindling hours of the afternoon. Robbie explained their meeting with Sarah Perlan and said that he was going to have to drive Evon back to her place. Something struck him as he spoke, a wayward implication in the detail, and Rainey responded at once to his apparent anxiety. In the faltering moment in which Robbie vamped to cover, explaining that Evon was new to town and still without a car, a different air came into the room. Rainey Feaver had heard her share of tales from her husband, especially regarding other women, and she clearly knew she was hearing one now. Her narrow, long-jawed face could show little in the way of expression, but even at that, her eyelids fluttered in a labored way and her lovely eyes grew darker.

"Co' heah," she told Evon. Evon pitched a look at Robbie, but his doting manner with his wife apparently comprehended no way to deny her. He let Evon take his place beside the chair. She bent closer because she could not hear when Rainey first spoke.

"He rise." It took a moment. Great, Evon thought when she understood. Perfect for the government witness. A testimonial to his dishonesty from the person who knew him best. Rainey, after a moment of recovery, had more.

"He rise a-bow everfing," she said. "Rememb'."

Evon suddenly understood that she was receiving a warning, vengeful in part, but also perhaps shared in a sisterly spirit. Robbie was not to be believed. If he said he cared, pay no attention. If he said he'd marry her when Lorraine was gone, it was only another lie. Rainey's eyes bore in as her message fired home. Robbie intervened to save Evon.

"She already knows that, sweetie. Everybody who hangs around me for a while knows that." Back beside the chair, Robbie was alone in smiling at his joke. "It'll just take her a few years to see my good side."

"Yes," said Rainey. Years, she meant and went on deliberately in her watery monotone. "Then I be dea'. And you be happy."

Robbie took quite a while with that. His tongue was laid inside his cheek. He gave her a look, a dignified request: Don't talk that way. But he said nothing. He bent to adjust Rainey's legs on pieces of foam cut to cushion them, and, still without a word, turned to take Evon back to the city.

In the car, after some time, he said, "They say things. PALS? People with ALS. It's part of the disease. Because of the neurons that get affected in the brain stem. They lose impulse control. It's actually funny in a way. You know, ironic. Lorraine was always one of these people who couldn't say anything. It just built up. She burned holes in my suits. She threw my Cubans down the toilet. She once put cayenne pepper in my jockstrap. You can imagine what that was about." A brief smile flickered up in admiration of his wife's spunk. "But she couldn't say what was on her mind. Now? Criminy. God, what I've heard."

Facing him, Evon had no idea what to say. Her sense of the size of what was bearing down on Rainey and Robbie was still gathering. The whole episode had left her heart feeling as if it wanted to scurry around her chest.

The car slid to the curb beside the brown awning extending from her building. Pedestrians rushed beneath it along the refurbished brick walks in their hats and heavy coats, eager to reach the warmth of their homes. She still knew none of her neighbors. There was an insular mood to the area. Despite extensive renovation and renewal, bums and addicts could often be found in the mornings, asleep in the sandblasted doorways or beside the struggling saplings in their fancy wooden planter boxes. Local residents were in the habit of moving on with their business without greeting anyone.

She reached for the door handle, then looked Feaver's way. Somehow, after all her ungainliness, she managed something in her expression. In response, a hundred emotions seemed to swim through his face.

"You know what a Yahrzeit candle is?" he asked her then. She didn't. "It's what Jews do to commemorate a death in the family. Mother. Brother. Every year, you light this candle. On the anniversary. And it's the saddest goddamn thing. This candle burns for twenty-four hours in like a water glass, and even if you get up in the middle of the night, the thing is flickering, the only light in the house. My ma always lit one for her sister. And right before her stroke, I was there, you know, I go see her early in the morning, it was still dark, and I looked at this thing, sitting on the stove, this forlorn kind of light, spurting and wavering, charring the sides of the glass and getting lower all the time, and I suddenly said to myself, That's Rainey. That's what she is now, just a long sad candle melting, burning down to this soft puddle of stuff which will finally drown the light. That's Rainey."

He'd drooped against the wooden steering wheel. She waited what seemed to be forever, but he never looked her way. Instead she left the car and watched as he zoomed from the curb and executed a smooth U-turn despite the heavy traffic, speeding back toward home.

CHAPTER
12

UCORC'S PROTOCOLS AIMED AT AVOIDING trials in the contrived cases. A full courtroom showdown with witnesses for two sides would require both the manpower and the budget of a Hollywood production and would greatly enhance the risks of detection. Plan A was that Robbie would either win a motion that disposed of a whole case, or prevail on some other significant ruling, then declare the matter favorably settled and make a payoff. Thus, Judge Malatesta's denial of McManis's motion to dismiss set the stage for Robbie to make his first recorded drop, this one to Walter Wunsch. With that, the Project would move beyond what the agents called 'talking dirty' to real criminality. Assuming no foul-ups, Walter would become the first trophy, the first dead-bang conviction, and the first person to squeeze when Stan began the ultimate castle siege meant to bring down Brendan Tuohey.

About two weeks after the session in Malatesta's courtroom, Robbie phoned Walter, imparting the good news that the judge's ruling had forced McManis to settle *Petros v.*

Standard Railing and arranging the drop at their customary site, the parking garage adjoining the Temple. That afternoon, Klecker arrived at McManis's with another of his clever devices, a portable video camera with a fiber-optic lens that fit into the hinge of a dummy briefcase matching Robbie's. McManis looked it over, then quickly vetoed its use.

"Robbie's never passed money before wearing hardware. It's tough enough to keep up the cover without worrying about aiming and focusing. We'll use the camera later."

"Jim," argued Sennett, in obvious distress, "Jim, a jury will want to see the money change hands. If it's only audio and Robbie can't get Walter to say something about the dough, this whole thing won't be worth much."

Jim would not budge. He rarely asserted the authority that UCORC had given him over operational details. In theory, Stan determined what evidence was needed, and Jim made the tactical decisions about how to obtain it, but usually Jim let Stan have his way. The best Stan could manage now was cool courtesy to hide the fact he was bridling.

Instead, the discussion turned to how Robbie could make an overt reference to the money, something which this dark world's strict etiquette severely discouraged. Feaver came up with the idea of delivering $15,000 to Walter, instead of the usual ten. The rationale for this largesse was found, oddly, in a problem that had been irritating Sennett for several days.

By now Sennett had ground out six more fictitious complaints. To Stan and McManis's amazement and chagrin, half of the new cases had been drawn to Malatesta, while none went to Barnett Skolnick. Sennett was especially eager to get to Skolnick, the one judge who dealt with Feaver without a bagman, but Robbie had no reason to complain about the assignments. His only interest was supposed to be having the case before a judge he could 'talk to.' However, with three specials recently added to Malatesta's calendar, Feaver had need to be particularly ingratiating, and the additional sum would provide an excuse to address the amount of money Robbie was bringing Walter.

But this left the agents five thousand dollars short. With some anguish, McManis wrote a check to cash on the Law Offices' account, knowing it would require hours of paperwork for D.C., only to find the bank downstairs closed when he arrived. Ultimately Sennett had to make a series of calls. The United States Attorney returned half an hour later and drew five thousand dollars in cash from an envelope in his topcoat. He'd requisitioned the funds with his own IOU from the Drug Enforcement Administration, which kept tens of thousands of dollars in currency on hand as 'buy money.'

Every bill was then photocopied so it could be identified if it turned up in a search. The stack of almost two hundred bills, mostly hundreds and fifties with a sprinkling of twenties, was nearly an inch thick, even banded. Accordingly, Robbie's habit with Walter was to deliver the cash in a cigarette carton. Wunsch was a heavy smoker, one of those nicotine fugitives regularly pacing back and forth before the Temple, coatless no matter what the weather and looking as if he was attempting to suck the cigarette dry in his race to get back to the courtroom before the judge returned to the bench.

Finally, Robbie was wired. He let his trousers down this time without much forethought. Afterwards, Robbie grabbed the cigarette carton with the money and Evon also put on her coat. She would be in the car while Robbie and Walter met. It would be far too unsettling to Wunsch if Feaver handed over the money in front of her, but the need to overcome standard courtroom defenses meant she had to catch sight of Wunsch to confirm it was his voice on the recording. She also had to watch Robbie so she could testify at trial that he'd had no opportunity to keep the money himself. To corroborate the drop, McManis would frisk Feaver carefully as soon as he returned.

"Now you have the scenario?" Sennett asked, reminding Robbie yet again to talk about the money. "And see if you can find out what the hell Malatesta does with all this cash. The Service," he said, meaning the IRS, "can't see anything."

That remark appeared to prick McManis, who looked up abruptly. Inter-agency rivalries are fierce, and Jim apparently knew little about the IRS's continuing participation in the investigation, although he must have anticipated as much. In a world where catching bad guys gives life meaning, the IRS agents who'd knocked on Robbie's door would never settle for being entirely cut out of the case. Nevertheless, knowing Sennett, I suspected Stan was putting Jim in his place, reminding him who still held the most secrets in the game of need-to-know.

Given the significance of the first payoff, Stan wanted to listen as it was made, which meant that I, too, was invited to join McManis and Klecker in the back of the surveillance van. We each walked separately to the new federal building, where a guard cleared us to enter the garage in the basement. The van was a boxy gray Aerostar, with flashy ivory detailing on the side. The only light in the rear came from two frosted observation bubbles on either side of the vehicle, which provided a dim, wide-angle vantage on the passing world. Cables snaked all over and Klecker knelt on the rubber floor mats, hovering close to the readouts and dials of the banks of electrical equipment secured with steel belts bolted to the floor. The stale air had a strong rubbery smell. As we left the garage, Sennett, McManis, and I were seated on narrow fold-down seats hinged to the wall, under strict instructions to stay there and be quiet, so that we did not impede the work of the agents.

The van was driven by Joe Amari, a middle-aged FBI veteran who'd clearly worked with Jim before and who posed as the law office's investigator. Joe had coppery Sicilian skin, and black hair so thick and perfectly groomed that it looked like something from a furrier's shelf. He had the appearance of a squat tough guy, and he was. He'd been under a dozen times, almost always on mob cases.

The municipal parking structure adjoining the courthouse was a five-tier open-air affair built in the same buff-colored brick as the Temple. By plan, Wunsch, in an old Chesterfield topcoat, would already be lurking on the ground floor. Robbie would drive by him with no sign of recognition, racing up the circling lanes to the top floor, which, at this hour, was largely deserted. In time, we heard the Mercedes gearshift jammed into park and Robbie's tread as he crossed to the elevator. If all went according to the standard arrangement, when the elevator's brown doors rumbled back, Wunsch would be inside.

Robbie and Walter had been using the elevator for drops for years now. The tiny carriage was a squeeze even for four persons and a hopeless wreck. The tiled flooring was gone in most places and the elevator reeked from its use as a pissoir by various urban vagabonds. The contraption rose and descended at an infinitesimal pace, and with awful sounds, the cables squealing and the brakes clanging like steam pipes whenever the machine slowed to an actual halt. It was used by virtually no one, particularly on the way down. Robbie was speaking even before the doors labored to a close.

"Jesus, Wally, the old man had me wetting my socks with that Hamlet routine up there. I wrote him a great brief. What else was he looking for? Smoke signals?"

"Shit. Silvio? Half the time he don't know if it's today

or tomorrow. And besides, you could give the old fuck a heart attack if you said 'reversed on appeal.' Any chance the boys upstairs'll bounce a case back gives him the willies. He figures somebody somewhere's keepin track." A reversal on appeal would draw suspicion to a case. Malatesta, as Stan had deduced, was determined to eliminate even the remotest risks of discovery. "Believe me, I had to carry on with him a long time on this one. I deserve the freakin Oscar. I had to wipe his nose and diaper his behind before he did the right thing. Anyway," Walter concluded, in a tone meant to get down to business.

Robbie said he'd brought some smokes. The sound of the cardboard ripping was distinct.

"Yeah," said Walter in time, "that's the right brand okay."

"Fifteen long there."

"Mmm-mmm," Walter answered quietly.

"Cause I want the old man to remember I'm a righteous fella. You're gonna be seeing a lot of me." Robbie reminded Wunsch of the three new cases. Walter, predictably, was more ornery than grateful.

"This better not be the miracle-of-the-month club," he answered, "because after this one, Silvio's neck's back in his shell for a long while."

"This wasn't a miracle. I had great authorities."

"Shit," Walter answered. "That wasn't what I was hearing. You better make sure Santa's got me right on the top of his Christmas list. Santa better *love* me this year."

"We'll write you down for a bushel and a peck and a hug around the neck."

"Fuck."

"No, here you go, look at this." The distinct crinkling of what I knew to be a travel brochure could be heard, along with the scuffing of fabric as Feaver removed it from his pocket. Walter, like the other bagmen, expected a tip. But he preferred no cash. He had told Robbie that he had enough cash, a reference, presumably, to the share Malatesta provided from his end. More pertinently, over the years Mrs. Wunsch had figured out where Walter was likely to hide his stash and, by his reports, regularly looted it. As a result, he preferred tangible items and thought nothing of calling Robbie with requests for merchandise that had caught his eye. Robbie had it all shipped to Walter's country cottage, where his wife seldom visited. Recently, he'd been paying Wunsch's way to various golfing havens. He extolled the resort in Virginia portrayed in the brochure.

"Yeah, well, I'll go," Walter said, "but listen, since I had to carry your water so far uphill on this thing here, I had a thought. I been looking at some irons. Oversized Graphite shafts. You seen these Berthas? Nice clubs."

With appropriate grumbling, Robbie now agreed to add the irons, then slid the conversation toward the topics Sennett wanted him to cover.

"Listen, Wally, I gotta ask you one thing about the old man that's always bugged the hell out of me. I look at him up there on the bench. The guy dresses like a hobo." From the sound of it, Walter enjoyed the description. "And whenever I see him tooling around the courthouse, he's in some old heap, right?"

"'83 Chevy."

"And he and the wife still live in his mom's old bungalow in Kewahnee, right? Isn't that the story? So what gives? It makes me nuts wondering: Where's it going?"

Over the speakers, there was a momentary lapse, during which the grinding motion of the elevator mechanism and the stiff wrinkling of the brochure going inside Walter's topcoat were audible. It was clear Wunsch did not welcome Robbie's curiosity.

"Feaver, this ain't a fuckin game show. You think *I* ask questions. I don't care if he's using it in the outhouse. What's it to you? I can't make no sense of whatever's goin on in Silvio's little noggin, anyway." Another silence followed, punctuated almost at once by the terrifying sound of the elevator brake being applied. The doors rumbled again as they retracted, followed by the scuffling of Walter's departure. Then there was an unexpected bouncing noise and Walter's voice was heard once more. He had apparently thrown a hand between the rubber bumpers on the closing elevator doors. Across the van, McManis tensed, anxious about the meaning of Wunsch's return.

"And listen," he said. "They got a big demand on these clubs. They're on back order. Okay? So you know, to get em, you know, they gotta be ordered right now."

"Gotcha," Robbie answered. The doors, finally closed, sealed off the sound of the city clamor heard in the background in the open-air garage.

In the van, as we listened to the elevator creak, to Robbie padding back to the auto, to the engine rumbling to life, there was an immediate air of celebration. Walter Wunsch now had a confirmed reservation in a federal penitentiary, and he'd said enough damaging things about Malatesta that the recording would be useful both in forcing Walter to turn on the judge and in corroborating him once he did it. Stan shot a thumb in the air and unfastened his seat belt so he could move around the van, hunched from the waist, shaking hands. I noticed he made it a point to start with Jim.

Yet as Amari drove back, I felt somewhat removed. I was happy enough to see the Project succeed, but I was more stunned than I'd anticipated by the events. I had always known there were monkeyshines of some kind going on in the Kindle County Superior Court. When I began practice as a new assistant State Defender, late in the 1960s, Zeb Mayal, a bail bondsman and ward boss, still sat in open view in the Central Branch courtroom issuing instructions to everyone present, often including the judge.

But in the felony courthouse, on the other side of the canyon created by U.S. 843, I was always an outsider. I'd come to the law at my father's table, listening to him speak about the great principles of decisions, moments that remain in memory magical and intense, like the spotlight's circle of white on a darkened stage. I didn't understand those who saw the law only as either a commodity or a social lubricant, nor, frankly, did they know what to make of me. I had no committeeman, no parish to name, and was primly disdainful whenever someone suggested that I take steps—selling tickets, for example, to a fund-raiser—to overcome these deficits. Over time, I realized that the system that existed, whatever it was, had as one of its principal aims closing out fellows like me, with my faint Southern accent, my unfaltering manners, my Brooks Brothers apparel, and my Easton degree. I was someone who had prospects in the Center City among the suits and the towers. Most of the regulars in the felony courthouse knew they counted for little in that realm, which was one of their foremost, if unspoken, excuses for taking care of each other. And eventually, as they expected, I departed for that other world, to the federal courts, where there was officiousness, but virtually no known corruption, beyond what was suspected about a few rogue drug agents.

Robbie's tales of retail justice were appalling, but also somehow titillating to me, because they suggested again some stifled secret I'd been searching for during my years across the highway. And now in the banter between Robbie and Walter I heard it, the hard wisdom of their clandestine world. A strange message was communicated in the passing of cash: I know the worst about you, you know the worst about me. The claims of law, rules, the larger community, the fabled, phony distinctions of class, are all, in the end, as insubstantial as dreams. Palaver aside, the black truth, which only we dare speak and which, as a result, gives us insuperable power, is that we are all servants of selfish appetites. All. All of us.

All.

"FIELD HOCKEY?"

"Yes, field hockey. It's been an Olympic sport longer than basketball."

"I know. Really, I know that. Guys get killed, right? In Pakistan? Somebody's always getting brained with that thing. The cudgel."

"The stick."

"Stick. It can be dangerous."

She stopped and lifted her lip to show him where there was still a pink scar. His black eyes, silvered by the streetlights, shifted back and forth from the traffic. Now that he was past his initial surprise, he nodded gravely, almost slavishly, clearly hoping to forestall any dread on her part that she had finally told him.

But she felt little regret. It was a good night. Neither one of them was down yet from the thrill of getting Walter. And, in truth, he'd guessed. About two weeks ago, he'd bought something called *The Olympic Factbook* and once or twice on the ride to or from work, he'd toss an event at her, usually as a non sequitur. He'd started with archery and went right through the alphabet. He was cute about it, of course, making his determination a joke, putting on a poor-mouthing, little-boy look. This morning he'd gotten to fencing, and tonight he'd had no trouble reading her smile. She was revealing only a fraction of what would come out about her eventually, now that there was certain to be a prosecution. And he'd been right at the start; he was too good an actor to blow the cover.

"The Olympics," he said, in dazzled admiration. Guys were always like this, staggered that a female had lived out their fantasies. "You probably couldn't even believe it was real."

Some would say it hadn't been. It was '84, so the Soviet bloc didn't show, but none of those teams were a power that year, so for her the glow had been largely undiminished.

"And you were great, right?" he asked. "To make the Olympics you had to be great."

Great? There was too much heat in the car and she was almost groggy. She had thought she was great. In high school, she was the best in Colorado, where no more than half the high schools even played. She was runner-up for Female Athlete of the Year in-state, and received a scholarship to Iowa, one of the great programs in the country, the absolute tops west of the Mississippi. She had gone off with high hopes. She was selected for the National Senior Team as a sophomore. It meant she was being groomed for the Olympics. But two of her teammates at Iowa were also on the squad, one a defender/midfielder like her, and both of them better than she was. They were stars, bigger stars than Evon. She played in the Olympics. But she did not start. Whenever she heard people talk about the Peter Principle, rising to your highest level of incompetence, she thought about her experience in field hockey. She had worked and strived and played against the best in the world and found, in the end, that the very best were better than she was. When the team took home a bronze medal, she thought, How appropriate, how doggone appropriate.

For Feaver, she kept it simple: she didn't start.

"But you were *there*." He was excited by the idea, clearly gripped again by some revived feeling of his own passionate hope for stardom. He was questioning her as an expert, as someone who'd arrived, who could tell him, perhaps, how he had missed the goal. How had she found the fortitude to pay the price? Where did it come from? The drive? The spark?

Her responses were laconic. She described practicing until long after dark, the way she had fallen asleep with a stick in her hand, not once or twice but a hundred times, reviewing moves in her head. She'd been through a stretch at Iowa when she had not spent even a single holiday with her family, a period in which Thanksgiving to her only meant prep time for the NCAAs and Christmas the "A" Camp in New Jersey, when even the Fourth of July was lost to the National Futures Tournament and in which the time devoted to sport meant it took six years for her B.A. Field hockey became a tunnel in her life, a long passage in which there was little external light. When it was suddenly over, she was like some underworld person returned to daytime, blinded, dazzled.

But beyond detailing her devotion, she could not share an answer to his questions. She was just not as open, or sloppy, choose the word, as he was; she could never take the joy or comfort he seemed to find in revealing himself. It had just been the path that was clear to her. Her father had been a baseball star. And it turned out his ability had leaped generations like an electrical arc. Evon had his power, his surprising speed from such a bandy build, and the precision to make that astonishing triangulation about where a flying ball, her body, and her stick were going to arrive. In the game, with the moving hand of the clock feeling as if it were winding her heart tighter, with the dimension of the known universe shrunk to 100 yards by 60 and its population reduced to the other twenty-one women on the field, with grace and fury possessing her as if they were visiting from somewhere else—at those moments she was finally, fully herself, not the odd, unknown, scowling girl lost in her tumbling home.

Her father lit up like a lantern when she played, paced

the side, at times too stirred up to watch, but her mother never really seemed to care for the sight of her, even when she ran from the field in victory. Her hair clung in damp ringlets to her cheeks, her uniform was mud-spotted, and her knee pads and socks were dragging down. Often, at the end of the game, she could see that she was where she had started, odd and vaguely unwelcome. Not simply because she was a girl good at what many still thought was reserved for boys, but because in her passion, in the explosive furious way she crossed the field, she was revealing something about herself, much like her scowling, which others did not want to know.

"I had the talent," she said. "And I worked it. For whatever that was worth." She shrugged, unwilling to express much more. The Mercedes by now had glided to a halt in front of the awning and the handsome refinished doors at her building.

"How far did you get? The team? Did you guys get close to a medal?"

She waved a hand, barring further inquiry. She heard her mother's corrosive warnings about being boastful and showy, and she was still wary, on principle, about going too far, too fast. But neither concern was the real problem.

"I did my best, Robbie, but it's over now. I've had to let it go."

The streets glistened in the warmth of a night thaw that would bring fog by morning. In the reflected light, she could see the fixed way he watched her. He knew about that, she realized, letting loose of the grandest hopes. Loss freighted his expression.

"Yeah," he said. He took quite some time before he spoke again. "If I said, Let me buy you dinner, that wouldn't be right, would it?"

Would it? She sighed on reflex, weighing it. But it was still too chancy. He was dashed, of course.

"Well, okay," he answered, but was too raw to look her way for long. His hurt, like almost everything else, was so open.

What the hell, she thought. What the hey.

"We took a bronze," she said.

"No way. Really?"

She indulged them both by absorbing his momentary worship. A medal. An Olympic medal! You could see his heart fly at the thought. She did not surrender often to pride, fearing she could remain stuck there for life, but tonight, under his influence, she felt it fill her out. She had done that. Set her mind, scaled the heights, and returned with the vaunted trophy. Ironically, he recognized the cost, too.

"That's a lot to climb down from."

"It is," she answered. "You realize you're a lot later than other people in getting started on a life."

They talked another moment. Before she left the car, he held out his hand to shake. Congratulations, probably. Alighting, she had another thought.

Peace.

CHAPTER 13

"PEOPLE TALK," ROBBIE TOLD US, "ABOUT Brendan, because Kosic and Milacki are always stuck to him like gum on your shoe. You know, it's like, What gives? Especially with Rollo, cause Rollo's lived for more than thirty years in the basement apartment in that big stone house of Brendan's out in Latterly on the West Bank. And Rollo's sort of been Brendan's loyal liege his whole life. The story is that they're both from the same parish, but Brendan's a few years older, so they didn't really get hooked up until they ended up in the same platoon in Korea. Anyway, they're in some hellacious firefight charging up Pork Chop Hill or wherever, the Commies are kicking their living ass, and Brendan looks around and some Chink jumps out of a bush and just about empties his rifle in Rollo. When they tell the story, and I've heard it only about seven or eight hundred times, it's like in the movies where the guy sort of stands there raffling from the bullets, dead already and only the recoil keeping him on his feet. Rollo's ripped to shreds, but good brave Brendan, under no circumstances will he say quit, he throws Rollo over his back and carries him up the hill for half an hour until he gets him to a corpsman. And this, by the way, is not just a story. Brendan's got the Silver Star at home to prove it." Robbie paused to direct a look across the conference room table at Sennett, a warning that Brendan Tuohey would risk his life to defy his enemies.

"Anyway, when Rollo recovers, he's like some character in an old novel or the Book of Ruth, My life is yours, whither thou goest. I don't know exactly what he pledged, but he's had his nose in Brendan's hind end ever since. Brendan becomes a cop, Rollo becomes a cop. Brendan becomes a deputy P.A., Rollo gets assigned to the P.A.'s investigation unit. Brendan becomes a judge, and pretty soon, Rollo's the bailiff in Brendan's courtroom."

Given the living arrangements, Robbie said, there was occasional sniggering. But his bet was what you saw was what you got—two crusty old bachelors, farting and walking around in their underwear. For one thing, Robbie said, Brendan'd had a thing on the side, his secretary Constanza, for more than twenty years now. Constanza was married, which suited Brendan just fine. He had once told Robbie he would no more care to live with a woman than with a parrot. 'Love the plumage,' he said, 'but too much jabber. Easier this way.' Indeed, in one of his acidic, if antic, moods, Robbie told us Tuohey had delivered a fairly entertaining monologue about why liquor was a more dependable companion than a woman. Kosic, who said almost nothing to anyone, seemed to share these attitudes. He, too, had a girlfriend, a widow, his second cousin, whom, conveniently, he could never marry.

In Robbie's opinion, the motive for Kosic's and Tuohey's living arrangements was not sex but money. Brendan had extended Kosic's duties as bagman far beyond the usual role of a simple intermediary. The 'rent,' as Robbie

called it, which certain Common Law Claims judges paid
to remain in their courtrooms, was delivered to Kosic and
never went farther. For more than a decade, Robbie had
never seen Brendan reach into his pocket, even for a quarter for a newspaper. Kosic handled everything—he paid all
household expenses, the light bill, the phone company, with
money orders purchased at random currency exchanges and
banks. Brendan had no credit cards and rarely used his
checking account. Meals, vacations, clothing, his debts from
his card games at Rob Roy, his country club, even the little bit on the side he had always given Constanza, were
always handed over by Rollo. 'Forgot my wallet' was the
excuse with those who did not know him well; others did
not bother to ask. Occasionally, apropos of nothing, Brendan would mention his mother's Depression-learned lessons
about the evils of credit and the virtues of hard cash. Robbie had never heard anything similar from Sheilah, Mort's
mother. It was just Brendan's play, always a step or two
ahead of his imagined enemies.

This debriefing about Kosic followed Robbie's payoff
to Walter by several days. It was occasioned by Wunsch's
warning that Robbie couldn't expect a 'miracle-of-the-
month club' regarding the three new contrived cases that
had landed on Malatesta's docket. From the start, Sennett
and McManis had known that there was a finite number
of complaints they could file in a short period. Tuohey's
cohort would feel put upon and suspicious if there were
too many 'specials'; Mort could become curious about the
extraordinary volume of referrals coming upstairs from me;
and the judges might grow wary if Robbie and McManis
kept showing up as matched opponents, like Tracy and
Hepburn. On the other hand, Stan was under continuing
pressure from D.C. to keep the Project moving forward.
By now he'd taken a small coterie of Assistant U.S. Attorneys into his confidence, never seen by us and rarely

mentioned, but whose presence was indicated by the volumes of paperwork forthcoming in connection with each of the new complaints Stan had produced every ten days or so.

But the judicial assignments on the new cases continued to fall out inconveniently. Besides Malatesta, two cases had gone to Gillian Sullivan, who was temporarily unapproachable. At the moment, Judge Sullivan was under intense media scrutiny that resulted from some ridiculous inebriate remarks she'd made to a Hispanic attorney who'd arrived late in her courtroom. Only one case had gone to Sherm Crowthers, who was proceeding with it at his usual phlegmatic pace. And none had been assigned to Barnett Skolnick, the only judge who accepted money from Robbie directly and the one whom Sennett was dying to bag as a way to quiet the doubters in D.C. When Sennett had suggested trying to transfer a case or two from Malatesta to Skolnick, Robbie had scoffed.

"Sure, Stan, I'll just give Rollo Kosic a bang on the phone and tell him the FBI prefers Judge Skolnick." Besides, Robbie pointed out, Kosic was clearly favoring Malatesta at the moment, probably because his docket had been consumed by a lengthy environmental tort case that had limited the business he could do on the side. But now McManis had recognized that an opportunity was presented by Walter's warning that for a while Malatesta wouldn't risk more favorable rulings for Feaver.

"That's your excuse to talk to Kosic," McManis said. "Because you need results on one of these cases right now."

Naturally, Stan was excited by the prospect of breaching Tuohey's inner circle so soon. But Robbie continued to insist it was impossible.

"I don't do Rollo. I mean, I talk to him. He'd bounce into my usual pop stand now and then, so sometimes I'd buy him a beverage. But Rollo's the kind of guy, you hear from him when *he* wants. I *never* call him. And no matter what, I don't talk dirty to the guy. I couldn't sell it. 'Always act in your own person,'" Robbie concluded, another quote from Stanislavsky.

"Sure you can, Robbie," said McManis soothingly. Jim had removed his glasses. He did this whenever he became intent, so much so that I'd become convinced that the glasses were windowpanes, merely part of a disguise. Now he extolled Robbie's abilities as an actor and a salesman, and told him there'd be no problem setting up a meeting to appear accidental. "We have this little thing we do called surveillance," said McManis. He pointed outside, meant to indicate Joe Amari. "We'll tail Kosic for a while. When he shows up at your spot, you'll get a call."

Jim had never pushed Feaver before. He was a model of reason and caution, but he'd clearly noticed what I had in Robbie's quick-eyed resistance, something I hadn't observed in the months I'd been his lawyer. This wasn't a down mood, or even pre-game butterflies. Robbie Feaver was flat-out scared.

ONE AFTERNOON IN LATE FEBRUARY, as Robbie and Evon were prepping a client, Heidi Brunswick, for her dep, Bonita put a call through to Robbie. He was sitting in the tall leather chair behind his desk, and as he listened he did not move. Evon assumed Lorraine had taken another bad turn. Instead, he ended by saying, "You're the greatest," and buzzed Bonita to get Mort, who was defending a deposition in the Palace. "Let's go," he told Evon. Suzy, the other paralegal, was summoned to finish with Heidi, and Robbie, with apologies to the client, ran to the door.

"New one," he told Evon in the elevator. By now she recognized the look. After nearly eight weeks in his office, she'd seen Feaver through major depositions, even one day of a trial that settled after jury selection. Yet nothing excited either Robbie or Mort like the prospect of signing up a new client. They reached a state of high alert, as if they'd smelled gunpowder on the air. The fact that Robbie's days in practice were limited and that he could expect to share in the fee on these cases, even from a jail cell, did nothing to lessen his enthusiasm. But for Robbie, charming and landing a new client was a thrill in its own right, a supreme moment of performance in which success meant he'd persuaded at least one person he was a better lawyer than anyone else in the tri-cities.

The present matter was what Robbie referred to as a "*good* case," meaning there were prospects for a huge recovery. The would-be client was a thirty-six-year-old mother of three. Yesterday her doctor had sent her home from his office telling her that her chest pains were bronchitis. The paramedics had just brought her in to Sisters of Mercy's emergency room, unconscious and fibrillating in the aftermath of a major coronary infarct. Evon understood enough of the grim alchemy of this practice, in which misfortune was turned into gold, to realize that the damages could escalate dramatically if she died, leaving three motherless children. Feaver pushed the Mercedes toward eighty on the highway. He had been tipped on the case by the administrator of the E.R.

"We were real good friends for a while," Robbie explained.

He clearly knew his way around the hospital, slamming the pressure plate on the walls that swept open the doors to the E.R. with a hydraulic whoosh. His open topcoat floated behind him like a cape as he hustled to the administrator's office.

The woman was striking, African-American and something else, Polynesian perhaps. There was a trace of some high-cheeked ancestral beauty. She was in her mid-thirties and carefully put together, wearing a large designer scarf that covered her shoulders and was knotted mid-chest. Robbie kissed her on the cheek. She placed an arm around him in greeting and directed him at once down the corridor into the waiting area for the emergency room.

The space was crowded, most of the people in the four rows of plastic chairs evincing the beleaguered blown-apart look of anxiety so intense it had grown numbing. A bloated young woman, with a ratted hairdo in some disarray, cradled one child, a newborn, while two more, both boys, near three, climbed around the seats, raising a commotion. She spoke to them harshly and occasionally flicked out a hand to deliver a swat that each child was already skilled in avoiding. She finally caught one of them and his howls filled the small area.

In spite of the cold, an African-American teen was dressed on top in nothing but a white T-shirt, on which blood had already dried brown. He held one arm with the other. A crude bandage of gauze and tape was visible near his shoulder. An older woman, his mother, Evon guessed, sat beside him, humped up in a bulky brown winter coat, tossing her head in chagrin every now and then. The boy, Evon took it, had been stabbed.

In the very last row were the people Robbie and the administrator, Taylor, were looking for, the family of the woman who was somewhere behind the curtains a hundred feet away, struggling for her life. A lumpy-looking younger man with the pallor of a potato and thinning hair appeared to be the husband. He had his hands folded piously and looked completely bewildered. Beside him was an elderly couple, a porky, hard-faced man with black hair and a pack of cigarettes bulging in his shirt pocket, and his wife, whose jaw was already trembling from the strain of prolonged weeping. She cried again as soon as she saw Robbie with Taylor. She could not wait to tell her story. Still in his coat,

Robbie slid into the chair beside her and immediately took her hand.

"Robbie Fever," he said. Evon was sure he'd pronounced it that way: Fever. From a gold case in his suit pocket, he offered his card.

By herself, several seats down, sat the oldest child, who, perhaps, had insisted on coming along. Neatly dressed, she was about nine, with dishwater curls. She'd sunk down in her chair, looking into her lap. She alone seemed to have fully taken on the gravity of the situation, recognizing the emotional abyss over which the entire family now teetered.

After a while, Robbie took out his yellow pad and began to write. He followed each of the family members intently as they related the story. About ten minutes later, Mort arrived, with his slow-paced, shuffling limp, and took up the seat between the daughter and her father. He spoke first to the child. He was quiet and made no effort to humor her, but hovered, awaiting her responses. When at last he received a decisive nod, he reached into his briefcase and removed a book of crossword puzzles and a pencil, Mort turned next to the father.

The two lawyers were like that, literally enveloping the family from both sides, when a doctor called out, "Rickmaier, who's with Cynthia Rickmaier?" He was in operating scrubs, including the green head cover, and he was followed, somewhat timidly, by two female residents, one also dressed for surgery, the other in a long white coat with a stethoscope at her throat. The surgeon, eager to get this over with, apparently took Robbie and Mort for family members. He motioned them all to an adjoining room and began speaking as soon as he had closed the door. He did not get very far before the old woman let out a primal shriek. Grief drove her to a corner of the room, where she looked up to a crucifix above her and cried out expressions that did not quite cross the threshold to words. Her husband cast a puzzled look her way and shook his head. The doctor had continued speaking and Robbie scratched a few things on the yellow pad beside him until one of the residents seemed to take note, causing him to lay the pen aside. At that point, he followed the dead woman's mother to the corner and put his arm around her.

Mort, in the meantime, had steered the little girl to her father, who, even standing, still clasped his hands. He had said almost nothing, but tears coursed beneath his glasses, as his daughter leaned against him. Mort, on the other side, took her hand. He was quietly weeping himself. More startling to Evon, Robbie, when he returned to the other family members, was weeping, too, real tears leaving trails of light on both cheeks. She never cried. That was another lesson from the playing field. No tears, no matter how bad the blow.

Robbie, in time, began talking to the family about arrangements, offering assistance with a funeral home. He motioned to Evon and gave her a phone number. As she left, she saw him reach into his briefcase for the contract. She knew the form by heart now. "We hereby exclusively retain the firm of Feaver & Dinnerstein to represent us . . ." He passed it and the Mont Blanc pen down to the husband, now sitting limply in a chair. His arm was around his daughter and his eyes were fixed on the large clock. His mother-in-law was demanding he sign. They were going to get the shits who did this to Cynthia. She couldn't leave this place, she said, without knowing the process had begun.

When Evon returned, Robbie was on his feet. His eyes were dry now. His coat was buttoned, the muffler was in place, and his briefcase was under his arm. No doubt the contract was in there. Robbie kissed the mother-in-law goodbye and said another private word to her. Before he left, he reminded the two men, even the little girl, to talk to no one else about the matter, especially not anybody from the insurance company. Refer all calls to them. Mort remained beside the little girl.

"Make a note," Robbie said to Evon, as soon as they were in the Mercedes. "Call Ozman County and find out when the coroner's inquest is. We need to be there. There's a lot riding on when the coroner fixes the time of the major infarct. If he says it was three days ago, then the doctor's going to claim all the damage was done and even if he'd made the correct diagnosis yesterday, it wouldn't have saved her." Robbie gave Evon the name of a pathologist he wanted to attend the inquest with them, an expert witness who could come to an opposite conclusion from the county coroner's, if need be.

Feaver was pensive as he drove, allaying Evon's worst fear that he might even celebrate. They were on the highway now and the Mercedes was a placid environment. Sisters of Mercy was far out, beyond the suburban sprawl. Here the frozen corn shocks of the autumn lay fallen, elbowing through the snows that filled the vast fields beside the road.

"Can I ask something?" Evon said eventually. At her center, a storm of odd feelings was agitating. "When I met you, you said your name was pronounced Favor. Like 'Do me a favor.' But just now you said 'Fever.' You say it like that most of the time."

"Fever. Favor. I answer to both. When I was going to be a star, I thought Fever was better. Hotter, right? I go back and forth. Maybe I was trying to be a hit with you that first day." He shrugged, with his usual whimsical appreciation for his own deviations. Most of the people around him said 'Fever,' in fact. "And besides," he said, "there's the public relations thing."

She didn't understand.

"The name was Faber. In the old country. It's one of those Ellis Island stories. The immigration officer couldn't understand the accent and my grandfather tried to correct him, so F, e, a, v, e, r ended up on his papers. But, you know, some people who think this way, they'll look at me, they'll think Favor. Faber. Jew. So I'm Fever. With the Rickmaiers. Part of the play."

She took her time with that. Robbie smiled briefly, pleased as always to gall her.

"And what about the crying? Is that part of the play, too?"

"I guess. That's sort of our trademark. Mort and me. You know, out on the street, we compete, every guy, every gal in this business, we all think we're the greatest trial lawyer who ever held a legal pad, we all want the work, it's greed and ego. Like with these people. This is a good case, okay? Real good. Word'll get around fast. Probably a dozen guys'll have some kind of in, the aunt or the neighborhood cop or their minister, and all of them will come beat on the Rickmaiers' door to say they know lawyers better than Feaver & Dinnerstein. I'm gonna have to stick closer to these people than the label on their shirts for at least three weeks just to deal with that. But anyway, when these other lawyers put the knock on us, they'll ask, Did they cry for you? You know, like that's our trick. Did they sit up and fetch?"

"But is it?"

"What?"

"A trick. Can you just do that?"

He asked her to hold the wheel and pressed his hand to his nose. He might have been meditating. When he finally faced her, beads of quicksilver brimmed in both eyes. He blinked, sending the tears down each cheek, but his grim expression gave way at once to a sly smile.

"I'm good," he told her as he resumed the wheel. She watched him, easing back into the gray leather, his cheeks still moist from his dramatics, while he luxuriated in the shock he inevitably inspired. He found her contempt so reliable, she realized. And with that, some premonition broke through the inner commotion. Was *she* being played?

"And you can just tell yourself to cry? The way I tell myself to open and close my fist?"

"Not exactly. I think about stuff."

"What stuff?"

"Sad stuff."

"Well, what kind of sad stuff did you think about now?"

He gave his chin a querulous little shake. He wasn't saying.

"I told you about the Olympics."

"That's different," he said. "That's like a fact. And besides, I guessed."

"And I admitted it," she said, adding, "like a fool."

He glanced over, apparently seeking to determine whether the self-rebuke was sincere. She stiffened her face a bit for his benefit. They drove on a mile, the only sound the unnerving hum of the tires on the cold road.

"The girl," he said suddenly.

"What?"

"I was thinking about that little girl. I was thinking about what it's going to be like for her tomorrow morning. When she wakes up. When her eyes spring open and she's thinking something dopey, about school or the movies or something she dreamt, and then, like an arrow right through the heart, she's going to realize that she lost her mother. And she's just going to fall down and down into fear, horrible fear, because she's smart and she'll know she can't even figure out yet how huge and horrible this is. That's what I was thinking."

"So it's *not* a play. The crying?"

"Huh?"

She repeated herself.

"I thought I explained this to you," he said. "About the

play." Irritated, he revolved his head between the road and Evon. "Don't you see this whole thing? What am I doing at that hospital? Or a funeral home? Or anyplace else I go to pick up business? I say to these people, Hey, you're in pain, terrible pain, but I can make it better. Trust me. I hurt for you. I'll get you money. I'll calm your outrage. But it's a play. Remember chaos and darkness? I'd need the power to raise the dead before I could really do anything for that little girl. Right? The money'll be nice. But hey—"

"So you *don't* care?"

"What? You think I stay up four nights in a row when I'm on trial because I don't care?" Staring at her, he was suddenly paying no attention to the highway at all. He directed the Mercedes into a small wayside, where the picnic tables had been turned over so they would not be crushed by the snow load. The brown legs, cross-membered, looked like arms waving for someone's attention. "Is that really what you think?"

She was afraid to answer. In ire, his eyes had darkened. He was going to spout again, speechify. And she didn't mind. She was glad actually. Except for remote moments of anger, Robbie Feaver could rarely be motivated to be fully sincere. But now something elevated was transmitted into his overorchestrated handsomeness.

"Look, I love the spotlight. I dig the bucks. I adore getting the chance to strut around on my victory lap down Marshall Avenue whenever I win a case. But hell," he said, "you actually think I drop to these judges *just* for myself? Get real. I can't bear to come back to these people and say, I lost, you lost, fuck hope, it's only pain, and it's only going to get worse. I can't do that. That's why it's a play. They need it. And *I* need it." Carried away, he had briefly taken hold of her hands. She did not know if he drew back then because he had woken to the precariousness of that gesture, or simply in refuge from what must have flooded from her eyes. He touched his bright muffler and softly said one more thing before he again put the Mercedes in gear.

"It's a *play*."

CHAPTER 14

A FEW DAYS LATER, AS ROBBIE AND EVON
were about to leave for the night, McManis called. Amari
had followed Rollo Kosic to Robbie's old hangout, an up-
scale spot called Attitude. After a hurried stop downstairs
for their equipment, Evon and Robbie buffeted through the
after-work crowd, the walks illuminated by the autos grid-
locked in the avenues. Feaver was surprisingly chipper. His
apprehensions about Kosic seemed momentarily eased by
the prospect of returning to the place where many good
evenings had been spent until about a year ago, when
Rainey's debility was no longer impending doom but a
calamity that had arrived.

Attitude's long windows fronted Cahill Street, but the
bar was entered through the lobby of a fancy retail arcade
where headless mannequins posed elegantly in the windows. Dr. Goodbody's, the health club at which Robbie
had formerly exercised every evening, was also here in the
basement. He said that the serious fitness types remained
in the cellar after their workouts, sipping carrot juice and

eating soy burgers. The crowd that hurried up to Attitude was more to his liking. They went to step classes, played racquetball and tennis, lifted weights for an hour, then stopped in here for tequila and cigarettes, to see if their strict physical regimen could yield any benefits more immediate than good health.

A stylish black sign hung over the doorway and the decor within was sleek—granite tables and polished chrome railings, Italian fixtures in the shape of inverted calla lilies casting a low light. The crowd was all suits. Some prowled the tumbling scene around the bar, a long arc of granite and wood. Others were settled in for the evening at the narrow tables in the slate loft, suspended overhead amid the smoke.

A chorus rose up as soon as Robbie came through the revolving door. "Hey, ambulance chaser!" a man yelled and arrived through the bustle to embrace him. He was a beefier version of Feaver, dark, elegantly dressed, with shining black hair moussed back into a bullet-shaped do. "Where you been for Chrissake? You hanging out at the rehab hospital, trying to get the nurses to pass out your card to all the quads? I'm waiting for this guy to get a toll-free number. 1-800-PARALYZED."

This was Doyle Mersing, a commercial real estate agent. He put an arm around Evon as he was shaking her hand.

"Come on, have a pop," said Doyle. There were two women beside the stool he'd briefly vacated, one in her late thirties, the other slightly older, both with big hair and bright manicures, both smoking cigarettes and pleasantly drunk. Divorcees, Evon guessed. Neither wore a wedding ring and there was something beaten-down beneath their good cheer. Evon watched as one of them, Sylvia, darker and thinner than her companion, began focusing on Robbie. It seemed astonishingly predictable, like something in nature, a flower turning toward the sun. Sylvia began asking him questions and tossed her hair back from her face so she could give him her full attention. At Robbie's wisecracks, Sylvia and her friend rattled in delight. After one of these explosions, Evon noticed that Sylvia had laid her hand on Robbie's arm, apparently regarding Evon as no impediment.

Turning away, Evon lifted her face to the smoke, the music and laughing, the smug but desperate emanations that lingered like fumes in Attitude's atmosphere. She had never been much at ease in this kind of place. They could have used a plastic surgeon and an erector set to make her over at Elizabeth Arden and she'd still never count for much here. Even pretending to be someone else, she couldn't project the air of frank and fearless interest that wafted off the Sylvias of the world. How did they do that? To Evon, it remained an enduring mystery.

The bartender, Lutese, was a gorgeous black woman with strong features and perfect makeup, including dramatic shadings around the eyes. She was nearly six feet tall and in beautiful shape. She had yellow nails the length of talons. Lutese was a fortune-teller by profession, Robbie told Evon. She took that at first for a joke.

"Speaks the truth," said Lutese. "Happens every now and then. You better keep your eye on this boy around this place," she warned Evon. "He's got more lines than a zebra." Robbie laughed but Lutese wouldn't let up. "Watch him, I'm tellin you. He's like a snake, strike anything that moves."

"I'm a one-man menagerie."

"Part jackass, too."

Mersing, who'd gone off for cigarettes, beat the pack on the heel of his palm as he returned to his stool.

"So what's going on in here?" Robbie asked. Despite the din, Evon could hear Robbie clearly in the earpiece. The way the instrument imposed Feaver's voice on the hubbub was slightly disconcerting. Klecker had applied the FoxBIte units to Feaver's thigh hurriedly, complaining about the idea of recording in a crowded saloon. 'Way too much ambient sound. You get glasses clinking. Other people's conversations. The defendant always ends up claiming that the guy saying "I did it" was sitting at another table.' Robbie remained adamant that his only chance with Kosic was here after Rollo had had a couple of belts. For the moment, however, Feaver seemed in no hurry to search for him.

"Same old," Mersing answered. "Your friend, the one you used to call s.b.d., she's been coming in again."

"Oh yeah? Tell her I say howdy." Robbie tilted his glass back and watched the bubbles rise. "S.b.d.," he said softly and smiled.

Short black dress, Mersing explained when Sylvia asked. Robbie and he then conversed about a fellow named Connerty. He'd had three marriages which, all told, had not lasted a year. Currently, he was seeing someone whom Mersing referred to as "the Sicilian girl."

"Glows in the dark," Robbie said.

"Really?" The two men shared a laugh.

Sylvia was fully entwined with Robbie now. Her arm was wrapped around his and she'd drawn him close as she sat on the polished steel barstool. Her knees, on which her nylons shone, were parted vaguely, and Feaver's hip occupied the resulting space. A huge swell of laughter rippled through Mersing and Robbie and the two women. Evon had missed the joke.

Looking away again, from nowhere she felt herself nearly knocked flat by longing. It arrived something like her period, always a little surprising and unwanted, with such sudden focused intensity that for a single instant she was afraid she might even cry out. And then blessedly, as ever, it passed, leaving her in the aftermath still throbbing like a bell after an alarm. The thought of a real drink, instead of her Perrier lime, tempted her briefly, but Feaver suddenly shed Sylvia. He'd spotted Kosic. He left a large tip for Lutese, before motioning Evon onward.

Robbie had said Kosic looked like an anchovy fresh out of the can, and with that description Evon had no trouble spotting him, a stringy, sallow, silent man, who sat at the end of the bar. Just above him, a pianist played show tunes in the loft. Rollo was alone. He was always alone, according to what Robbie had said. If somebody sat down beside Rollo, he moved to the next stool, and if there were no stools left, he just stared at the wall or the bottles on the bar in front of him. He generally spoke only to Lutese or the other bartenders. He was genial with them, if you could call the exchange of a few words geniality. He laid two twenties down when he assumed his stool and quit when there was only a ten, which he left as a tip. As they came upon him now, Kosic had stolen a look at himself in the bar mirror and was patting his thinning hair back into place.

"Rollo the K, how's tricks?" Robbie slipped into the usual open space beside Kosic. Rollo nodded a bit and worked on his cigarette. Up above, the pianist began a rendition of "Yesterday." Dressed entirely in black, the musician crooned along lethargically, bearing up through one more night of indignity in which any attention he received came only when the patrons reached an awkward juncture in their come-ons. Evon knew the music was going to be a problem on the recording, but there was nothing to do about it now. Kosic had yet to say a word, anyway.

When Robbie introduced her, Rollo cranked his face over his shoulder and looked her up and down in far too frank a manner. He was out of place in here, where the air throbbed with pretense and fashion. He wore a very old tweed sportcoat and a washed-out plaid shirt. His black hair, the soggy remnants of an old d.a., spilled over his collar. His face looked dried out by drink.

Robbie motioned to the piano bar up above and told Kosic a quick joke: A guy comes into a joint, opens his briefcase, and on the bar puts down a miniature Steinway and a little man one foot tall. The little man plays for an hour and the guy collects a number of tips. When the barkeep expresses his admiration, the man with the briefcase grimaces. 'Whoever heard of a genie with a hearing problem? You really think I asked for a twelve-inch pee-nist?'

Rollo took it the way he might have tried to shake off a punch, twitching out the sour leavings of a smile. He crushed his cigarette and shook his head. He drank old-fashioneds, and kept his right hand on his glass most of the time, his index finger curled inward. Robbie had explained that the nail had a sinister look, a little like the shell of a rotting walnut. It had been crushed in the service while Rollo was hauling an artillery round. It grew back black and rimpled, and was ordinarily hidden. Feaver said that was the only way to tell when Rollo was angry, since he otherwise maintained a morbid and haunting lack of affect. But when he extended that index finger at you, with that ugly token at the end, it was not a good sign.

At the moment, Kosic took the stem of his cherry between his thumb and third finger. He gave it a twirl, then knocked the glass back, draining it and taking one of the ice cubes in his mouth. He chewed on it as Robbie and Evon stood beside him in silence. When Lutese came their way, Robbie put a fifty on the bar and surrendered his stool to Evon, asking Lutese to refill Rollo and to tell Evon her fortune. She and Robbie, even Kosic, watched while Lutese shuffled and smoothly dealt out the tarot cards, despite the glistening obstruction of her yellow nails, each curved like a parrot's bill.

"Home?" she heard Kosic ask Robbie very softly, apparently thinking Evon was distracted. His voice was high, a virtual countertenor. She wondered if its feminine quality accounted for his reluctance to speak.

"Not good," Robbie answered.

Kosic grunted. It was not clear if that was a response to Lorraine's condition or to the fact that Lutese had just put down his drink.

"Listen," Robbie said to Kosic, "I'm happy to bump into you, I got a little something. I've been trying to figure out who to talk to. Maybe you can give me a pointer. You don't mind listening, right? It's a barroom. Everybody's gotta tell you their problems." Robbie laughed. When Evon's eyes drifted sideways, she saw Kosic toss another ice cube into his mouth.

"Anyway, I got some problems in a case I filed a couple weeks back." Robbie named it.

"Who'd you draw?" Kosic asked neutrally. There was no way to tell if he truly didn't recall.

"Malatesta."

"Good judge," said Kosic, then added, "Knows the law."

Lutese continued dealing on the granite bar top, talking to the figures on the cards as if they could hear her.

"Right," Evon heard Robbie say in her earpiece. "Normally, you know, I'm really happy to get him. But I got a very big problem. Case is a Structural Work Act. Client's painting an atrium and a scaffolding collapses. Serious, serious back injuries. Herniations, L-4 and -5. So I call to tell him we filed, they always want to know, and he says, 'I'm a little numb, I just saw my internist and I've got stage four cancer of the lung.' Cancer! Now I got a hellacious problem. Case is worth zip if the insurer finds out he's a goner, right? No loss of future earnings."

With considerable circumspection, Robbie detailed his troubles in having the case before Malatesta. For Robbie to have any hope of recovering much, the judge would have to quickly suspend the discovery process while Robbie attempted to settle. But Malatesta never agreed to stay discovery, a practice only Judge Skolnick ordinarily allowed. Walter's warning made it certain that Malatesta would not consider a deviation in this case.

"So I got a bellyful on this one," Robbie told Kosic.

Robbie, as usual, had laid down the pitch just as Sennett and McManis had scripted it. He wasn't asking for relief so much as issuing a warning. Everybody would end up a loser if the case remained before Malatesta. As he spoke, Robbie concentrated on the TV over the bar where mud bikes were spinning through glop. Evon was pretending to watch the piano. Looking back, she saw Kosic's small eyes aimed at Feaver. A pure, deadly light beamed from them. He was flicking nervously at the notch over his lip, touching it again and again with his blackened fingernail. He said absolutely nothing.

Taking the cue, Robbie shifted at once to talk of the Indiana basketball team which had clobbered the Hands, the U.'s team, last week. Kosic showed no interest. He got off his stool and threw back the diluted remains of his drink. Lutese, at that moment, laid out the last of the cards, a red queen, and stared down at it. When her wide brown eyes rose to Evon, they held a look of alarm.

"The two-faced queen lives a lie," she said.

It was not clear Kosic had heard that as he pushed out, with no word of goodbye.

THE RECORDING WAS TERRIBLE. At the critical moments, Robbie, just as Klecker had instructed, had rounded his shoulders and hunched forward to funnel sound toward the mike, which tonight had been placed under his tie. But the piano and the singing intruded into every sentence; it was as if Robbie was speaking between measures in a karaoke bar. A woman to whom Evon had paid no attention could be heard distinctly now, whining along. 'Now I long for yes-ter-day, ay, ay, ay.' The recording offered no proof Kosic had even heard Robbie.

But he had. Evon had been palpably frightened by the wave of primal menace he transmitted. As had Robbie. Sennett and I had hurried to McManis's conference room to hear the results and Feaver now directed his attention to Stan.

"They're gonna make me dead," he told him, "if I keep pushing like this. I said way too much."

Sennett frowned.

"Listen, Stan," said Robbie, "you may think I'm just afraid of the big bad wolf, but Brendan's the only guy I know who's an actual killer. I mean, killed with his bare hands in Korea. And would do it again today, if he thought he had to. He's ordered hits. I mean it. That's why he's stayed hooked up. It's not just for money. He wants to be able to push a button on somebody if he has to."

Even I had trouble believing that. Most talk of violence, even in mob cases, was gas, and I had a hard time imagining a Presiding Judge orchestrating a murder. Robbie looked around the table, where he was encountering similarly skeptical expressions from Alf and Jim and Joe Amari. As McManis had told him long ago, c.i.'s were always scared by what they were doing.

"Here, I'll tell you a story," Robbie said, looking about to each of us. "I've told you before that Brendan's had the same thing on the side now for more than twenty years with Constanza in his office. Constanza is like a jewel, this tiny, exquisite thing, five feet tall, perfectly shaped, and this noble Mexican face, Irish features and Indian cheekbones. Fifty plus now and still this very quiet, dignified beauty. Married lady—which is another story—with two kids, a boy, never meant for much good, and a daughter, completely the opposite.

"And Brendan, you know, he's been good to these kids, like he's been to me, frankly, always looking out and concerned. Anyway, the daughter goes off to the U., with a full boat ride, and does the college-age breaking-away stuff, takes up with a boyfriend. Black kid. And not a bad kid, really. Full of himself, but hell, he's nineteen years old. Constanza was having none of it. Not just cause he's black. I think if he was black and Catholic, she maybe could handle it. But that's a two-fer with her. And the daughter, of course, she kicked and moaned originally, but eventually, you know, she loves her mom, life goes on, she adioses the black guy and meets a nice boy, Puerto Rican, which is next worst to Mom, but this one's been in the seminary, so he otherwise fills the bill. Only this black kid, Artis, he won't take no for an answer. He calls. He follows the daughter around. He won't back off. And his life is going to hell in the process. He drops out of school. He gets strung out on something. He's more and more desperate, and finally one night, he's dusted his brains out, he jumps the daughter and the P.R. boyfriend, he pistol-whips the Rican, holds the girl at gunpoint, threatens to rape her, and finally, for whatever kind of jolly this is, makes her watch while he pulls his own pud.

"Well, Constanza goes straight to Brendan. Now, Brendan, when it comes to power, Brendan gets every channel. So he's never let go of his alliances on the Force. If he gives the call, he can have thirty uniformed coppers looking for this kid. He can make sure Artis doesn't get bail, that he gets the treatment at the jail till his anal sphincter has the same consistency as Cream of Wheat. But that's not good enough. Because Brendan, I guess, personally told this kid on a couple occasions, Cut it out or else. So now it's Or Else. He gets on the phone. He calls Toots Nuccio, who was always his connect. And Brendan's Brendan, he doesn't ask for anything out loud. He just shoots the breeze with Toots, he tells Toots this story in passing, about this horrible thing that happened to his secretary, Constanza, and her family. 'Can you believe this gorilla son of a bitch, what zoo'd they let him out of? It's a shame to call yourself a human being with the likes of that walking around on the same planet. I can't stand to breathe the same air.' That's all. T, h, e end for Artis. Ciao, au revoir, sayonara, bye-bye. When they found him, he had battery acid dumped on his genitals sometime before they finished him off. And it goes on the police blotter as a gang hit. 'Pity what they do to each other.'

"And here's why Brendan's a genius: because he made sure everybody close to him knew the story. His fingerprints aren't anywhere on the hit, of course. But he tells the tale about poor Artis and smiles. 'Makes you think there's a God in heaven.' But he was trying to make a different kind of believer.

"So Uncle Brendan, he ever finds out I set him up, it'll be the same for me, if he gets the chance. He'll have them gut me like a fish and come by to watch my heart beat its last on the pier."

As it turned out, no more than a week later, Judge Gillian Sullivan, still under relentless press criticism for her insobriety, took a ninety-day administrative leave from the bench. Officially, she was hospitalized for 'stress.' In the interval, much of her docket was reassigned. The two contrived cases Robbie'd had languishing on her call were both transferred, one to Judge Crowthers, one to Judge Barnett Skolnick. In the course of that reshuffling, the suit of the painter who'd developed cancer was also sent to Judge Skolnick from Judge Malatesta. The only explanation on the order was 'Reassigned for the convenience of the court.' Kosic, whatever his suspicions, had done just as Robbie had asked. But we did not know that, that night. What we knew was only what Robbie with his skills at impressing himself meant to convey.

These were dangerous men. Anyone who crossed them was in peril.

AFTERWARDS, IN THE MERCEDES, the shadows of fright and disappointment kept them silent for quite some time as Robbie maneuvered through the dwindling traffic in the dark streets. At a stoplight, they were caught under the flickerings of a mercury lamp going bad. It reminded Evon of a question.

" 'Glows in the dark'?"

"Implants," he answered, smiling wearily.

She laughed, but there was no admiration in it. She made a remark about men.

"Hey," he said, "you think the women in there are better? They're looking for rich guys and a free ride."

"It's *so* angry. That kind of talk."

"They're all angry. Most of them. Because they're lonely and setting themselves up to feel worse by the time the evening is through. And they know it. Every one of them. The guys. The gals. They're lonely and they're burnouts. They know they're taking what they can get. If I was gonna rename that place, I'd call it Sadder But Wiser."

"So why did you like to go?"

"You telling me you've never hung out in joints like that?"

Not like that. Not that she hadn't had her nights, her sorties to secret places. After the Olympics, after her body stopped being such a holy shrine, she'd go out to get juiced so she could see what she'd been missing. She'd been part of the good-time group getting smashed on Friday nights in agent hangs across the nation. And there were evenings of abandoned, obliviated drinking aimed really at nothing more than getting ready to have sex. But none of it lasted.

For her, these evenings were at best mistakes, at worst harshly struck notes of personal shame. And she remembered none of it with Robbie's wistfulness. Far from sad, he'd ignited the minute they were through the door. When she repeated that observation, he seesawed his head, something short of a denial.

"Well, I was always chasing the Myth. Like everybody else in there. You know? The myth of love. Right? Love will make me different. Love will make me better. Love will make me dig myself."

"But it doesn't work," she said. It was the first thing she'd said for herself. Naturally, he didn't notice she wasn't speaking about him.

"At the time? Romancing, getting there? It worked. In the sack? It worked. A lot. Because I was really there. And she was really there. The whole experience is beyond bullshit, right? It's beyond everything else in my life I've fucked up. I don't have a past or a law practice or a sick wife at home. And neither does she. I can be happy. And so can she. We can make each other happy. I can be something great and good to her. And she can be that way to me. And for an hour or a night, for a while, man, we can *love* each other for it.

"You know, sometimes, I'd just sort of wake to it, like, Here I am, sharing this experience, intimacy, I mean close this way, all ways, to a person I didn't even know existed six hours ago, and I'd ask myself, Is this so bad? Is this really so goddamn wrong? For me, you know, I'm not one of these guys who thinks sex is the only thing in life, but it was glorious. That's all. Glory us." He spelled it. "That's how I'd think of the word."

He'd gotten caught up and looked across to her in the dark auto. There was something soft on the radio and she found herself unable to answer him. The unguarded way he spoke about himself, as if he were somebody else, open to himself and anyone within the sound of his voice, was often breathtaking.

"It's just when it was over," he said. "By the end, it didn't work. Jesus, afterwards, it was always like I could never get out of there fast enough. I don't know what it was. Embarrassed, I guess. You know, that creature need made such a big jerk out of me. Or that I'd thought she was more beautiful. But what was worst was probably just seeing how separate we were. At the end of things. She was here, with whatever it was—her classes tomorrow at cosmetology school and her dad, a copper cold-cocking himself with brandy every night, and her mom saying novenas. She had her life and our minute hadn't really changed anything. All the women—I never spent the night. Even when I was single. Even Lorraine. After we were engaged, you know, naturally. But not before. And even there, the first few times—I mean, she was like, Robbie, come on already. So I stayed. But I didn't sleep. Not a wink.

"But next year, two years from now, whenever it happens," he said, with the same unruffled knowledge of the future and himself, "give me three single-malt whiskeys on a Friday night, give me the whole scene, the jostling by the bar, the jokes, the cigarettes, the shouting over the music so loud it feels like big wings beating the air—give me the whole shot and I'll believe it. Big time. The Myth. I'll be right back there, spotting somebody across the room and thinking, Yeah, she's it, if I can get with her, I'll be great."

Evon had no trouble envisioning that. She could see him, with two or three Sylvias attending him, the dashing millionaire lawyer catching sight of someone else, younger, prettier, more perfect, the one who for a second could make him better than he was. A throb of what had passed through her in the bar briefly revisited and Evon looked out the window at the hulking dark buildings of the city. He'd ask that perfect young woman what numbers she liked, even or odd. She knew that much. He laughed when she predicted that, asking him what would come next.

"Everybody likes even numbers," he said. "That's how it turns out."

"So what do you say then?"

"I don't know. I'd probably tell you about me. What I like, don't like. I didn't like horror movies when I was a kid and I still don't. I bet you do, right?"

"Right."

"Sure. But I like thunder. Most people don't like thunder. Bam! I think that's a gas." He smacked his gloves together.

And then? she asked.

"I'd probably ask you what you're afraid of. You know, really scared of. That's a great one."

"And what kind of answers do you get?"

"Well, it depends how drunk you are, how honest. I've heard it all. Breast cancer. That's a very big one. Driving at night or on snow. Rape, naturally. Spiders. Rodents. Elevators. One woman—I really dug her for this—she told me that there's some little piece of her that still gets scared when she hears the toilet flush. And there's a lot of stuff people can't really name: Things that go bump in the night. The bogeyman."

"And what do you tell them you're scared of?"

"Truth? I make it up. Whatever will play. If she says breast cancer, I'll say, 'Amazing, God, my old man died of breast cancer. What man gets breast cancer? Two in ten thousand. But I'm scared to death of that.'"

"That's not true, though, right?"

"My old man may be alive for all I know."

"But they buy it?"

"Some. The ones who want to go with me. Either she buys it or she knows at least that I care about making her comfortable. So she's not afraid to get on to what happens next. You know?"

Evon didn't answer.

"If it's perfect," he said, "we have a good meal, and we split a bottle of some red wine so fantastic it could burn a hole in your sock. And then we drift back to her homestead or the Dulcimer, and I always ask this . . ." He dared for a second to look her way. "Where should I touch you first?"

She was briefly aware of the river of sensation rushing past her shoulders.

"Maybe you want me to come up softly from behind and put my palms on your hips. Maybe you like having your breasts touched in just this way. Almost not a touch. A hint. A grazing. Like a breath. So that your nipples get so hard it's a little painful in your clothing."

"Not me," she said quietly. "Don't talk about me." The words had not quite cleared her throat. She had thought when she started to speak that she was going to tell him to stop completely.

"I take my time with the clothes. I've never cared for the strip-down-and-do-it stuff, like there's a meter going in a taxi. Some people, all this buildup, and then it's, Hey, let's get it over with. I take my time. A skirt, a blouse. I like the layers. I like to say hello to each new part like it's a jewel. Hey, look at this elbow! This shoulder. Then something sudden. Maybe I slide my tongue halfway down her ear. But I want it to be right. Everybody's *so* different when it comes down to, you know, the little mannerisms of pleasure. Hard or slow. Touch me here but not there. I always want to know. I want both of us to be free. This one gets off by rubbing my business with her titties, and that one can't come unless my finger's up her fanny. But it's always a gift. Always. Even if it was a five-minute stand-up in a phone booth, I've kept a piece of every woman I've ever made love to with me. Glory us," he concluded.

She had not said a thing. Sometimes it was amazing that life had gone on. It went on and you didn't know exactly what had happened. She didn't know now. Across the city, somewhere, a lowing truck horn boomed out. She was going to tell him to stop. For good. If he went on, she'd tell him. But he didn't.

"So what are you scared of?" he asked. She laughed, but he insisted. She didn't have to reveal any details of her forsaken identity, he said, but she couldn't simply be the interrogator. "What's your Big One?" he asked her.

She looked out the window. Near nine o'clock, a young boy who had apparently been sent down the block to the corner store waited for the light, coatless in the cold as he clutched a brown sack.

"Death," she said.

"That doesn't count. Everybody's scared of death."

"No, I mean, it's very strange. Some moments, I just *know* it. As if there's a record stuck in my head. 'This will end. This will end. This will end.' I just see the light closing off, me disappearing. I can't even move I'm so scared." Alone. That was the worst part somehow. Fully, inalterably alone. She did not say that.

He took his time. Reflections from the road ran up the front window as the car started forward again from a light. With his serious mood, his handsomeness once more took on depth.

"And you?" she asked. "What's your Big One?"

"Me?" He shook his head.

"Come on."

"No laughing, right? That's definitely part of the deal. I never laugh. I mean, a girl once told me she was afraid that as she got older she'd get ugly feet. And she meant it. I didn't even laugh at her."

She promised, but he took another moment.

"Sometimes I wake up at night—I mean, this is ridiculous—but sometimes I wake up, it's dark, and I don't know who I am. I'm just petrified. I don't know if I can't remember because I'm so terrified or if it's the other way around. I mean, I can remember my name. If someone called me Robbie, sure, I'd answer. But I don't really feel a part of anything else. I'm just sort of floating, groping along in the dark, waiting, waiting and waiting, until it comes back to me, who I am, what I am, the center. And I'm just terrified. Does that sound too weird?"

"Uh-uh."

"You're being nice."

"No, I'm not." She tried again for one second to call herself back, to think about what she was doing, and then once again succumbed. "Now. Doing this. Being UC. Undercover? I wake up and that's exactly how I am. 'Who am I? Who am I?' As if I have to wait to be told."

They were in front of her apartment.

"Frightening," he said.

"Really," she answered.

She turned to him then, but he had the good sense, whatever you'd call it, the intuition to make no move. He was going to let her come to him and in some infinitesimal fraction of time seemed to know that even now that was not what she'd choose. She endured an instant of pain so intense and familiar that it seemed almost a friend, then with a single solemn nod in his direction she left the comfort of the Mercedes and, in the harsh wind of the midwestern winter, picked her way between the ice patches on the street, returning to the place where she lived.

MARCH

CHAPTER 15

"THERE ARE DEAD MEN," SAID ROBBIE Feaver, "who are not as dumb as Barnett Skolnick. You stand before the bench, you think, God, how did this ox ever pass the bar exam? Then you realize he didn't. Knuckles, his brother, fixed it."

Knuckles, long gone now, was said to have fixed much more in his time than the bar exam. An associate of Toots Nuccio, he drew on the same wellsprings of influence, political clout enhanced by substantial mob ties. His nickname referred to his right hand, misshapen as the result of an infamous racial brawl at Trappers Field in the 1940s. He had been a downtown party committeeman, and the proprietor of a vast insurance agency that enjoyed uncanny success in underwriting municipal agencies.

"As the story goes," Robbie told us, "Knuckles had to put Barney on the bench because he was too dim to practice. The guy can't zip his fly without an instruction book. These days, at least, he *looks* like a judge. Beautiful head of white hair. But he just sort of sits there with this sweet, terrified expression. 'Gosh, I like you all, please don't ask me any hard questions.' Rules of evidence? This schmo's been on the bench twenty-six years and he couldn't guess what hearsay is if you gave him multiple-choice. God only knows what Brendan owed Knuckles. Skolnick's been here since Brendan became Presiding Judge."

It was late afternoon. The sun was dying with style, looking, in its descent, as if it might burn a hole in the river. We sat with pretzels and soft drinks in the conference room while Robbie went on. By now all of the UCAs would make it a point to crowd into the room for Robbie's debriefings, extended adventures, as they were, in the oral tradition. With his shirtsleeves rolled and his hands flowing through the air, Robbie worked his audience with care, aiming some gesture of connection—a deft smile, a decisive nod—at every person. Watching, I often thought about how magical he must have been before a jury.

"For all of it, it's still hard to hate Barney. I know you'll never believe this, Stan, but he's a sweet guy. Doesn't want to hurt a soul. Honest to God, he takes the money because his big brother told him to. They even tell a story about Skolnick, Lord knows if it's true, but it's a great tale. About twenty years ago, he's sitting in Divorce, not long after he first came on the bench. I can't remember who the lawyers were, two of the gods over there, guys who can talk to the judges. Well, apparently Skolnick's getting ready to start trial, and all the sudden he calls the attorneys back into chambers, just them, and he gets the two into the far corner and in this iddy-biddy little voice he says, 'Just so you know, the dough is even, so I gotta decide this straight.'"

According to Robbie, Skolnick had been bagged for several years by his court reporter, a Hasidic Jew by the name of Pincus Lebovic. Blue-eyed and foxy-looking behind the dense brown growth of his beard and pais, Pincus in his dark, outdated suits presided over the courtroom in a style bordering on tyrannical. He was cold-blooded and peremptory. It was even said that, on occasion, Pincus would halt proceedings, purportedly to change the paper in his stenographic machine, but actually to take the judge back to chambers to give him directions or, even, a scolding. The recognized brains of the team, Pincus handled all arrangements with the lawyers who 'talked' to the judge.

Then, last spring, Pincus's seventh child, his first son, was struck with encephalitis. Like a body on a bier, the boy floated toward the gates of death and lingered there for days. Pincus and his wife and their daughters sat beside the boy's hospital bed, singing to him, praying over the small, somnolent form, and begging the boy, whenever he could be roused, not to leave them. He did not. No one knew exactly what the terms were of the bargain Pincus had struck with the Almighty, but he was a changed person. He grew almost affable, and was unpleasant only when approached in his role as intermediary. He was now adamant in his refusal to take part in any further ugliness.

For some months there was, in effect, a corruption embargo in Skolnick's courtroom. Skolnick was far too kindhearted to dismiss his court reporter and not quite certain anyway what Pincus, in his reformed state of godliness, might say when questioned about the reasons for his departure by the likes of Stew Dubinsky, who covered the courthouse for the *Trib*. For a few weeks, the judge succeeded in convincing his secretary, Eleanor McTierney, to handle the envelopes, but Eleanor's husband was a police lieutenant, whose scruples stretched no further than to live and let live. At sixty-eight, Skolnick might have simply gone without, but that would have meant cutting off Tuohey as well. As a result, Skolnick would have had to accept demotion to a less esteemed courtroom—Housing Court or, worse, the ultimate hellhole, Juvenile—the kind of ego blow that Barney, like most victims of justifiable self-doubt, would have found devastating. Thus, in desperation, Skolnick began dealing hand to hand with a few well-accepted insiders, Robbie among them.

Skolnick, at least, had the sense not to allow money to pass within the courthouse. Instead, he established a schmaltzy routine in which the briber-to-be left a message from 'tomorrow's luncheon committee.' The next day, at 12:30 p.m. sharp, the attorney would take a position curbside, right in front of the Temple, possessed of a cash-filled envelope and a vexed expression. Skolnick, in his Lincoln, would tool by and, noting a familiar face, pull over, inquiring if there was a problem. The lawyer would then impart a tale of automotive woe—car wouldn't start, had been towed, stolen, sideswiped—and Judge Skolnick would offer emergency transportation. Skolnick would then circle through the Center City, while the lawyer in the passenger seat stuffed the envelope into the breach between the red calfskin backrest and the front bench.

Robbie had done this once last September, not long before Stan and his companions from the IRS had arrived on the flagstone stoop of his home. Feaver was due for another visit with Skolnick now, in early March, because Skolnick had ruled in Robbie's favor only a day or two after the case reassigned from Judge Sullivan had arrived on his docket. In that matter, *Hall v. Sentinel Repair*, Skolnick had ruled that Robbie's client, a driver paralyzed when the brakes failed on his truck, was eligible to receive punitive damages from the repair service that had found the vehicle roadworthy. Unlike Malatesta, Skolnick had dealt with the matter summarily, issuing a brief written order. Robbie would now tell the judge that the case had been settled favorably and would leave the envelope behind in appreciation.

Sennett was under increasing pressure from D.C. to justify the expense of the Project by scoring against one of the primary targets. Given that, and the fact that this would be Petros's first direct payoff to a judge, Sennett wanted it in Technicolor. The afternoon before Robbie was scheduled to see Skolnick, Klecker visited the section reserved for judges' cars on the first floor of the Temple parking garage, the same building where Robbie and Walter had met. With local agents covering Alf from all sides, he drove an ice pick through three of Judge Skolnick's tires. When Skolnick trudged out of the courthouse for the day, in an old rabbit hat and a lumpy muffler knitted by his granddaughter, the agents had him under surveillance. They radioed Alf, and just as Skolnick reached the lamed automobile, Klecker came ripping down the concrete ramp in a tow truck with a huge smoking engine. He jumped on the brake and leaped from the vehicle in a greasy jumpsuit and a seed cap. Alf had a bridge, a memento of his years as a high school ice hockey player in Minnesota, and he had removed his front teeth as part of his disguise. The agents said that when he talked he was pretty much a dead ringer for Sylvester, the puddy-tat.

"Got you too?" asked Alf.

"Hah?" replied Skolnick. He was still shaking his head in embittered wonderment at the sight of the flats.

Alf related that miscreant youths had apparently gone through the parking garage popping tires on a number of cars. He offered to tow Skolnick's Lincoln. Given the hour, he could not return it that night, but he promised to drive the car back to the judge's house by eight the next morning. He'd give Skolnick a great price on tires and would even reduce the towing fee, assuming the judge wouldn't forget Alf next time he needed to talk to somebody with a little pull in the courthouse when one of his guys got in a scrape on a repo.

When the vehicle was returned to Skolnick, it was somewhat enhanced. As promised, it had three fresh Dunlop

X80s. It also sported a new rearview mirror, a one-way, into which a fiber-optic lens and a mike had been inserted. The input devices were wired to a 2.4 GHz cordless sound camera resting on the ribs of the auto's ceiling. Leads ran down from the roof, through the hollow temple beside the windshield, to an existing junction box under the hood, so that the car's battery powered the camera.

"Fry the guy with his own juice." Alf beamed at his achievements. He described the apparatus to Robbie when we met at McManis's about eleven-thirty on the morning of March 5 to prepare for the encounter with Skolnick. The camera, which was turned on and off by remote, operated much like a cordless phone. It emitted a black-and-white video signal over four channels. Along with the audio output, the impulse could be picked up from a surveillance van as far away as four hundred feet. The transmission was admittedly subject to occasional interference, and as a backup, Robbie was also wired with the recording component of the FoxBIte. It was Velcroed today to the small of his back in order to avoid any revealing bulges at the thigh when Feaver sat with the judge on the lipstick-red leather seat of the Lincoln.

Along with Sennett and McManis, I had my reserved spot in the surveillance van. We circled in front of the Temple, waiting for Skolnick to pick up Feaver. Amid the thick electrical odors, Klecker crawled around on the van floor in a snake pit of cables. A small monitor with a twelve-inch screen and a VCR had been added atop the pyramid of equipment that had been there the day Robbie paid off Walter.

"We're going," Joe Amari called from the front, meaning that Skolnick had arrived and Robbie was on board. Joe's responsibility on Petros was surveillance. Sennett had allowed him to put together a select group of local agents from the Kindle County Division to help. As he weaved through the traffic, he made hand signals to the other cars. He wore a radio headset with a mike, which dented his smooth hairdo, but Klecker wanted him to stay off the air, if possible, to avoid disrupting the camera's signal, the same reason he'd removed the broadcasting component from the FoxBIte.

For the moment, Joe's assignment was to pull close enough to Skolnick that the camera could be activated by way of the remote Klecker held. Although the camera functioned from some distance, the infrared remote that controlled it worked only within thirty feet. It was plain from the tense instructions Stan issued to both Alf and Joe that he'd had some trouble convincing Moira Winchell, Chief Judge of the Federal District Court, to sign the warrant authorizing installation of the camera. The nature of the intrusion had seemingly mortified her, inasmuch as Moira was both a judge and a car owner. Stan had reminded the agents that Judge Winchell had directed that the camera could be turned on only when Feaver was seen with Skolnick in the auto.

"Hit it," Amari yelled out now. The small black-and-white monitor sprang to life, and we all canted forward in anticipation, while Klecker activated the VCR.

The bribery of judges is eternal. At common law, before there were statutes and codes, the word 'bribe' meant only this: a benefit conferred to influence a judge. It began as soon as King John signed Magna Carta and set up the courts. Probably before. Probably when Adam tried to reason with God about Eve, the first man offered Him something on the side. What we were there to see held the fierce primal attraction of any elemental wrong.

The initial picture was unfocused, a Hadean scene in which Robbie and Skolnick were reduced to images as indistinct as smoke. Klecker called directions to Amari, while Alf frantically squeezed buttons on the tiny remote. As always, the picture got worse before it got better, and then Skolnick detoured through Lower River, a covered roadway where the light was poor. But when he emerged, a relatively crisp image appeared, Feaver and Skolnick each slightly distorted by the wide-angle lens. If we fell farther behind, the digital imagery became weirdly aligned, so that little pieces of Robbie and Skolnick slid off the screen. But when Amari was able to stay within seven or eight car lengths, there was good reception.

The two men started out with warm greetings and ranged companionably over a number of topics. At McManis's instruction, Robbie also complained about having had his tires punctured yesterday in the courthouse garage, and he and Skolnick bemoaned their shared misfortune and the deterioration of society.

"These kids! What *momzerim*," said Skolnick and held up a thick finger. "They're almost as bad as we were!" He laughed, very much the genial, bovine creature Robbie had described. He was portly and florid, with a large broad nose, and that majestic spume of pure white hair cresting in a high old-fashioned pompadour. Skolnick asked after Mort, whose father he apparently knew from some shared affiliation with a Jewish organization, and then, more gently, about Robbie's wife.

"Ay, Robbie," he said after Feaver finished his matter-of-fact rundown on the crushing grip of the disease. "My heart goes out. Truly. You've been a rock for this girl."

"Not me, Judge. She's the one who's amazing. I look in her eyes every night and it's solid courage." Robbie's voice curled around the edges, and Skolnick, while driving—and in the very center of the broadcast image—briefly touched Feaver's hand. Watching across from me, Sennett scowled, apparently contemplating the effect of Skolnick's tenderness on a jury.

Shaking off despair, Robbie reached into his briefcase

and circumspectly removed the envelope the agents had prepared. Knowing the sight line of the camera in advance, he held the package against his chest so it was fully visible. Then with the stylized rigmarole these scenes apparently required, he let the envelope slip from his fingers to the seat and, not quite on camera, jammed it into the crevice under the backrest. Skolnick, who was supposed to remain blind to these maneuvers in order to have deniability later, predictably forgot his role. At one point he actually turned from the road to watch Feaver, although he was wise enough to avoid any direct comment.

"So, Robbie, what's doing?" he asked neutrally. "I haven't seen you in a while. I was surprised to see you called."

"New case, Judge," he answered, and described the matter which Kosic had transferred from Malatesta. Stan insisted Robbie had to ask for a favor now on that matter. If Robbie simply delivered a payoff on the first case, the one concerning the truck driver that had passed to Skolnick from Gillian Sullivan, a defense lawyer might attempt to characterize the payment as akin to a gift, inasmuch as Robbie had never spoken to Skolnick about the trucker's lawsuit. Thus, Stan wanted to make sure that money changing hands was linked to a request for favorable action, albeit on another matter. Robbie told the story of the painter with cancer movingly. But he made it plain he was hoping to bamboozle his opponent.

"See, Judge, I gotta get a stay of discovery. The defense, this lump McManis, they've got no idea about the c.a., the cancer? If we start with deps and medical records, then boom bang bing, they find out. After that, the lost-wages component in my case? Out the window. 'Sorry for your disability, but you're gonna be dead anyway.' So I need the stay, while I try to *hondle* with McManis. And the worst part, Judge, this poor bird's a widower. So if I

don't bring home the bacon, we got three kids with no
mother, no father, and not even a pot to pee in."

"*Oy vay*," said Skolnick. "How old, the *kinder*?"

"The oldest is eight," said Robbie.

"*Vay iz mir*," said Skolnick.

Sennett winced again at the last part. Robbie was making this up as he went, lying with his customary éclat, but
by painting a bleak picture of the consequences to the family, Robbie was lending an element of humane justifica-
tion to the misconduct he was requesting. Skolnick, in fact,
was quick to explain that from his perspective the whole
matter was rather routine.

"In my courtroom, Robbie, you know how it is, somebody makes a motion to dismiss, a motion for summary
judgment, something that can dispose of the whole case, I
stay discovery. Everybody else, these days, they want litigation to be like an express train. Who cares what it costs,
so long as it moves fast? But I stay discovery. That's my
practice for twenty-six years. So you make a motion, say,
for judgment on the pleadings, I stay discovery. That's how
it is. *Nu*?" Skolnick shrugged as if it was all quite beyond
his control. "Now you want help with your judgment on
the pleadings? Don't talk to me. My angina will act up."
The judge quivered with laughter. A judgment on the pleadings would have declared victory for Robbie on the sole
basis of his complaint and McManis's answer, something
that rarely occurred. Across from me, Sennett's frown had
deepened, as the judge had cheerfully outlined the bounds
of propriety. Skolnick was suggesting he wouldn't really
do anything wrong.

"I hope that's not why you're monkeying with the seat,"
Skolnick added. "Cause of this new case."

Robbie was briefly drawn up short by the unexpected
reference to the money. All of us were.

"No, Judge. That's *Hall*. We got a great result after you

stuffed them on their motion to strike my claim for punitives. I mean, that's why I'm here." In shadowy terms, Robbie reminded Skolnick of the first case about the injured truck driver whose brakes had failed. Skolnick searched his memory, his eyes thick with the effort. He concluded with a robust shake of his head.

"*Neh*, that's Gillian, Robbie. She'd drawn the order when I got the case. We just filed it. You oughta see her, poor thing." He gossiped sympathetically about Judge Sullivan's battle with drink. Adroitly, Robbie promised Skolnick that he'd visit Sullivan, too, but Skolnick continued vigorously revolving his head. "*Neh*," he said again, "take that there"—he dared to motion in the direction of the envelope—"take it home."

"Oh *fuck*!" Sennett shouted. His scream shot through the van. Up front, Amari pounded the brake and jerked around to see what was wrong. Stan waved him ahead, but it was too late. We'd missed the next light. As Robbie and Skolnick cruised on, we watched the small screen waver and flicker and finally dissolve to snow. Then the sound began to break up, too, sizzling into static. Klecker spun the dials futilely as Sennett cursed, his hands and face twisted in anguish.

By the time Amari raced back into range, Robbie and Skolnick's business was completed. There was no further reference to the envelope. Until he dropped Robbie off on a corner near the LeSueur, Skolnick instead regaled Robbie with a series of Jewish jokes. The best was about Yankel the farmer, who, years ago in the old country, went to buy a dairy cow. Two were for sale. One, the seller explained, was from Pinsk and would breed an entire herd; it cost one hundred rubles. The other, from Minsk, cost ten rubles but could be expected to bear only one calf. If anything, the cheaper Minsk cow looked better to Yankel than the Pinsk cow and Yankel decided to save his money. He bred the

Minsk cow successfully once, but subsequently she kicked and bucked savagely whenever a bull tried to mount her. Baffled, Yankel went to consult the shtetl's wise rabbi, who had something to offer in almost any situation.

'This cow,' asked the rabbi, 'is it by any chance from Minsk?'

Yankel was astounded at the rabbi's perspicacity. How did he know? The rabbi stroked his beard at length.

'My wife,' he said, 'is from Minsk.'

Alf couldn't restrain his laughter, but he popped a hand over his mouth in deference to Sennett. On his little fold-down seat, Stan was brittle with disappointment and rage. After Robbie had disembarked from Skolnick's red Lincoln, Stan pointed at McManis and demanded to know how the hell Joe could have just stopped. No one was willing even to look in Stan's direction. Sennett let his eyes close in their bruised-looking orbits and suddenly held up a hand which settled on his own chest.

"My fault," he said. "All my fault." He repeated that several more times. After close to thirty years, I knew Stan's demands on others were second to what he required of himself. It would take him days to recover from screwing up. Frozen on the narrow seat, Sennett was what he became most rarely and least wished to be—someone for whom everybody felt sorry.

BECAUSE FEAVER WAS GOING TO RETURN to the LeSueur Building first, Evon had been assigned to await him in McManis's office so she could turn off the FoxBIte. She sat there, knocking her thumbnail against her teeth, irritated by the suspense, until Shirley Nagle, the undercover agent who posed as the office receptionist, put a call in to the conference room from Jim. He was on the secure phone in the van and explained what had gone wrong. Amari had lagged behind Skolnick in the traffic, taking his time before getting close enough to turn off the camera, hoping that in the interval they might see Skolnick retrieve the envelope. But that hadn't happened, suggesting—at least to a defense lawyer—that the money was no longer there.

"Don't let Feaver know what's wrong," McManis instructed her. "But before you deactivate, you have to get him to describe in detail what went on. Then frisk him carefully. If he says Skolnick took the money, that'll be our only corroboration."

Feaver sailed into the conference room a few moments later. When Evon asked how it had gone, he raised both thumbs in his cabretta gloves, but signaled toward his back, where the recorder was still rolling. One of the protocols Feaver attempted to follow with mixed success was to avoid idle chatter while wired. Even the most innocuous remark could come back to bite him on cross-examination.

"Today we need to talk." Evon promised to explain later.

Robbie said he had simply waved off Skolnick's suggestion to take back the money. There had been a few quarreling gestures between them, but in time Skolnick had succumbed with an elaborate shrug.

She then asked him to stand. "I have to frisk you."

His eyes narrowed with an odd light, veering between disbelief and lechery, but he came to his feet with his arms thrown wide. All yours.

She had frisked men before, of course. Regs didn't favor it. But when you were first to the subject on an arrest, you didn't twiddle your thumbs waiting to see if he'd pull a six-inch switchblade. But she'd never frisked someone she knew. It was strange. As when they'd wrestled, he seemed larger and more solid than she imagined. She squeezed her way up his pants legs, turned out his pockets, and passed as quickly as she could over the crotch. She had a sudden fear he'd try something awful, hold her hand there or boost his hips forward. At that moment, she realized she should have asked Shirley to be here. But Robbie did not react. He had enough stage sense to realize how bad he could make both of them sound on the recording. She was the one who was tense. She turned him around and repeated the procedure from behind. At the end, she searched his briefcase and his overcoat, then described all her findings, before grabbing the remote and turning off the FoxBIte.

"Was it as good for you as it was for me?" he asked then.

"Listen, buster, I nearly said I found absolutely nothing in this boy's trousers."

He clutched his heart but he was smiling. The insinuations, the joking. She knew he felt he had her going his way.

He had figured out by now that the camera had not worked. McManis had asked her to listen immediately to what the FoxBIte had captured and to let them know in the van. Robbie pulled the mike back through his buttonhole and removed his shirt, and happily unhitched the unit. His back was sore from sitting against it. Klecker by then had left instructions with Shirley about how to load the recording magazines in the computer. Shirley, a curlyheaded woman in her late forties, helped, and the three of them listened together. At the critical point, as Feaver and the judge had exchanged their dueling gestures about the envelope, there were a few words—both of them, in fact, said "Come *on*"—but nothing clearly indicated what had become of the money. The only direct proof that Skolnick had accepted would be Robbie's word. From the start, Sennett had known that an admitted felon against a judge was a losing contest before most juries.

"Figures," said McManis, when Evon called him. "Everything that can go wrong will." He asked to speak to Robbie so he could tell him he'd done a great job.

Afterwards, Feaver, who'd draped his shirt unbuttoned

around himself, took it off again and asked for Evon's help removing the FoxBIte harness. It had been secured with yards of tape circling his abdomen.

"Pull the tape fast," he told her. "It's going to hurt like a bastard." He was right about that. Unruly black hair stretched densely over his upper body, gathering to the thickness of a pelt across his chest and down the medial line of his stomach. He looked like a lemur or something else you might want to pet. Klecker had suggested shaving, but McManis said no, it could lead to too many questions at the haberdasher's, or the doctor's office, or the locker room of the health club where Robbie still appeared occasionally on weekends.

"I lived my life pulling off adhesive tape," she told him. She cut through it with scissors, then peeled back the ends, making an opening right over his hipbones where the flesh became soft. She was standing inches from him, close enough to take in all his cosmetic scents and his body heat and his size, the coarse feel of all that hair on his upper body. Beautiful people—women *and* men—knew it. Pride, a sense of attention, and confidence in his effect radiated off Robbie Feaver at all times. With him half-unclothed, it was as if some lead vest containing that emanation had been removed.

"Ready?" she asked.

He put his hands on her shoulders to brace himself. "Tell me you're not going to enjoy this."

"Mommy brought me up not to lie. Hold tight." She squared her knees against his for leverage. There was a pulse of something at that moment. Perhaps he shuddered, or his grip on her shoulders tightened. It lasted only a second and she avoided his eye. Then she pulled off the front layers with a single heave, amazed by the vigor, the sheer wildness of the laughter that raced through her as he emitted a half-stifled outcry of pain.

CHAPTER 16

HAVING PROMISED D.C. A JUDGE AND HAV-ing failed to deliver Skolnick, Sennett turned his attention to Silvio Malatesta. Stan told us he had proposed bugging Malatesta's chambers, but Judge Winchell would not approve an overhear that risked prolonged eavesdropping on innocent judicial functions. She wanted proof, just as she'd had before the camera went into Skolnick's car, that a specific criminal incident was about to take place.

Thus, the only way to get direct evidence against Malatesta was if Robbie had a wired encounter with the judge. Outside court, Feaver had never had a conversation with Silvio Malatesta that lasted longer than thirty seconds, and he regarded the idea as far-fetched. But Sennett felt that without a judge, D.C. could pull the plug within a few weeks, at the next review. The case against Walter was solid, but there was no certainty he'd roll on Malatesta. If not, there wouldn't be enough evidence against the judge to charge him if the Project was cut short. Therefore, Sennett reasoned, it was better to send Robbie in against Silvio now. McManis reluctantly agreed, even though Feaver continued to predict it would be fruitless.

Amari began round-the-clock surveillance on Malatesta, but it showed that the opportunities for a chance meeting between Feaver and the judge were limited. Aside from work, Malatesta seldom left home without his wife on his arm, a miniature human being four foot eight or nine, who minced along on huge high heels. Amari referred to her as 'Minnie Mouse,' and Minnie Mouse was omnipresent. She was with her husband when they went to church, when they visited their daughter and her children, when they attended concerts at the symphony. Minnie was a harpist and Judge Malatesta was observed hauling her instrument to and from their ancient station wagon several times a week. Most evenings, he accompanied her to her performances at weddings or other large events where her gentle playing was usually lost in the clatter of china and voices. Silvio sat unobtrusively, studying briefs and memos and applauding demurely at the end of every selection.

After a week, Amari concluded the one moment to accost the judge was when he taught. Now an adjunct professor at Blackstone Law School, where he'd previously been full-time, Malatesta continued to meet a single Torts class. Each Tuesday and Thursday at noon, he trudged the two blocks from the courthouse to Blackstone's seventy-year-old building. Head lowered as he recited today's presentation in his mind, he passed beneath the law school's elaborate concrete façade into the interior of dark oak. Outside his classroom, Amari said, Malatesta invariably observed the habit of many older gentlemen and took a moment in the rest room. And it was there Robbie would get his chance. In order to prevent intrusions, Klecker would play the role of janitor, barricading the entrance with the little yellow plastic signs used by Blackstone's regular service, whose crews actually visited each day at 4 p.m.

Klecker was certain no one would think much of some-body swabbing the floor in the john. There were a hun-dred ways this could fail, especially if another person followed Malatesta in, but the risks were viewed as toler-able. If questioned, Alf would answer in Polish and go on his way, while Robbie made small talk with the judge.

I have mused now and then on the ubiquitousness of men's rooms in public corruption prosecutions. From the time I entered the so-called white-collar practice, where bribery cases are a staple, there was at least one case a year where some matter of consequence took place in the john. Why two fellows would choose to pass cash as they stand at the urinal has continued to puzzle me. Because they have only one free hand and no one can reach for a gun? Because they are, so to speak, exposed? Because all know this is truly dirty business? There must be something deeply symbolic. Whatever the reason, it happens with suf-ficient frequency that a bribe case which is largely hope-less for the defendant is routinely shorthanded as 'folding money in the men's room.' Jurors are inevitably unwilling to believe the parties were up to anything good.

So at 11:30 a.m. on Thursday, March 18, Robbie was wired and marched off to Blackstone. He had gone to law school there and, if need be, would explain his presence as related to alumni activity. Evon was along as a witness, again to corroborate that Malatesta was the only other per-son to have gone in and out of the facility and, accord-ingly, that his was the other voice on the recording.

Feaver came to a standstill as they entered Blackstone's Gothic front hall. There were fusty odors of floor wax and deteriorating plumbing, and he surveyed the surroundings right up to the ribs of the buttressed arches. He hadn't been back, he told her, in years.

"Bad memories?"

"Sort of. I didn't care to run into the old dean. He'd

have had heart failure if he knew I was actually practicing law."

"Why else did he think you went to law school?"

"Oh, he knew that's why I came. But by the time I left he'd caught my routine. He wouldn't have been my top reference for Bar Admissions." Robbie, as usual, was amused by his past antics.

In a moment, he'd entered the men's room, where the plan called for him to lock himself in a stall. Evon took a seat on an oak bench with a good view, and Alf, faintly whistling a Chopin polonaise, appeared less than a minute later with his bucket and his sign. He held the door half-open as a successful inducement to get the one other occupant on his way.

At 12:05, Malatesta showed up in his overcoat, which, like all his clothing, seemed slightly too large. He stopped in his tracks when he saw Alf and his sign, but Klecker bestowed a bountiful wave and Malatesta entered, smiling in humble gratitude.

Outside with the earpiece, Evon could hear the stall door open and Robbie's shoes scraping on the tiles. The script called for him to place himself at one of the urinals. There was no mistaking the sound of his lowering fly. Malatesta arrived beside Robbie, quietly humming some musical theme, perhaps the one he'd overheard from Alf.

"Judge, hey," Robbie said. "Robbie Feaver."

"Oh yes, Mr. Feaver. Nice to see you. Very nice to see you."

Robbie apologized for not offering his hand. A laugh, somewhat stillborn, emerged from Malatesta, who was predictably shy of bathroom humor. Robbie asked what brought the judge around and Malatesta offered a thumbnail of the cases he was teaching today on assumption of risk.

"That *Ettlinger*," Robbie said. "That's a half-ass decision."

"Well, it's somewhat more interesting than that," said Malatesta.

"I mean for a plaintiff. It's bad."

"Well, yes," said the judge. The cloacal waterfall roared. Feaver had been instructed by Klecker not to attempt anything of significance before then, the apparent lesson of sad prior experience with this environment. Now Robbie's voice dropped.

"Say, Judge," Robbie said, "that *Petros* case. Thanks. Okay? That was a great ruling. We got a terrific settlement."

There ensued a silence of frightening length. Malatesta, Robbie later reported, was plainly startled. He reached up to touch the black temple of his glasses. Given Silvio's caution and the limited chances for success, the scenario did not call for Robbie to make any brash declarations. He was to cut things short at once if Malatesta veered toward anything overtly defensive. From Feaver's stillness it was plain to Evon he was already afraid he'd overstepped. She heard him padding along and water running in the sink. Afterwards, over the wrinkling of a paper towel, Malatesta unexpectedly spoke.

"I really should thank *you*, Mr. Feaver."

This time Robbie lost a beat.

"That's okay, Judge. My pleasure. Really. I've got a lot of respect for you, Judge. I just want you to know that I appreciate what you do."

"It showed, Robbie."

"I tried."

"Your papers were excellent. Excellent. Most lawyers, frankly, don't show that kind of respect for the court. I regret to say that not all are as resourceful. You were thoroughly researched. The lawyers in my court so seldom use an out-of-state or federal citation, especially one of any precedential currency. That was helpful to you. Very difficult issue, too. But you convinced me you had the stronger hand. No telling if the Appellate Court would have agreed. We'd both be holding our breaths. You know, out of law school, I clerked in the U.S. District Court for Judge Hamm and he always said to me, 'The lawyers think they're getting reversed. They think they've lost. But it's my name on the opinion. I'm the one they say made a mistake.'" Malatesta laughed mildly, recalling this wisdom. "He'd tell me I should be pleased to hear you settled."

Robbie, at a loss throughout the conversation, stumbled again. "Didn't you know?"

"Did I? Perhaps it slipped my mind." The revolving lid of a trash bin banged. "But I'm sure it was a good idea. Better that way for everyone. Right? Naturally. The parties want an outcome they can live with, not their names in a casebook. Of course, I'll always have a grain of curiosity about what the Appellate Court would have said. But I suppose we can just move on to the next one. *We* know, correct?" Malatesta coughed up another thin laugh and the scuffing of his shoes drifted farther away. "See you in court," Malatesta called. "I hope I find the next one as interesting."

"It will be."

When Evon saw Malatesta emerge, he seemed to be smiling. He had his overcoat folded over his arm and started into the large, tiered classroom. Two students greeted him with questions as he was on his way down.

"Jesus," Robbie said as soon as McManis stopped the FoxBIte, back in the office. "What a wacko! This guy is one bubble left of level. One minute he's right with me and then—" Robbie made a whooshing sound and shot his hand into space.

I had been summoned as soon as Feaver returned.

Klecker had finished the dupe, and fast-forwarded to the rest room encounter when Sennett arrived.

"Very clever," said Sennett after it was played. He was beaming. "Very clever. He got his message across. He said his thank-yous. I loved the line about your papers being excellent. The fifties and hundreds especially."

Several of the UCAs who'd crowded into the conference room chortled.

"And the federal currency," said Evon. Nobody else had caught that line and Alf rolled the recording back to play that part again. Robbie had moved a little and the words were somewhat obscured. But we all heard them now.

"What a fox," Sennett said. "I love the visitor-from-another-planet routine. But we've got him. I enjoyed the warning about steering clear of anything that can cause trouble in the Appellate Court." Stan avoided 'I told you so,' but it bristled off him anyway.

McManis directed a look toward me. This was less than the clean head shot Stan imagined. Malatesta's defense lawyer would say it was no more than a discussion about a case. Why the wistfulness about the Appellate Court if Malatesta was acknowledging a bribe? And if he'd been paid off, he would have known the case had settled. But Stan had some evidence now, particularly if he could first get a jury to regard Malatesta as crazy-cautious. The sly remarks would take on shape then.

"We need more," McManis said suddenly. It was pointed as Jim had ever been. The struggles between Stan and him were growing more overt daily. Sennett took McManis's measure starkly, but, with reflection, managed a nod.

"We do," Stan said. "And we'll get more. We have to keep working cases in front of Malatesta. But we've got him talking now. To Robbie. And I may be able to pitch Moira again with this." Sennett allowed a little more of the flush of victory into his smile. "But we're going the right way, Jim. Aren't we? You have to admit that. D.C. will see it."

McManis answered only with a sidewards nod. It was the first occasion I could recall when he'd been something other than gracious. Instead he looked away from Sennett, and complimented the agents and Robbie on their work.

PERSONAL INJURIES / / 199

this way, Jim. And I’m...You know it’s about that I’ll—
will not...

Stabbing: something only with... pecuniarily had. It was
the.? Not on scene I could mouth when he’d been that doing
other than practice...Maestro he passed away from himself
and complicated the wrath and to keep on that week.

CHAPTER 17

"WE HAVE A PROBLEM." IT WAS LATE IN THE
day, close to 4 p.m. on March 22, the Monday after Robbie's law school encounter with Malatesta. On the phone,
Sennett was in imperial mode. He did not say his name,
but simply directed me to meet him at Jim's in ten minutes. Arriving, I found McManis and Alf Klecker with
Sennett in the conference room, each of their faces slackened and grave. Stan was in his well-pressed blue suit and
the grip of his public persona, jaw prominent, very much
in command. He circled a finger and Alf opened more of
the red oak cabinetry to reveal a large reel-to-reel tape
recorder, a stainless steel Grundig that began turning at
once.

The sounds took a moment to identify. There was paper
crinkling with an odd distinctness, the chuffing of various
items being pushed about close to the microphone. Something clunked down with an impact like a log.

I asked Klecker if this was an 'overhear,' the feds' delicate term for a bug.

"The mike's in the desk phone. Sound comes right here over the existing lines." Alf smiled with innocent pride, until Sennett swiveled about and burned him with a look for violating the strictures of need-to-know.

There were now voices, both female. From a distance, someone was talking to the nearer woman about the interminable length of a cross-examination.

"Anyone you recognize?" Sennett asked.

I didn't.

"I'll give you a clue," he said. "Two years ahead of us in law school." Nothing struck me until the distant voice addressed the first woman as 'Judge.'

Magda Medzyk! Magda had had a lengthy career in the Prosecuting Attorney's Office, supervising appeals, then had gone on the bench. She was a stolid, frizzy-haired spinster, one of those folks who seemed to have reached middle age even in her law school days. Her wardrobe had never changed, her suits always heavy enough to appear armorplated, guarding a figure of matronly proportions. I asked Stan where she was sitting currently.

"She's been hearing Special Motions in the Common Law Claims Division. Stay tuned. We're getting to the good part." Stan permitted himself a lean smile. It sounded as if Magda had gone back to writing at her desk, when her secretary announced a visitor. Mr. Feaver.

"Robbie!" A happy full-throated greeting. He addressed her as 'Judge' and made a joke with the secretary about the fact that he'd caught her eating a box of chocolates for lunch. When she departed, there was quiet padding, and a barely discernible click, which I instantly recognized as the door lock. I sickened as I realized what was happening: Robbie was about to fix a case with a judge we'd heard nothing about.

There was precious little small talk.

"Come 'ere, you," Robbie said. You could hear him

shuffle nearer. The springs in her chair sang out, there was a coarse rubbing of clothing, and, to my astonishment, Magda Medzyk emitted a rapturous little groan. I knew for sure I'd guessed wrong when he told her she had the greatest tits in the world.

Things progressed rapidly, to the usual percussion accompanying the human animal in heat—zippers, shoes hitting the floor, exerted breathing. Robbie and the judge eventually moved away from the phone, to a sofa I imagined, but their sounds remained telling. Magda was a groaner. As it developed, she was also wildly amused when Robbie employed certain Anglo-Saxon words. He could not have made a more explicit recording if it were a travelogue. As he described his forthcoming activities, unbounded laughter spilled from her. Big pink cunt. Big hard cock. The running brook of Magda's happy sounds was the only element that kept this from feeling entirely like a peep show.

"Enough?" asked Stan.

Plenty, I said. Klecker had his fingers over his mouth, but he jiggled with laughter. McManis, on the other hand, had turned away from the speakers as soon as the tape rolled. He'd spent most of the time staring at his thumb.

"So?" asked Sennett.

Odometer on his zipper, I reminded Stan. I didn't see the big deal.

"You know the definition of bribery, George? A benefit of any kind intended to influence the action of a public official."

I actually laughed at him. Prosecutors! Robbie sounded like the beneficiary to me.

"The lady on that tape isn't going to launch a thousand ships, George."

And he's not picky, I reminded Stan.

"Look, George, you say what you like. Moira Winchell didn't have any problem signing the warrant."

Stan had been playing on home court. Chief Judge Winchell, frosty and officious, would have been scandalized by this, especially as a woman entrusted with similar power. But I couldn't believe Sennett would actually prosecute, and I told him so.

"I don't know what I'll do, George. But I do know this much"—with gunslinger eyes, Stan leaned over the Parsons-like conference table—"your guy's holding out on us. He's banging the lady judge and then appearing before her on motions. On which he has a stellar rate of success, I might add. I want to know what else he's holding back. I haven't gone to D.C. with this yet. And you know full well I don't want to have to roll the Project up. I'd like to present this as additional information developed in the course of the investigation. But I can only do that little dance step once. Next time, they'll shut us down and cart Robbie off to do forty to fifty-two months. So this is it, George. Amnesty day at the library. I want all the books open and on the table."

I sat in one of the leatherette swivel chairs, confounded. I was long hardened to the dumb things clients would do. I was unsettled, rather, by a legal conundrum. No matter how supportive Chief Judge Winchell was, the law required probable cause, reliable evidence portending this supposedly corrupt encounter, before a bug could be authorized. Where had that proof come from? I asked Stan, and regretted it promptly, as he simpered.

"You're supposed to be wondering that privately, George. The government's response to the question is none of your business. But I warned you. I told you we'd know."

I groaned when the answer struck me: They'd bugged Robbie, too. Sennett was utterly stoic when I ventured this thought. He strolled to the electronic equipment in the cabinets and looked it over astutely, like a buyer in a show-room.

I told Stan this was too low, to make a deal with a guy and then undermine him, whatever the madmen at UCORC were demanding. But it was a mistake being so direct with Stan, given our audience. The personal side of our relationship had not really been exhibited to the agents. Sennett felt required to defend himself, particularly because McManis's continuing silence telegraphed a deep uneasiness with present events.

"George," Sennett said, "you may like this guy. But to me he's a Trojan horse with a body recorder, that's all. He might as well be a robot. I need two things to win these cases: Dead-bang recordings. And proof that the government held him to his bargain and didn't let him just bag the judges he hates. If a jury thinks that happened, then they may well cut everybody loose rather than let a creep like Robbie play favorites. And frankly, from what I hear, that seems like it's happened."

But *bugging* him, I insisted. A deal to cooperate didn't authorize this kind of gross intrusion into his private life.

"We're legal," Stan shot back. Like every prosecutor, he resented the suggestion of abuse. "We're completely legal. That's all I'll say." He bulleted me with one more angry dark look and put on his coat, which had been slung over a chair.

"No, I'll say something else, George. Because I resent your sanctimony. Your beloved client is what people have in mind when they use the word 'lawyer' as a pejorative. He treated a profession which you and I are both proud to be a part of as if it's tantamount to pimping. And he got rich doing it. And when we caught him, he made a deal to tell us the whole truth and nothing but, a deal which he doesn't seem to be living up to. And you and he both better understand that I'll do whatever I have to within the limit of the law to protect these prosecutions. Because I have to, George. Because the people on the other side, your client's buddies, the Brendans, the Kosics, they're a law unto themselves. For them, there are no limits. These are ruthless men, George." My friend Stan Sennett stared from the door, his eyes now hidden in the shadow of his snap-brim hat. He was pointing at me, a gesture meant to indicate he had no present use for courtesy or any of my other pretenses.

"And if I'm not willing to be as tough as they are, to seize every advantage allowed—if I'm not willing to do that, something terrible will happen, George. They'll walk away. And they'll do all of this, again and again. They'll win, George. And we'll lose. You and me. And the profession we're proud of." He looked back from the threshold. "And I don't want to lose."

FEAVER PACED in my office and raged.

"Is that corrupt?" he asked. "Letting a lonely woman have a little affection?"

According to the recording, I offered, it wasn't so little. The locker room humor, an effort to soothe him, drew a fleet smile, but he barely changed stride.

"So I'm her jocker. So what? This is a lady, a person for Chrissake, she's a great person. You think she was looking for this? I was whispering sweet nothings in her ear for years. Do you know who Magda is? She was a novice, she lived in a convent until she was nineteen. She's still in an apartment with her eighty-eight-year-old mother. And we fuck in her chambers because she'd rather die than be seen coming out of a hotel room with a man. This lady, George, didn't have sex with anybody until she was forty, and then just because she couldn't stand thinking of herself as a virgin. So she got keelhauled and let the super in her building have at her one day while Mom's visiting an aunt. Quite a story. This guy wooin her a mile a minute in Polish, not a word of which she happens to speak, and smellin, so she says, a little European. And then, of course, she was so embarrassed she moved out the next month. I mean, she's pretty goddamned funny about it. Did you know Magda was funny?"

I'd had a four-week trial in front of Judge Medzyk when she sat in the Felony Division, and I didn't remember a moment that warranted more than a momentary smile. She had good demeanor and better-than-average ability, but for Robbie's purposes and mine there was only one thing about her that mattered—she was a judge, before whom he had appeared often over the years.

"I *like* Magda, for Chrissake. I really like her. We have a great time together. I'd like her whether she ruled for me or not. And she doesn't rule for me all the time. I get this little tiny smile and a shrug when it goes the wrong way, like, What can I do, this is my job?"

She had no business ruling either way, not in these circumstances. It was shame, I could see, that had been her undoing. She hadn't recused herself from Feàver's cases because she would have expired if she were ever called upon to explain the reasons to the Presiding Judge.

"So they're gonna put her in the penitentiary for getting laid?"

Probably not. There was no mention of any case on the tape I'd heard, and Robbie insisted there never had been. But that didn't obscure Sennett's larger message that Robbie was not entitled to pick and choose whom he'd talk about.

"Who would I be holding out on?" he asked. "Really?"

Mort was my first answer. Robbie jolted. I'd scared him or caught him, perhaps both. My continuing worry was that Sennett and I would someday be having a heart-to-heart much like today's, but one where it was Morty on the tape, up to his ears in all of this. I told Robbie that the train was leaving the station. Anything that should be said about Mort or anyone else had to be heard now. He insisted, as always, that Mort was clean.

"Don't you believe me?" His dark face was a beacon of baptismal innocence.

Conveniently, my phone rang. Even before summoning Robbie, I'd called a private investigator named Lorenzo Kotrar, whom I'd represented some years before when he was charged with violating the federal wiretapping statute. Poor Lorenzo had gotten the goods on his client's cheating husband, a police captain, but the captain took more than his pound of flesh when Lorenzo went off to the Federal Correctional Institution at Sandstone for sixteen months. When Lo was released, he found the notoriety of his case had led to significant demand for his technical expertise. He now worked the other side of the street, so to speak, sweeping and debugging, usually for major corporations, but also for persons wary of snooping by spouses and partners, not to mention the government. He was calling from Robbie's office, to which Feaver had admitted him before coming to see me.

"It's clean," Lo told me, but he could not say that Sennett hadn't shut down, anticipating the sweep. Klecker had had such free access to the line cabinet in the building that it might have been no more than a matter of throwing a switch. Lo offered to do Robbie's car and house next, but Feaver was certain his two calls to Magda had come from the office.

I looked out to the river below, where the city lights swam on the currents. It remained possible that Sennett had tapped Magda's chambers for other reasons. Perhaps Robbie had wandered into a trap set for someone else. But he found that idea laughable.

"Magda's a quality person. She wouldn't even know

how to be a crook." So where? I asked, Where did Stan get probable cause for the bug?

Feaver's black eyes were still, but if he knew, he wasn't telling me.

CHAPTER 18

MCMANIS PHONED EVON AT HOME THAT
night. He had never done that before and he stayed with
the cover, telling her he hadn't received a copy of Feaver's
brief in a case in which his reply was due the next day.
He insisted, cordially but firmly, that she bring it to his office right now.

He unlocked the door himself. Past 8 p.m., the LeSueur
Building had a ghost town feeling. A cleaning man ran a
floor buffer down the corridor, but aside from the security
guards, he was the only person she'd seen about. Somewhere, young lawyers were toiling, but they were confined
like secrets, given away only by the occasional scattered
lights visible from the street.

McManis told her the story in bold strokes. Her heart
rippled at one point when she thought he was about to play
her the tape, but Jim proved too old-fashioned for that.
Shame was her predominant reaction anyway. It felt as if
someone had poured battery acid into her veins. She had

been placed in Feaver's office to prevent, or detect, episodes exactly like this.

"So I look real good on this thing," she said when Jim finished. From experience, she'd have expected something forgiving from McManis, his usual faint, silent smile. But his light eyes were still as he studied her. Jim had his tie down, his sleeves rolled. Two cartons of Chinese were at the end of the long conference table, one of them emitting an overpowering odor of garlic.

"And you had no clue on this?" he asked. "No idea about this judge?"

'Clong' was the agent term, the rush of shit to the heart when you suddenly saw you'd screwed up. Sure, she knew. There was that remark about messing around with a judge which Feaver had made after the first time they'd seen Walter.

"Anybody else hear about that?" McManis asked. He was fully focused, intent.

She drummed her fingers. She had told Alf, who had a persistent lurid curiosity concerning Robbie's catting about.

"Alf?" McManis looked to the fake grain of the conference table as he pondered. Behind the steel door, the night sounds of the city were held at astonishing distance. "Somebody backdoored me on this," Jim finally said. "Alf must have let it slip. Maybe to the local agents on the surveillance. But Sennett knew. And he went around me. He handed me a signed warrant on Friday morning, told me to get Alf to do the installation. No details. He must have used the IRS guys to nail down the probable cause. I didn't understand what he was ticked about." McManis flexed his hand, on which the fingers were slightly clubbed. His usual comfortable manner had worn down. If he was from D.C.— and his comments over the weeks had largely confirmed that—he'd been through this before. You ran with the big dogs in that town. Got crackbacked and bushwhacked and cut down at the knees. Still. It wasn't Jim.

"He was sending us a message," Jim said. "Me. And you. About staying on our toes. He wants you inside this guy's shirt from now on. He already said as much. You're with him whenever he leaves home."

Her impulse as always was to defend herself. Robbie had made it sound as if the relationship was long over.

"Then learn the lesson. Anything like this in the future, some mention of other judges, any hints, you better let me know." The rebuke was mildly spoken but it burned through her. "And when he starts talking—" McManis weighed what he was saying. "You've got to try to draw him out. More. See if you can. God knows what else there might be like this."

More. Evon nearly laughed. More and she'd need to borrow a couch from a shrink. Or somebody's wet suit. But McManis's expression allowed no room for humor. Jim's mouth worked around what he was going to say next.

"This isn't the nicest part," he said and looked at her directly, so she didn't miss the meaning. She considered the advice in the strange hush of the building and tried not to shake her head. "It's not easy," Jim said. "UC is the hardest. And you know, Feaver—" Jim shrugged. "I've sort of gotten to like the guy. In his way."

"In his way," she agreed.

McManis smiled. "I like him—" He checked himself there and gave his head, and his boyish do, the tiniest shake. There was a leased car for her in the basement garage, McManis told her. She'd see Feaver in and out the door to his house every day now.

As she drove home, she felt her emotions collecting in a familiar way, sliding into humiliation. She felt hammered down by it, more ponderously now that she was alone. When it came back up again, by the time she'd closed the dead bolt inside her apartment, it had made its inevitable transformation to anger, her ferocious companion. She'd been *played*! Played by Robert S. Feaver, future felon and full-time slimeball. She was even enraged with McManis, who was doing what bosses do in bad situations, sending her in two different directions at once, asking her to be warier at the same time she was supposed to lead the guy along. They had the wrong girl for that. There wasn't that kind of art to her. If she didn't respect McManis so much she'd have told him so.

"Fucking Sennett," she said aloud. Game player. Powermonger. "I hate that shit." Playing the Mormon girl, she'd reverted for months to the vocabulary she'd used in high school. The curse words resounding around the apartment struck her as childishly amusing. Fucking Sennett. She laughed then. She'd just realized what it was McManis was going to say. About Feaver. At the end.

He was going to say, I like him more than Stan.

AT 6 A.M., SHE WAS PARKED outside Feaver's house, blocking the driveway. He didn't ask why. He knew it was coming. For cover, though, they'd still travel in the Mercedes. Settling in, she slammed the door with a powerful heave. He did not look her way as she frumped around in the seat.

"I'm gonna be out here every morning now, bucko. And I'm gonna be seeing your wandering behind through the door every night. And I'm calling every two hours to make sure you've stayed put. I'm even tying a string around your ankle when you go to the potty."

He flirted with a smile, then apparently reconsidered under the circumstances.

"Do you have just the smallest clue how *bad* you made me look?" she asked.

When he turned, his expression—its harshness—was shocking.

"Cut the crap. I know you dimed me out on this. I know you went right to Sennett when I said I'd had a thing with a judge."

"I only wish I had, Robbie."

"Did you listen in on my phone calls, too?"

"Sure," she said. "Absolutely. I record them on that wire I'm wearing. Sennett's up all night listening to the output."

They were driving. There'd been a frost again last night and the windshields of the cars at the curbs were glazed with what looked like large snowflakes. He made a bitter remark: Everything with her was business.

"You're not gonna do this," she said. "You're not gonna embarrass the hell out of me and then try to make me feel bad cause you got caught with your hand in the cookie jar. You're not going to do that, Feaver."

"Hey, I'm a big boy. I took a chance and I lost."

She battled herself. He was always saved by intuition. Because of course there was a piece of her that inevitably needed to explain.

"You barefaced lied to me and now you want an apology?"

"Lied?"

"Didn't you tell me that you'd stopped that stuff?"

"Oh, please."

"Didn't you? What was it you said. 'It seems disloyal'?" He'd be single again soon enough. She skipped that part out of sheer mercy.

"What's it to you?"

"Only my job. That's all. Just what I get up every morning to do. I'm lyin in bed last night, ripping the hell out of myself. 'How'd you miss it?' Then I realized you'd looked right in my dumb green eyes and told me that whopper."

"You didn't believe it anyway."

"Stop making excuses, damn it! What kind of person are you? How can you just flat-out say stuff that isn't true? That you *know* isn't true?"

"Aw, don't give me that production number. 'Men were deceivers ever.' Shakespeare, right? Everybody lies. 'Oh, I love your hair.' 'What a great idea.' 'The dog ate my homework.' Jesus Christ. Every minute you're living is a lie. Look at you. 'My name is Evon Miller. I'm a Mormon girl from Idaho.'"

"But that's for a reason. For a good reason."

"So, I had a good reason, too."

"Yeah? Fooling around and getting favorable rulings?"

He tried to speak, then stopped. His hands moved first.

"Listen, you know, when I went romping around up on the stage, I always felt like I was trying on things about myself. Little pieces of myself. Seeing if they could be ginned around to fit. Like making stained glass. You can call me a liar, and people do. But at least I've tried. I haven't sat around with the same looney-tune fantasies as everybody else, keeping them in some hot dark box until they start to stink. If you talk, if you tell, if you make the play, if you say, That's who I am, at least it gives you the chance to figure out if you're right."

She thought of a million old sayings. So full of it his eyes were brown.

"And who did you think you were trying to be by b.s.-ing me?"

His Adam's apple wobbled.

"Somebody you liked."

She didn't say anything. He was an actor, she reminded herself. An actor. At a stoplight, a woman in the next car was making up her face, sharpening her brows at the moment, as she hiked herself up to the rearview to peek at the results. They drove on quite some time without speaking, the morning burble of two high-powered drive-time jocks filling the car, the pair yelling at each other to revive their audience.

"So'd you listen to it?" he asked.

She just slid her eyes over. He knew the look by now.

"Oh, come on. Fess up. I know you listened to that tape." They went through that a couple of times, each run-through stoking her anger again.

"Why would I *care*?" she asked him.

"'Cause you've got this burning interest in my scintillating personal life."

"Me?"

"Oh, come on. That's all you want to talk to me about. Almost from day one." He went down a list he'd apparently been keeping, beginning with the girl with the flag. He didn't mention the other day when she'd frisked him, but it was clear the incident had emboldened him. By the time he finished, she could barely hear over the blood rush throbbing in her ears.

"Hoo boy. Here we go again. What do they call this? A recurring theme? I just can't resist you."

"You're curious about something."

"Drop dead." She said it as if she meant it. Which she did.

Instead he repeated himself. She was curious.

"You know, Feaver, you ain't as smart by half as you think you are. I thought you told me you had the picture? When you gave me your big lecture about Shaheen Whatever Her Name Is who you kissed onstage? I thought you said you had me all figured." A little voice within asked what in the Lord's name she was doing. But it was the stuff with McManis. The only way she could translate it was just to let fly.

In spite of traffic, he'd turned full about to look at her. She did not shy away, just let the anger burn from her eyes.

For the moment she had him confounded. Not because he didn't remember. But because he couldn't get the words out of his mouth.

"I never said that," he insisted.

"The hell."

"I didn't."

"Well, what if I said you were right? What would you say, smarty-pants?"

He took an awfully long time.

"You dig girls?"

"What would you say?"

He drove in silence. But she could tell he was thinking. His eyes seemed to have shrunk back some infinitesimal measure into his face.

"I'd say, Good."

"Good!"

"Yeah," he said, and finally cheated a glance her way. "I'd say we have something in common."

"YOU KNOW, I KNOW that was just a line. Yesterday? About you being a—"

She arched an eyebrow awaiting the slur. They were in the Mercedes, on their way into work.

"What should I say?" he asked. " 'Sapphist'?"

" 'Lesbian' seems to be the word if you're straight."

"But you're not, are you?"

"Straight?"

"Not-straight."

"Look, whatever I am is none of your business."

"So why'd you tell me?"

She'd been contemplating that for a day. She'd needed to knock him off his high horse, to regain some control, let him know he didn't have her completely pegged. But whenever her mind lit on what she'd *said*, she wanted to crawl away.

"I think it's a play," he said.

She told him to think what he wanted, but she couldn't settle for that. After a moment, she pivoted on the smooth leather of the passenger seat.

"It's just a hoot. I'm tellin you things, my Lord, sayin things to you I haven't told my sisters. And you're sittin there goin, Prove it. What do you want me to do? Describe my first time?"

He actually seemed to consider that.

"You know, I've done that," he said, a block or two farther on. "Said I was that way. 'Inverted'? Isn't that the word?"

"*You* said you were gay?"

"Yeah, I did. I did it a lot. As a play."

"Naturally," she said dryly.

"What does that mean?"

"Forget about it."

"You think I'm always on the play, right?"

"Look, just tell me the story. That's what you're gonna do anyway, isn't it? You think I'm giving you a line about being a lesbian and you'll prove it by telling me how you've said you're gay. Which, *of course*, is a play, because nobody could ever believe *that* about *you*."

He stared at her for some time. They had just pulled into the garage at the LeSueur and he slammed the car into park. God, where did that come from? She was mean. She could hear her mother's voice clearly, delivering that judgment: she was *mean*. She grabbed his wrist.

"Look, tell me the story."

"Another time," he said. He patted his muffler into place, inspecting himself in the vanity mirror on the visor as he prepared to present himself to the public in the lobby of the LeSueur.

"Okay, be like that."

"Look, it's not a big deal. I told you it was a play. You're going to hate me for it, anyway."

"Then I'll try to forgive you," she said. Her mother had always said that forgiveness was a virtue. He took the chance of looking her way to see if she meant it, before he stared out the windshield into the murky reaches of the garage.

"It was just in college, all right? It was a line. I'd tell girls that. You know, that I was having a crisis. That I thought I was that way. That I was really worried about it. And in those days, they'd be horrified. For my sake. You know, they'd say, 'No, not you, you can't be that way. Have you ever done anything?' 'No, no,' I'd say, 'but I just worry about it sometimes.' Look, it was the dark ages. Nobody ever talked out loud about this stuff. It probably sounds ridiculous now. But to an eighteen-year-old girl from Great Neck, it was pretty convincing. And you realize what the point was, right? You know what I was really after."

"And it worked? Girls fell for it?"

"All the time. They were always so proud of me afterwards. Even girls I never called again didn't mind. It was our little secret that they'd sort of healed the leper. I guess I shouldn't laugh. Right?"

"Right." She looked away.

"You said you'd forgive me."

She'd said she'd forgive him. Her mother, who preached that lesson, seldom seemed to forgive her. Some woeful guttural escaped her. Every time she sat her large pink fanny down in this automobile something went awry.

"Who cares?" she asked. "I forgive you, you forgive me. Who we kiddin? You're just talkin dirty and I'm lettin you do it."

"It's not dirty."

"No, what is it?"

He took a moment.

"It's friends. Isn't it? Aren't we? We're talking like friends, that's all."

Friends. She couldn't believe it. She felt the weight of him watching her.

"So do they know?" he asked.

" 'They' who?"

"Your bosses. Headquarters. Whoever's on the homo patrol, now that they missed J. Edgar Hoover."

She could see how this was going to turn out. A cataclysm. It was never going to end. She refused to answer.

"I thought that was an issue," he said. "They don't want anybody blackmailed."

"Are you threatening me?"

"No. God no."

"You're threatening me. I tell you I'm a lesbian—"

"Hey," he said. "I don't care if you say, 'I'm a little teapot.' That stays here. I don't rat my friends, Evon. No matter what. That's why everybody was on my case yesterday."

She wondered what Walter Wunsch or Barnett Skolnick would say about that. This guy would never make sense.

"I was just thinking," he said. As he paused, a little ironic wiggle flexed through his even features. She knew what was coming. Something of dubious taste, surely insulting. Something that would treat her life like a dirty joke.

"Don't you dare," she told him. She popped the door lock on her side.

"No." He reached after her. "No, I just realized."

"What?" What could he possibly have realized?

"You're always undercover."

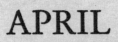

APRIL

CHAPTER 19

AT THE TIME I MET SHERM CROWTHERS, I was a young State Defender and he was one of the stars of the criminal defense bar. Throughout my career, there have always been gifted black men renowned in court, great orators who borrow from the style of Baptist preachers. But Crowthers was unique. He was a stone fortress of a human being, nearly six foot six. His huge proportions had paved the way for a college scholarship to State, where he became a legendary football star in the fifties. After he had literally knocked down a wooden goalpost while catching a touchdown pass he had acquired the nickname Sherman, in reference to the tank, and I seldom heard anyone call him Abner, which was his given name. His size was also the foundation of a uniquely imposing personality. In court, he was seldom anything but belligerent. He terrified witnesses, including cops, treated judges with disdain, and did not even spare juries. He attempted charm in the early phases of a trial, but in summation he worked himself into a state of absolute fury in which he delivered virtual orders to the jurors, which, to the chagrin of the prosecution, were all too often followed.

Sherm was brilliant. But it was the aggressive character of his mind that especially impressed me. He was never back on his heels. He accused and quarreled and ridiculed and rarely met any argument head-on. His accent was still strongly flavored with south Georgia, where he'd been a shoeless boy, but it was no drawl. He spoke at bullet speed, never quite getting to the end of words before another thought was coming at you, the better to batter you down.

In my early days, I tried one case with him as co-counsel. I was scared of him throughout, just like everybody else I knew. Our clients were charged in a dice game murder; Sherm's guy had been cheated, and my client's prints were on the gun. Their defense was that the murder weapon had actually been drawn by the victim, whom, they said, had been killed as they attempted to wrest the .38 from him. The onlookers didn't seem to remember it that way, although they admitted things had happened quickly. But the pathological evidence appeared to show that the gun had been fired from at least three feet.

Sherm's cross of the police pathologist, Dr. Russell, was astonishing. He took the murder weapon and loaded it while Russell was on the stand, cleared the chamber, then put the weapon in the pathologist's hand and forced it back toward his face, engaged all the while in a barrage of questions about the physiology of wrists and fingers. As the gun lingered at his temple, Russell's voice grew watery and he appeared to have no confidence whatsoever in his opinions. Afterwards, the Chief State Defender asked me what I'd learned from the experience of trying a case with the legendary Sherm Crowthers. The answer was nothing. He was inimitable. It was hard to convince anyone that I'd actually seen a defense lawyer point a loaded gun at a witness during cross-examination, much less that the judge and the prosecutors never thought to object.

Nevertheless, the case left me with much to ponder. Sherm saw life in terms of angry essentials, inescapable categories—rich and poor; black and white—which as far as he was concerned defined everything and whose existence enraged him. Even worse, in his view, was the hypocrisy practiced by virtually everyone but him in refusing to acknowledge the all-determining power of these factors. When the jury went out, I was astounded that Sherm had no doubt they'd acquit.

'We gone win this case, don't you know that? No problem here. Cause it's just a nigger shootin a nigger. Happens every day. We gave that jury all the excuse they need. This here was just some drunks at a dice game, not somebody gone bust into their house. They don't care now. This idn't gone take two hours 'fore they send these two fellas home, don't give a hoot if they get drunk and shoot another nigger or two tonight.' Sherm was huge in every part, with a massive face, a long wide brow, and large throbbing eyes. His hatred for a moment stood magnified in all of his dark features. He despised me, not so much for being white as for not seeing what was plain to him. And the jury returned a not-guilty verdict in about ninety minutes.

When he was nominated for the bench, I was astounded. Sherm lived the black bourgeois life, not a lot different from Robbie's: big cars, diamonds, snappy clothes. And I couldn't imagine him enjoying anything in the law more than combat in the courtroom. Furthermore, every lawyer I knew, black or white, was terrified of facing Sherman on the bench. In the Bar Association there was a restless current of opposition. But it was the early eighties; the dispossessed African-American electorate was demanding more black hands on the levers of power; and no one could doubt Sherm's abilities. As my friend Clifton Bering, probably the county's most respected black politician, told me, 'He's a son of a bitch, George. But he's the son of a bitch we all need.'

The two contrived cases Robbie had in front of Crowthers, one assigned to him directly, the other transferred from Judge Sullivan, had dawdled along. The first of the cases, *King v. Hardwick*, was supposedly a sexual harassment suit, whose plot Robbie had dreamed up, apparently inspired by the story he'd later told about Constanza's daughter and her ex-boyfriend. In this version, a young woman, whom we called Olivia King, had been secretary to Royce Hardwick, an executive at Forlan Supply, who was two decades her senior. In her first year of employment, she and Hardwick had had a brief fling. Eventually, she met a man closer to her own age and broke off the relationship, enraging Hardwick. His wounded antics, ranging from pitiful entreaties to furious ridicule, had forced her to quit her job. Even then Hardwick persisted. He followed her to work, harassed her by phone, and sent silly defamatory letters to her new boss, which, while unsigned, were clearly from him. Finally, in desperation, Olivia had contacted a female superior of Hardwick's. An investigation was initiated in which a company attorney interviewed him. Hardwick casually admitted virtually everything Olivia claimed, laughing it off as a prank. He was astonished when the company fired him.

Now that Olivia had brought suit, Hardwick's story had changed. He defended with a mixture of outright denial and failed recollection, explaining objective evidence like phone records and Olivia's coworkers' sightings of him lurking around the elevators as simply part of his efforts to retrieve needed information from his departed secretary. As for Hardwick's confession to the company attorney, his present lawyer, James McManis, asserted that it could not be admitted into evidence because of the attorney-client privilege. The central question in determining whether the interview was privileged was whether Hardwick could have reasonably believed Forlan's lawyer was acting in his behalf, rather than for the company. On April Fool's Day, Robbie and McManis appeared before the Honorable Judge Crowthers to argue the issue.

As a judge, whatever else might be said against him, Sherm never had problems arriving at an opinion about a matter. He was pontifical and often brutal with the lawyers before him. Today he shook his mighty head as he read through the papers Robbie and McManis had filed.

"Where's your client?" he demanded of Jim. With the bench elevated six feet over the well of the court, Crowthers appeared the size of Zeus. McManis was wordless as Sherm leered down at him. "You want me to deny this motion, don't you, Mr. Mack Manis?"

"Yes, sir," said McManis when he finally found his tongue.

"And the reason's cause your client believed he was speaking under the confidence of the attorney-client privilege to this lawyer from Forlan Supply. Isn't that what you're sayin here in your papers?"

"Yes, sir."

"Am I gonna take your word for that?"

"Sir?"

"Am I supposed to let you tell me what your client thought, or is your client gonna get up on the witness stand here in my courtroom and tell me for himself?" Crowthers always took a particular glee in eluding attorneys' expectations. Practicing before him was a little like hitting a ball toward the front wall of a handball court without realizing that it could come back and smack you from behind. "So where is your client?" Crowthers demanded again.

The matter was set over for one week to bring in Hardwick. McManis sent a Teletype to D.C. to find an FBI Special Agent from out of town to play the executive. But UCORC intervened. It was one thing for Robbie and Jim to make misleading statements to Crowthers and the other judges who were under investigation; the courts had long approved of that kind of governmental deception as part of an undercover operation. But an FBI agent, sworn on oath, claiming he was Royce Hardwick and testifying about events that had never happened looked and smelled a lot like perjury. That was one of the reasons UCORC's protocols had sought to avoid trials of the contrived matters.

Both McManis and Sennett had to fly out to make a personal appearance at Main Justice, and supposedly the decision to go forward was made by Janet Reno herself. In any case, on the morning of April 8 a rock-jawed agent from somewhere in America was in McManis's office, prepared to play Royce Hardwick.

Jim remained unnerved by his performance the week before and amazed at the primitive awe Crowthers was capable of inspiring with that murderous stare compressed beneath his graying brows. Robbie and Stan spent more time coaching McManis than our pseudo–Mr. Hardwick. The agent was relaxed and seemed to understand his part, although he'd be less convincing if he was required to show Hardwick's seedy side.

As they were all heading for court, Sennett pulled me into McManis's office.

"Go with them."

I was incredulous.

"You're the referring attorney," Stan said. "It would make sense if you're there. And I'm worried about Jim with Sherm. We don't want people to start wondering if McManis is really a lawyer. If he needs some cues, it'll look less peculiar if they're not all coming from Robbie."

This was exactly the kind of thing I'd been afraid of. But Stan claimed the request had McManis's blessing, and

Jim, in fact, repeated it. Crowthers was a lot to handle, even for courtroom veterans, and Robbie had no objections, so I tagged along, vowing to myself to do nothing, unless there was a four-alarm fire.

McManis had rehearsed the direct examination with the visiting agent at least a dozen times and he was quite poised going through it. 'Royce Hardwick' testified according to his script that he'd believed the Forlan lawyer was there to act in his interests and that he had figured what he'd told the lawyer was confidential. McManis tendered the witness for cross-examination, but Sherm never allowed Robbie to stand, or Jim to get out of the way.

"Now just a second here," Sherman demanded. "You mind if I ask your client a couple questions, Mr. Mack Manis?" Caught again in the headlights, Jim failed to answer and Sherm flipped a dismissive hand in his direction. He could do pretty much as he liked on a matter like this. "Now listen here, Mr. Hardwick. You tellin me that when that lawyer from the company asked you what happened you were thinkin he was gonna keep what you told him a secret?"

'Hardwick' took his time with the question. His hands were folded on the shellacked birch rail of the witness stand and he maintained an impressive executive timbre in answering yes.

"So you must have told him the truth, then, huh?"

Caught short, Hardwick sat back. Sherm had scooted his chair all the way to the partition between the bench and the witness stand, but that apparently was not advantage enough. He now stood, looming seven or eight feet over Hardwick.

"Heard me, didn't you? You wouldn't lie to your own lawyer, would you?"

"Well, Judge, I really—I don't know."

"You don't? You mean you'd send Mr. Mack Manis here to tell lies to *me*?"

Hardwick, who'd had to lean back to about forty-five degrees to face Sherm, said of course not.

"No," said Sherm, and shook his huge head. "I didn't think so. So if this lawyer's got some notes and memos about what you said had been passing between you and Olivia King, those things must be true. Right?"

"Well, I don't really remember what happened back then anymore," Hardwick said, repeating the lines he'd rehearsed. "My whole life fell apart. It's just a big jumble."

"I been hearin you say that. But you don't have any memory of lyin to that lawyer, do you? That's what I'm askin you now. Did you lie, far as you remember?" Sherm put his hands on the partition and pushed his large face down toward Hardwick's, breaching a space between interlocutor and witness that he would have drawn and quartered any lawyer for violating. Hardwick actually let one arm rise up defensively before he said no.

"That's what I'm sayin. Course you wouldn't lie. So if that lawyer says you admitted you were all worked up over Olivia King, that you'd been bothering her and pestering her, following her to work and calling her vile names in these letters, you were tellin the truth, weren't you, best you remember?"

Hardwick's eyes lit first on McManis, who still stood mute, then revolved past him as the witness searched the courtroom for help. I had some dwindling thought of passing Jim a note to tell him to object, but that only figured to inflame Crowthers more. Besides, I reminded myself, McManis was there to lose.

"I guess," Hardwick finally answered.

"Idn't any reason to think otherwise, right?"

"Right."

"Okay," said Sherm and finally beat his large head up

and down. With that he returned his attention to McManis at the podium. "Okay. So what I'm tryin to figure is what we-all are doin here, Mr. Mack Manis. Client just admitted on the record in this case same things he supposedly said in confidence to that lawyer. Di'nt he?" Sherman revealed his large irregular teeth in a mischievous smile. "Nothin for me to rule on, is there? Dudn't matter whether the statements he made before are privileged, cause there's no way what he just said right here doesn't come into evidence—is there?"

Sherman, when he laughed, let his tongue slide through his teeth, and he emitted a wet sputter under his heavy gray mustache. He enjoyed himself while his mean lesson sunk in around the courtroom. He'd obviously demanded McManis produce his client so he could batter a new set of admissions out of Hardwick, avoiding a difficult ruling in the process. Sennett, when he heard about this turn of events, was delighted. Talk about a judge on the take! But, sitting there, I had no thought that corruption played any part in what Crowthers had done. It was just Sherm being himself, savoring the gratification he got by clobbering a jerk like Hardwick and by demonstrating that the best attorney in the courtroom was the one up on the bench.

As Sherm took his seat again, still chuckling and tossing his head in amusement, McManis came out with his only line of protest.

"But, Your Honor!" he said.

Crowthers threw his big hand Jim's way, disregarding the objection, and went on drafting the order.

We all left the courtroom together and climbed into an elevator, where we were alone in the car. Robbie, who'd had the good sense not to speak a word during the hearing, finally piped up.

" 'But, Your Honor,' " he wailed, just once. Hardwick had no comprehension what the laughter was about.

CHAPTER 20

FEAVER JOKED THAT EVON WAS WORKING
half days, since she was with him every minute now, 6
a.m. to 6 at night, seeing him back and forth from his
house. The Feaver residence was English manor-style, with
a long shake roof and yellow stucco between the outer
members of the upper story. The structure was surrounded
by a crisp lawn and decorative landscaping, but it looked
entirely out of place here amid the prairie flatlands west
of the city where the only trees had been planted by gar-
deners a few years before.

Glen Ayre, the suburb, was a former cornfield on which
some developer had set down dozens of gigantic houses.
Everyone here was like Robbie, rich and eager to show it.
Huge luxury cars sat out in the driveways, and the alarming freakish shapes of satellite dishes reared up along the
rooflines. The kids were obviously spoiled; you could tell
just by the basketball standards the parents had driven into
the earth beside the driveways, with cranks to raise and
lower the rim, and snappy acrylic backboards.

The rich to Evon were Other People. She'd never envied much of what went with money. Merrel's husband, Roy, was a businessman, an MBA, who traveled all over the world and seemed to ship dollars home by the suitcaseful, but Evon wasn't certain it had done her sister much good. Clubs and fashion, the competition to keep up often seemed to have constricted Merrel's life.

When Evon climbed into the Mercedes each morning, Robbie was cheerful as a sunbeam. He zipped along, entertaining her with chatter, while she remained in the sullen funk of the sleep-deprived, still grieved that his circus act with Judge Medzyk had cost her another hour in bed.

Their first stop, a few miles in the wrong direction, was his mother's nursing home. While he was inside, Evon read the paper. She pushed her seat back, reclined, took in the aroma of the leather. The engine ran and she had the enormous solid machine to herself. One morning he decided to invite her inside.

"Hell, come on, you'll meet my ma." It seemed unthinkable to him that she would have no interest. And she did, actually. She was curious about the woman who'd borne him.

The result of Mrs. Feaver's stroke last year was a nearly total hemiplegic paralysis. She had no use of her left leg and only marginal ability to move the arm on that side. But she still could speak, much as Robbie occasionally wished that weren't the case; after therapy she had no audible impairment. Mrs. Feaver's home, the apartment in which Robbie had grown up, was a second-story walk-up, which she'd had to abandon as a result of her disability. Robbie had wanted to take her into his house, but his mother, even in her weakened state, would hear none of it. He had enough on his hands with Lorraine. After much discussion, this nursing home seemed to be the best alternative. It cost him a left lung, he said, which made him feel a little better.

Today Estelle Feaver sat upright in a padded day chair, dressed and ready for breakfast, which was still some time away. She held on to her heavy black-framed glasses with one hand, as if this might improve her vision, while she extended her neck turtle-like in the effort to follow the TV suspended on the opposite wall. Judging from the volume, her hearing, too, was failing. The utter immobility of her left side was apparent even from the doorway. Her arm hung down like wet laundry. She did not realize they had entered the room until Robbie was quite close to her. When she saw her son, she threw her right hand in the air, then recovered enough to whisk the glasses from her face and bury them in the folds of her skirt.

"*Rob*-bee!" She fell into his arms and lifted the one good hand to his shoulder. She held him for quite some time until her cloudy, dark eyes found Evon.

He introduced his new paralegal. To account for the fact that they were together so early in the morning, Robbie claimed they were heading to court. His mother's mouth went through a series of sour reflexes that signified disbelief, but she looked away rather than castigate her son for his antics. Robbie, as always, happily avoided unpleasantness.

"She looks great, doesn't she look great?" he asked Evon. Mrs. Feaver in fact looked simply old. Her skin was engraved by heavy wrinkles which the thickly applied base and makeup did not really hide, and the chin beneath her neck hung in several folds that no doubt displeased her. It was clear she continued to take pains with her appearance. Even if Robbie had not told Evon that he engaged a manicurist and a stylist to come to the home weekly, it would have been plain. There was no missing the incredible orangutan orange of the hair dye or the popping red paint on her nails; they contrasted too pointedly, both with the glum surroundings and with her decrepitness—the bent spine, the pallid spotted hands, the rattling cough. Looking at Mrs. Feaver, Evon found it difficult even to say that she might once have been attractive. Her nose was hawkish and her false teeth, on which some of her bright lipstick was smudged, seemed to have altered her jawline. But she was a force. You could feel that much. She brushed aside her son's compliments with a show of bashfulness.

"Well, it's just for him," Estelle said. "Who else sees me in this place?"

In his cheerleading fashion Robbie again extolled the way his mother took care of herself, once more inviting Evon to chime in with praise of her own. She'd have been willing to flatter an old woman, although she'd never had much enthusiasm for ladies in war paint, the way they felt it was a female's responsibility to be so much more colorful, more glittering and glamorous than God and nature had made them. These days her own hair was barely combed; she was growing more perfunctory with her Elizabeth Arden makeup every morning, and she'd taken the color off her nails several weeks ago.

But there proved no need to patronize. Mrs. Feaver continued as if Robbie had not invited Evon into their conversation. Evon saw quickly that, at least as far as Mrs. Feaver was concerned, no one really intruded on her relationship with her son. And in fact, as Robbie and his mother went on chortling over events here in the home, Evon realized that the same was true for him. They were so happy in each other's presence! Robbie tended to speak of his mother as if she were a drain. But it was his disinterest, his objectivity, that was feigned. The man was really a through-and-through fake. He was as clearly bound to her as she was to him; his litany of compliments even, as her body failed, seemed sincere, a measure of the comfort he took in her physical presence. He held on to her hands as he questioned her about the doctor's latest report, while his mother lingered contentedly in the hot light of his interest.

"Oh, the doctors. What do they know? You think you get Nobel Prize winners in here?" She squinted at Evon, her harsh voice reduced to a whisper. "They're all foreigners. They're here for the Medicare. They give them I don't know what, six bucks for every old bag they glance at. They run through here like their pants are on fire. I can't even pronounce the names. Shadoopta. Baboopta. God save me if I ever needed to call one. I'd just be dead."

Robbie received this speech, like everything else the old lady said, with great mirth. He hugged her again, and then, after further banter, motioned Evon to go. To detain him, Mrs. Feaver inquired after Lorraine.

"Eh," he answered.

"My son. His wife and his mother, one sicker than the other. Sometimes I'm alone, I cry for him, it's such a terrible thing. Who takes care of Robbie?"

He was jiggling the water pitcher throughout this speech. But he heard her, apparently. He reminded her about Mort.

"He always sees the bright side," answered Mrs. Feaver. "He makes jokes anyway. He's on the economy plan with Hospital Supply. My God."

"Hey, shaddup, willya?" He leaned over and kissed her brow.

"So you'll come tomorrow?" Mrs. Feaver asked somewhat plaintively.

"Wouldn't miss it for the world. End of the day. I got court in the morning." He waved, then shot down the hallway. Mrs. Feaver watched his departure with dismay and did not respond when Evon lingered at the threshold to say it had been a pleasure.

"So that's my ma. A pistol, right? There's only half of

.ier left and she's still full of beans." Advancing down the corridor, each doorway revealing another frail body, shattered by age and disease—the skin parchment-colored and like a luffing sail, mouth toothless and desperately agape—Robbie managed another thrilled laugh.

Seeing what was required, Evon made the previously suspended remark about how well Mrs. Feaver kept herself.

"Yeah," he said again. "She looks great. She's always looked great. I mean, when I was a kid—" He rolled his eyes. "You look at the pictures now, I don't know, it's not like she was Liz Taylor or anything, but she had something. Pizzazz? Vitality. What was Jackie Gleason's old line. 'Va va va vooooom!' She was always put together really nice. She was going out and selling and looking good at it. Still today, I'll smell Chanel Number Five—Channel Five, I used to call it—and I'll think about my ma, hugging me before she ran off to the store.

"Guys dug her. I could tell that. And she was like a lot of pretty women I've known, she liked being dug. She liked the power of it, I think. I could always tell that she loved walking down the street on the way home from work. In those straight skirts and high heels? The neighbor guy, in his sleeveless undervest, smoking a cigarette and pushing a hand mower over the little strip of city lawn, would stop and draw a smoke and take a real long look, even shake his head for mercy once she went past. She loved that. Half the wives in the neighborhood wanted her arrested. They called her 'Sophia Loren,' and not to be nice."

They were crossing the parking lot by now. The temperature had increased and the sun was seen some days now, but winter, a stubborn old witch, held on. The sky was piled with ugly soiled messes of clouds. Robbie, caught up in his reverie, looked to the pavement where oily rainbows had gathered.

"I think, you know, when it came to the actual act, she was probably pretty prudish, like a lot of ladies that age. I mean, I don't really know. She had one boyfriend for a while, a few years after my old man skipped, but that came to the usual sad ending, and after that she pretty much scrapped the whole notion. I caught her crying one night and telling herself and me it was for the best. He was a *goy*. A gentile. And younger than her. I was frantic. I couldn't stand that she was crying. I was eleven years old and I wanted to go after this guy with a bat, especially when I began to get the picture. With *my mother*?" Robbie had a sudden laugh. "I *still* would," he said. "I'd still like to kill him." His breath, turned to smoke by the cold, raced upward and he smiled at Evon, inviting her to laugh with him at his sudden recognition of himself.

CHAPTER 21

THE HASH SENNETT HAD MADE OF THE first encounter with Judge Skolnick left him with serious tactical problems. Robbie could have employed the usual gambit, announcing that the case of the painter with cancer had settled and making his drop. But Stan felt he'd be left with a relatively weak case on the judge, much less imposing than what he needed to finally get Washington off his back. Skolnick's lawyer would argue to a jury that the first payoff had been refused—the recording supported that—and that the second, even if accepted, was not intended to influence any official act, since Skolnick had emphasized in the Lincoln that he would stay discovery for any party.

Instead, Sennett decided that Robbie should appear before the judge with McManis and actually ask Skolnick to grant his motion for judgment on the pleadings, a claim that his client deserved to win the liability phase of the lawsuit without a trial, or even discovery. In his car, Skolnick had said flatly he'd never grant such a request. Sennett, therefore, felt there was little to lose, particularly since Stan thought there was some chance Robbie might even win.

"If you show up," Stan explained to Robbie, "that tells the judge that McManis won't settle. So if Skolnick denies the motion, he knows discovery starts and McManis finds out your client has cancer. You'll get nothing, the kids will get nothing—and Skolnick will get nothing." Stan was convinced he had the judge cornered.

"You're missing one thing," Feaver told Sennett. "Barney isn't smart enough to figure all of that out."

When McManis and Feaver arrived in court to argue the motion, Skolnick sat on the bench with his perfect judicial hairdo and his florid face scrunched down among his many chins. He seemed to understand nothing but the fact that a plaintiff's motion for judgment on the pleadings was virtually never granted. Just as Robbie had predicted, the judge swiftly denied his motion.

Yet this setback proved only momentary. After ruling, Skolnick invited Feaver and Evon and McManis back to his chambers. He was entirely agreeable as he sat behind his desk, still in his robe. He offered coffee, told a few of his usual jokes, and then began mercilessly pressuring McManis to settle the case.

"You got out of here with your *gatkes* today, Jim," he said, addressing McManis, who'd never been in Skolnick's courtroom before, as if he were a friend through the ages. "You know what that means? Rough translation, you got out with your boots on. But who knows about next time, when Feaver makes another motion? Not that I'm prejudging. I'm not. I'm keeping an open mind. Completely open. Believe me, after twenty-six years on the bench, that's one thing you learn to do. You have to learn all the facts and hear both sides. Next time, who knows, maybe I'll still see this exactly your way. But I could grant plaintiff's motion. I very well could. I was about this far." The judge held up his thumb and index finger, which were not parted at all. "Then where are you, Jim? The insurance companies, I don't know why they like to hang on to their money so long. It's like those cartoons where the moths fly out of the wallet. A case like this. Does he have a family?" Skolnick asked Robbie innocently. "The plaintiff?"

At the end, Skolnick stayed discovery another month to allow the parties to consider his remarks. He could not quite bring that off with aplomb; his eyes never left his leather desk blotter.

The FoxBIte had captured the judge's song and dance perfectly. Sennett accepted congratulations without preening, knowing, as we'd all seen, that there was no end to the way things could yet go wrong. Skolnick still had to take the money, and the complicated equipment in the Lincoln had to function. On April 12, Robbie, having reported to Pincus that the painter's case was now settled, prepared to visit the judge again in his car.

"We need this," Stan told Feaver before he departed from McManis's. Considerably shorter than my client, Stan laid his narrow hands on Robbie's shoulders and looked at him almost plaintively. The brotherly appeal, the fact that Stan was asking and not commanding, seemed to impress all of us, even Robbie.

"JUDGE, I'M SHAVING YOU a little," Robbie said, almost as soon as he was on the nail-polish-red leather of the front seat. Feaver had seen the prior tape a number of times and had his mark exactly. He held the envelope containing the cash in his left hand and waved it in front of the lens. The picture today was noticeably better. Alf had added a signal booster, and at considerable expense, Sennett had requisitioned a second surveillance van from the Drug Enforcement Administration, which was also receiv-

ing the picture as a backup. Alf manned the dials feverishly, while Stan and McManis and I were belted to our
little tin seats on the walls.

"Hah?" asked Skolnick. The judge had been providing
his own windy analysis of what the Clintons should do
about health care reform and had seemed sincerely oblivious as Robbie prepared to deliver the payoff. Even with
the camera, Feaver had to find some way to get Skolnick
to talk about the money. If the envelope was simply stuffed
into the seat unnoticed, a defense lawyer would argue Skolnick knew nothing about it. Thus, Feaver had employed a
variation on the ruse with Walter.

"Judge, you know, like I say, it's a little less, but to get
this done, I had to undercut myself on the settlement. And
I'd like to leave the family, the kids, with as much as I
can. Only I don't want you to think I'm stiffing you."

Skolnick's large face labored through the calculations
inspired by this deviation from form. He finally looked
straight down at the envelope.

"*Veefeel?*" he asked quietly, meaning 'How much?'

"Eight. If that's okay."

Skolnick laughed out loud. "My God, they should all
worry like you. *Genug.* We're friends, Robbie. We've done
a lot together. What you think is right, fine. Besides," said
Skolnick, "you gave me last time. For nothing." Robbie
played dumb and Skolnick added, "With Gillian."

Across from me, Sennett rattled his fist in the air, but
issued no sound. He'd learned better.

In the Lincoln, Skolnick's garrulousness had overtaken
his caution.

"See, you know, you hear stories, some of my brethren,
they're like bandits with pistols, really, what they do, it's
a stickup. Here, with me, it's good for you, okay, so it's
good for me. I'm not for grudges. I appreciate what you

do. And if you did nothing, it would be the same, you know that."

"I do," Robbie said. Sennett recoiled, but Feaver quickly sent things in the proper direction. "It's just this time, you really went out of your way, Judge. You know, when you denied that motion, I was—"

"I could see," said Skolnick. "You looked like I had my finger in your *kishkes*. Right? Come on. I could see. You were thinking, What's this guy doing to me? Am I right? I could see that."

"Well, you know, Judge, I just saw this guy, his kids. But what you did, in chambers. That was brilliant. Really. That was just terrific. That scum-sucker, McManis, he wouldn't have come up with a nickel if you hadn't given him a poke."

"Well, thank you, you know, when I saw that look on your face, I said, So what can I do so this works out like it should? Same as always really, this isn't different from some other case, you talk to the two sides, you tell them to be sensible. That's what I did."

Stan was still making faces—Skolnick's continuing insistence that he hadn't behaved improperly would be a small impediment—but the fact was the judge had annihilated himself. He was already driving back toward the LeSueur, but he detained Robbie in order to finish another joke, this one about a priest and a rabbi who have a collision. After a cautious start, each agrees that he's partly at fault. To cement their amicable resolution, the rabbi offers the father a drink from the sabbath wine which he happens to have in his trunk. The priest takes a long draught, then offers the rabbi the bottle.

" 'Right after the police get here,' the rabbi says." Skolnick reddened further as he roared over the punch line, and even in the van there was a current of suppressed laughter. Robbie departed the Lincoln chuckling, but Amari continued to follow Skolnick's car. Given the results of the first recording, Stan had persuaded Judge Winchell to expand her order slightly, allowing the camera to remain activated for an additional ten minutes to see if Skolnick retrieved the envelope from the front seat. The second surveillance van was by now in the Temple parking garage, near the section reserved for judges where Alf had punctured Skolnick's tires five weeks before. We stayed on the street, where, despite Alf's apprehensions, the picture was clear.

Alone, Skolnick used his car phone to call his wife about a set of race cars he was supposed to pick up for his grandson's birthday. Afterwards, as he circled up the ramp, the judge actually began quietly singing "Happy Birthday to You," wagging his large head on the beat. Parked, he turned off the motor, which sent a jolt of static across the picture. The camera would remain on only for another two minutes, as it automatically powered down once the ignition was off to avoid draining the battery. But that figured to be long enough.

For a troubling instant, Skolnick started squeezing out from under the steering wheel without the money. Then he rammed himself in the head. "What a *draykopf*," he complained about his absentmindedness. He squinted through the windshield and looked up and down the dim structure, then grunted audibly as he twisted around and heaved. The envelope came out like a weed he'd uprooted. He held it aloft, only inches from the camera, then jammed it into an interior pocket of his raincoat. With that, he grabbed the rearview mirror where the lens was secreted and angled it down so he could look himself over. His large features swelled across the screen as he straightened his tie. The pores on his nose were distorted to craterlike dimensions and he ran his tongue over his teeth. Then the poor bastard smiled with all his empty-noggined good humor and again began humming to himself, "Happy Birthday to You."

ALL THE UCAS GATHERED to watch the tape. Evon briefly stole away from the office to join them. It was, as Klecker said, more fun than the movies. Afterwards, Sennett addressed the group. Today's success made Stan seem more determined, more vital. He stood straight in his white shirt under the recessed spots.

This was a great achievement, he said, a relief of a kind and a tribute to the enormous hard work and sacrifice each one of them had made, to the months away from their families, and the strains they'd endured in living undercover. None of them had to worry any longer about saying it was all for nothing. They had put together a case Skolnick could never defend, and another one, on Malatesta, that would soon be at the same point.

But no one should forget these were simply first steps. Men like Skolnick, Sennett said, weren't the deepest problem. They could roll up dozens of Skolnicks, and with luck they would. But the Skolnicks had been born into this system. They went along with no ability to change it. Altering things permanently meant reaching the people who were in command, who willed this to continue as a matter of personal privilege and gratification.

"Tuohey," Sennett said, and let his determined look tick over each of them. "When we get to Tuohey, all of your magnificent efforts will have culminated not just in stats or headlines or stroke letters from D.C., suitable for framing"—there was appreciative laughter—"but a lasting change in the life of this community."

Evon felt high from all of this, the success with Skolnick and Sennett's address, but she found Feaver in a decidedly different mood when they drove home an hour later. The aftermath of these wired showdowns was beginning to assume a pattern. Much as Robbie enjoyed the moment, it demanded an intensity, a state of high alert and toe-dancing nimbleness, which left him depleted and also somewhat depressed as he confronted the results.

"Sometimes I sit up at night and think about all the people I'm fucking over," he said now. "It's starting to be a lot." As the number of solid prosecutions mounted, Feaver often seemed caught between warring impulses of self-congratulation and loathing. She understood in a way. You couldn't hate Skolnick. Even for her, there was no rush at the thought of him in a cell. But she felt no regrets.

"He knows what he's doing," said Evon.

"Do you? I mean, bringing out the worst in people and making them pay the price? You really think that's okay?"

"Necessary," she answered. She didn't think what they were doing was terrible. There were good deeds and bad, like the two different sides of the highway with a stripe in between. And once people crossed over, they could just keep going. That was the sorry lesson of experience.

"I wouldn't mind," Robbie said, as the big car galloped up the ramp onto the highway, "but I know damn well you're gonna scoop up the small fry and never land Brendan." It was a jolt hearing that on the heels of Sennett's halftime speech. But Robbie nodded to cement his opinion. "Never," he said. "And I'm not saying anything about me. We get there, I'll march in a straight line, do like I'm told. Stan's got me by the short ones anyway. But Brendan's way beyond crafty. He'll see your shadow in the dark. My prediction is you guys aren't gonna get close."

"We get em all, Robbie," she said.

"FBI's like the Mounties?"

"You betchum." She meant it, too. Inspired by Sennett, she felt starched by pride. People asked all the time, A nice girl like you, FBI, huh? And the truth was that she was hard put to say where it came from, being an agent, Effin

Be I. The end of field hockey was like falling into a hole. Most of her Olympic teammates planned to be coaches. Life for them would remain the field: green Astroturf wet thoroughly before game time, the continual sharp crack of the ball on the stick, and thinking about how great they were when they were young. For her it was done. Because somehow the illusion that had gone with it had been exposed. She was twenty-four years old. She'd been to the Olympics. And there was still no place in the world where she felt right.

Just to look at options, she'd done the paralegal course at the law school at Iowa while she was finishing the degree requirements for her B.A. In the same kind of mood, she went to a job fair in the field house. Behind a folding table, sitting around with the recruiters from places like RJR Nabisco and American Can, were two guys from the Bureau in gray suits and government-issue glasses, types if they'd ever existed. But it clicked. Her mother's father had been the Sheriff. He was a lifelong deputy who got the top job when his boss died on duty, buried in an avalanche he'd brought down on himself trying to blast loose a cornice that was threatening a road. Valiant. That was the word her grandfather used in mourning his friend. Like the prince, she thought, with his beautiful pageboy that resembled Merrel's. It had become, in the tangle of things inside a little girl's head, improbably large. The Sheriff's star, a heavy gold medallion twice the size of what the deputies wore, looked to her as though all the power and obligation were pinned right there on her grandfather's chest. She was halfway through Quantico when she found out that she wasn't going to get a badge. Hoover never wanted the national police force to look as if they were police. That's why they wore suits instead of uniforms, and carried credentials instead of a shield. But she still longed for a star of her own now and then.

Yet she'd never regretted the Bureau. She could lecture you until the next Flood about what was wrong, all the dumb acronyms that made them sound as if they were speaking in tongues, or the callous way women were treated. At Quantico, during training, she had the highest firearms scores in three years; the instructors would take her over to FATS—Firearms Automated Training System, where the guns fired laser beams, not bullets—and marvel at her reaction times. But they wouldn't let her come out there as a full-time instructor because somebody was convinced women couldn't handle .45s. She was lucky if every eighteen months she got to teach a two-week in-service, a training session for cops or other federal agents, most of whom were there for a boondoggle.

But being the Bureau meant being the best. They told you that at Quantico, so loudly and so often it seemed to echo from the rolling hills. And it was true. There was McManis, and Alf and Amari and Shirley Nagle to prove it. And her too. She believed every word about mission and duty. She lived it and liked it and liked herself for doing a good job right. And they'd get Brendan. Together. The FBI.

"That's fine with me," Feaver said when she repeated that prediction. "You put Brendan behind bars, I'll take photos and frame them. I won't feel bad for a minute. I mean, maybe I should. The guy's always treated me like gold. On account of Mort, and his ma, and my ma. I'm in Brendan's in crowd. Which is why Sennett thinks I'll have such a good shot at putting a knife in his back." He shook his head again over his current life's work of betrayal. She gave him the line, the shopworn agent's special, for whatever comfort it offered.

"He'd do it to you, Robbie. Don't worry."

"Brendan? Never. Sennett came to Brendan's doorstep, a moth can't beat its wings as fast as he'd have told Stan to hit the road. Brendan kneels to no man. That's like a credo. I can say a lot of bad stuff about Brendan, but these tables would never turn."

"So what do you have against him?"

Robbie screwed up his face the way he did when he thought she was being difficult. But after a second he seemed to yield to her point.

"Meeting Brendan the first time," he told her, "you'd say he's charming. Likable. Poised. Humorous. Especially if you've got any power. Reporters, politicians, celebrities, anybody who can do him some good, he'll bark like a seal if he thinks it'll make you beholden. But when you get down through the layers, Brendan is an absolute fuck-hole of a human being. Here, this'll tell you something. I mentioned Constanza, didn't I?"

Tuohey's secretary. Evon remembered.

"To this day, she's sitting right outside his office. Beautiful little lady. But listen how Brendan got his mitts on her. All this time, twenty-some years now, Constanza's married. Constanza had better English than her husband, Miguel. She made it through secretarial school, but Miguel, you know, he's a busboy and, after all that time working around all the liquor he can steal, he's also a drunk. The world beats him and he beats Constanza. And she's pouring out her woes to her boss, of course, Judge Brendan. He's touching her bruises and pretty soon other parts, but you know, Constanza is a Catholic girl of great virtue, Miguel is the hand God dealt her, she can't be bad with Brendan and look her husband in the eye at night.

"Brendan, naturally, acts very understanding with all of this. 'Well, we'll just have to make Mike a better man. He needs a fresh start, a new job, a chance to feel some pride in himself.' And Brendan gets him into the jail as a fry cook, standing behind the griddle suddenly, not carrying the slops. Miguel is *muy contento*. And then bad news for

Miguel. He's been riffed. All the Department of Corrections can offer him is a transfer downstate to Rudyard. 'Oh, but that's three hundred feefty miles from *mi familia*.' A pity, they say. Of course, there's a three-thousand-dollar raise, and a travel allowance. A travel allowance for a fry cook, right? Needless to mention, when Miguel gets there, he finds that his two off days are Monday and Thursday. He can go home maybe once a month. And never seems to notice his side of the bed is still warm. To this day— he's the head of Food Services by now in the penitentiary, and, by magic, they keep extending his retirement date— whenever he sees Brendan, he actually kisses his hand. And Brendan, the fuck—" Robbie stopped to shoot the finger at a hard-looking fellow in a pickup who'd cut off the Mercedes. "Goddamn Brendan lets him. How can you not hate a guy like that? Whenever Miguel comes by chambers to pick up Constanza, Brendan's number one thrill is to call her in for a little late dictation and get her to honk his horn while her hubby's on the other side of the wall."

"Oh, Lord."

"Yeah," he said. "And you think your sex life's strange."

Robbie was just talking, but the remark hit her hard. She was afraid from the start that he'd put her down.

"My sex life's not strange." She eyed him severely.

"Then you're the only one," he said. "Sex is always strange. Whether it's Brendan-strange or me-strange or you-strange, it's strange."

She hadn't heard this theory yet.

"I mean, this is the most private, inner thing in life, isn't it?" he asked her. "It comes out just a little bit differently in each of us, like a fingerprint. Who you do what with. And your fantasies. And what part you like best. And what you're thinking. It's unique. That's why it's intimate. That's why it's magic."

She had once been at a sex club in San Francisco where

she'd watched one woman fuck another with a dildo strapped to the crown of a leather hood on her head. There hadn't been much magic in that. Not for her. But it was no business of his.

He took her silence to mean she required convincing.

"Here's what I'm saying," he said. "I picked up a woman one night. Well, 'picked up.' I wouldn't say picked up. She works in the clerk's office. I've known her forever. Single gal. Joyce—Well, forget her name, but you know, I like her. Anyway, we're both pretty toasted. And we get to her place, she says, Sit down. And she takes out this photo album. Said she took the pictures herself. And they're of her. She's doing a sort of striptease for the camera. More than a tease. Very explicit. I don't know if she sent this in to Collected Kinks of America. But she was ramping up to show it to somebody. And it was me. And you know, if I was a jerk, I could have laughed. But I was fascinated. And very touched. And also really turned on. Even though I wouldn't exactly say she showed to advantage. She had pretty legs, but just about zip on top and, you know, the camera, it can be pretty harsh. But she was sharing it with me. Her strange little secret. Which was cool." He peeked her way to see how she'd received this. "So," he concluded, "you ought to ease up on yourself."

"Myself? How'd I get into this?"

"Don't give me that. I got you figured now."

She laughed and, as soon as she'd done it, felt a tremor.

"Laugh all you like," he said. "I know why you always wanna talk about it."

"You're the one always talking about it."

"But you wanna listen."

"A-*gain*?"

"It's true."

"The hell."

"You can't," he told her.

"Can't?" She felt a stab of apprehension. "Can't what?"

"Be like that. Or at least what you think I am. Free. You can't be like that." He squared around to face her at a stoplight next to a shopping mall, teeming in the early hours of the evening. "I mean, I don't know if your thing is girls or boys or lightning bugs, but whatever it is—you can't. Not the way you'd like. Maybe you can't come. Or maybe you're too frozen up, inhibited, whatever you call it, to actually get it on with anybody. Or maybe you've gotten tanked and gone out for anything that comes your way and there's still a whole big country of pleasure you know you can't get to. But it's something like that. Don't tell me I'm wrong, because I know I'm not."

It was a form of punishment to have to meet his eye. The heat of her flush had reached her scalp and her gut pinched. But she didn't look away. And in the few seconds that passed, another of those things that seemed to happen between them occurred. He was the one who emerged looking abashed and somewhat caved in on himself. He was the first to break off, to flip up the switch for the sunroof and fiddle pointlessly with all the other dials in the walnut console. He was the one who didn't dare look at her the rest of the way home.

CHAPTER 22

"GEORGE, I'VE BEEN MEANING TO CALL you," said Morton Dinnerstein. I had just stepped into one of the elevators beside the grand lobby of the LeSueur. As soon as Mort saw me, he lit up with his silly off-center smile. I was a referring attorney now, a source of income and someone to whom he was obliged to show gratitude and charm. He pumped my hand several times. But it turned out he had serious business on his mind. "You didn't by any chance get the settlement check on this *Petros v. Standard Railing* matter, did you? The guy who fell out of the balcony at the Hands game? The thing was over two months ago and this McManis is stringing Robbie along."

In the brass-ribbed elevator, with the artful festoonery adorning the grillwork, I suddenly felt like a bird in a cage. I remained determined not to lie for the government.

Not so far as I know, I told him.

"And the client, this Peter Petros, he isn't banging your door down? That's a miracle. Where'd you find this guy,

George? There must be a couple more like him somewhere on earth."

I laughed far too robustly at Morty's humor and looked up desperately at the old-fashioned clocklike mechanism that counted the floors.

"I'm going to get this taken care of this week, George," Mort promised as I alighted. It was nearing April 15, and I guess Mort, like most Americans, was scrounging for tax money.

Again and again, Petros confirmed the lesson I'd learned over the years watching my wife, Patrice, practice architecture: you can never plan well enough. Life will always outwit you. The devices employed to avoid detection of the Project were elaborate. With no questions asked, the General Counsel at Moreland had agreed, as part of their continuing cooperation with Stan's office, to confirm Mc-Manis's role with the company. Every plaintiff and defendant in the contrived cases had a listing with directory assistance and a phone number that forwarded to Amari's desk, as well as post office boxes from which the UCAs dutifully collected the mail. The companies created, like Standard Railing, were registered with the Secretary of State. But there was no controlling random events.

The day Skolnick had pressured McManis to settle the painter's case, Klecker had rushed to the courthouse to correct a problem with the FoxBIte only to find, as he went through the metal detector, that he'd left his gun on under his jumpsuit. Amazingly, he'd gotten away with rapping on it and telling the deputies it was a tool. But the whole Project might have come down at that moment. Then last week a law student in Malatesta's class had called Feaver. He happened to have been in court, watching the judge on the bench, the day Silvio had ruled on the motion to dismiss in *Petros* and the student was now thinking of doing a paper on the case for a seminar. Feaver told him he couldn't discuss the matter without the client's consent, but everyone was living in dread that the student might decide to investigate on his own.

No one, so far as I knew, had given much thought to the fact that Dinnerstein would expect to see money. It had been enough just to maintain all the pretenses in court. Yet if you believed the paperwork created to dupe Mort, he had several hundred thousand dollars coming, something he was unlikely to forget. In the office with both Robbie and Evon, he was, naturally, far crankier than he'd been with me. She had been around several times recently when he'd reminded Robbie to get after McManis, and Feaver's failure to produce results had even made Mort slightly mistrustful.

"You sure spend a lot of time with that guy," Mort said one day this week. "Don't forget you're supposed to be kicking his ass."

"Hey," Robbie answered.

Mort turned to Evon. "He falls in love with people, you know."

Dinnerstein had come to accept her regular presence, inured to the random women who became enmeshed in Robbie's life. Evon, for her part, had learned to enjoy the gentle needling between the two men and, even more, the intimate undercurrents that inevitably overcame Mort's frequent exasperation with his partner. But finances were one of Mort's responsibilities in the firm, and despite his good nature, he was exacting. He could tell you the monthly income within a few dollars without a financial report. He invested shrewdly, too, Robbie said.

'That dippy head-in-the-clouds stuff,' Robbie had once told her, 'that's partly a schtick he got into as a kid so he could ignore a lot of hairy stuff. You're too young to remember how it was, but until Salk found his vaccine, mothers would sort of hover over their kids all summer, watching for even a runny nose, knowing that somebody—some kid from school or the third cousin of your downstairs neighbor—but someone was going to end up with this horrible plague. And Morty was the one. He was in an iron lung for months. That can weird you out some. The paralysis pretty much receded. But afterwards, his ma was always hanging on him. Sometimes when he was sleeping, she'd put a mirror under his nose to make sure he was breathing. And she made him wear this leg brace, so he felt like the world's biggest dork. When he'd get out of the house, we'd take it off and hide it in the bushes. It was leather with steel rods and laces like for shoes. I must have tied that thing a hundred times, helping him put it back on. Sheilah was never the wiser. He'd go home to Mommy with that dopey out-of-it smile.'

Feaver found this story, like everything about Mort, endearing, but the point was well taken. The same day Mort had seen me, Shirley Nagle burst into McManis's conference room to announce that Dinnerstein was in reception. As it happened, Evon was with Jim, doing a status check on the paperwork outstanding on each of the contrived cases. Shirley described Mort as polite, but determined. He'd already made a couple of unanswered phone calls to McManis today. He'd now announced that he'd just wait out there until Jim could see him. Dinnerstein had taken a seat in one of the upholstered chairs, reaching into a full briefcase to draw out a draft on which he began marking out changes in his small careful hand.

"Should I hide?" Evon asked McManis.

"Hell," said Jim, "you better go see what he wants."

In reception, Evon explained her presence with something close to the truth: she'd come down here to confirm briefing schedules on a number of cases and, hearing Mort's name, thought he might have been here to find her. It was the money, of course, that he was after.

"Why don't you stick around," Mort whispered. "I wouldn't mind a witness."

Eventually they were ushered back to McManis's office. Mort never stopped smiling throughout the visit. He said that after all those months of hearing Jim's name, he thought they should meet. Trying to build a bridge, he even tossed out the names of a few people in Moreland's legal department whom he took for mutual acquaintances. McManis was not completely convincing in response, but owing a fellow several hundred thousand dollars didn't generally foster a relaxed appearance.

When Mort finally reached the subject of the money his firm was due, Jim, in usual lawyerly fashion, blamed the client.

"Well, we have a client, too." Dinnerstein laughed. "And we're going to have a hell of a time explaining to him why we didn't file a contempt motion." Mort happened to have a draft of such a motion in his briefcase and, with no lapse in his jovial manner, handed it to Jim before Evon and he went on their way.

Naturally, Sennett and Robbie and I were urgently summoned in the aftermath. This problem was only going to get worse. Beyond *Standard Railing*, Dinnerstein would soon be looking for a settlement check on the case of the poor painter with cancer which had been before Skolnick, and also on *King v. Hardwick*, the sexual harassment suit on which Robbie had informed Judge Crowthers' clerk of a settlement two days after the hearing. Things were only half as bad as they looked, since Feaver would immediately refund his end to the government. But retrieving the money from Mort, whenever the Project was over, might be a complicated legal undertaking, especially if Mort was angry, as he figured to be. The folks at UCORC, who were forever hounding McManis and Stan about the significant costs of the Project, seemed unlikely to let go of $250,000 they might never see again.

We all watched Sennett calculate, banging his fingers against his lips. It reminded me a little of one of those game shows I watched in childhood, where the audience waited for the correct answer to come spinning down in a sheaf of IBM cards dropped from the bottom of Univac.

"They'll do it," he said suddenly. "I know how to handle it." Around the table, we awaited a further explanation, but it wasn't forthcoming. Sennett gave us a dry smile, but his idea, whatever it was, was locked in the need-to-know treasure chest. Yet he was right. The money was wired from a code-named account to McManis two days later.

"You know," Robbie told Evon the night he'd presented Mort with the check, "I wasn't really scared. I've always figured with Morty that if push comes to shove, I can just tell him to shut up and trust me."

Sennett would not like that—what if Mort let something slip to his uncle?—but Robbie was right. For all his lapses and deceptions, Robbie was committed to Morty's well-being, and Dinnerstein knew it. Years ago, despite some qualms from Joan about Robbie's philandering, Mort and his wife had named Robbie in their will as their children's guardian, recognizing the powerful bond Robbie had formed with both boys. He was 'Uncle Robbie,' and had coached Mort's older son, Josh, in Little League for several years, in 'the good old days' as Robbie called them, when he would show up for practice at eight on Saturday morning still in his suit. The younger boy, Max, was not an athlete. But from an early age, he'd been an exuberant performer, a talent Robbie had helped cultivate by directing the annual children's theater production at the local Jewish Community Center. Last summer, for the first time, he had bowed out because of Rainey's deterioration, but

Evon heard Robbie on the phone with the boy often, coaching him for different parts.

"You have any friends like that?" Feaver asked her now. "Like Morty and me?"

"Me?" Evon was somehow startled by the thought. Her first impulse was to mention her sister. But family wasn't quite the same. She knew that. No, was the honest answer. The bare facts sank her, but she told him the truth.

"Not many people do," he offered for comfort, clearly having read her reaction.

But it was not a good night after that. When she got up to the small apartment, she was reeling. She felt fierce anger at the way Robbie managed to sneak up on her, and she hated herself for being who she was, so simple and manipulable in her longings. She sat on the couch in a blanket for quite some time, before she even had the spunk to put on Reba singing "It's Your Call." She was going to have to go out and call Merrel. There was no choice about that. Downtown, in a couple of the fancy hotels there were luxurious phone booths, elegant enclosed spaces, with brass fixtures and a little shelf of granite, a place where she did not feel in peril when she spoke in her old voice.

She took a box from the freezer, unsure exactly what entree was in it, and punched the beeping buttons on the microwave. She went to shower while her dinner twirled under the rays. When she'd stripped down, she considered herself in the small mirror on the bathroom vanity, whose corners were already being glossed over with vapor. Good tits. She had that much going for her. The sight, without any expectation, brought on the first vivid fantasy of being with Feaver that she'd experienced in all these months. It was sudden, enrapturing, and brief: just an intense image of him in darkness. An exact tactile memory of the unanticipated male hardness of his limbs revisited her. Her nipples peaked at once; she knew if she lowered her hand for consolation she'd be wet. But she twisted away from that, almost like a wrestler escaping from a hold. No. *No.* And then she prepared herself to recoil from the shock. But she wasn't upset. It was just a piece of something she'd tried out, knowing all along it would never fit, just one more thing rocking and rolling inside her.

She looked to the mirror, hoping for some confirmation from the woman there, but her face was already obscured by the steam.

CHAPTER 23

THE DAY AFTER ROBBIE'S TELEVISED PAY-off of Skolnick, Stan had met with Chief Judge Winchell and played the tape for her. He wanted her to know Petros was on the right track, that Feaver's accusations were proving out. Stan's hope, yet again, was that she'd be willing to authorize the installation of a bug in Judge Malatesta's chambers. The Chief Judge was careful not to give him any advice; she was the judge, not the prosecutor. But Sennett felt that if he could specify a limited time frame, a few days in which the government was watching for a particular event, she'd sign the warrant. Therefore, Sennett sought Robbie's help in devising a scenario for an emergency motion, one Malatesta would have to rule on quickly, which would give the government an event to earmark in applying for the bug.

There were still two contrived cases on Malatesta's docket. Given Walter's warnings, they had remained largely dormant, supposedly snoozing along through the interrogatory stage in discovery. One of the cases, *Drydech v. Lan-*

caster Heating, concerned a gas water heater that had supposedly exploded in the barn of Robbie's client, a farmer. Drydech, based on an out-of-state decision Robbie had read, was known as 'The Fart Case' around McManis's office. The planned defense was that combustion resulted not from the water heater but from a buildup of high quantities of methane emitted by a barn full of cows.

To create the emergency, Robbie now proposed that he file a motion to advance the deposition of a company engineer who allegedly had warned of the potential for flash explosions if the heater was installed in an enclosed space occupied by livestock. The motion would require an immediate ruling because the engineer, supposedly, was seriously ill and slipping downhill.

As soon as the papers were typed, Robbie and Evon dashed to the courthouse to file them and visit with Walter. The predicate for the bug would be a conversation, much like the one in Peter Petros's case, in which Feaver told Wunsch that the outcome of the lawsuit would hinge on Malatesta's ruling. The government would then watch to see how Wunsch brought this news to the judge and how Silvio reacted.

When they arrived, Walter was already in the courtroom, getting ready for a hearing at 2 p.m. Once court started, Robbie would have a hard time holding any conversation with Wunsch, and they galloped across the corridor. As Evon flew through the swinging door behind Robbie, she nearly knocked over a burly guy twice her size. He was somebody she'd seen around here before, a cop or a deputy from the looks of him. While she apologized, he stared incredulously, not so much angry as unaccustomed, Evon figured, to taking that kind of wallop from a female.

Walter was walking back and forth on the yellowish birch tier beneath the judge, with his customary ill-humored expression, giving directions to the bailiff and court reporter regarding the session about to get under way. Evon hung back, allowing Robbie to approach Wunsch on his own, although the voices were clear through the infrared. Handing over the motion, Feaver declared, between his teeth, "This guy is my case, Wally."

Walter's rumpled face shrank with distaste, but he said nothing. When Robbie asked how soon the judge would decide, Wunsch recited the court's rule on emergency motions: McManis would have two days to reply, and the judge could then take up to two days to rule. That meant he'd consider the motion on Thursday or Friday.

"You gonna ask me to add one plus one next?" Walter asked Robbie, before shooing him away.

When Stan called midday Friday to ask if Robbie and I could join him at McManis's, I figured we were being summoned for another celebration. But there were no upbeat greetings from the UCAs. In the conference room, both Jim and Stan sat with long faces. The dead gray eye of the video monitor was exposed in the red oak cabinets. When I asked what was wrong, the two looked at one another. Robbie arrived then, and even before he was seated, Stan pushed the button on the VCR.

The screen sprang to life with a black-and-white image. The date and time, down to tenths of seconds, were displayed in a running count of white block letters in the upper right-hand corner. The footage, whatever it was, had been taken at 5:05 p.m. yesterday and the perspective was strange. The camera was positioned somewhere near the ceiling— in a phony smoke detector, Klecker told me later—and the lens was a fisheye, foreshortening the sides of the room much like the gold-framed parabolic mirror that hung in my parents' foyer. The halftones blurred to white in the weak light.

Eventually, I recognized a large desk, ponderous as an anvil, with Old Glory and the county flag on standards behind it. Two figures were at the edge of the picture. When they moved into the frame, they were, as anticipated, Malatesta and Wunsch. The judge held a sheaf of documents, which, it developed, were rulings on various cases. Silvio, in his Harry Caray glasses, looked over each one, then entered his name at the bottom. Hanging over his shoulder, Walter picked up the order as soon as it was signed. As he went along, Silvio made remarks to Walter and himself. A settlement conference was due on this one. The trial in *Gwynn* would last a lifetime. In response, Walter showed none of the dourness so much in evidence elsewhere. While the judge worked, he was a fountain of compliments about the wisdom of each decision.

"Figures," Robbie said. "What a toady."

Klecker had entered and Stan waved at him to cue the tape ahead. When the imagery began moving forward again, Malatesta was taking some time with the draft order in his hands.

"What's this, Walter?"

"*Drydech*. You looked at the papers last night, after defendant filed, Judge. Remember? This is the case where the defense is that the cows had gas. It's some discovery baloney. Same as usual. Defendant's got his wheels in the mud."

Malatesta touched the center of his frames to push them back up on his nose.

"Walter, how do you keep track of these cases? I can't remember half of them. It's a blessing to have you. Remind me again of the issue here."

Walter explained that Feaver wanted to depose, out of order, an engineer who supposedly was on death's doorstep.

"It's a complete blank, Walter."

"Judge, you read it."

"Did I?" Absently, Silvio tugged up the sleeves of his cheap shirt, which swam on him, and reset the garters over his negligible biceps. "Get the papers, Walter. I just want to be sure I didn't do something temperamental at the end of the day."

Malatesta had finished the stack of remaining orders by the time Walter was back with Robbie's motion and Mc-Manis's response. The judge shook his head as he read.

"Walter, I must have paid no attention at all. This is quite a complicated issue. I'm not sure that the defendant doesn't have a point." McManis had argued that it was unfair for Robbie to take the engineer's deposition before staking out a position on various technical issues related to the testimony. If Feaver wanted to expedite this dep, he had to expedite expert discovery as well.

Hovering behind the judge, Walter was silent at first.

"Well, all right, Judge. But one thing. The plaintiff here, Feaver, he's going straight to the Appellate Court."

Malatesta rolled back in his large chair. "Is he?"

"Straight up there. That's the impression he gave me. Says he can't put on his case without this engineer. He'll stipulate to a verdict and go right up."

"I see." Malatesta covered his mouth and studied Robbie's motion again.

"I don't know, Judge, you're the judge, but you know, that whole appeal thing doesn't happen if you rule for the plaintiff. Why not see what this engineer has to say? If it's nothing much, Feaver loses. If it's hot stuff, the Appellate Court'll never reverse you. They'd have no use for a defendant tryin to sweep bad testimony under the rug."

"Well." Malatesta swung his head back and forth. "I'm sitting here to render my best judgment, Walter, not to handicap the Appellate Court."

"Yeah, well, naturally, Judge, but you know, you got such a great record. Judge Tuohey talks about that all the time. How you're leading the league upstairs. Nobody down in the Superior Court is close, Judge."

Malatesta, a man little inclined to laughter, actually giggled, an oddly childish sound.

"True, true enough, Walter. I saw Brendan last week and he was praising my name to three or four other judges, how well regarded I am up there. It was a trifle embarrassing, actually. Still, I confess I'm proud of my record. There are some very fine jurists here in the Superior Court, Walter. It's an accomplishment to be the least often reversed."

"And, Judge, I don't know, but I got it in mind the Appellate Court threw a case back in the last few days—I thought it was just like this. 'Let the plaintiff have his discovery.' Ain't that what they usually say?"

"Well, yes, normally, Walter. But there has to be some even-handedness." Malatesta continued to deliberate. He fishmouthed and tapped on one cheek. "I don't see the parties citing a case like that."

"Just came down, I thought. Brand-new opinion. Not even published. What's the name?" Walter walked around, pounding his fingertips on his forehead. "Why don't I remember this?" he asked himself. "But they reversed whoever it was. Almost exactly like this case."

"A reversal?" Malatesta asked again.

Walter nodded soberly. In a gingerly way, Malatesta threw up his hands so as not to loosen his sleeves.

"You've got good sense on these things, Walter. I acknowledge that. Well, all right. File the order, Walter. First instinct's always best in this business. I granted the motion last night; that was probably the right thing to do."

"Right." Walter almost bowed as he turned heel.

Stan stopped the tape. He lifted his chin as he faced us. He asked what we thought.

"You're kidding, right?" Robbie answered. He'd been unable to hide his amusement for some time. "For Godsake, Stan, Walter's leading the poor little son of a bitch around by the nose. He's getting him to sign orders blind. Isn't that what it looks like? He goes and splits the money I give him with Rollo Kosic and has a laugh about how Silvio is thinking so hard he can't tie his shoes. And then Brendan, just to keep it all moving, Brendan comes along and pats Silvio on the keester for his great record of never getting reversed."

Behind Stan, McManis flashed me a look. I took it Robbie's dialogue with Sennett was a replay of what had already gone on between Stan and Jim.

"So you mean you've been cheated all along?" Sennett asked.

"Cheated? Christ, Stan, who am I to complain? I get what I want. Walter takes the money and keeps it? So what? For me it's the same thing."

Sennett bristled. "It's hardly the same thing. A devious minute clerk isn't a corrupt judge." He cast a hard look at Robbie. "Not for either of us," he added with a menacing flash of candor. He was right. Walter was a flunky, both in the court of public opinion and in that of a sentencing judge.

"What I'm thinking," Sennett said, "is that you got made."

Feaver stared, insulted. The cover for the Project, maintained by huge mutual effort, was a shared treasure. The person who was detected as a government operative would have let everyone down.

"Think about it," said Sennett. "There must be a way they found out the camera is there. Walter knows he's rare roast beef, so he's helping Malatesta wriggle away. If—" He stopped, brought up short by our reactions. McManis and Robbie and I seemed joined in a moment of awe and wonder such as the Scripture describes, not of celebration or joy, but of amazement and dread. The power and speed of Stan's thinking and the way it could divert him from even the most glaring realities was stunning.

"What?" he asked, in response to the staring. He folded his hands and sat forward stiffly. "It's possible. It's completely possible," he said. "Completely."

CHAPTER 24

THE NEXT THURSDAY, APRIL 30, EVON found herself sitting alone in the Mercedes on the top floor of the Temple parking garage. The car was within sight of the glass vestibule housing the ruined elevator, and she'd watched as the doors wobbled open and Robbie had joined Walter Wunsch. After a few words of hearty greeting, they passed completely out of range of the infrared while the elevator groaned and rattled as it made its descent. She sat there, unknowing, isolated, hoping like hell it didn't go to fudge, and feeling an unexpected irritation in her bladder.

Following a few days of confused debate, the best tactical option seemed to be to proceed with another payment to Walter in gratitude for the favorable ruling in *Drydech*. It would put to the test Sennett's theory that Wunsch was somehow on alert. No matter how loyal he was to Malatesta, Walter was not going to buy more time in the pen by accepting a second envelope.

Even before the elevator had arrived back on five, Evon

knew something was wrong. The sea rush of static in her earpiece began to yield to voices. Instead of having high-tailed it on the first floor, Walter was still with Robbie. They were talking about a woman, with the usual unpleasant undercurrent. Feaver was laughing, in his humoring fashion, and Wunsch was growling in a low way that made his words difficult to discern.

The elevator doors, engraved with rusty gang signs and markered graffiti, slowly parted. Unharmed, Feaver stepped forth smiling, still in the company of Wunsch. In spite of a heavy topcoat in the mild spring weather, Walter's narrow shoulders were hunched, almost up to his ears.

"Not possible," she heard Robbie say. He tossed a wave at Wunsch and pushed off from the vestibule. Walter stood his ground. He stared through the smeared plate glass toward Evon in the car, his complexion like a bowl of oatmeal, his look ugly as it loitered on her. Unexpectedly, she heard Feaver speaking to her over the infrared as he advanced on the Mercedes.

"Okay, now when I get into the car I'm going to say something to you, blah, blah, blah, and I want you to laugh out loud. Hysterical laugh. Okay? I just told you something that's a living, fucking riot."

Feaver bounced into the driver's seat and, as he'd said, mouthed several sentences, making no sound whatsoever, a pantomime intended for Walter. "Laugh!" he then exclaimed through his teeth. She did it, while he continued offering stage direction. His hand was lifted to obscure the movement of his lips, as he told her to shake her head, laugh so hard she was coughing. Eventually, Robbie turned to the windshield and mushed up his face. He shrugged at Walter, and Walter shrugged in response. The elevator car had opened behind Wunsch, and he turned for it.

She waited for a hand sign, something, but Feaver gave no explanation. Instead he rammed the car into gear and peeled from the garage. Several blocks down, he veered into an alley, bucketing along until he'd pulled into the graveled parking lot behind a small store. Its back doors were protected by a rusted security grate. Robbie pointed emphatically to his belt line and mouthed, "Off."

She did not have the remote today. They were only a few blocks from the LeSueur and she had figured to de-activate the FoxBIte at McManis's.

"Shit," said Feaver out loud. "Frisk," he told her.

She asked what was going on.

"Goddamn it, frisk," he answered. He sat through it stiffly, looking off through the window. He told her to state her findings and the time, and then, without another word, plucked the microphone bud out of his shirt and tore it from the lead. "Show time's over," Robbie said.

"He didn't take the money?"

"Ate every bite. Same as always." At Klecker's advice, Feaver had bought custom-made boots as a safer and more comfortable spot to hide the FoxBIte, and he jacked up his calf now to wrestle one off. He had considerable difficulty in the cramped confines of the car. She asked repeatedly what was wrong, but he refused to answer. Finally, he tore the FoxBIte from the ankle harness and slapped it down on her purse.

"For God's sake, what's the problem?"

"The problem is," he said, "as Walter and I are about to go our separate ways, he tells me a story. It's half a joke to him, half maybe not. Apparently, when we were in Malatesta's courtroom last week, you plowed into some guy? Well, he's a copper. Old chum of Walter's from when they were both around felony court. This guy's got a law-suit going, administrative appeal from a ruling of the Fire and Police Board. He caught thirty days for something. Name is Martin Carmody." Feaver stared, waiting for a re-sponse. "Wanna buy a vowel?"

"I've seen him around. I thought I had."

"Yeah, well." She followed Robbie's eyes as he looked out the window again toward the unfaced brick at the rear of the low building. A little tendril of something green twisted around the rusted rainpipe. "He says about five, six years ago—this is what he tells Walter—he was sent to Quantico for a couple weeks of advanced firearms instruction. Out there he gets to know his instructor, female FBI agent, DeDe Something. Real well he got to know her one night. Biblical 'know.' And he could swear, so he tells Walter, that this chick he plowed into, meaning you—that's her. DeDe. Dyed her hair. Lost the glasses. A little less country-looking, but, Christ, that's hard to forget. The only reason he's asking Walter is because Missus Carmody is attending the hearing every day and he'd rather not have any howdy-dos."

Evon had her eyes closed by now.

"So I did the big ho-ho," Robbie said. "FBI? Ridiculous. Let's go ask her. Walter, thank God, is too much of a prude to actually stick his nose in the car and inquire of a lady about who she might have been bopping, and of course, his act is what-me-worry-about-the-FBI, but he was still curious enough to come up and watch."

"Fuck," she said, when she could talk. She had never used that word in front of him, she realized. Her Mormon routine.

"So, DeDe, baby, you better tell me what we're going to do now."

"Goddamn." Her mind was like a ship stuck in ice. The engine revved but the prow couldn't break through. If Walter had taken the money, she hadn't been made. But there was no way to be sure. Her whole torso was rattling. And as always, she felt her heart being carved on by shame. It was worse, somehow, that it had been broadcast to the surveillance van. Everybody knew. By now, Sennett was spinning like a weather vane in a tornado. They were all going to be nuts.

"So do I understand?" she asked. "He was just being cautious? Carmody? He wasn't really sure? I mean, we were drunk, Robbie. Knee-walking drunk." She drummed her fingers. "He's not sure. That's why he asked Walter."

"Probably. But Wally's still a little spooked. It looked like he was cooled out by the time he left. But the question is out there."

She talked mostly to herself I couldn't place him. I really couldn't place him. I walked right past him." It had to have been around 1986, because they were still building Hogan's Alley, a little town where crimes were staged for training purposes. It was the first time she'd been invited back to Quantico to teach firearms. Ancient history. Another life. A tiny inappropriate burp of laughter jumped up to her throat. Naturally, she remembered him as so much better-looking.

"Yeah," he said. "A one-nighter. Just a stray dick at closing time. I've been there." When she caught Robbie's look, she understood the rest. The emotions tumbled through his dark face. He was gripping the walnut wheel with both hands and the deep eyes flicked up at her the same way they had the first day when she told him they'd already caught a bad guy.

"Robbie," she said, then stopped.

He gunned the car, backing into the alley.

"Great cover," he told her.

MAY

YAM

CHAPTER
25

"DO YOU REMEMBER?" SHE ASKED. "WE talked. That night. After Kosic. Do you remember that? And you described lying in the dark. And feeling so uncertain. Do you remember?"

She heard the hollow glottal echo as he drank. "So are you saying—?"

"I'll tell you what I'm saying," she said. "But answer me first. Do you remember that?"

"Sure."

"Well, here's what I need to know. Was that a play?"

He made a low sound, perhaps a groan. "Nope," he said at last. "That was straight shit."

"So then, can you imagine reaching inside yourself and being uncertain about what's there? Not being sure you can really feel what you crave. Can you imagine that?"

In the dark, he took his time to ponder. After he'd removed the FoxBIte and told her what Walter had said about Carmody, they had driven around before heading back to the LeSueur. Contempt bristled off him—him of all people, enraged because he thought he'd been deceived. But his anger proved strangely hard to bear. She felt lost and mangled as it was, still trying to calculate the costs of this breach of cover to the Project and to herself, shocked that out of nowhere her former life had come, like some unwelcome relation, to reclaim her. If Feaver had dropped her on a corner, she could never have wandered home.

He'd finally asked her what was true. Was she or wasn't she? She refused at first to answer.

'We're not going there, Robbie. It's not appropriate. I have a job to do.'

'And you've fucked that up, too.' As the dust from that wrecking ball rose, she received a darting sideward look, softer than anything she'd seen since they left Walter. 'Not fair,' he said after a moment and reverted to silence.

Somehow they reached a consensus not to remain at the LeSueur. Feaver circled the block, while she tossed the FoxBIte to McManis from the door to his office. Jim didn't say much. He wanted to know if Walter had looked sold when he'd turned back to the elevator. She thought so. So did Feaver. But, she'd realized, even if Walter had doubts, there were no odds for him in confronting her.

She asked if Sennett had gone crazy.

'Yes,' Jim answered. 'He thinks the Movers should have picked this up on background.' Grave as the situation was, he smiled at the notion of that questionnaire: List every wild and crazy evening for the last ten years. He nodded kindly when she told him she just wanted to beat it. 'This isn't on you,' he told her.

She knew that was true. It was nothing more than wicked coincidence. UCAs got made most often by cops or prosecutors who recognized them. But that was logic. If the Project cratered now, it would always follow her. Back to Iowa and whatever might come next. Don't embarrass the Bureau. The Quantico watchword was burned like a brand onto the mind of every recruit. McManis and Sennett were talking anyway. Balancing risks. That was why he was just as happy to let her go. They didn't know yet what they were going to do with her.

Back in the Mercedes, Feaver had asked if she needed a drink, which God knows she did, and he volunteered to go into a package store to get her a bottle. Until they abandoned ship, the Mormon girl shouldn't be seen buying liquor. She was not really ready to be alone, and it seemed at least a form of recompense to finally let him into her apartment. She mixed the vodka with some frozen lemonade she had in her freezer and, after they had drunk much of it in silence, impulse had welled up in her, almost like the piston push of sickness. She wanted to explain. Why? she asked herself, hoping to find a clear rationale for restraint. Why?

Because. Because silence would be fatal to something fragile in her.

Because it seemed unbearable to have the precious truth, so hard to speak, taken for a lie.

The light had disappeared. She'd never closed the drapes. Refractions of the streetlights and a neon sign across the avenue limned the room. Her eyes were closed for the most part. Robbie sat on the floor against the flowered sofa the Movers had rented. In the cushions, when she lay on it at night watching TV, she could detect the trace remainders of stale cigar smoke and the gassy chemicals that had failed to remove it. Feaver had taken off his suit jacket and his boots. His toes wiggled in his fancy patterned hose as he drank, but he'd gone still now while he deliberated on his answer. Could he imagine?

Yes, he said, in time. He could imagine that, yes.

"Is that how it is for you?" he asked her.

"How it was," she said, "for years. Years. I thought I was just not interested or didn't care. I wasn't sure. Maybe

I was putting all of it into sports." Athletes *were* their bodies. After a game, there was a supersensory awareness: the bruises, pulls, the aches within. Her skin felt as if something keen had been drilled through every follicle into the deeper layers of the derma. For most of her teammates, that electricity must have flowed into sexual expression. But for her, the game was the excitement. Her inchoate sensations of herself seemed almost superstitiously forbidden. Not merely because of the church-taught sense of plague or peril. But because it would deplete her somehow, put at risk the radioactive core of passion that sent her storming down the field.

In high school, she was the great jock, too much for many boys to want to take on. And it was a Mormon town anyway; more than half the kids weren't allowed to date until they were sixteen. She wanted to go out, naturally, once all that swung into motion. She wanted to belong. She was seventeen years old. She went to the senior prom and had sex that night, as if it were part of the same ceremony, which for many in Kaskia it was. She lay out in the grass on the lee side of the local ski mountain and let Russell Hugel wrestle off her undergarments and plunge into her. It didn't last a minute. He helped her up. He carefully plucked every leaf and grass strand from her dress, then walked her back down the hill in silence. The poor boy was probably embarrassed, probably thought he'd made a hash of it. A rooster in the barnyard, flapping his useless wings, went at it longer than Russell had. Such was sex. She reviewed it in her mind periodically. The interlude passed like the dance itself. Long-anticipated and brief and disappointing. She put away the dress. And concluded, as she went off to college, it was all too much of a mess.

Gay—the thought that there was anyone on earth like that—was still kind of a legend, as far as she was concerned, one of those terrible things that people tell you about the world that you suspect is exaggerated or not even true. She sounded like a hick, she knew. But she'd grown up on a ranch. Rams with ewes. Bulls with cows. She'd heard about Sodom in church. But God had destroyed *them*.

"I made it through hockey camp the first summer with no clue. And some of those girls were so dykey, so out, one of them, Anne-Marie—the girls joked about not being alone with her. I *still* didn't get it."

She had a teammate at the time, she told him, a woman named Hilary Beacom, a good midfielder but not quite a star. Two years ahead of Evon, Hilary was from the Main Line near Philadelphia. Field hockey, weirdly, had a high-class heritage. There were all these women out there, running, whaling at balls, smashing each other in the legs and even, now and then, the head. Blood flowed often. It wasn't what Evon thought of as a finishing-school game. But that's where many of the girls came from. Private schools. Rich schools. Hilary Beacom had emerged from that world. Blond hair thick as velvet, pulled back in a tartan headband. Clothing by Laura Ashley. And the contented charm of someone who truly owned the world.

She looked after Evon, sat beside her on the bus, told her secrets about the coaches. Away from the field, they rode horseback together. One night in May of Evon's sophomore year, they got drunk. Drinking was forbidden in or out of season. They'd all signed pledges. But Hilary was graduating soon and they drank wildly, rolling through half a dozen frat parties before they made their way to Hilary's room. They were just silly. They were imitating people on childhood TV shows ("Oh, Mr. Grant!") and then *Star Trek* stuff, all the different species who were human except for a single trait that had been amplified, or mutated, or replaced. Spock, without emotion.

'I see your aura,' said Hilary across the room, pretending to be a character from the Canis galaxy, who supposedly had the ability of dogs to see the halo of emotional discharge around a human being. 'I see your awe-rah,' she said and waved her hands swami-like as she approached. Evon had collapsed on Hilary's bed with her head against a bolster. They were both laughing.

'And what do you see?'

Hilary came closer, spreading her opened palms over Evon's head, as if massaging some presence in the air.

'I see,' said Hilary, whose eyes seemed to clear briefly, 'I see you're drunk.'

They crumbled against each other. Hilary finally righted herself and began the same routine.

'I see you are uncertain,' she said. Her eyes lit upon Evon. 'I see you are afraid.'

'Okay,' said Evon, laughing, though she realized then that the time for laughter had passed. Hilary moved her hands again, first around Evon's head, and then allowed them to drift along her entire torso, separated from contact by some barely visible micrometer.

'I feel yearning,' Hilary said.

Evon didn't answer. Hilary's face, thick with makeup to hide the blemishes on one cheek, was inches from hers. The shades on the room were drawn.

'Do you know what's happening here?' Hilary asked her.

Yes, she knew. She knew. Somehow. They watched each other, measuring the uncertainty. And then Hilary brought her face to hers. Evon lingered there, in the sweet, powerful smells of Hilary's face. Beyond the phony scents, her flesh had the vague sweetness of milk. Evon's eyes were still open when their lips met. Dry from sport and the anxiousness of the moment, they felt like the fragile crust formed on an orange section left in the air, and, like the orange, some thrilling sweetness lay below. Hilary slowly brought her full weight down upon her.

Feaver spoke: So, she knew.

"No. It was something that happened. I didn't know what it meant." She never failed to admit there was pleasure in it. But afterwards, she told herself she had not known what else to do. It was, oddly, not much different than being on that hillside with Russell. She remained aloof from Hilary, whose patrician grace—more than that, her kindness—prevented her from ever speaking a word. A month later Hilary graduated. The event receded with time, its contours lost in the murk of memory. There were lots of things about her, Evon reasoned, that weren't the same as most people she knew. She came from a tiny little town nobody'd ever heard of. She'd been selected for the national team in an Olympic sport. And she once slept with a girl. That was how she was.

But did that mean she wasn't going to get the happiness everybody else wanted? That she wasn't entitled to it? If you'd asked her, then, after Hilary, she'd still have predicted she was going to get married, have kids, the house, the husband, a good guy, quiet and sincere, the way she thought of her father and her little brothers. When that happened, Hilary wouldn't matter. None of it would. She was thirty-four years old now. Thirty-four, and the vision of that waiting serenity still swam through her as a comfort from time to time, and when she realized it was never going to occur, she was still, at thirty-four, crushed.

A little more than three years ago she had been detailed to San Francisco on an investigation of suspected bribery of Agriculture Department inspectors at the seaport. Another agent had taken her to this strip club for a laugh. One of the girls there was a source of his, she bounced around with a lot of would-be wiseguys and had some good information. But Evon wasn't laughing. He thought it was because she was uptight and they left after a drink. But what seized up everything in her was the way one woman looked at her while she was dancing. She had her naked breasts in her hands, massaging them, drawing them together, the nipples slender, very red, and visibly erect, and she turned a yearning, willing, knowing look on Evon. It was a come-on, she realized, part of their routine, the girls played to everybody in the crowd, knowing nobody was there by accident, everybody came looking for a little thrill. And Evon got hers. She went home and did not sleep all night. When she poured a vodka for herself, her hand shook so that she could barely get the liquid in the glass. She sat in an easy chair in the little monthly studio where the Bureau'd put her and tried to calm down. And after an hour or so of drinking she finally said it to herself. So that's how I am.

"And I went back. I didn't have the remotest idea what I'd say if anybody I knew showed up there. 'I expected to find you'? I guess that was what I'd worked out in my head. I went back like it was business, an investigation. I sat in the front row. I watched this woman—Teresa Galindo, it turned out, was her name—I watched Teresa, I smiled at her, she looked at me again that way, and now I just sort of gave in, succumbed. I felt my body rise to her—" Even now, the memory was stunning. Stunning.

"Anyway, they circulated, the girls, you know, they wanted you to buy drinks. And this girl, Teresa, she wasn't a special beauty. The girls in the clubs, most of them, the main attribute they brought to the job was that they were willing to take off their clothes and dance in front of people. Teresa was all kind of pockmarked. When she went walking around in this skinny bikini and this little bathing shift, you could see she was made up all the way down her chest. But I was *so* turned on. Because I didn't have to work for what I wanted, because Teresa just saw it and knew what was there. When she came back with the drinks, she dropped a napkin in my lap and whispered, 'I do privates.'

" 'Private what?' I nearly asked. 'Dancing' is what she'd have said. But I didn't think she was really talking about dancing. I saw a phone number and just crumpled the napkin up in my hand. And I called. That night, so I didn't lose courage. And she came to my apartment the next morning. 11 a.m. Broad daylight, before both of us went to work. It was so weird. Not because of what we were doing—and it went past dancing in about two minutes— not because it was a woman's hands on me, not because of the incredible little toys she'd brought with her—there was one she called the Magic Wand with these three little revolving balls at the end?—but because in the middle I thought, This is a dream, God, I *have* dreamed this, I have dreamed it a thousand times.

"I paid her. And she always took the money. She said she only did this with women and not very often, but I had no idea whether that was true. She liked me. She figured out really fast that I was law enforcement, but she never guessed it was the Bureau. She thought I was a county sheriff's deputy. She made up this whole tale about me. I worked in the jail. I hated the men in there. Just the way she and most of the other girls hated the men in the club. That's why they seemed to do it. For the chance to look down on men, who want it so badly, so openly, and who're not going to get it. She had her reasons, too. She'd been messed with for years by her grandfather, a big *patrón* who everybody was afraid of. She'd been to college; that was a surprise. She had a degree in accounting. But she made more money doing this.

"So I knew. Out loud to myself, I knew. And people who're straight, I listen to them talk, and sometimes they seem to think that knowing is the only hard part. As if straight people have an easy time hooking up with someone else and aren't miserable about the fact they can't. I tried hanging out with this woman, Teresa. Sometimes, before or after, we'd go for a drink. But she'd made up her story about me, and I'd made up my story about her. Mine was that she was soft and kind and really just wanted somebody to turn to, and that wasn't so. Her crowd was tough. They liked pain. She took me to the sex clubs. They call them clubs, but it's just somebody's loft where you pay at the door. And I didn't care for what I saw. A woman with an Idaho potato? I wanted a life. That was a freak show. At least to me it was. So," she said wearily.

"I mean, sometimes I think about it and I'm just appalled. A stripper. A *strip*-per, for gosh sake. It's like my life was something dreamed up by a wino in a bus station. A stripper."

That was a play, Feaver said. She stiffened, but she'd misunderstood.

"It's a rehearsal," he said. "You're not bringing a stripper home to Mom."

She laughed at the idea. She wasn't bringing anybody home to Mom. She'd never have the fortitude. But she knew what he meant.

"So where the hell does Carmody come in here?" he asked. "After this?"

"Before. That was a pretty predictable period. I mean, I knew I wasn't getting the same thing from it as other people. From the Act. I thought I was frightened. Well, I was frightened. So I thought if I could get drunk enough— And I was away from home. That wasn't the only time. Hardly. The mechanics, they were okay, actually. This isn't about mechanics. It's about passion. Being the kind of woman who feels passion for other women. And who wants a woman to feel passion for her."

He asked who she was feeling passion for now, who

she'd left back home, and somehow she laughed again at the idea. Des Moines wasn't exactly San Francisco, and she had to be sensible, there was a lot the Bureau wasn't ready for yet. Iowa City was another story, but it was a distance, and there was an uncomfortable aspect to what she encountered there, reminiscent of what she'd seen in San Francisco. A lot of those women were on a mission and sort of demanded you be queer their way. It was fine all right to walk around in leather panties with your nipples covered in duct tape, but God forbid a girl liked Lee Greenwood or Travis Tritt. Or George Bush. Over all, though, she was still uptight. She realized that. Even now, there must have been some little part of her that was waiting for it all to go away.

About eighteen months ago something started to happen with a woman from church named Tina Criant. She was married to a trooper Evon had worked with, and Tina and she had a lot of things in common, the same funny mix of hobbies, needlepoint and pistol-shooting. They did those things together. Tina liked to give her books. They laughed. She was just a warm, special person, and Evon could see something beginning, probably the kind of thing Hilary Beacom saw in her. She never said a word, neither of them did. In retrospect, she knew she'd let it get away somehow. If she'd been bold, she might have been an example or supplied the courage for both of them. But perhaps it was just as well. Tina and Tom, her husband, had two little boys, five and seven. For about two months, Evon watched Tina work it out with herself. And decide. She quit the needlepoint circle. She stopped coming to the range. It had hurt a good deal. Evon hadn't realized until then how hard she had been hoping.

Sometimes now, she told him, in her worst moments, she would see one of those women who turn up in completely male settings—on road crews, or the lone white person among a Hispanic gardening gang—one of those bulky types with short hair and a dried-up face devoid of makeup and a bunched-up sweatshirt to hide what, for some reason, was always a humongous set of tits. She'd look at those women and think, Is that who I am? Is that who I'm going to be? Some self-declared misfit with her pistol collection and three sports channels on cable?

"Cut it out." He spoke unexpectedly, softly.

"Huh?"

"Don't do that to yourself. I mean, you can say I don't know you, but I know *that's* not you. Christ," he said, "you don't have it that easy."

It probably wasn't funny. But she laughed for a long time, and he laughed with her. Tonight, right now, she was ready to laugh. Because he was right. Both ways. The good news and the bad. She wasn't a type. She was herself. Square peg, all right. Cranky. Awkward. Confused, of course. But not *completely* ill suited to the world, not so dominated by these questions that they took over everything else. She had her secrets. Everybody did. Stuff swirled around inside her, undetermined, like the dust in the cosmos that wasn't yet a comet or a planet or a star. But who wasn't like that? Everybody. Everybody's sex life was strange. Right?

"So what else do you need to know, Robbie?" she asked after a time, in a drier tone. Across the room she heard the ice cubes rattle in his glass. Next door, a neighbor who'd played the *Bodyguard* sound track often enough since January to wear out the plastic was at it again.

"How'd you come up with 'Evon'?"

It was the name of her first cousin, a girl about her age, an Americanized spelling meant to be pronounced the same way as Yvonne. But people got confused. The teachers. Other kids. They came to call her cousin 'Even' and she got tired of correcting it. At times, it was a source of torment, kids being like they are. 'Even worse.' 'Even dumber.' 'Even uglier.' 'Even fatter.' But this girl, her cousin, she had some stuff. She wouldn't dent. 'Even better,' she would answer, and meant it. She was a doctor now in Boise, divorced, two kids, pretty happy on her own. They'd seen each other only once in the last ten years, but it had been a warm occasion. 'Even better.' She always wanted to be able to say that the way her cousin had.

A motorcycle gunned by in the avenue. She asked him if there was anything else.

"Once and for all," he finally said, "are you wired or not?"

She had to laugh. She'd laughed quite a bit by now.

"You think I'd have said all this to you with a tape recorder running?"

He'd considered that, though. He said he'd always figured they let her, as an agent, turn it on and off. She faced him in the dark. They'd been careful up to now not to look at one another.

"Just tell me no," he said. "I'll believe you. Just *tell* me no."

"I've told you no before. You want to look?"

"Huh?"

"Look." She stood up. She lifted her arms. "Go ahead and look. Go on. Frisk me. You won't believe anything else."

He was startled, but he eventually padded, shoeless and with a strangely light tread, to where she waited.

I don't have to do this."

"Yes you do. Only don't mess around," she said. "Do it the way I would. Check the purse."

He stood there for some time, embarrassed or simply unskilled in laying hands on a woman without the usual involvements. Finally, he gripped her shoulders. But he went no further. Instead he pulled her toward him slowly, until her head was directly beneath his chin, and then he bent and kissed her squarely on the crown, much as he'd done in the courthouse with Leo, his elderly cousin.

After that, he collected his coat and wiggled one of his feet awhile getting it back into his boot. A blade of light edged the door.

"You're okay," he said.

"Don't sound so surprised."

"I'll see you tomorrow."

"If they don't close us down tonight."

He shrugged. They'd done their best, he said. Both of them. He left her in the dark, feeling he was right.

THE NEXT MORNING, when Evon left her apartment, she was followed. She took a taxi out to Glen Ayre, where she'd left her car overnight, and even as she was getting in, she saw the headlights come on in a car positioned in a no-parking zone across the street. Daylight Saving had recommenced, and there was little light at this hour. She used her makeup mirror to watch behind her. The car fell back on the highway, yet it appeared now and then, and soon she noticed a second auto, sometimes floating a little ahead of the taxi in the right lane. At one point, that vehicle, a jacked-up Buick, rode alongside, its occupants black guys, older fellows with a thuggish look. The passenger had a beard and prison muscles and wore a dark do rag and shades, even though the sun was not over the horizon. He turned to Evon with a quick, knowing smartass smile that froze her heart.

Both cars stopped a quarter block away while she paid the taxi driver. She told Robbie as soon as she was in the Mercedes. He didn't seem to buy it, but she'd described the cars and he recognized them himself in his rearview within a few minutes of leaving the subdivision.

"Should I ditch them?" he asked.

"Let McManis decide. I'll call him." Her cell phone wasn't really secure, but there was no choice. There was no answer on the emergency number.

Robbie's car phone rang a minute later. McManis didn't even say good morning.

"They're ours," he said. "We've been covering you since last night. Just in case." Before he hung up, Jim told Evon he wanted to see her once she got in.

She came straight up from the garage. Jim greeted her from behind his desk and asked her to close the door. He drained the last from a Starbucks cup and took a long time to look her over. He was well groomed, but there were little gray swells from sleeplessness beneath his eyes.

He'd prepared a speech. The assumption from the start, he said, was that they were dealing with rough company. Undercover agents who'd been unmasked had had some heaping bad times, McManis said. Shot. Some UCAs had been tortured to find out what they knew. His tone remained unruffled, but he did not spare details graphic enough that for a moment it was almost as bad as if he'd laid those corpses on his desk. As McManis figured it, he said, she was entitled to get out now.

"I'm a big girl," she answered.

"You have to think about it. Don't just sing from the hymnal."

She had thought about it. Much of the night.

"It's starting to get exciting," she said.

"We might be able to do it without you."

That was ridiculous. They both knew that. If she cut and ran now, she might as well wire Walter Western Union to tell him Carmody was right. She tried to be level and unflappable, like McManis, as she shook her head.

At ten, we met. Jim stood up in his white shirt and addressed the assemblage—Sennett, Robbie, me, and the remaining UCAs. D.C. had punted. The decision whether to go on had to be made on the ground, where the operatives themselves had the best vantage to judge how close they were to blown. Evon was willing to go forward, he said. But he urged everyone to take a second to reconsider. Around the table, no one moved. It wasn't clear to me whether Stan would have offered Robbie the same chance to opt out, but Feaver and I had talked already, and he was convinced that, for the moment, Evon was the only one in serious peril.

Stan received the community resolve with a taut buttoned-up smile and took over. To reinforce the team, he had decided to share news previously sequestered in the realm of need-to-know. Everyone had realized that Amari and his surveillance squad had tailed the targets after the drops. Both Walter and Skolnick, it developed, had visited with Kosic within a few hours after Robbie passed them money. And the surveillance hadn't terminated there. Amari and his watchers had been dutifully following Rollo when he bought a newspaper, or blood sausage at the market, or visited a currency exchange. As he approached the register, an agent would sidle close enough to catch a look at the bills Kosic was using to pay. Then, as soon as he was gone, another agent would make a purchase with something larger. The idea was to get Rollo's bill back as change in the hope it would prove to be part of the prerecorded money Robbie had delivered. And it had worked. They'd hit the bull's-eye three times now, picking up two bills Robbie had passed to Skolnick, from one of which D.C. had even lifted Rollo's prints. This morning at Paddywacks, the notorious hang of county pols, where Rollo, as always, had paid for Brendan's breakfast, Amari had recovered a fifty that Robbie had given Walter yesterday at 5 p.m. Stan was prepared to ask the Chief Judge to approve a bug in Kosic's office the next time money changed hands.

"The game is changing," Stan said. "We're in the second half. After yesterday, we have to figure the clock is running. But, folks"—Stan's dark eyes were bright as a grackle's—"we're literally, *literally*, right outside Brendan Tuohey's door."

CHAPTER

26

CHAPTER 26

SINCE SHERM CROWTHERS TREATED ALL souls on earth as likely enemies, he refused to employ the usual courthouse bagman. Instead, according to Robbie, Sherm did business through his half sister, Judith McQueevey, the proprietor of a successful soul food restaurant in the North End. Judith had begun with a simple storefront and had expanded over the years. Although only the hardiest of white folk ventured into the neighborhood after dark, it was not unusual at lunch for all colors to gather there, drawn by the legendary fried chicken, or the Southern-style ribs, simmered until the meat parted from the bone.

Robbie and Evon had arrived at noontime one day in late April. After their meal, Robbie approached Judith at the register. In paying the check, he handed over an envelope intended for her brother in gratitude for the fine settlement supposedly achieved after Crowthers manhandled McManis in the sexual harassment case of Olivia King.

Like me, Stan had known Sherman for years, although he had a far dimmer opinion of him, as a result of tangling with him as an opponent. But with that advantage, Sennett had figured a way to trap Crowthers. Ordinarily, the envelope Feaver offered would have been almost an inch thick, containing a hundred $100 bills. Employing the familiar gambit, Sennett decided Robbie should short Crowthers, figuring in this case Sherman would confront Feaver rather than abide being dissed.

'I gotta talk to him,' Robbie had whispered to Judith amid the restaurant's luncheon clamor. The air was heavy with frying smells and the piquancy of greens. 'There's something he doesn't understand.'

Judith, who was far too shrewd not to know what was occurring, steadfastly refused to acknowledge anything. She was a big person, taller than Robbie in her high heels, and clearly a fan of her own cooking. At noontime, she wore a snug spangled evening gown, profuse purple eye shadow, and a heavy Ghanaian necklace, apparently solid gold. When Robbie handed over the envelope, Judith, adroit in these matters, pouched out a heavy vermilion lip as she hefted the package. There was only $2,000 there.

'Mmm-mmm,'she said to herself.

'That's why I have to see him,' Robbie whispered.

'I wouldn't know a thing about that,' Judith said, a well-practiced line. Her dangling earrings, little African gods, and her long straightened hair rambled about as she shook her head.

'Please,' Robbie answered. Usually he paid Judith two hundred dollars for lunch, declining the change as her tip. But today he peeled five hundreds off the roll in his pocket. Judith, a woman of prosperity, looked at the money through one eye. Her usual animation drained, and she cheated a glance at Evon, who stood a safe distance away, while she'd overheard their exchange on the infrared. The kitchen was just to the rear, and around them rattled the voices of waitresses, in their pink uniforms, demanding their orders from the chefs in a characteristic tone of weary disappointment in the performance of men. One thing Judith had learned in this life was that money was money, you couldn't have too much, and she finally picked up the hundreds and crushed them in her fist. She waved Robbie on his way, even as he begged her for reassurance that she'd speak to her brother.

Whatever she'd told Sherman, however, did not work. Crowthers made no effort to contact Robbie. Instead, the next time Feaver appeared before Crowthers, in the first week in May, coming in with McManis on the case that had been transferred to Sherman's calendar from Gillian Sullivan's, the judge had scalded Robbie with a furious look. Without explanation, he granted McManis's standard motion to dismiss the suit.

"Figures," said Stan. "He's crunching your nuts because you didn't come through." Sennett was probably right, although a defense lawyer would argue that the judge had just called this one as he saw it, much as he had in *King*. Besides, there was a more ominous explanation now for Sherman's conduct: they knew. If Walter gave credence to Carmody's suspicions and circulated the news, that might account for both Sherm's rage and his eagerness to rule against Feaver.

Either way, McManis and Sennett agreed that Robbie had to force a meeting with the judge. There was not much to lose. With the potential of suspicions arising about Evon, there was less time for patience and the case they had against Crowthers was too thin to prosecute. Judith was unlikely to flip on her brother, and Walter's stunts with Malatesta had emphasized the fallibility of treating a payoff to a bag man as proof of a judge's involvement. Amari's surveillance had never traced Robbie's money from Judith to the judge. They met, but nobody could ask a jury to draw a criminal inference from a get-together between siblings.

On Thursday, May 6, Robbie appeared in the small reception area of Crowthers' chambers and asked to see him. Sherm's sheer size and his aggressive character presented a new risk. There was no telling exactly what he would do if he felt cornered or provoked. For that reason, Evon, again equipped with the infrared earpiece, was lurking right outside the chambers' door. Stan and McManis and I were in the surveillance van, which was parked on Sentwick, one of the side streets bordering the courthouse.

Amari's watchers had confirmed that Crowthers was in his chambers. After a long wait, during which Robbie entertained us with a softly whistled version of most of the score of *Phantom of the Opera*, Sherm's secretary announced the judge would see him. Sherman's firm basso cut off Feaver's cheery greetings.

"What brings you here, Mr. Feaver?"

Robbie seemed to hesitate.

"Judge, I guess this is a personal thing. I just—"

"Feaver, I never meet lawyers alone. Seems to me you've been round this courthouse long enough to have heard that. I always ask Mrs. Hawkins to stay here. Or to be sittin right outside the open door. Nothin personal. Just good practice."

Crap, mouthed Sennett from his fold-down seat across from me. Robbie, who'd never approached Crowthers directly, was clearly taken by surprise.

"Well, Judge, this is really awfully embarrassing this way."

"Nothin embarrassin about it. Just say your piece."

Inspired, McManis pulled his cell phone from his briefcase and dialed Crowthers' chambers. We could hear the phone pealing over the FoxBIte, but Mrs. Hawkins, apparently, was not about to move. Robbie, however, had had an inspiration of his own.

"Well, Judge, there was a young lady in my office this morning, Judge, and she wants to bring a paternity suit against Your Honor."

Mrs. Hawkins reacted first, a startled trill, as if she'd been pinched.

"Pa-ternity suit!" Crowthers thundered. "Who's this? Who in the hell is this female scalawag gone try shake some money out of my tree? No. Wait. Mrs. Hawkins has no need to hear this. Wouldn't want to, I'm sure. You go on, Mrs. Hawkins. Not a word of truth in this, Mrs. Hawkins, I assure you. Mr. Feaver and I are gone get to the bottom of this thing right now."

The door closed soundly enough to suggest Mrs. Hawkins was miffed.

"Hey, Judge, I'm sorry about that." Robbie's voice had grown smaller and he was clearly moving closer to the heavy paper-strewn desk where Crowthers sat. "I've been trying to get with you for weeks. I gotta explain. About *King*?" he said, meaning the case about the ornery executive who'd harassed his former secretary.

There was no response. Crowthers did not so much as clear his throat.

"See, Judge, this is really embarrassing. I know you didn't see what you were expecting, but this chick, the plaintiff, Olivia? She didn't sign, Judge. I thought the paralegal'd gotten her to do it, she thought I had. But, bottom line, I don't have a fee agreement. And you know, Judge, she's an operator. Olivia? She knew what she was doing. She's already got another lawyer telling me he's going to Bar Admissions and Discipline if I don't release the whole check to her. I mean, it's a pisser, Judge. I say implied contract, he says, Okay, $300 an hour, send her a bill. Can you imagine, Judge? Five-hundred-thousand-dollar settlement and she's looking for an hourly fee."

Nothing. As I imagined the scene, Crowthers, an immense presence, sat behind his large desk, his eyes and the huge whites turned upward to Robbie and almost throbbing with anger, his nostrils widened in a primal flare. Anyone's first instinct would be to cut and run. But Robbie kept scraping out his apology for shortchanging the judge.

"If I get five thousand out of the case it's a lot. I mean, what can I do, Judge? That's why I was light with Judith. Between you and your sister, you figure taxes and expenses, you guys got everything on this one. The whole chile relleno."

Still no sound. There was nothing, not even a grunt that might have passed for assent. Facing this recording, a defense lawyer was likely to maintain that the judge was no longer there, that Robbie was talking to himself as a desperate way to enhance the body count and improve his sentence.

Beside me, McManis whispered, "He's getting smoked." Sennett nodded.

Then it turned worse.

"What the *hell* is this?" Crowthers asked suddenly. "What kind of crazy shit are you talkin? In my entire life, I have never heard such stupid, crazy shit."

Even Jim groaned on that one. As with Malatesta, Robbie's instructions were to cut it short if he began eliciting denials, and his clothing shifted roughly over the microphone, as he started for the door.

"Right, judge, you're right, I was just really stupid. I know that. I'll catch up next time. Scout's honor. And I'm going to tell her out there, Mrs. Hawkins? I'll tell her it's a mistake and all, that— What?" At the edges, Robbie's voice raveled in alarm. A spring sang out. You could hear the chair rolling with velocity and a rocking sound as it hit the wall.

"What?" Robbie said. "There—"

The smack of flesh on flesh was distinct. I was certain Crowthers had slapped him. The mike jostled harshly as Robbie rocked and he cried out simultaneously, but that was stifled quickly, even as Robbie tried to speak. Sherm had gotten hold of him. By the mouth or the throat. Doubled over, McManis scrambled up toward the front and told Amari to alert the covering units. In the meantime, from Feaver's gargled sounds and the thumping of his bootheels, I decided he was being dragged along. A door slammed, in an oddly resonant way, then there was a whooshing sound, some kind of whispering in the background almost like static.

"Who you?" It was Crowthers in a harsh whisper, somewhat muffled by the persistent noise in the backdrop.

"Water," said Amari in front, identifying the sound.

"Christ," said Stan, "he's got him in the john."

Jim had the cell phone out of his pocket. He was dialing a number, Evon's pager, I imagined, ready to signal her to go in.

They had to be standing very close in the little bathroom that adjoined Crowthers' chambers. I'd seen the facilities in the Temple on a number of occasions and there was barely room for one person, especially somebody of Sherm's size.

"Listen, here," the judge said. "I'm just standin here wonderin who the hell you're thinkin you are? What'm I suppose to call you, Chatty Kathy? What the hell you doin, man? You know better'n that. I don't want to be hearin bout this crazy shit."

"Judge, I'm not trying to mess with you." It was a relief to hear Feaver's voice. "I just wanted to be sure you're not creased."

"I'm creased, okay, specially about the way you goin on. Now, cut that shit out. If I'm not satisfied with the way you attend to your business, you gone know that. And seems to me, you do. Am I right?"

"Yes, sir."

"So next time you gone attend to your business, right?"

"Yes, sir."

"That's all. Just don't talk that crazy shit to me." His voice dropped. "Get us both in a trick bag."

Sennett shot me a look, marked by a fleeting grin. 'Trick bag! We both knew it was one of those lines that turn a case in front of a jury. Feaver's shoes resounded on the tiles, but Crowthers spoke up harshly.

"Close that door. Did I say we're done?"

"No, Judge."

"And come'ere. Right here. Come right here. Now what you mean bout my sister? Between me and my sister. What's that about?"

"Sir?"

"You heard me. Don't give me that dumb ofay look. I know better than that. What'd you give her?"

Feaver seemed dumbstruck by the implications. Crowthers repeated the question.

"Five, Judge."

"Five dollars?"

"Five hundred. Five hundred for her and two thousand for you."

"So she gets quarter what I get? And I'm the judge. Somethin ain right about that."

"Well, I told you, Your Honor. That was just so I could talk to you. Apologize. That came out of my own pocket."

"Well, they any more in that pocket?"

There was a discernible gurgle of surprise from Feaver, but I thought he was in role.

"You know, Judge. I mean, I've got an office. I've got overhead."

"Aw shit. Who you think you talkin to? You think I'm just some boy off a walnut plantation?"

"Oh, God no, Judge."

"Now you come round here, bother me like this, that gotta cost you. Mmm-hmmm," the judge told himself "You go see Judith—you bring her what you brought me before. You hear me?"

"Absolutely."

"And don't ever come talkin this shit to me again. Fact, now that you got me thinkin on it, you bring her what you oughta brought her before."

"Jeez, Judge. Another eight thousand?"

"No, ten. You keep poor-mouthin, gone be twenty-five before I let you outta this damn bathroom. And don't you go whinin to anybody either. I don't want to hear any more about this. I just want this to be one of those unpleasantries everybody resolves ain gone be mentioned again. Come talk this crazy shit to me," said Crowthers to himself. He was worked up.

In the outer office, Robbie passed a word with Mrs. Hawkins. Talk about a mix-up! He just called on his cell phone and the client said Carruthers, not Crowthers. Mrs. Hawkins laughed. She knew it all along.

"Judge gets up on himself," she said, "but he's a righteous individual."

In a moment, there was another distinct smack, not all that different from the first one. After a momentary qualm, I realized that Evon, with her earpiece, had just given or received a high five from Robbie in the corridor. Stan had risen from his metal seat and, crouched to three-quarters height, actually danced a quick buck-and-wing at the first stoplight. "Outright extortion," he kept repeating.

Yet as the van headed back to the federal building, I

couldn't share in the mood. My father was always reviled as a racial agitator because he'd attempted to integrate our county bar in 1957, but despite that, I grew up full of guilt about what had been ingrained in our way of life. I had made the vows, like many other persons of my age, to live in a better world. It had disheartened me to hear Sherman's name from Robbie. But it wasn't hard to believe. Sherm was the grimmest of cynics. And I'd been down the same road only a few years before with my pal Clifton Bering.

Clifton was a classmate of Stan's and mine at Easton, the first African American ever to make the *Law Review*. He was charming and gifted, handsome and overjoyed by the great prospects he had in life. His father was a Kindle County cop, and Clifton always had his feet in both camps, at home with civil rights progressives as well as Party figures. He was the councilman from Redhook in the North End and was regarded as a serious candidate to become Mayor when Augie Bolcarro finally died. And then, not long after Sennett's induction as U.S. Attorney, an investigation of corruption in the North End started, and I began hearing Clifton's name. He fell prey to all of today's finest technology. He'd come to a wired hotel room to accept $50,000 to secure a downtown zoning change for what proved to be an FBI front, and he had, in the parlance, barfed all over himself. He had not just taken the money, not merely promised to rig the change, in just those words, but baldly stated that next time he'd appreciate it if there was a girl in the room for afterwards. Then he added the one word that sealed his fate, unpardonable to a jury of any composition: 'White,' Clifton had said.

After he was convicted, he asked me to help with the appeal. I went over to the jail, and when I saw him in the orange jumpsuit, I couldn't help myself. I asked the question I had vowed not to: Why? Why, Clifton? Why with all his good fortune, why this? He looked at me solemnly and said, 'That's how it is, that's how it's always been, and it's our turn. It's our turn.'

I knew if I talked to Sherm Crowthers, I'd hear something similar. The tone would be angrier, he'd be more disparaging, telling me I was a fool for believing life would ever be any other way. But in the end his explanation would be rooted in the unfairness of being asked to behave better than the generations of white men who'd wielded the same authority he did and had used it to feather their nests.

There was a logic there, I suppose. But I couldn't believe it when Clifton had offered that answer. I couldn't believe that Clifton Bering, wise and wonderful, would turn against every other value I knew him to adhere to so that he could, almost out of duty, exercise a privilege long denied others like him. He didn't even fully understand the white men he thought he was imitating. The Brendan Tuoheys of the world had bagmen and intervenors and a thousand layers of protection; they never showed up in person so they could catch a piece on the side. They were wily and arrogant, but not brazen. How could he not recognize that his picture of white power was a grotesque cartoon? But so he saw it. Just as I had never recognized how isolated he felt—and no doubt often was—notwithstanding all his great talents. Our true continental divide, the one between black and white, fell open, leaving us, friends of thirty years, on either side, watching as Clifton and all the good he'd been destined to do disappeared inside.

And now Sherman had dived into the same chasm. He had sounded proud and happy, even as he plummeted. And most painful of all, he was entirely unaware that he'd actually been pushed over the edge, driven by the very forces he'd long boasted he alone had understood and mastered.

CHAPTER 27

DESPITE THE INTERMITTENT SUCCESSES of the Project, Robbie's mood was swinging noticeably lower, plainly out of concern over Lorraine. The day after his encounter with Crowthers, he received a distressed call from his wife in the middle of the afternoon and told Evon he was headed home. Even for this reason, she wouldn't let him out of sight, and she descended with him to the garage and the Mercedes.

Rainey's deterioration now seemed to be picking up speed. Last month, as her ability to swallow had begun to disappear, she had been hospitalized for the insertion of something called a PEG, a percutaneous endoscopic gastrostomy, a little plastic button that allowed a liquid diet to be fed directly into her stomach four times a day. It was a simple procedure, but she had never seemed to recover the same energy. By now, many functions had gone from impaired to nonexistent.

Her speech had slid to the point that neither Robbie nor Elba could make sense of it. Rainey had briefly made do with a letter board, using her right hand, in which she still had good movement, to pick out the words she was trying to say. Finally, last week, they'd made the transition to the computer voice synthesizer. Lorraine had quickly mastered the software, which spoke the words she selected from various vocabulary trees, but the hardware had been balky. The replacement module, which had arrived over the weekend, functioned well, but had a male voice. It had been an unexpected blow to find that Rainey's speech was not restored but essentially gone, transmogrified into the atonal bleat of a masculine android. The deliberate pace of the machine with its blank tone had made her feel more thwarted, not less.

"And in the middle of this shitstorm, my mother-in-law arrives," Robbie told Evon in the car. "She flew in from Florida for the weekend, and you know, you'd think family would make it better, but we just can't wait for her to leave. Betty walks through the door and she's crying and she doesn't stop for two days. She hangs on me and says, 'Robert, Robert, I want to help, but this tears me up so bad, I just can't stand to see it.' She's that kind. If she's not lookin, it'll go away. Christ."

When they reached the house, Robbie turned to Evon.

"Just come inside for one second, will you? Tell her the voice box sounds good. Do you mind? Betty went to pieces every time Rainey tried to talk to her."

Evon was less frightened than last time. But the sense of the breach between this house and the rest of the world remained appalling. Once over the threshold, you dived off the edge of a cliff. Far above, in the daylight, the healthy danced to the tune of their small delights, but down here, amid darkness and sewer smells, the base, dogged game of survival was being played out with every breath its own struggle.

"Touch her," Robbie whispered before they entered the

room. "She likes to be touched. Take her hand when you say hi."

At the thought, Evon felt a stricken quiver. She was already worried that her presence might provoke another sad scene between Robbie and his wife, but he had plunged around the corner into the equipment-crowded room where Rainey was attended by her caregiver.

"Say hello, boys and girls." He kissed his wife. He was a song-and-dance man now, bright as a new penny.

These days, Rainey slept in a water bed, where she rested more comfortably. Beside it roosted a mess of pill bottles—antispasmodics, sleep aids—and an electric Barcalounger that she used as a day chair. She looked drained among her bedcovers, which remained oddly undisturbed over her. Evon approached slowly and gripped Rainey's cold hand. There was a desiccated feel to the skin. The flesh had almost no tone; she could squeeze to the bones amid the softness.

"How. Are. You?" said the boy robot who was Rainey Feaver now.

Evon carried on. What a great improvement! Things would be so much easier. But there was no mistaking what had gone on here over the weekend, and it was neither machinery nor even the appearance of Rainey's inept mother that had caused the disruption. The end was beginning. When Evon had met Rainey, less than three months ago, she could not imagine how a human being could get any worse, but Lorraine had. You could somehow see vitality withdrawing from this body, as from a fallen leaf. Robbie's increasingly frank remarks had given Evon an intimation of the hugeness of what lay ahead. Rainey's upper body was losing strength with alarming speed. She had only three fingers that moved on her left hand. Far worse, the muscles that supported her breathing would soon no longer function.

Some ALS patients let go at that point. But ventilation was an option. A machine could inflate Rainey's lungs for her; there was even a portable device that could be carried on her wheelchair so she would not be immobilized. But it remained a momentous decision. Once Rainey was ventilated, there was no logical stopping point. She could go on for quite some time, awaiting the opportunistic infection that eventually claimed most ventilated patients, living beyond the time when even the remotest voluntary impulses could stir her body. ALS patients had been known to end up entirely inert, with gauze patches over their unblinking eyes and attendants applying wetting solution every five minutes, to prevent the agony that would result if the tender membranes of the cornea became air-dried. These people existed—seeing, smelling, hearing, suffering—with no means of communication of any kind.

Rainey and Robbie had agreed to take it a step at a time. He had asked her to live; *he* wanted her life to continue and said so plainly, so emphatically that no one could imagine it as some ultimate chivalry meant to remove from her the burden of clinging selfishly to life. At some point soon she would have to decide whether she was willing to oblige him.

For the present, Robbie characteristically accentuated the positive.

"She can talk on the phone. She hasn't been able to talk on the phone for more than a month. Who'd you call?"

"Tired," the voice answered. "Too. Tired. My Mother. Wore Me Out."

"Yeah," Robbie said.

They spoke about the spring, now arriving. Evon leaned Rainey's way to take in the apple tree visible from her window, a pillowy mass of pinkish blooms. Yet Rainey was clearly exhausted, and even after a few minutes, Evon felt she'd overstayed. Rainey lifted the fingers on the one hand that freely moved as a goodbye.

"I'm going to show Evon out. Then we can do your massage, and maybe get through Act IV." On the winding stairs, Robbie explained that he rubbed down Rainey every night as a matter of ritual, then read to her, sometimes for hours. "When I pick, I like plays. You know. I get to ham it up. Read all the parts. Right now, we're nearly done with *A Midsummer Night's Dream*. Then she'll choose something."

"Isn't that Shakespeare?" asked Evon.

"You don't think there's room for Shakespeare in my common little mind?"

"I didn't mean that."

"Yes you did. Hey, listen, we've done all the classic comedies in the last year. *Tartuffe. The Importance of Being Earnest. The Man Who Came to Dinner.* We're having a great time. You know, sometimes she likes a break, so I'll read her a novel. She likes all the law guys." He showed her the next one they'd take up, *Mitigating Circumstances*, which was on a table downstairs. His mother-in-law, with her fatal touch, had brought a number of books that neither Rainey nor he much cared for, self-help guides, even a couple of picture books of far-off places written for juveniles.

"I just wish she wasn't such a dip. I mean, I like Betty. Not a mean bone in her body. Just this poor girl from the South End who thought she'd like the fast life and married this complete loser who happens to be Lorraine's father. Now, this guy. J, e, r, k. His picture's in the dictionary next to the word. Really. He's got a boat. Supposedly, he sells real estate. But his whole life is this fucking boat. The fish he caught, the dames he screwed there, the six days straight he was drunk at sea. If it doesn't happen on water, it doesn't count with him.

"Anyway, he marries Betty cause it's the kind of girl his mom wanted him to bring home. And then, you know, he drinks. Well, she drinks, too. They drink together. Picture the house: it reeks of cigarette smoke and spilled beer. They have the kid. And he says, This ain't for me. Betty eventually remarries. Which is good. But Lorraine sort of gets lost in the shuffle. She's living with three other kids, but the stepdad doesn't like to ante up for anything. He wants Neptune to come ashore and pay a bill now and then. So there's a lot of tension and crap. I don't know. Betty did her best. She says she did, anyway. Isn't that what they always say? Not that it did much for her daughter.

"Rainey was actually sort of in trouble when I met her," Robbie said. They had reached the foyer. There was an enormous chandelier above the circular stairs, five feet across, with a million baubles. The floor was Carrara marble, the walls were mirrored. The affected grandeur seemed almost painful at the moment, in its sheer inadequacy to make any real difference.

"I mean, I didn't know it at first. It was back in the days. I'm living it up on the Street of Dreams. Morty's been married since childhood and I'm like, They'll never catch me. Ho, ho, ho. I dig the routine. I work my ass off. I try cases. Then I go down there and get slightly sloshed every night and, the general trend, laid. It's A-OK. I see one girl. I see another girl. I'm thirty-four or what, and you can't say I've really been steady with anybody, not more than three or four months' worth, since junior high.

"And Lorraine's just one of them. Well, great-looking. Super-great. She's so damn beautiful she actually seemed to glow. But I've known some beautiful girls. Anyway, those days, I was in my snowman phase. Well, everybody was. It's the standard good time. 'Hey, baby, come on back to my place, we'll do a couple lines.' Which we do. And I really like this girl. Sense of humor. Very smart. She's a computer geek, before most people even know there's such a thing. You know, she sells computer systems, inventory software. And she's so bright, such great company, that it takes me a while to catch on. But when I'm with her, I can feel she's nervous. Laughs too loud. All the wrong places. Very edgy thing scraping along underneath. Well, I know nervous people, too. A lot of women have that sort of frantic, tight-ass thing, am I perfect enough, and boy, this girl looked perfect, so that made some sense. Sometimes I'd flatter myself and think, It's sexual tension, she can't wait to get back to my boudoir to do the deed. And it was some mind-numbingly, unbelievably, sky-high fanfuckingtastic sex. And that seemed to be the only time she was really relaxed. But that's not what it was, either. I don't know how I caught on. But when you're connecting with somebody, you just do. And suddenly one night, we're lying there on my silk sheets—geez, I was a terrible lounge lizard—and I get it: she didn't come here for my charm or company, or even to get her brains fucked out. She's here for the dope.

"I'm devastated. Kind of amazing. Because when you're living that life, it's endless, frankly, the stuff you just don't know about somebody. I mean, you can be semi-serious with a woman, keeping fairly regular company, and you come to pick her up one night and there's a note taped to the mailbox: 'Moved to Tucson.' Laugh all you want. I laughed myself. But that kind of stuff happened to me. So I've had a lot of practice saying, Hey, what the hell.

"But this time, I go around crying in my beer, 'Damn this bim, she only wanted the dope,' and guys are yukking it up. I mean, really. Always the last to know. Mersing, you met Mersing, he gives it to me real good. 'For Chrissake, Robbie. You didn't know the nickname? Cocaine Lorraine? The Snow Queen? But hey,' guy says. 'Great tits, right? You weren't exactly there for a sleigh ride either.'

"Snow Queen. I guess I'd heard it. But I figured it was because she was, you know, not warm, let's say. I took it for a challenge. That's the kind of asshole I am.

"Man, and I don't know what got into me. But I just thought, Shit, this isn't right. This person has got too much on the ball to be shagging every creep with a connect because she's too scared to go out and cop on her own, and that, frankly, was about the size of it. So I confront her. 'What the hell is wrong with you? A beautiful, brilliant person like you?' First she's shocked. Then she's pissed. But when I pulled out the nickname, it's boohoo. Man, Niagara Falls. She was so goddamned ashamed. 'I'm gonna help you beat this,' I say like I had any idea what that meant. But I checked her into Forest Hills. I paid the bill, too. And six months later we got married.

"That was the best thing I ever did for her. I'm the man who saved her life. That's what she called me." He opened the door then and finally looked Evon's way. "Until, of course, I became the guy who ruined it."

CHAPTER 28

WHEN PATRICE IS OUT OF TOWN ON A PROJ-
ect, I tend to make camp in the den off the kitchen, everything I need spread out in reach of the comfortable chair
where I spend the late evenings. I was there when my doorbell rang near ten-thirty, several nights after Robbie's visit
to Crowthers. Through the door-eye, I saw Sennett kicking my stoop. McManis was beside him, in his suit coat
but no tie, shaking out a long umbrella. This could only
be disaster, I knew. Ordinarily, Stan would never have risked
a meeting where the three of us could be seen together. I
slid back the dead bolt. I have seen executioners who looked
more lighthearted.

Is it bad? I asked first thing.

"Terrible," Stan answered.

Had Feaver screwed something up?

"No," Stan said. "Well, yes. Only 'screwup' isn't enough.
George, for Chrissake," he said then, "let us in."

Even anger had been unable to fulfill its usual function
of holding Stan aloft from despair. His suit had gone limp

in the rain. McManis, on the other hand, looked scattered. He managed a soft smile when he came through the doorway, but stood still there, baffled. Both said okay when I offered a drink.

Stan swished his scotch around in the tumbler. "Why don't you just show him?" he told Jim. McManis handed over a red expandable folder and I removed a file. He said it was a run of the Roll of Attorneys-at-Law in this state, all those whose last names began with 'F.'

"Look for your client," Stan instructed.

Not there. Didn't pay his dues? I suggested.

Stan delivered a look hotter than magma. He took it I was being a defense lawyer, as I was, instinctively seeking excuses.

"He's Not A Lawyer," Stan shouted.

I laughed, naturally. It was ridiculous. Perhaps Robbie had been admitted under a stage name or a different spelling, or maybe in another state. There was an explanation. Walking through the streets of the courthouse triangle with Robbie, as I occasionally did these days, I'd been introduced to half a dozen attorneys with whom he'd gone to law school.

McManis directed me to the other items in the folder, but Sennett had no patience.

"He attended Blackstone," Sennett said. "He's in the law school yearbook. But he's never been licensed to practice law. Not in this state or any other we can find. We've been on the phone all day."

After the panic over Carmody, they'd begun to wonder how easily Jim could be discovered. That had caused them to check the Roll of Attorneys. One thing had led to another.

I was still too stunned to figure out what this meant.

"What it means?" asked Stan. "It means that every day for almost two decades Robbie Feaver has committed an ongoing fraud—on his clients, on the courts, on you, and on me. It means every letter he's signed, every motion, every business card he's handed out has been a lie. It means every nickel he's earned as an attorney is ill-gotten. And it means that every fucking thing we've done on Petros is probably out the window, since Rule One from UCORC was no fraud on innocent bystanders. And now it turns out we've left a one-man fraud wave in place for the better part of a year.

"And that means Robbie is shit out of luck. It means his deal was a fraud to start, and every horrible thing I said would happen if he dealt us dirty is coming down. It means he's going to the penitentiary as fast as I can get him there, wife or no wife, and that he's going to be inside until the fucking hair on his empty head has all turned white." Sennett closed his eyes and took a breath, perhaps reminding himself that I was his friend, or at least that I wasn't my client. "That's what it means."

That's what it meant. But that wasn't why Stan was sitting in my den as the minute hand swung closer to midnight on the Howard Miller clock in the corner. I had an obvious assignment. My job was to figure out how to save them all.

"IN LAW SCHOOL, there are lots of required courses. You know that. Torts. Contracts. Criminal. Corporations. Yadda yadda yadda. I took all of that. And passed. Not by very much. I was jumping around like a grasshopper, clerking in a law firm, still reading for parts in commercials. But I got by. I'd always tell Morty, 'You know what the guy who finishes last in the class gets? A diploma.'"

He peeked up to see if he could get a smile. I rotated one finger forward as a bare command to continue.

"So it gets to be my senior year, 1973, it's Watergate, and all of a sudden, son of a bitch, we've got a *new* requirement. Now nobody can graduate without taking Legal Ethics. Like that would have stopped Nixon. Only I *can't* take Legal Ethics. Cause it's Tuesday and Thursday at four, and that's when I'm working for Peter Neucriss. It was a bigger miracle than the loaves and fishes that he'd hired me in the first place. *Blackstone* Law School? Law Review from the U., you weren't even worthy to run Peter's Xerox machine. But I got to know him down on the Street of Dreams, he liked the girls I ran with, I guess, so he gave me my shot. This to me is bigger than Broadway. Cause if I really carry the load, then I can get a full-time job as an associate in the best P.I. shop in the universe, known and yet to be discovered. It's all in lights: try cases, make money, be a star. So no way am I taking Legal Ethics on two of the four afternoons when I'm supposed to be at Neucriss's office. And besides, the registrar's office, they couldn't hold a fire drill in a phone booth, they'll never know the difference. Right?

"Wrong. The week of graduation, the dean whistles me in. 'Robbie, Robbie, what the fuck are we going to do with you? You didn't take Legal Ethics.' If it was just me, he'd have flunked out my fanny faster than I could scratch it, but there's about half a dozen other folks who've pulled the same stunt, including, bless his heart, a fella who's number three in the class. So the deal is, we can go to graduation. And take Legal Ethics over the summer, which means write a paper while we're studying for the bar exam. Pretty square deal. Frankly, I was so grateful I cried, because the idea of telling my mother she's not going to this law school graduation, for which both her sisters are flying in from Cleveland, that's inconceivable, that's like the idea of antimatter.

"So that summer, I'm working for Neucriss, who still hasn't firmly committed to a full-time job for me, and going to Legal Ethics and to a bar exam review course. I'm busier than a bunny in spring and then Peter got this case—it was a huge plaintiff's class, one of the first toxic torts in the country, even before Love Canal. I'm working with Neucriss directly, at the right hand of God, no sleep, and of course, I blow off the final paper in Ethics. All I know is this is it, once in a lifetime, bottom of the heap to the top, and nobody's taking it from me.

"So three weeks before the bar, it's back to the dean's office. 'Jesus Christ, Robbie, we can't certify you for the exam, you've got an incomplete in Legal Ethics.' You know, I tried every angle. I'd donate organs and half my income for life if he'd just stamp the little blue sheet. No sale. 'Finish the paper now, then you can take the bar in December with the group that flunks the first time.'

"And I don't know, I thought I was going to do that. Of course, there's no way in the world I'm telling Neucriss that I didn't get my law degree. And, naturally, all of this works to my advantage. Peter thinks I'm a Trojan, cause the other two clerks, they're wimping out to study as the bar comes up, and I'm like, I got it handled. I even came in the afternoon the first day the exam was given. Neucriss was really impressed!

"So I got the job. Now what do I do? The bar results come back. Everybody's crowing. And you know, the third of November the three new associates—Robbie from Blackstone and two hotshots from Easton and Harvard—get the afternoon off to be sworn in. The ceremony's just a cattle call over in the Supreme Court, eight hundred kids all standing on the front steps. So I raised my hand with everybody else. The only difference was that the rest eventually got mailed a certificate to practice law and I didn't. That's how it happened."

He sat in the leather club chair in front of my desk with an unfaltering, fawnlike expression, utterly compelled by his rationale for ridiculous behavior. He took no responsibility for the thousands of hours of work to which he'd laid waste—by Stan, by the agents, by Evon, by me—or the peril and pain to which he'd exposed himself and Lorraine. The Robbie I'd come to know and like was elsewhere, like a spirit released from a body and hovering in a corner of the room. Observing my reactions, he made a face and looked out the window.

"I'm sorry," he said. "You do stuff as a kid and then you're stuck with it. I was a kid."

He was a grownup, I pointed out, when he didn't tell me.

He brought a hand to his temple protectively. It was no later than 8 a.m. and he appeared to be watching the light crawl, like a gentle hand, down the sides of the big buildings along the river—anything rather than face me.

I asked if Lorraine knew.

"Nobody knows. *No* one."

I could take the usual consolation: my bills were paid. And I'd realized all along there were reasons we were each sitting where we were, on either side of the desk. Nor could I pretend that similar things, perhaps not on this scale, but not entirely unlike it, hadn't happened before: clients who lost their deals because they tried to hide money they were required to forfeit; an executive who'd recently gotten probation to testify against the grubby smack-dealer he'd scored from, and then blew his first monthly urine drop and spent a year in the pokey. There was no end to the way clients could disappoint you. But I'd seldom been as thoroughly taken in.

Feaver finally seemed to be absorbing the weight of it. He was slumped with both feet in his close-soled loafers flat on the floor. Eventually, he went to the door.

"Are you my lawyer?" he asked from there. It was the right question, not so much for focusing both of us on the pragmatic issues, but because the fragile look that accompanied it redeemed him somewhat. Robbie was an eternal beacon of need, like those dead stars which, even imploded, continue emitting a radio signal through space. But his baddog truckling made it seem that he actually cared about what I would answer, and not simply because it would represent a monumental inconvenience to him if I withdrew. I realized what had been implicit from the start: he had come to me not out of regard for my courtroom oratory or my connections but out of personal respect. I seldom thought of myself as an example, or of the valor of what I tried to do every day. I whisked him out the door with a backward wave and no answer, but I'd already settled the matter with myself. I was his lawyer. In the better sense of the word.

NEAR 2 A.M. the lobby buzzer had roused her, a honking duck in her dreams.

"This is your Uncle Peter," rasped a voice distorted by the intercom. 'Uncle Peter' was the Project code word, a fail-safe i.d. for times of trouble. It was McManis who showed up at Evon's door. He was too proper to step any farther into the apartment. He just leaned back against the steel jamb.

"It's about Robbie," Jim told her. Her first thought was that he was dead. And he was, as far as she was concerned, once she heard the story.

"I was wrong," McManis said before he left. He was wearing a light suit spotted with rain. "I always said that Mort was the most dangerous person to the Project. Which was foolish. We knew where the risk was from the start and we forgot. Heck, that's why you're here. We knew he was a con. And he conned us anyway."

"Played us," said Evon. It was more impulse than humor, but Jim responded with his mild smile.

"There's never a bottom with these people. It's like facing mirrors. You just go down and down." McManis instructed her to skip the morning pickup, just go to the office, so she'd be at hand when they started to sort things out.

Around 9 a.m., Robbie appeared at the opening to her cubicle. His tie knot was already wrung down six inches below his open collar. He wanted to talk.

"I don't think so, Robbie."

"Look, I'm sorry. I want to say that." He was too weakened to raise his hands; he simply opened his palms at his side. "It was the past to me. A mistake in the past."

She propelled her chair to the credenza behind her and, waiting for him to leave, hovered over a phone-book-sized printout of hospital charges she'd been abstracting. But what was the reason for that? she thought suddenly. A case she didn't care about, clients who weren't really hers. The months, the time, the work, the hope for something of value—the staggering size of what had probably been destroyed, of what was being wrenched away from her, brought a whirling moment of desperation and, as ever, shame. He took a step closer.

"Don't be a jerk," she told him.

"A bigger jerk, you mean."

"You couldn't be a bigger jerk, Robbie. You're maxed. You busted the meter."

The cover occurred to her remotely, whatever it was worth now. They were out in the open here. Yet it fit. Lovers' tiff. If she wanted, she could throw something at him. Instead, when he tried to speak to her again, she stuck a finger in each ear.

In time, she felt his shadow move off her. She sat still, contending with her rage. Once lit, it could incinerate everything else, including normally reliable means of restraint. She tried to sit in this chair, be in this place, step aside, but it was useless. In a minute, she was tearing down the corridor.

"What *matters* to you?"

He looked up abjectly from his chrome-armed desk chair.

"Did you hear what I asked?"

"Yeah, I heard." He motioned to close the door. She slammed it.

"Then what's the answer?"

"What do you mean?"

"You know what I mean. What counts. With you? I can't figure it out. I really can't."

"Shit, what counts with you? Getting merit badges from the Bureau? You think your bullshit's better than my bullshit?"

"No way, bub. I want an answer. What matters to you? Can you even tell me? Or is it just whatever play you can work. That's it, isn't it? So you can look down on us poor morons when we buy it?"

"Is that what you think?"

"Yes, Robbie. Yes, that's what I think."

"Well then, that's what you think."

"Don't you blow me off. Don't you dare. Tell me what matters to you, goddamn it!"

In his face, she could actually detect a fluttering aspect of fear. He had no idea how far down she'd drive him. Nor, in truth, did she.

"Can you tell me?"

"I don't know. Probably."

"Then I want to hear it."

His jaw rotated.

"It's love. Okay? It's the people I love. That's what counts. My friends. My family. A lot of my clients. That's all. Everybody else? They can take a leap. Everything else? It's just that crap floating in the sea. Flotsam and jetsam.

The rest of life is just people doing things to other people for their own good. Except for love."

She closed her eyes, so angry she felt as if she might fly apart.

"Is that why you did this? For love? Is that why you walked through that door every day, where it says 'Attorney-at-Law' right under your name, and didn't just fall down from shame?"

"I don't know. I guess that was part of it. There were people I didn't want to disappoint. Christ, what are we talking about? Not writing a twenty-page paper? It's not homicide. I didn't try to hurt anybody. Just the opposite. For twenty years, I've been doing my job, caring about people and winning their cases."

"That's a play, Robbie. You wanted it for yourself. You wanted the job, the status, the money. But you hadn't earned any of it, and you took it anyway. just like a thief. And because of that you've screwed over anybody who didn't have the good sense to wonder if you were lying when you said 'a,' 'and,' 'the.' How do you keep yourself from seeing that? Look what you've done to Mort. Or to those clients you say you love. My God, think about the poor Rickmaiers—that little girl you cried about when she lost her mom? What'll you say to her, Robbie, if somebody sues her to get back that great big settlement check you handed that family last week? How'd you just forget about stuff like that? For twenty years?"

"I don't know. I did it. I knew it, but I didn't think about it. I kind of forgave myself, or put it away, I don't know. I don't know how I lived with it. I lie, okay? I lie all the time. You think I really kissed Shaheen Conroe? I never got closer to her than clomping around in the chorus. That car I drive you around in? It's an S500, thirty grand less than the S6. I owned it a week when I saw Neucriss breezing down Marshall Avenue in the 600. Suddenly I felt like such a river-bottom turd that I went back and paid some stock boy five hundred bucks to replace the plate on the trunk lid and the steering wheel so it looks just like a 600. But it's not."

The car! She actually groaned.

"I'm a weak, fucked-up person. What can I say? I never told you I made sense to myself." He had another quotation from theater life handy for trouble: "'Ask me to play myself, I will not know what to do.'"

Even in anger, she had to give him that much. For months she'd had an intuition, a vision almost, of a steaming jungle, full of hairy-barked trees and thick vines, teeming wildlife in all forms, and rank greenish waters that bubbled with stinking hot gases venting from inside the earth. That was the great primal wilderness that lay at the center of Robert Simon Feaver.

Sitting in his tall leather chair, backed by the dramatic shapes of the city, he continued to seek mercy from her assault.

"Did I ever tell you when I knew I was in love with Rainey?" he asked.

She looked at him coldly, unwilling to be entertained, but it did not deter him.

"Funny story, actually. Very funny story." He chortled once to prove that was true. "I was taking her to a hockey game. And she got hung up. I can't remember why. She was late and she was, you know, upset. These were great seats. Third row. Right behind the glass. She was like falling all over herself. And I said one of those things I say. 'I heard they're starting late tonight. No, no, really. The Red Wings' plane was late.' I can't imagine what I was gonna say when she saw they were in the middle of the second period. But I said it. 'No. No, really. They're late.' And like I could see this smile, half a smile, and this thing behind her eyes. She got it. That I wanted it to be true. I mean, she got me, really. Not it. But just that I believed it myself. Right then. And it was okay with her. That's when I was in love."

"Fuck you," she answered. "That's the whole problem. You think the world owes you that. You want everybody to give you a big goddamned hug, when you oughta be feeling terrible guilt, Robbie, or at least a little regret. And I don't understand how you let yourself off so easy. *How* do you do that? Every blasted day? How do you not level, even with yourself? How do you look people in the eye, knowing they think you're something you're not? How do you get out of bed every morning to do that? I don't understand."

"*You* don't?" His look remained bleak; he was not being underhanded or snide. He was startled only by the lapse of some fellowship he thought they shared. But when she took his meaning, the ignition of anger nearly lifted her off the floor. She eyed the scalloped silver letter opener on his desk, which she used to open the mail every morning, with half a mind to cut his treacherous tongue from his throat.

Instead, she flew from the office. She did not say a word to him for the rest of the day, or the day after. She spent as much time as she could around McManis's, but Amari, with little to do, got on her nerves referring to Robbie as often as he could as 'the pussbag.'

As the week wore on, with the status of the Project still in doubt while they hashed things over in D.C., her anger somehow subsided to gloom. It was like being trapped in a pastepot. She couldn't get out, and seemed to exhaust herself with the inevitable effort. Although it was supposed to be for her own safety, she'd come to hate being under constant surveillance. She felt exposed and somehow less secure. On Thursday, the super, buffing the brass mailboxes, reported that a man had been asking about her and a number of the other tenants on the third floor. In alarm, she'd beeped Amari, but Joe's guy had been watching and ran the plate. A local—a Kindle County cop, on the dick squad, presumably working a lead. The pointlessness of her fear seemed only too typical of where things were. It was all screwed up, everything. Her. And Feaver. Everything. She walked on the streets and felt solemnly unmoved by the tulips with their bright faces popping up in the spring air.

CHAPTER 29

MY PLAN TO SAVE PETROS—AND ROBBIE—
required him to withdraw at once from practice. He would
never again see clients, go to court, or sign documents.
There was no other alternative. Even if we could somehow wangle Robbie's law degree, BAD, Bar Admissions
and Discipline, would never license someone whom they'd
inevitably discover had been illegally masquerading as a
lawyer for the last twenty years.

Accounting to Dinnerstein for Robbie's changed status
would require a pretty fancy story, but whatever we cooked
up, Mort was virtually certain to keep the news about Robbie secret so that opponents did not attempt to take advantage of him while he was scrambling to hire another
courtroom lawyer to replace Feaver. In the meantime, Robbie could still pass money to Crowthers, through Judith
McQueevey, and to Gillian Sullivan, who was about to resume the bench and was still owed for her favorable ruling in the case transferred to Skolnick. More important,
Robbie could remain a player in whatever endgame Stan

aimed at Kosic and Tuohey. That in turn would give me the leverage I needed to bargain. Robbie was all but certain to end up in the penitentiary; my goal now was to minimize his time.

Most of my negotiations with Stan were conducted during our resumed morning trots in Warz Park. Neither winter darkness nor anything short of a blizzard deterred Stan from running, but I had taken a few months off until the weather eased. Now I met him there several times to talk things through. Although UCORC threatened for a week not to allow the Project to go on, they were in too deep, with too much money expended and too much crime uncovered, simply to throw everything aside. Ultimately, Stan and I agreed that the government would no longer promise Robbie probation. Instead, they would advise the sentencing judge of all relevant matters—Robbie's extraordinary cooperation and the full range of his misfeasance, including his unlicensed law practice—and let the judge impose whatever sentence the court found appropriate. My best guess, when the whole story came out, assuming there were some significant convictions, was that Robbie would do about two years inside. The restitution order relating to Feaver's unlawful practice might be staggering, but most judges would let the financial issues fall out in the inevitable morass of civil law suits for fraud that the insurance companies would file. Even with all that resolved between us, Stan needed D.C. to sign off.

"We accept," he finally advised me one morning in the middle of May. "But there's one more condition you're not going to like." Somehow, Sennett finished six miles every morning looking a picture of order. He had perfect equipment—neopropylene shorts and a sleeveless jersey, footgear the size of snowshoes, and a water bottle in a holster at the small of his back. His wiry Mediterranean hair was unmussed and his sweat always seemed to evaporate. His cheeks were already razored clean. Now he gave me his elevated look, chin ascendant, attempting to appear impregnable in the face of my expected complaints.

He had many excuses for what he proposed. Every prosecution, he said, even Skolnick and Crowthers, was in danger. The government could probably beat back the inevitable defense motions blaming them for Robbie's fraud, but the chances had grown significantly that a jury might just flush the cases out of disgust with Feaver. The future of Petros, therefore, rested more than ever on justifying the government's deal with this devil by demonstrating the widest-ranging success in uncovering corruption. Yet they'd already lost Malatesta, and Feaver was done going to court on the contrived cases, since that wouldn't square with his pose with Dinnerstein. Instead, Sennett had a plan for a new matter, a fictitious motion to reopen one of our old cases, a motion in which Robbie's role, in essence, would be not as a lawyer but as a defendant under attack.

"It'll have to be heard by the Special Motions judge." Stan watched to see how long it would take before I got it, then he confirmed the worst. "We want him to try to fix Magda."

He was right. I didn't like it. We stood in the park fighting for quite a while. He had no predication, I pointed out, no reason to think Magda would corrupt herself. But he claimed that D.C. had decided the long-concealed personal relationship between the judge and a lawyer appearing regularly before her met the threshold. He said this actually had been UCORC's idea.

To me the whole business sounded like trial by ordeal, the medieval ritual where the hands and legs of a suspected witch were bound before she was thrown into a pond to see if she could float. Stan took my criticisms the way he usually did—without patience.

"George," he answered, "how many times, how many

hundreds of times have you had a guilty client walk away? Not an acquittal, but some guy we just never found out about. How many scared-shitless executives have you had in your office, a guy who's caught a subpoena and is terrified about what might come out if he's asked the wrong question, or a fellow who's in the middle of a divorce and gets a spastic colon every time he thinks about all the naughty secrets his angry ex might spill? You've had a thousand of them, George. And they stroll. Most of them. Because we never know. It's not that we can't catch them all. The truth is we hardly catch anybody. And so it goes, George. I can't get ulcers over what I don't know about. But when I do know, George, then I've got a responsibility. It's not my job to be a sweet guy or say it's just an accident we found out. It's my job to protect the folks who live in this district. I'm not supposed to hope Magda won't do something worse in the future. It's my job to catch her, if she deserves to be caught."

His intelligence kept his self-image as spotless as stainless steel, but I gave him a hard look that rang up No Sale.

"I told you, you wouldn't like it," he replied as he turned to jog back to his car.

Robbie, bless him, said no.

"She's not a crook. I'll give them crooks. But I'm not going to try to sucker an honest person just because she's dumb enough to like me."

I loved him for it, I admit. It wasn't brass or the flatulent bluff of a coward. He was ready to do the extra time, years, frankly, it would cost him to defy Sennett. I admired his fortitude and his loyalty, uncertain whether, in his circumstances, I'd have the same resolve. And then I did what I had to as his lawyer. I explained why he had to go along.

If Robbie was anything other than a remote-control automaton, the government would have no choice about pulling the plug on the Project. They were taking a risk as it was, because a defense lawyer already had a howitzer load to lob at them, portraying the U.S. Attorney as the naïve handmaiden of the worst kind of double-dealing snitch. Allowing Robbie to veto their selection of targets would just go to prove that point and pave the way for disaster in front of a jury.

"But Stan would give up a vital organ for Brendan," Robbie said.

He would, but to the people in the Department fortress in D.C. Brendan barely mattered at all. They cared about Congress, the President, the media, the national bar organizations. And when UCORC shut Petros down, Sennett would vent his wrath. The cases he'd be left with—on Skolnick, on Crowthers, on Walter—were preserved on magnetic media and could be proved now without even putting Robbie on the stand. And if the government decided to call him as a witness, they'd prefer he be dressed in a pair of prison overalls, a visual aid demonstrating to a jury that they hadn't let him get away. Stan, therefore, would arrest Robbie right now and use his deception about his law license as compelling evidence that he couldn't be trusted on bail. In the end, Stan had the same leverage he'd had from the start: Lorraine.

When I spoke his wife's name, Robert Feaver did what many other strong persons have done as they've received grim news from me. Positioned in that maroon chair he always sat in, he turned again to my window. Then as the sad facts took root, he raised his hand to his forehead. The resolve not to give in fixed in his face and then passed through him. He wrenched his circled eyes shut and succeeded, except for a few seconds, in his effort not to cry.

THE OTHER COMMITMENT I'd made to Stan was that I would 'explain' Robbie's new situation to Dinnerstein. Evon would remain in their law office as an observer who could testify that Robbie had forsaken further action as an attorney. But Mort had to understand where the lines were drawn, since any failure to comply could end up endangering his right to practice as well. Stan was not about to trust Robbie to deliver the message.

To effect our plan, Robbie presented Mort with a somewhat desperate invention: In the wake of a particularly anguished scene with Lorraine, in which she'd assailed him with the thousand ways he had betrayed his commitments to her over the years, Robbie had supposedly raced to the offices of Bar Admissions and Discipline—BAD—and, in the most dramatic gesture to his wife imaginable, surrendered his license to practice law. Now she would know she was his absolute priority. He had purportedly thought only afterwards to check with me, as an ethical adviser, on the implications of this emotional act. As Robbie's counsel, I'd agreed to help him explain them to Mort.

Feaver & Dinnerstein had existed for fourteen years now. After law school, Mort's uncle had found him a cozy spot in the County Law Department. The original idea, Robbie had told me, was for each of them to get a year or two of experience in other offices, then join forces. Once Robbie had hired on with Neucriss, that plan had been put on hold until Robbie had begun to establish himself in the P.I. trade. Only after Feaver had been out on his own for a year did he persuade Mort to come in with him.

At the moment, Mort was undoubtedly ruing that decision. In my job, I dispensed a lot of bad news. Oncologists who routinely deliver fatal diagnoses were the only professionals I knew of who had it harder. It was my responsibility many times every year to tell people—many of them kindly, okay human beings who'd made a single mistake or who suffered from character failings that did not prevent them from being loving parents or friends—it was my duty to tell these individuals that they were going to be scourged by their community, captured, and caged. Even worse, I often helped them explain these unimaginable facts to their spouses and children, most of whom inevitably felt, with some reason, that they were the true victims of the penal system. Listening, Mort had that kind of frantic expression. He sat across from me, a hand over his mouth, his small eyes zipping back and forth behind the heavy lenses, as he tried to come to terms with my long list of restrictions.

"I still don't believe it," said Mort. "It can't be true. I still can't believe you did this," he said to Robbie, who was sitting beside him. Mort tried smiling. "It's April Fool's six weeks late. Right? You're trying to get me. George," he said, "don't let him do this to me."

Although I'd had a large role, within the security of the attorney-client relationship, in concocting the latest fantasy, I had my usual reluctance about advancing any fabrication myself. I felt safe, however, in telling Mort that he could call BAD and ask them to check the Roll of Attorneys. Robbie's name wouldn't be there. As that affirmation sank home, Mort grabbed his forehead with both hands.

"This is impossible," said Mort. "Can't you reverse this? What if he just goes over to BAD and tells them he changed his mind."

I said, stoically, I was certain that wouldn't work. Robbie added that he didn't want to change his mind. He wanted to be with Rainey, no matter how long or short her time.

"*Be* with her," said Mort. "I want you to be with her. We could have worked that out. You know that. You didn't have to commit suicide as a lawyer. Look what you've done to *me*."

Mort sat in his chair making noises and hugging himself. He ran his hands again through the frizz of hair that was haloed by the strong light emerging from the window.

Then, without a backward glance at his partner, he bolted to the door as quickly as his awkward gait allowed.

"Morty!" Robbie called and took off in pursuit.

At my desk, I felt awful for Mort, and even worse when I thought how enraged he'd be when he discovered the whole truth. He was going to be buried for years in litigation with former clients and vengeful ex-opponents. God knows what he'd say about me.

I didn't sit still long, however. I requested the men's room key from the receptionist, Danny, and moved urgently in that direction. Male-pattern baldness, hair in all the wrong places, the swells of fat that took permanent residence over the hipbones—a friend of mine had suggested that the changes of male middle age were the Darwinian mechanism to ensure that younger women were not persuaded by our attempts at romance. Under this theory, the prostate enlarged just to be certain that we couldn't sit still long enough to try. I circled out the side exit, heading down the dim service channel between my space and my neighbor's. The heavy door to the main corridor had been propped open and, from the darkness, I saw Robbie arrive by the elevator where Dinnerstein was already waiting.

I expected remonstrations or, on the other hand, efforts at rapprochement. Instead, Dinnerstein gave Feaver a faint smile. After a second, Robbie reached in his pocket for change and flipped a quarter in the air; Dinnerstein immediately did the same thing. I'd seen them play this game a few times before, as they awaited the elevator in the lobby. It had been ongoing since childhood, one of the few forms of physical competition where Mort stood an even chance. The contest combined juggling and gambling. They flipped coins simultaneously, each calling his coin in the air while the other caught it. There were complex rules about how to win, doubled bets in some circumstances, and a provision that missing a catch forfeited all winnings. After almost forty years, they sent the coins back and forth at astonishing speed, catching and releasing in a single motion, while the quarters sparkled in the air. They played happily for a moment before the elevator dinged at their rear. Feaver sprinted ahead to hold it as Mort limped in.

I continued staring into the empty corridor, adding it up. I knew nobody reconciles that quickly. Even so, I was disconcerted enough that it took me a second to accept that I'd been taken in again—and this time not only by Feaver. Figuring out why came faster. Mort knew. Mort had known all along that Robbie had no license. Suddenly, it was not really imaginable that Robbie Feaver, Mort's soul mate since the age of six and his law school roommate, hadn't shared his plight. In fact, it explained why Mort had been slow to come practice with Robbie. They'd waited until it was certain that Robbie could actually get away with it. Then they'd proceeded with an obvious contingency plan. In the event of discovery, to protect Mort's license, both of them would deny Dinnerstein ever knew.

I was beyond being shocked by Robbie. But Mort—I'd completely bought his routine in my office. Mort knew, I thought again, and with that realized he almost certainly knew much more. About his uncle. And Kosic. About the judges. Robbie had been shielding him from the start, just as Sennett, a stiff-necked cynic, had always insisted and even as I had frequently feared.

All of this provoked the predictable responses, chagrin and frustration, and several random curse words. Given what Robbie had already done to himself, I shuddered to imagine the kind of time inside he would catch if Stan could ever prove this. But Robbie knew that and was doing it anyway. As I rushed the last few steps to my destination, I was afflicted by a feeling I didn't expect—envy. I envied Mort, envied him everything he got from Feaver. The dedication. The fellowship. And, especially, the truth.

CHAPTER 30

"MAGDA, IT'S ROBBIE."

"Robbie?"

"Feaver."

"Robbie Feaver?" There was nothing for an instant as she tried to parse her confusion. It was May 17. The lead from the recording earpiece Robbie wore ran directly to the tape machine in the cabinet where the seven-inch reels turned with the slow precision of doom. McManis and Evon were beside me at the table. Neither they, nor Klecker, who was standing, had the heart to look long at Robbie. Sennett had not even shown up, recognizing that his presence would be inflammatory.

"I was thinking I could see you."

"See me?" Magda was cautious by nature, precise. "Robbie," she started. Beginning again, she took up the strict tone of the courtroom. "I think that's a very poor idea."

"No, I *need* to see you. just for a minute. I need to talk."

"Talk?"

"Talk."

"No." She took a beat to think about it and said again, "No."

"Magda, this is really important. Life and death. I mean it. Really. Life and death."

"Robert, what could be life and death at nine o'clock in the evening?"

"Magda, I can't do this on the phone. I have to see you. I have to. Please." Robbie drew his lower lip under his teeth to gain control of himself, then went on cajoling.

"Only a minute," she stated at last and gave him the address.

Earlier this afternoon, McManis had filed an emergency motion under the Extraordinary Writs Act to set aside the prior judgment in *Hall v. Sentinel Repair*, the contrived case that had gone from Judge Sullivan to Skolnick. The original complaint had alleged that Herb Hall, a truck driver, had suffered severe burns and been rendered a paraplegic when the sixteen-wheeler he was driving for a hauling company had lost its brakes on a downhill grade. Hall had sued the repair service that had supposedly examined the truck immediately before it went out on the road. According to McManis's motion, Moreland Insurance, in behalf of the service, had settled soon after Skolnick issued Judge Sullivan's ruling allowing Hall to seek punitive damages.

Now Moreland had learned—through Herb's former mistress—that Herb in reality had fallen asleep at the wheel. It was this fact, not brake failure, that accounted for why no tire marks had been found at the crash site. McManis further alleged that the idea for Herb to blame the repair company, rather than himself, came from Herb's attorney, Robert Simon Feaver, who'd tutored Hall on what to say.

The hope, as always, was that if Robbie was successful in reaching Magda, the judge would rule on the basis of briefs. But if a hearing was necessary, I'd agreed with heavy heart to appear in court, acting as the attorney whom Feaver, if he wasn't being the proverbial fool, would be expected to hire.

As soon as the call to Judge Medzyk was finished, Klecker wired Feaver. They were sending Robbie out tonight not only with the FoxBIte but also with the portable camera Klecker had installed in the briefcase matching Robbie's. A fiber-optic lens was hidden in the hinge, and the camera, the same kind as the one installed in Skolnick's Lincoln, was powered by a lithium battery the size of a brick, concealed in the case. The point, however, was not improved evidence-gathering. Robbie's instructions were to keep the camera pointed at all times not at Magda but at himself. They wanted to be sure he didn't signal her somehow.

Before Robbie left, McManis took me aside, stating tersely, "We expect the usual Academy Award performance." He made no apology for not trusting Robbie, and Feaver, when I spoke to him alone to impart the warning, required none. His mind was on Magda, anyway.

"I want you to realize something," he told me, pausing to impart a stark look. "I did the right thing in the first place when I didn't tell these guys about her."

AT HER DOOR, Magda Medzyk grabbed her housedress by the throat and looked both ways down the hallway before letting Robbie in. With the weight of the case, Robbie couldn't keep from swinging his arm, and as a result they were both in and out of the fish-eye. But you could have seen from the street she was worried. Given the tight look of her hair, I imagined that she'd spent the time while Robbie was on the way taking down her pin curls. They stood in the dim front hall of her apartment.

"I hope this is really necessary? I'm *so* uncomfortable, Robert. I can't believe I allowed you to talk me into this.

I was hoping I was mistaken, but I have the papers right in my briefcase. A motion was filed this afternoon. Did you realize you're at issue before me?"

"Hey, I've talked you into a lot of things you think are terrible." Stepping forward, he set the briefcase down and was momentarily out of sight. But Magda's voice was clear.

"No, absolutely not! Not now. Really," she said. More quietly, she added, "My mother's asleep right down the hall." She'd stepped back into the picture again and cast a desperate look over her shoulder. In the fun-house mirror distortions of the lens, I could see the apartment behind her, a railroad flat with heavy dark furniture in the living room, including a console TV with a thirteen-inch screen, the likes of which hadn't been manufactured in at least a decade. As they moved off to the kitchen, the image bounced along impossibly on the monitor in the surveillance van. We were parked beneath one of the grand century-old elms that rose in the parkway in front of the hulking three-story tenement. The sound also took on a bit of a buzz under the kitchen's fluorescent lights as Feaver tried to make conversation. She cut him off abruptly.

"It's probably best, Robbie, if you just state your business."

As he pretended to wrench the cover story from himself, she sank down to a wooden spindle chair by a small table. He had some trouble here, Robbie told Magda, referring directly to the motion McManis had filed. It hadn't been the way they made it sound, he'd never trump up a case that way, but he'd beaten the tar out of Moreland over the years and the insurance company wanted him. They were cutting a deal already with Herb Hall to roll over against Robbie. If she granted this writ, Robbie said, the company would sue him, instead of Hall, to recover everything it had paid out. Then, once they'd picked a million bucks out of his pocket, they'd turn him over to BAD and the Prosecuting Attorney. He'd be lucky to stay out of Rud-yard, and the only thing of value in that license on his wall would be the frame.

Robbie had set the briefcase down on the kitchen counter and we had a good view of the scene. He was opposite Magda at the small maple table where she and her elderly mother had dinner each night. With his long hands, he reached toward her and tossed his head about in distress. She listened at first with her hand over her mouth. By the time he had finished, she refused even to look at him or to speak.

"I *need* this, Magda. And I'll make it okay, for you. I'd *want* to. No number's too high. But this is my life, Magda. This is my whole screwed-up life passing before my eyes. You can't let these bastards take it from me. I mean, for Chrissake—"

"Not another word." With her face averted from Feaver and the camera, her voice was somewhat disembodied. Even so, a sound of despair choked out of her with the effort of speech. "When you called, while I was waiting—" She stopped. "I actually prayed this had nothing to do with your case. I prayed. I actually called upon the Mother of God. As if I deserve her mercy. I have only myself to blame, don't I?"

"Magda, come on. Stow the melodrama. I've been be-fore you a lot in the last ten years. You've ruled for me."

"And against you. You know better, Robert. You know *much* better. I won't have you sit here pretending you don't understand the magnitude of this. Of what you're asking. This isn't business as usual and you know that." Merely contemplating it forced her to look away from him once more. "Oh, God," she said. "God."

"Please, Magda. Think about this. Magda, look, you don't know what goes on around you. You've never stopped to notice. You don't have any idea."

"And I don't *care* to know." Her sharpness seemed to surprise even her, and she planted her mouth on the heel of her palm.

He went on pleading until she covered her ears.

"Go," she said weakly. "Go."

Even then, he begged—she had to, *had* to—until she had finally lost even the power to tell him to stop and her head of tight graying curls appeared to droop in assent.

"Thank you," he told her. "For seeing me. For doing this. Thank you." He repeated that a dozen times more. When he came around the table to embrace her, she recoiled with her thick arms held aloft. In the last frames before he jerked the camera off the counter, she was bunched in her simple frock, virtually formless in her grief

"She's gonna do it," said Alf in the van, while Robbie was on the way down. I had reached the same melancholy conclusion myself. McManis and Evon both nodded.

But Robbie had a judgment of his own. Once inside the Mercedes, Feaver had apparently taken hold of his briefcase, bringing the lens right up to his face. On the monitor, his features flattened monstrously in the fish-eye. But he didn't want anyone watching to miss a word.

"That's the worst fucking thing I've ever done in my life," he yelled. Then, I took it, he'd hurled down the camera, because the screen first jumbled, then went completely black.

CHAPTER 31

THE NEXT MORNING, WHEN EVON CAME
to pick up Feaver, he was gone.

She'd waited fifteen minutes for him at the foot of the
drive, her car window opened to the sweet morning air.
Eventually, she went up to the house. Punctuality was normally his sole reliable virtue.

The home care worker was new. Elba had returned to
the Philippines for two weeks for her niece's wedding, and
her place had been taken by Doris, a stooped African-
American woman who looked as if she needed assistance
herself. She had no idea where Robbie had gone, other than
having heard him depart in the middle of the night.

Evon had told herself that she would never feel sorry
again for Robbie Feaver. But as she'd watched his silhou-
ette plunge wearily toward his door last night, that resolve
had eroded. The truth about Feaver was that he wasn't actually anything he said he was. Not one thing. He wasn't
a lawyer, obviously. And he'd never amounted to dip as an
actor. He wasn't even a husband, if that meant keeping to

your commitments seven days a week. But his answer to all of that was that at least he was a friend. That's what he'd told her when she demanded to 'know what mattered.' His friends. And as punishment for getting caught in one of history's all-time whoppers, Sennett with his treacherous genius had pointed his shotgun at Robbie and brought him to his knees, making him look down both of the dark barrels and find out that even the one thing he said for himself was no truer than the rest.

Maybe he'd just gone out to get drunk, she figured now. Or to stare at the river.

After another half hour she realized he'd probably run.

She called McManis from a nearby pharmacy so she could use a wire line. Jim was silent so long she had to ask if he was there.

"He couldn't run," Jim said finally. "He wouldn't leave his wife." McManis stopped then. "Christ. You better get back and make sure she's still there."

She raced back down the clean suburban streets. He'd run! What had Jim said? There was never a bottom with his type.

When she arrived, Robbie was in the driveway, just emerging from the Mercedes. He walked slowly toward her. It was probably the first time she'd seen him looking sloppy. He was unshaven. His hair was stirred up and his face seemed withered by lack of sleep. A placket shirt hung limply over the belt line of his fancy slacks. He was clearly not heading to the office. From the dullness of his eyes, she thought she'd been right in the first place, that he was drunk, but he was moving too well. He turned his head to follow some thought as if it were a butterfly before his attention fell to her again.

"My mother died," he said, "last night. She had another stroke. She was DOA at the hospital, but they went through some stuff in the E.R." He flopped up a hand from his side, acknowledging the futility of those efforts, and somehow it landed on Evon's. It seemed almost accidental, but he permitted himself a brief squeeze before letting go. He looked off toward the apple tree in the yard that was heavy with pink blossoms and made a face. The stroke had been on the other side, he said, so he figured it was, all in all, better this way.

Two years ago, Evon's father had gone in for bypass. Her mother and she and five of her sibs, all the girls and one of her brothers, sat together nearly six hours in the contour chairs of the surgical lounge. In her anxiety, her mother had been herself, only more so, carping about the nurses and going from child to child finding fault. Evon had decided to leave, had actually gotten to her feet, when the doctor came out to tell them that her father hadn't made it.

He had been a large red-faced figure, with thick arms and a substantial belly straining the buttons of a gingham shirt. His thick fingers were calloused, the nails always cracked and never free of dirt. He smelled of the land at all times. She had known him mostly as a presence. He spoke little, even when he was sitting around joshing with the neighbors. He treated her mother kindly, but with the same somewhat distant air they all experienced. He was uncomfortable with feeling and always wanted to be away from it, safe in the realm of chores and routine. He'd split with his own family when Evon's mother quit the Church. He spoke to his brothers occasionally, but not his parents. In her entire life, Evon couldn't recall his mentioning his mother or father more than twice. How had he done that? He was gone, never fully known, and yet he still reared up in her dreams and thoughts countless times a day, and always with a lingering twisted pain, as if somewhere in her something had been torn up by the root.

Robbie said he had already called Mort, who was working on the funeral arrangements. Now he had to tell Rainey. Before he started up the driveway, he asked Evon to go to the office, to take care of the mail and help Mort reschedule the deps and other appointments for the next few days.

"No problem." She had no will left to rebuke him.

He looked at her pathetically, unwilling to move. She realized what he wanted. In the house, his wife would not even be able to lift her arms to him in consolation. She reached out just to touch him, but he flowed toward her and swarmed her in an embrace, which she reluctantly returned.

"You're a tough cowpoke. You're gonna make it. You let me know what I can do."

He didn't let go of her, even then. He had begun to burble. When he stood back, he grabbed his lip and continued to cry, his face crushed by the pain.

"She was just so much," he said. "She was *so* much."

News of the death had circulated through the office by the time she got there. There was a dismal air that seemed to go beyond mere respect for the boss. Mort was on his way out to sit with Robbie at his home, and asked Evon to follow up on several details related to cases. He stood at the opening of her cubicle. He was in his suit but his tie was already removed, an emblem that business as usual had been suspended.

"How's he going to take all this?" Mort asked her. He, too, appeared on the verge of experiencing his famous vulnerability to tears. "It's too much," Mort said. He sobbed then and smashed his face into his hand, but could not move, desolated by Robbie's future.

The funeral was the following day. Jews traditionally buried with speed, Eileen explained. Everyone from the office was going, so Evon was spared any decision.

Mort phoned as she was leaving her apartment. "We have a big problem," he said. Doris, the home care aide, had not shown up. Robbie had suspected from the start that the job was too much for her, and the notion of a hundred people traipsing through the house for visitation had apparently pushed her beyond her limit. Mort had sent Robbie off to the funeral home, promising to handle this, but he had called a number of agencies and none of them could produce someone before the early afternoon.

"My mom was a nurse," Mort said, "so she could do it, but you know, I think he'd really want her there. Considering the circumstances. I can call one of his cousins, but I thought you might be able to think of somebody. Lorraine's sleeping most of the time now anyway, but it would be nice if it's somebody she's met."

She could tell Mort was angling. His cagier side grew more apparent each day. He kept minimizing what he was asking. There was less than an hour to the funeral, the service wouldn't last long, and a number of people would then return to the house. There seemed no way to say no, and he thanked her enthusiastically when she finally offered. But she felt exasperated once she put down the phone. She decided to call back and wriggle out. It didn't really fit the cover. People would wonder, wouldn't they, about Robbie's girlfriend caring for his wife on the day of his mother's funeral? No, she saw then, they wouldn't. They would think that's Robbie Feaver all over.

By the time Evon arrived in Glen Ayre, Mort had gone off to the funeral parlor, leaving his wife, Joan, behind. She was a tiny, thin woman, pretty in a way, but drying up and bowing just a bit in the hormonal retreat of oncoming middle age. She was dressed in black crepe and pearls and had been setting up coffeepots for the crowd that would arrive here from the cemetery. She showed Evon what Mort had shown her about Rainey's care, as he'd been instructed by Robbie. There was no telling what had been forgotten or misinterpreted in the many retellings. But the basics were apparent. The bedpan. The Sustacal in the kitchen for Rainey's lunch. When Evon realized moments later she was alone with Lorraine, she nearly sent a scream rebounding through the empty house. My God, what if she killed her? Then she sealed off all of that like the hatches in a submarine on the verge of descent.

Rainey slept for nearly half an hour after Evon arrived. She was wearing a full oxygen mask now, a transparent plastic shape covering her mouth and nose. Her breathing was growing more shallow every day. She had no energy to leave the bed, and Evon knew that soon she would be engirded in something called a cuirass, a negative-pressure device to assist in drawing air into her lungs. But that could put off only so long the ultimate crisis of whether she would allow the installation of the mechanical ventilator. Robbie remained hopeful of persuading her as the time for decision drew nearer.

When Rainey woke, Evon reminded her who she was and swung into place the hospital tray that held the computer mouse and its pad, lifting Rainey's fingers onto it. Lorraine was far more adept with the speaking machine than she'd been only a few weeks ago. She scrolled through lists of words, clicking rapidly.

"Oh I Know Who You Are," the bleating boy's voice said. Even without any emphasis, there was something ominous in the choice of words. Evon had no idea what to do if Rainey began to pelt her with the kind of abuse she sometimes hurled at Robbie. He said he'd actually turned off the volume on the speakers on a couple of occasions, but she had no right to be so callous. She busied herself instead. She pulled the covers back on the bed and buttered Lorraine's flaccid arms with almond-scented lotion, but Rainey was not about to be put off.

"He Is Such A Great Liar," Rainey said. "Do You Know What He Says About You?"

Evon stopped. A clutch of devastated feeling was already gathering in her chest.

"He Says You Are A Lesbian."

Evon laughed, longer than she might have but for the relief.

"I am."

Expression remained alive in the submerged depths of Rainey's eyes, which contracted somewhat in doubt.

"He Talks About You."

"We work together. We're friends. Robbie has lots of friends." Evon found a pillow and pulled Rainey to her side and put it behind her. She'd seen all of this done with her grandmother. Her skill was amazing to her, the ease and naturalness of it once she started. At the side of the bed, she placed her face near Rainey's on the pillows.

"We aren't lovers," she told her.

Even with her body wrecked, Rainey clearly craved to believe her, but she had been hardened by the disappointments Robbie regularly delivered. Rainey circled there in the ruinous back-and-forth of doubt and longing.

Evon read to her for some time. Robbie had begun *Mitigating Circumstances*, and Evon went through several chapters. No doubt she was a poor substitute for Robbie and his stagecraft. Even to herself, she barely sounded more dramatic than Rainey's voice machine and she was not surprised when Rainey dropped off again. She awoke with a pathetically contained shudder that reached only her right arm and foot. Her eyes sprang open and the palest rasp of sound emerged from her, almost certainly meant to be a scream. Evon could feel the pounding when she touched Lorraine's cheek.

"I Dream I'm Dead. All The Time."

Evon closed her eyes, caught on the barb of her own dread. It came back to her a second, like some bitter, regurgitative mess rising with a hiccup.

"That must be frightening," she said.

"In Some Ways." Lorraine took her time in thought, then described the dream. She had seen her mother-in-law. "We Were Wearing The Same Hat. It Had A Peacock Plume On The Front." Rainey paused for several breaths amid the bare whooshing of the oxygen tank. "But Then I Wanted To Take It Off. And Realized I Couldn't. That Was Frightening. But It's Not Usually That Way. They Say Dreams Are Wishes. Have You Heard That?"

She had been a psychology major, so she probably had. She'd figured she was going to learn to understand people that way. These days the thought of it made her laugh.

"You Know He's Promised Me." Somehow Evon was beginning to discern expression in the squawking from the computer speaker. It wasn't possible, she realized, yet this dry adenoidal male voice corresponded more and more to the broken person now shaped like a question mark in the bed.

What was it he'd promised? Evon asked. She took Rainey's hand and touched her brow.

"He's Promised. He'll Help Me. Whenever I Tell Him. He Swore To Me."

Unconsciously, she had tightened her grip on Rainey's fingers and barely had the presence of mind to release them. Lorraine was undeterred. She went on describing the arrangement she'd reached with Robbie long ago, when she learned about the disease's inevitable progression. She'd made him reaffirm the agreement only recently when she'd begun to lose the last control of her limbs. It petrified Evon to listen to this. Rainey's voice poured from the speakers at the same volume as before, words that should have been hushed. It was not the act or the idea that frightened Evon so much as contemplating the moment it would be for both of them. But Rainey seemed at ease. The certainty of a reprieve, an outlet, a way to end the suffering seemed a part of bearing it.

"Don't Let Him Back Out. Don't."

"No," Evon said, more as a reflex.

"Promise."

God, she was a cluck, Evon thought of herself, never even to suspect this, particularly given Robbie's long-standing desperation to be certain he was free throughout Lorraine's decline. Robbie, she thought. Good or bad, you'd just never get to the end.

"You can't ask me that, Rainey."

"I Suppose I Can't. But I Ask All His Friends."

She slept again, and Evon herself drifted off, waking at the sudden sound of voices downstairs. Joan had returned, along with Mort's mother, a stout woman with a white bun. Linda, one of Robbie's cousins, wore a hairdo that looked harder than an insect shell and so much jewelry she glittered like a Christmas tree. The women had returned following the service to ready the house for the remainder of the crowd, which would begin arriving after the interment. There had been nearly nine hundred people at the mortuary, they told her, enough to fill a second chapel, where the ceremony was broadcast on closed-circuit TV. Center City must have been a ghost town with the exodus of Feaver's friends—lawyers, clients, court personnel, the legion whom Robbie amused and aided. Joan worried that the house could be overrun.

Evon helped the women carry in a dozen heaping trays of cold cuts, which had been sent to Mort's house by friends offering comfort. The new home care person, a grandmotherly Polish immigrant, came in at the same time. She had a heavy suitcase, and Joan, who knew the house, showed her where she would be staying.

Rainey was awake when Evon went back up.

"Cavalry's arrived. I guess I'll be going."

"Come Back."

She promised that.

"I'm Sorry. For Before. I Say Things Now. Sometimes I Don't Believe I Even Thought The Words That Are Coming Out."

Evon took her hand again. She didn't mind, she said. What Rainey feared wasn't true, and she was glad she could reassure her.

"It's Your Loss Anyway," Rainey said. "That's What He Would Tell You."

Humor. Evon smiled. She was sure he would, she thought. Rainey's eyes darkened in the labor of a more serious effort.

"You Would Think I Wouldn't Mind Now. Finally. Sick And Twisted As My Body Is. But I Still Want Him. All Ways Too. I Can Still Feel That. There. And Do It. Did You Know That?"

Hardly. The astonishment must have crept through her face.

"It's The One Thing Left. I Think I'm Hornier Than Ever. It Probably Sounds Vulgar. Or Perverted. But It's Not. It's Wonderful. To Feel Him Around Me. To Think He Wants Me. Even Now. So Broken And Ugly. They Say It's The Partner Who Loses Interest. But He Hasn't. And I'm So Grateful. We Love Each Other You Know."

"I know," Evon said and found a tissue to blot Rainey's tears, creeping to the pillow even while her hand clicked away on the mouse.

"He Hurt Me. Too Much. And I Hurt Him Back. We Hurt Each Other Every Way You Can. But I Love Him. And He Loves Me. I Never Knew It The Way I Did After This Happened. But That's Why I'm Living. Isn't That Strictly Amazing? I'm Not Alive Really. And I'm Still Living For Love."

The new nurse's assistant entered energetically, talking

in an accent that Evon could barely decode, but she greeted Rainey lovingly and clearly knew her business. She propped up Rainey and straightened the sheets, transforming the bed in such short order that Evon was predictably embarrassed by her relative incompetence. After an uncertain moment, she leaned over the bed and embraced Rainey quickly.

Downstairs a short time later, through the large living room windows, Evon saw Robbie arrive in a long limo. His mother's younger sister from Cleveland was with him and he held tight to the older woman's arm as she wedged herself out of the car. Evon caught them in the foyer. Robbie was pale and his features appeared loosened by a bleary uncertainty. His elderly aunt, humpbacked from age, seemed temperamental and largely unmoved by the day's proceedings. Somewhat crossly, she asked for directions to the powder room. When he returned, Robbie offered to walk Evon out. He was on automatic pilot again, talking as they drifted down the drive.

Once, he said, when he was eight or nine, his mother had taken him fishing during the white bass run up near Skageon. He'd been getting in trouble, lifting stuff from the five-and-dime, and his mother was convinced the problem was a lack of manly activity and attention. In the retelling, Robbie marveled over the sight of Estelle, who would never leave the house with so much as a wrinkle in her nylons, appearing that morning in a flannel shirt and old hat. She later told him that after two hours rocking in the river she'd become seasick to a point where suicide seemed sensible, yet she'd given him no clue that day.

They were near Evon's car, parked at the foot of the property. The neighbor's lilacs, white and soft purple, were open and as sweet on the air as cologne. His mother had been laid to rest on a glorious day. Evon turned her face up to the perfect sky and found him watching her when she looked back.

"This was spectacular of you," he said. "I can't even tell you what it means to me, I really can't. This is one of the nicest things anybody's ever done for me in my life."

She answered with the thought that had been circulating unvoiced most of the morning. "You'd have done it for me," she told him and that harp string in her center sang out, plucked by the truth. You could never count on him for honesty, assuming he even knew what it was. He was unruly and incorrigible. But if she stumbled, he'd come running. She couldn't even say for sure she'd be able to reach out when he extended a hand. But he'd be there. She wasn't going to forgive him, really. But she had to stop pretending with herself. Nine hundred people had just turned out, all there to buoy Robbie Feaver in his grief, nearly every one a friend who'd experienced his openness and the soothing warmth of his care. And she was one, too. You couldn't fight facts.

She asked how he was holding up.

"Eh," he answered, and let feeling swirl him off elsewhere for a moment.

"Losing my dad was something," she said, "but my mom, being last and my mom—I can't even imagine."

"Yeah," he said. "But I read something once and I keep thinking about it now. 'Every little boy loses his mother the first time, the day he realizes he's a man.'"

Evon didn't understand and Robbie said he hadn't either. Not originally. But the idea seemed to be that boys had to come to terms with the fact that they couldn't be like their mothers, they had to be somebody else. He was still and his face was heavy in the light. He didn't seem entirely happy with these thoughts.

She had decided long ago she wasn't going to be like her mother, probably because her mother had let Evon know she was nothing like her. But the notion of her mother actually disappearing from her life still seemed to suck the center out of the world. It would be as if the force of gravity, which was down there at the midpoint of the earth and which kept it from flying apart, was suddenly missing. Her mother, past seventy, still hung out her wash every day, except in blizzards, preferring the touch of mountain air to the hot breath of the dryer. In her mind's eye, Evon saw her there, with the clothespins in her mouth, securing a tattersall shirt or a sheet to the line, standing her ground, asserting her intentions, while the wash gave in and snapped on the wind.

He asked if Evon got along with her.

"Some. She judges. You're always being weighed on her scales. But you know, she's strong." Her arms went out. "She's big, You know what I mean?"

He drifted down the curb line with her. They were interrupted by a neighbor who had awaited his return before bringing another huge tray, piled up like the others with pale mounds of foods Evon had never really seen and suspected she couldn't stomach. The woman paid her respects and then proceeded up the driveway.

He hugged Evon then, before she could withdraw. That was apparently going to be standard now. She only hoped he had the good sense not to do this in front of McManis or Sennett. When he was halfway to the house, he turned and shouted as he walked backwards, just before he disappeared into shadow, "You're great. I love you, I really do."

She realized that somewhere nearby there was probably a surveillance agent, covering her. God knows what he'd seen. Or heard. That'd be some 302. 'The cooperating individual then stated to UCA Miller, I love you.' Great. She'd recognize the agent by the size of the shit-eating grin he'd throw her through the driver's window. And what was she to respond? 'We're just friends'?

But when she settled in the Chevette she caught a

glimpse of herself in the rearview mirror and spied traces of a cheerful look. How could that be, amid all this anguish and misfortune and flat-out confusion? She took herself to task, then gave up. What the hell, she thought suddenly. Really. What the hell. She put the car into gear, and felt the spry, lively wind of spring as soon as she lowered the window.

CHAPTER

32

THE NEXT MORNING WHEN I CAME IN,
Danny, my receptionist, had taken a message from the U.S.
Attorney, Stan Sennett, asking if I could arrange to see him
in my office at 12:30, with my colleague, which was how
he referred to Robbie. Feaver, who was at the nursing home
to begin the dismal business of sorting through his mother's
effects, was cranky about being summoned, but he arrived
on time, still with bleared eyes and appearing vaguely di-
sheveled, as he'd been when I'd made a condolence call
the prior evening.

"What's this about?" he asked.

I hadn't a clue.

Stan's mood, when Danny showed him in, was quite
formal. He was in his usual immaculate blue suit and he
took the trouble to shake Robbie's hand, which I didn't recall him bothering with before. He expressed his sympa-
thies and, finding them tepidly received, put himself down
in the maroon chair Robbie usually occupied. Sennett spent

a moment arranging himself, reaching down to straighten the crease on his trouser leg, before beginning.

"I wanted to advise you both of a very unusual meeting I had the afternoon before last. I would have done this sooner, but for Robbie's circumstances. It was with an old friend of ours. Of all of ours. Magda Medzyk." Stan looked into his lap at that point, his expression taut.

"She had consulted an attorney that morning, Sandy Stern." Stan nodded toward me. Stern, who reviles Stan for reasons I have never fully understood, is my best friend in practice. "That was our good fortune. Mr. Stern declined to represent her, telling her he had an undisclosed conflict, but he suggested she approach me, rather than the P.A.'s office, where political allegiances could occasionally become problematic. She waited more than an hour before I got back, and when she came in, she told me a long, somewhat tawdry story about her relationship with a personal injury attorney named Robert Feaver.

"Mr. Feaver, she said, had asked her to throw a case the night before. He actually seemed to be offering her money to do it. She wasn't quite certain of that, because she was so upset, so alarmed, she didn't follow every word. But there was no mistake that he wanted her to alter the outcome of the case. The judge told me that she will enter an order recusing herself from the matter. But she wanted to inform me first because she was willing, if need be, to wear a wire against Mr. Feaver, prior to that." Trying to be grave, Stan still could not stifle a smile at the irony.

He said that Magda had willingly accepted his guidance. Aside from withdrawing from the case, she would undertake no action or alert any other party in order to allow the government to investigate. She'd await further word from Stan.

Sennett waved his chin around to loosen his neck from

the grip of his shirt collar, before turning to Feaver beside him.

"She's quite an extraordinary person," Stan said.

Robbie did not move. His shadowed eyes remained on Sennett, who, to his credit, declined to look away.

"'An extraordinary person'?" Robbie finally asked. "Stan, do you know how Magda Medzyk spent the night after I left there? Have you got a clue? Because I do. I was sitting there burying my mother yesterday and I saw Magda, like a vision, like it was on TV. I saw her at that little kitchen table all night long. She barely moved. She only got up once. To get her rosary. She just sat there begging the Mother of God to help her find some little piece of herself that could go on with whatever was left of her life, only some sliver of her soul, because the rest of it had been swallowed up by shame." He stood up then. "'An extraordinary person,'" he repeated. He directed one last harsh look at Sennett, kicked over my wastebasket, picked it up, and left.

Stan took just an instant to recover. At my door, he tipped an imaginary hat.

I found his behavior oddly consistent with my lifetime experience of Stan. Just when I was ready to give up on him, he'd redeem himself. As a line prosecutor he'd shown all the tenderness of a blunt instrument, but when he became Chief Deputy P.A. under Raymond Horgan, he exhibited monumental strength in reforming the office and especially in loosening the grip of the Police Force, with its political crosscurrents, over prosecutions. Shortly before he'd married Nora Flinn, her mother, expecting the couple to have children, chose to reveal the fact that she was not Portuguese, as Nora and her brother had always been told, but black. Stan, so far as I could tell, had never flinched. Instead, he had been an admirable support, even an example, in helping Nora come to terms not only with her anger at her mother but with the uglier stuff that would seep out of the hearts of most white Americans in the same situation. And when, as luck would have it, age later prevented them from being able to conceive, it was Stan who first suggested adopting a child of mixed race.

Today, he had arrived here, the Mountain to Mohammed, with the clear intent to be what was once referred to as A Man, knowing Feaver would dish out exactly what he had gotten. He'd come anyway, not merely to concede an error, not only to apologize to Robbie or to grant that my anger had been well placed, but to acknowledge that Feaver, disingenuous and compromised as he was, remained an able judge of character. Being as coolly objective as Stan, one could say that he was better with principles than with personalities. But as he went on his way, doing his best to look uncrimped, he left behind the saving information that he remained subject to the discipline of his own beliefs.

THE FOLLOWING THURSDAY, the week before Memorial Day, Robbie resumed his activities. With Evon, he returned to Judith's to deliver the money Sherm had demanded. Judith, who'd plainly had a merciless ruction with her brother, refused even to look at Robbie, but the envelope went in the register drawer. Amari and his watchers had better luck this time in trailing the funds. Crowthers himself arrived for a late lunch and casually took the small white envelope from Judith, his hand lowered to his side while he was joshing with the kitchen staff. His first stop in the courthouse, even before his own chambers, had been at Kosic's small office, adjoining Tuohey's.

The wiretap, briefly activated, revealed little more than greetings. Something hit the desk, but no one could say for certain it was money. Somehow Kosic knew the source of the payment already or perhaps, out of extreme caution, sources were never identified, because nothing about that had been said.

But there was no question Rollo had received a share. No more than two hours later, Kosic paid for steak dinners for Brendan and himself at Shaver's, an old-fashioned joint not far from their home. One of the surveillance agents, seated only two tables away, had watched Rollo lay a $100 bill in the plastic folder in which the tab was presented. The agent jumped up and asked if Kosic minded exchanging five twenties for the C-note, claiming he wanted to fill a graduation card for his nephew. Not only did the serial number match one of the bills Robbie had dropped to Judith earlier but lifts raised a thumbprint so large the agents were all convinced—correctly, as it turned out—that it was Sherm's. Kosic was now a long way to being cooked. And Crowthers was fully grilled. There would be no argument that anything Sherm had said to Robbie was merely a rambunctious jest. Despite the middling results with the wiretap, Stan was confident that Judge Winchell would agree to a full thirty-day overhear in Kosic's office. Something on Brendan was bound to turn up.

Sennett reported this information to the UCAs that night, clearly aiming to inspire everybody as they moved into the critical stage. Evon had come back to the Center City to attend the meeting, then returned to her apartment.

A large mirror with a frame of beveled glass hung as a wall decoration across from the elevator on her floor. Even when she glanced in the usual solemn fashion at her reflection, she knew something was wrong. She could never have identified what was out of place, but once she turned the corner down the narrow hall, she could see the door to her apartment ajar.

She stole to the threshold and lined herself up, shoulder to the left jamb, using the palm of her left hand to slowly push the door open. For the one hundredth time since Walter told Robbie that Marty Carmody thought she was an FBI agent, she longed for her weapon.

Inside, she heard someone clear his throat, and then another voice. Call the locals, she told herself, meaning the Kindle County police. Back out and dial 911. She had a cell phone in her purse. But this was the stuff she lived for. The cowboy types on a bust were always there for the power, sticking their .44 Magnum in somebody's ear and calling him motherfucker, hoping for a 'brownie'; she'd never been able to see that as a trophy, since you had to tolerate the stink when you brought the poor bastard in. But for Evon, all roads led back to game day, to the telling moment of precise reaction. She loved to win, loved herself when she triumphed, in the pure, uncompromised way she'd transplanted from that earlier part of her life. She was not calling the locals.

She was halfway down the front hall now, spidering along with her backside to the wall. Recently, she'd been playing softball, a Sunday pickup game in a nearby park, kind of a boys-meet-girls event, but many of the participants competed seriously, and she'd bought a black graphite bat last week, which was still propped in a corner a few feet from where she was now, in the living room. Ahead, she saw a shadow move. She flattened herself and held her breath. Voices sputtered up once more. She had just placed the source when a middle-aged slope-bellied copper stopped at the end of the hallway and looked her up and down. He was pug-nosed and fairly cheerful-looking, despite his eyes, which were so small they had barely any whites. He reached to his belt to turn down his radio.

"Lady of the house?" he asked.

"Something like that." She showed him her key.

"Got a report," he said. "Burglary in progress. But I guess we missed them. You want to step back outside, I'll just finish. Take a minute. Or wait in the kitchen. I've already covered that."

The whole apartment had been tossed. Cabinets, dressers. The officer had a flashlight in his hand and was stepping carefully over the drawers of her bedroom wardrobe and their contents, which had been emptied out here on the meal-colored rug. He was agile for a big man, for somebody his age.

In the kitchen, the back door was wide open. There was nothing subtle. The dead bolt had been forced right through the plaster, leaving, even now, bitter white dust in the air and a crater in the wall the shape of a bowler hat. A piece of wallpaper hung down, as if exhausted, and the molding had been pulled straight off, revealing the three-inch straight nails with which the finish carpenters had applied it. Crowbar, she decided and was surprised, stepping to the threshold, to see the tool outside, still resting on the steel fire escape.

"The crowbar they used is on the back porch yet," she called. "You might want it for prints."

She'd returned to the living room. The copper looked back into the bedroom for something and took his time in responding.

"You don't get much from that kind of surface," he said. "But I'll take it along." In the kitchen, an empty plastic bag from the grocery produce section rested on the counter. He asked if she could spare it and he grabbed the crowbar with that. He laid it on the white Formica breakfast bar, pulled a tiny spiral notebook from his back pocket, and asked her for her name and date of birth. She panicked for a second until she recollected that the birth dates were the same, Evon Miller's and hers.

"Probably kids," the cop said. "Doesn't look too professional, the way they went through that wall. Must have raised a racket. Anything special they'd want with you?"

She shook her head mutely. But his question unsettled her. Probably kids, she told herself. She asked if she could look around to see what was missing.

"TV's still there. Looks like most of the big stuff's in place. I must have scared them off. God knows what's in their pockets, though. You'll probably be finding stuff missing for days. But go ahead, look. Anything with some value could turn up in the North End. Be good to know about it."

She walked through the apartment. The wreckage was upsetting. Every closet door was open. They'd gone through her bedroom with vicious speed, probably looking for jewelry. Her dresses were all off their hangers and on most of the garments the pockets had been turned inside out. A small jewelry box on her bureau had been upended, the pieces strewn around the room. She'd never know what was missing, but it was all costume stuff anyway that the Movers had provided. Even her bed had been disturbed, The spread and covers had been ripped off and the mattress now sat crookedly on the box spring. A routine hiding place, under the mattress, jokes notwithstanding. Probably kids, she told herself again.

When she went under, the Movers had given her the option of keeping her FBI credentials. It was a rainy-day measure, worse coming to worst. But if a snoopy boyfriend found them, well, most likely you were blown. That was how the leader, Dorville, had explained it. Agents who were undercover in the world of dope, of fencing, many of them held on to their creds, because they were likely to get arrested. But she didn't figure to have that need and she was relieved now she'd made the decision to leave them behind. Even her gun, much as she missed it, might have been a problem. She finally saw the logic.

She went back to the living room. The drawers had been pulled out on a small desk there. She had been dictating today's 302 before she left, and she pawed around through what was on the floor, looking for her Dictaphone. It was gone, as well as the spare microcassettes that had been in the drawer beside it. To her best memory, there was not that much yet on the recording—the case file number, her voice referring to herself as 'undersigned agent.' Still, that cassette, in the wrong hands, would give her away.

"Anything gone?" called the copper.

"Hard to tell," she answered. There was so much disruption, so many odd things thrown here and there, that she knew the Dictaphone and the tapes could still be here. She picked through clothing, books, CDs on the floor. She went into the bedroom and systematically worked her way around the room. In the living room, she found the Dictaphone, but today's tape had been removed. Hoping, she checked her briefcase, but the microcassette was not in the side pouch where she routinely zipped the tape when she was done. Two inches by one, though, the cassette would be easy to miss. It was going to turn up, she told herself.

She walked around the apartment one more time, looking things over. Nothing else seemed to be missing. Then she realized that a birthday card she'd written to her mother, sealed in its white envelope and addressed, had also been removed from the desk. Fear darkly bloomed near her heart. She'd signed it 'DeDe.' Still, that was nothing, who'd make anything of DeDe? Only Marty Carmody, she realized. And Walter.

As the anxiety began knifing deeper, she added it up. Would kids skip the CDs and go for a birthday card? Would they take the tapes and not the Dictaphone? That's why the pockets of her clothing had been rummaged, why her bed had been overturned. Carmody's information had finally made the circle, from Walter to somebody who cared.

The cop was ready to go. He stooped for his hat on her

coffee table. As he did, the white corner of an envelope peeked up out of his rear pocket and Evon missed a breath.

Lots of things came in envelopes, she told herself. Lots of people carried stuff in their back pockets. But she recollected all of Robbie's warnings about Brendan's enduring connections on the Force. The brass, almost all of them, were Brendan's pals. He'd served on the Force with most of the Area Commanders and had cultivated the others over the years. Milacki, in fact, was still on the job.

"How'd this call come in anyway?" Evon asked, trying to sound casual.

The copper wiped a thick hand across his mouth.

"One of the neighbors, I suspect."

"You know which one? I really oughta go say thank you."

"Fraid not. Just a 911. Beat hell over here, you know how it is." He was looking around the living room as if he'd left something. Maybe he didn't want to meet her eye, Or perhaps he was already wondering what tipped her.

She'd gone back to the front window and looked through the miniblinds down to the avenue. There was no squad car outside.

"It was just a real surprise to find you in here," she said. "I didn't even see a police car outside."

The copper looked at her with sudden directness. His tiny eyes had hardened and she cursed herself. She might as well have handed the guy a note that he'd been busted. And like a bat suddenly flying through the room, Evon abruptly realized this man was weighing the thought of killing her. It was not necessarily something he wanted to do. It was just that he had never really considered his alternatives. But if she beeped the Bureau for assistance, if they searched him and found that card and her Dictaphone tapes in his pockets, his life was over. There was a Chief's Special, a .38 Smith & Wesson, on his hip. And he could use any excuse: she snuck in; he mistook her for another bandit.

"You know the old trick," the cop finally said. "Come up on foot. I didn't want the perp to catch sight of a black-and-white." He kept his pinkish face half-averted, check-ing with one eye to see how this was being received. "What kind of law enforcement you in?"

"Me?"

"You sorta sound like you know what you're doing. With the fingerprints and all. Way you were crawling the wall there." She noticed his nameplate over his shirt pocket for the first time. Dimonte. Then again, it might not even be his.

"I just watch a lot of TV."

She got a laugh with that, albeit somewhat obligatory. She desperately wanted to unheat this guy, put him at ease. Bad enough that they were on her, but even worse if they realized she knew. She went to her cupboard in the kitchen. It was open, too. The vodka was on the front of the shelf. Did she leave it there? Somebody trying to pick through her cover would be looking for liquor. She brought the bot-tle out with her, as well as a box of cookies, and offered Dimonte both.

"Not on the job, lady. I'm pretty much a beer guy any-way. Poor man's pleasures."

She made excuses about the bottle. Her boyfriend bought it. She didn't take alcohol herself, the way she was brought up.

"Methodist?" the cop asked.

"No, no. Mormon. Church of Jesus Christ of Latter-day Saints."

He shook his head to show he'd never heard of them. "Each to his own," he said. He looked her over one more time, plainly still deliberating, then seeing no harm, reached over and took a cookie.

He was gone a moment later. She thanked him lavishly and he tipped his hat. She leaned against the apartment's painted steel door as soon as she'd closed it. That had been a bad minute there. Her knees were jumping around like fleas. Back in the kitchen, she found the crowbar, still resting on the counter in the bag bearing the grocer's logo. But that made sense. Officer Dimonte had already found all the evidence he needed.

SENNETT DID NOT WANT TO BELIEVE IT.

"A birthday card?" he asked. "If I was a burglar, I might lift a birthday card. Maybe there's a twenty inside."

But Joe Amari had gotten agents from the Kindle County Division who worked regularly with the locals to tear this up. Over in Area 6, Dimonte had filed a report that said he'd responded to a burglary in progress. But Joe's guys had burned a copy of the 911 tapes and a number of evidence techs had listened to all twelve tracks. There was no break-and-enter logged anywhere in DuSable between 8 p.m. and 10.

McManis knew Sennett well enough to realize he'd have to hear this news directly. Heavyset but smooth, Joe sat calmly at the end of the table and delivered the report. Sennett began to speculate about why the call might not be recorded and Amari lost patience.

"Stan, nobody sends a single unit, let alone a one-man car, to answer a burglary in progress. You end up with officers down that way. And from what Evon says, this critter had way enough wear on him to know better." Amari, who was seldom reticent with his opinions tucked his chin against his chest and gave Sennett the full measure of his solemn brown eyes. "Face it, Stan. These guys are on her. They've got the Dictaphone tape. And they know that Carmody said he was fooling around with an FBI agent named DeDe, and that's the name on that card."

The weak light of a rainy morning leaked into the conference room through the open blinds. Trying to take this in, Sennett popped his middle finger rhythmically against the small dark 'o' he made of his lips.

Stan had his vision. He was going to round up every corrupt lawyer and judge in the tri-cities. He was going to use all of law enforcement's latest technological gadgets and put together a cinch case on every on of them, dozens, maybe a hundred. He was going to drive them like a herd of branded cattle down Marshall Avenue in the full sight of the world, clopping along with their heads down as they moved on toward Stan's personal slaughterhouse in the federal building. And at the head of this legion of disgrace would be Brendan Tuohey, the guy everybody told Sennett he'd never get. And now he wouldn't. The bad guys were on alert.

Finally, he turned to Evon and asked her what she thought.

"I'd like to stay out there," she answered.

Across the table, McManis's smile was almost sweet.

"We know that, Evon. We all do. But the boss wants your opinion. You were there. Do you think you're burned?"

She might have fooled around with Sennett, but she would never dis McManis. She believed in all the same true blue stuff he did.

"Cremated," she answered.

Even Sennett managed a smile. He got up and walked around the room for quite some time while he weighed the real question. What did they do now? Everyone else hung there in the usual suspense. The beeping and scraping of the traffic down on the avenue wandered up here. Suddenly, Sennett faced them with a vague smile and his head at the same inquisitive angle practiced by most mammals.

"What if we *go* with this?" he asked. "Assume they know she's FBI. We can't afford not to. But what says they realize what she's doing? Maybe Robbie's the guy under the microscope, the one she's investigating." Sennett, hurtling with the momentum of his idea, was happy again. No one else seemed to see what pleased him. "We can get a clean shot at Brendan this way. Robbie thinks he's got an FBI mole in his office. So he goes to Brendan for advice: What should I do? Knowing who she is, Tuohey can't afford not to warn Robbie."

Evon had always felt grudging admiration for this part of Sennett. He was like a screw that kept turning, no matter how impregnable the surface it was supposed to penetrate.

McManis took a minute.

"You want to do this while Evon's still working in Robbie's office?"

"Why not?"

"These guys have too many ways, Stan. They showed us that last night."

"Evon's a big girl," Evon said. Sennett opened a palm in her direction. McManis, who'd heard the line before, made a face, then stole a look at Amari, who also shook his head no. Stan continued pitching. After all the work, all the months, they had to take a shot at Brendan. They had to. And she had to remain in place to give Robbie credibility when he went to Tuohey to ask about what he should do. The fact that she was still here would mean she—and the Bureau—didn't suspect who that copper, Dimonte, had been fronting for, didn't realize she'd been uncovered.

"Stan," said McManis, "these boys don't lack for hormones. There's a real chance they'll make a move."

"All the better," Sennett answered brightly. At moments, it was shocking how little Stan cared whether or not people liked him. His logic was cold-blooded. If Robbie went to Brendan on Monday, and on Tuesday they found some punk snipping Evon's brake lines, it would close the circle, make the case. Jim, the steady master of his emotions, was visibly shocked. His lips parted once or twice before he spoke.

"I don't bait traps with agents. Not if I can avoid it. And neither does UCORC."

"Jim, I can handle this," she said.

His eyes came to her without the slightest movement of his head. She was out of place. He closed the file folder before him and said he needed some time with Stan. Evon and Amari quickly left together.

"Big stuff," said Shirley from behind the red oak receptionist's station. Evon had taken a seat across from her. Plump and reliably cheerful, Shirley, in her real life, had been a state cop somewhere before joining the Bureau. Neither she nor the other UCAs knew exactly what had happened last night, but they all seemed to feel something was up. Klecker came through from the other side of the space.

"¿Qué pasa?" he asked.

Evon shook her head as if she didn't know.

McManis came out in another ten minutes, and pointed her to his office. The Movers had decorated with a minimal concession to his tastes. There were photos of the Blue Ridge Mountains of Virginia on the paneled walls. The supposed mementos of a lifetime were displayed on the office's open shelves. He had a bronzed Letter of Achievement from the Chairman of Moreland Insurance in a brass frame, and a pewter triple block from his bygone sailing days. There was also a signed photograph of Mike Schmidt taken at the Vet in Philly, inscribed to 'Jim.' The autograph was a phony, but McManis had confessed to Evon that his family—the wife and the kids—were in the photo somewhere, probably, she supposed, in the stadium's seats. The only other thing Evon knew about Jim was that he had been an Eagle Scout. Literally. And at least one of his sons was as well. He'd said something about that at a party.

He sat, then thought better of something, and got up to shut the blinds. From now on they were going to assume that Tuohey had a full countersurveillance going. Jim leaned against his desk on her side. She knew before he started that he was pulling her in, and she began talking him out of it before he could find his words.

"Jim, I know what I'm doing."

"It's not your choice."

"You can put the whole surveillance squad on me."

"DeDe—" He hadn't called her that since the day he'd met her in Des Moines. "We *had* surveillance on you. And this creep walked right past them. We're lucky he didn't kill you. The next time they catch hold of you, it'll be guys in ski masks thumping you all night long to find out what we've got."

"Then make sure I've got company. Twenty-four hours. Have Shirley move in with me. And I can pack again now. I'll be safe. Jim, I know what I'm doing."

"No you don't," McManis said, but he was smiling gently again, much as before. With admiration. At moments, she was amazed to realize how much he liked her. He'd liked her from the beginning.

She begged. He had a thousand more objections. About UCORC, and the feasibility of Sennett's plan. But she could see he was wearing down.

"Jim, we all deserve the shot at Tuohey. I do. You do. Sennett does. We can't stop here." She was almost desperate with that thought. How could she just go back to Des Moines? To bank thefts and church choir and thinking about getting a new cat? "I mean, Jim," she said and spoke one of her errant pieces of humor, a joke that was not really a joke at all, "I'm Evon Miller."

JUNE

JUNE

CHAPTER

33

IN THE GRAINY REDUCTION OF THE
black-and-white monitor on which we watched, His Honor
Brendan Tuohey, Presiding Judge of the Kindle County Superior Court's Common Law Claims Division, was mus-
tached with confectioner's sugar when he first came into
view. The picture had careened as Robbie had entered the
restaurant, tossing off morning greetings with characteristic brio to the owner and several members of the staff.
When Feaver had reached Tuohey's table, he had apparently set his briefcase, and the camera within it, on an extra
chair, or perhaps on the next table. Whatever the perch, it
afforded a well-framed picture of the three men he was
joining.

Paddywacks was another venerable Kindle County institution. Its appeal was not in the overripe decor—brass
fixtures and tufted benches, and floors that were mopped
once a week. Rather, it was renowned for its gargantuan
omelets and its early morning clientele, which included
most of the county's important insiders: officeholders, Party

bigwigs—and the ward types and others who relished the opportunity to mingle with them. While Augie Bolcarro was living, he had appeared here at least once a week, and Toots Nuccio, the octogenarian fixer, had a large table in the corner where he kept court every day with his many vassals in politics and the mob. In the world of the Democratic Farmers & Union Party, where working-class values still forbade too much overt splash, one of the truest signs of stature was if the gregarious proprietor, Plato, released the red velvet rope with which he restrained the regular trade and beckoned you to a table at once upon your arrival.

From the surveillance van parked immediately across the avenue from Paddywacks' plate glass doors, Sennett and McManis and I, like *Macbeth*'s witches around their cauldron, watched the black-and-white imagery froth up on the monitor. The guessing game concerning what Tuohey's cohort knew about Evon left everyone uncertain about how they would react to Robbie. He might encounter anything— a beating, the cold shoulder, or some preconceived drama intended to portray their innocence. Amari and several local agents were circulating through the moderate early traffic, on radio silence, but tuned in for emergency direction. Depending on the turns in the conversation, Stan was prepared to respond with surveillance, or even, in his fantasy, a bust.

I had gone to see Robbie on Friday to tell him what would be required today. We sat in the perfect white living room, which had been restored to order for the days of visitation following his mother's death. Robbie remained gripped by that retrospective mood and, with little prompting, his conversation wandered to his childhood memories of Tuohey, which remained intense.

Hungry for men, for their smell, their ways, their company and example, Robbie loved Morty's uncle more, frankly, than Mort seemed to. He was allowed to address him as Uncle Brendan, and despite the fact that Sunday was Robbie's only full day with his mother, he rarely missed one of the afternoon suppers when Tuohey appeared at his sister's table. Brendan was still a cop then. With his gun and his blue patrol uniform, Brendan seemed as auraed and heroic to Robbie as Roy Rogers, and he was greeted with roisterous delight by the boys when he arrived in the entry of the Dinnersteins' home. After supper, he'd let Mort and Robbie gallop around the house wearing his heavy cap with its strip of silver braid along the short brim. Occasionally, he would even unsnap the polished black holster on his hip. He'd empty his service revolver and allow the boys to hold the weapon and inspect the brass-jacketed dumdum rounds, which he stood on end on the dining table, a lethal hollow cut dark and deep into the leaden tip of each bullet.

'Even then,' Robbie told me, 'I was scared of Brendan. You had to be. There was this thing that came off of him, like a smell. You knew he didn't completely like anybody, that he was pretending just a little bit with everyone, except his sister.' The stories he liked to tell were of his rough encounters on the street, shellacking some mouthy blackguard he'd caught up with in a gangway.

Sometimes on Sundays, Estelle also came next door with Robbie for supper. For a period, he said, she actually seemed to have taken some kind of shine to Brendan, and Robbie could even recall a cockeyed childhood hope that Brendan would become his stepfather. But Estelle was a decade older and not really of interest to Brendan, and Robbie's mom, for her part, would have no more considered marriage to a gentile than to an ape. She always came home talking about how much Tuohey and Sheilah drank, expressing a kind of sorrowing wonder that Mort's dad, Arthur Dinnerstein, could put up with it. For Robbie, starstruck by Brendan, these criticisms were incomprehensible.

Eventually, Estelle stopped accompanying her son. Brendan passed the bar, joined the Prosecuting Attorney's Office, and appeared on Sunday in the suit he'd worn to church, rather than his police regalia.

'It was all downhill,' Robbie told me. Something came apart. He wasn't specific, but his eyes froze in the past, pinched for the shortest moment by obvious regret. Then they swung back to me with a lingering dark look.

'So whatta you think, George. Is it just silly chatter when I talk about Brendan having me waxed?'

I didn't think it was silly. There were certain practical incentives. If Robbie's car blew up, if he were run down by a speeding auto, if his remains were found tangled in the limestone crags along the river, Tuohey's cause would be immeasurably advanced, not so much because Robbie would no longer be available as a witness, but because anybody else with thoughts of flipping would be bound to think several times.

But in twenty-five years in practice, I'd had only a single client who'd found turning fatal. John Collegio was an oil executive who'd played ball with the wiseguys as a young man and then, after he'd risen up the phylum, went to the G to complain about the way gasoline was distributed, the mobbed-up companies getting the first supply. He'd been killed with a shotgun blast when he answered his front doorbell at dinnertime. But within the outfit, that would have gone down under the rubric of internal affairs. They seldom took aim at civilians.

All in all, killing a federal witness was recognized as a very poor idea. The FBI did not take it lightly. As a threat to the entire process, it ranked just below killing an agent or a prosecutor or a judge. For that reason, it would bring down heat that would make the effort poured into Petros look restrained. The truth was that if Robbie was going to have a problem, the most likely time was afterwards, in prison. He'd go to one of the federal prison camps—Sandstone or Oxford, or Eglin in Florida—where the inmates played golf and tennis after work. In the old days, before Reagan and Bush had federalized street crimes, that was not really a concern for someone like Robbie. The worst damage another inmate was likely to inflict was to take you badly at cards. But these days there were plenty of thugs in the federal prison camps, dopers who were inside for clean offenses like money-laundering, the only crime the government could prove. Wounded, braggart, futureless boys, they had killed before and gotten away with it and would do it again for a lark and the right price. Robbie would have to do his time in segregation and, even at that, watch his back. But I had always regarded as remote the chance that Brendan would actually orchestrate something on the street now.

Robbie stared out the window, toward his neighbors' vast homes and smooth lawns, trying on my reassurance for size.

'No matter how you slice it, the best thing for me is to bag him. Right? Go in and get him. The whole thing topples.' He had thought this through clearly. Robbie would be safest the day Brendan was indicted and pried away from the levers of power.

Accordingly, Robbie'd had an air of resolve when we'd met today at 5 a.m. to go over the scenario. Then he'd walked by himself to Paddywacks, while we took up our station across the street. He held his shin-length Italian raincoat of a fashionable muddy shade closed at the collar, although the day was not particularly brisk.

Brendan had been easy to find. His morning rituals were unvarying. At 5 a.m., he attended Mass across the way at St. Mary's Cathedral, one of the few men among the elderly female devotees. Then he joined Rollo Kosic and Sig Milacki here at Paddywacks, where Plato customarily opened the doors for them long before the usual gala breakfast crowd had assembled. The three sat at a small round table near the windows, where Brendan, the master of public relations, could throw off a hale salute to the many important citizens approaching the front door. When I turned on my seat in the van, I could see them clearly through the pale whorls of the one-way bubble-window. Milacki chattered. Brendan showed occasional signs of amusement, while Kosic finished his breakfast first, then stared at his cigarette as it burned.

With Robbie's arrival, Tuohey smiled faintly at the mess he had made of himself, surrendering the Bismarck, still swollen with dark jam, to the plate in front of him. Then he tidied himself carefully with his napkin before extending a hand to Robbie. Kosic and Milacki offered greetings and Milacki drew his chair aside to allow Robbie to join them. Instead, mindful of the camera, Robbie moved to the opposite corner. It was a few minutes before six, and in the background two waitresses in their white uniforms stood in the corner of the smoking section, a few feet behind Tuohey's table, gabbing before the morning crush. It was the Tuesday morning following Memorial Day, and despite occasional ringing china and shouts from the kitchen, the restaurant, on the FoxBIte transmission, seemed sweetly still, as the world slowly shook off the slackened tempo of the holiday.

"We were just raising good thoughts about poor Wally," Tuohey said.

Robbie didn't understand.

"Wunsch," said Milacki. "You didn't hear? The Big C."

Walter, it developed, had been diagnosed last week with pancreatic cancer. In the van, Sennett moaned when he heard the news. It was hard to turn a man who had no hope of living.

"Doc gives him six months with the chemo and shit," said Milacki. 'Wally says his wife's already marking off the days on the calendar. Have to hand it to him. Same brick. Guy always looks unhappy and this didn't make it any worse."

The thoughts of mortality turned the conversation to Robbie's mother. Tuohey and Kosic had appeared briefly at Robbie's home the week before last to pay their respects. It was a predictable gesture from Tuohey, who favored ceremonial occasions, but Robbie now unctuously expressed his appreciation.

"Not at all, Robbie. Lit a candle for Mom this morning. Lord's truth. Estelle was a grand lady. I've been thinkin about both of you, son." In the image on the monitor—like a sight seen through a rainstreaked glass—Brendan daintily lifted his hand in Robbie's direction and took the occasion to dispense further advice. Along with Mort's mother, Tuohey had been born in Ireland, emigrating by the time he was five. On occasion, when he spoke, you could still hear the piping echoes of a brogue. "You're in a tough patch now, Robbie. We know that. With Mom, and Rainey in such a difficult way. You have to keep your faith, though. I can still remember the day I lost my Mame like it was yesterday. The best consolation is prayer." With a long gnarly finger, Brendan pointed his way.

Milacki, voluble in his appreciation of Brendan's many pieties, uttered Amen. Robbie in the meantime saw his opening.

"Shit, Judge, I'm praying, but not how you mean." His chair scraped the floor as he came closer and hunkered over the table. Like a bungled tape delay, the image ran some milliseconds ahead of Robbie's bare whisper as he told them about Evon. Sennett had wanted Feaver to try to get Tuohey alone, but Robbie said Brendan would be far more relaxed in the secure presence of his henchmen. Leaning in, Robbie had cut off a bit of the camera's angle and I turned back to the bubble, where I found the sight through the front window of four heads gathered in such plain conspiracy almost amusing. Life, generally so subtle in its textures, is disarmingly blatant now and then. Barely a foot separated the crowns—Brendan's tidy gray head, Milacki's greasy do, Rollo even now touching his thinning hair to keep it in place—each trained on Robbie as the story grew more dire.

He described what Walter had said about Carmody. The girl had laughed it off and he had consequently dismissed it. But it ate at him, Robbie said, and the following week, treating it as a dare, he'd asked her to let his secretary look her over in the john for a wire. She'd refused, then agreed the next day, when the secretary, predictably, found nothing. But the paralegal was getting buggy. She'd been burglarized last week and came to the office on Friday positively frantic. She'd spent nearly an hour searching her cubicle, asking her coworkers if they'd seen some Dictaphone tapes. The problem, Feaver said, was that no one in the office had ever used a Dictaphone—their system required different cassettes. What was she doing with her own tape recorder?

"I mean, Jesus, do FBI agents look like that?" he asked. "Hell, this babe was crawling around in the sack with me."

"That means she's G for sure," Milacki whispered. Everyone at the table laughed, even Kosic. It had sounded like a joke at Robbie's expense, particularly considering the source. A robust, big-bellied man, a plainclothes copper from central casting, Milacki always had a good time. He wore an old-fashioned hairdo, with slicked-back sides in which the comb tracks were grooved precisely in the Vaseline.

Milacki had been Brendan's partner during his brief time on the street. Tuohey had not remained a patrol officer for very long, but like all old soldiers, he maintained a permanent nostalgia for his period of fortitude and courage, and he carried Milacki with him as an enduring emblem. At this point, Robbie had said, he felt he had heard an account of virtually every day they'd had riding in Squad 4221. During Tuohey's years in the Felony Division, Milacki had been detailed by the Force to run the Warrant Office, losing the arrest warrants that Brendan wanted destroyed, usually for the benefit of his mobbed-up pals. In one of those mysterious arrangements that no one outside the Police Force could ever be made to understand, when Tuohey had moved to Common Law Claims, Milacki had gone with him. He remained a cop so he could qualify for his pension, but he was now assigned directly to the Presiding Judge's chambers as the police liaison to the sheriff's deputies in the courthouse. In reality, he did Brendan's bidding, everything from squiring him about in a black Buick owned by the Force to fielding calls like the ones Robbie made from time to time, aimed at denoting certain cases as 'specials.'

Milacki now insisted he wasn't kidding. He claimed to have heard lots of tales. It was a favored stunt of feds undercover, especially the females, to sleep with the suspects in order to establish themselves. Of course, they denied it on the stand. It was like the coppers who posed as johns and said they'd announced their office before the blow job instead of after. The four men laughed about that as well.

Robbie, in time, again asked what he should do.

"Fire her," said Milacki. Both Tuohey and Kosic sat stonily, as though Milacki hadn't made the remark. Looking at the tape later, I had the strong impression that Milacki knew less about Evon than the other two. Robbie, as always, held to his role, and doe-ishly turned to Tuohey to confirm Milacki's advice.

"If you have an employee you don't trust, it's probably sensible to consider firing her." The mildest shrug elevated Brendan's slender shoulders, The thought was hardly revolutionary.

"But does it look like I'm guilty, if I fire her? I mean, she knows I'm hinky because I talked to her after Walter. I mean, I keep wondering. Is there something I can do to throw her off the track?"

Tuohey was long and narrow, with a thin but agreeable face. With Robbie's last remark, he retreated somewhat. The tidy gray head came up and on the monitor you could see him appraising Feaver.

"These are questions, Robbie, I think you'd best ask yourself"

"Well, I thought you'd be concerned."

"Do *I* look concerned? A man shouldn't wear his troubles on his sleeve, Robbie."

"Well, Judge, you and I have never talked about things—"

"And we shouldn't be starting now." Tuohey took a measure and popped out a short exasperated laugh. "Robbie, you're past the age where I can be looking after the two of you every moment. I can't call the precinct house the way I did when you and Morton were fourteen and nicking lewd magazines."

"Well, this isn't about naked ladies, Brendan. You know that."

"I do? No such thing. How would I know that, Robbie? I don't keep track of your doings. I can't. You appear in my court. You understand how I must behave. If you've done something that scares you"—*skeers you*—"then I'm sorry, Robbie, but I'm a judge, not a father confessor. You start telling me your sins, I've got no choice but to turn you in, and Lord knows, neither of us would care to see that." Tuohey sat straight in his chair now, delivering his brief monologue with appropriate gravity.

"He's hosing him," Sennett said with anguish behind me. But it was a better performance than mere denial. Brendan was a master, the kind of man who did not say good morning to you with only one thing in mind. Ulterior purpose clung to every remark as if it had been greased, and he was actually letting Robbie down easy with this speech, explaining his position.

"He's got to go for it," Sennett demanded. "Right now. Lay it right there. Come on, Robbie. 'What do you mean you don't know what I'm doing?' "

But it did Stan as much good to coach the screen as any armchair fan. When Robbie repeated Tuohey's first name, the judge refused him with a stern rattle of his narrow face. He would hear no more. Milacki and Kosic, who had hung back, certain Tuohey would know best, now inserted themselves. Milacki actually raised a tempering finger in Robbie's direction. In the silence, Brendan Tuohey looked down and brushed some more of the confectioner's sugar from the lapels of his straitlaced suit.

"Robbie, it sounds to me like you should get yourself an attorney," he said. "Get an experienced federal man. You might want his advice."

"What am I going to tell an attorney, Brendan? What do you want me to say to him?"

Sennett had anticipated Tuohey and had fed Robbie that line word for word, but Brendan was nimble.

"Tell him what you like, Robbie. Tell him what he needs to know."

"Jesus Christ, Brendan, don't you understand? She's seen a lot of stuff."

A brief, derisive sound ripped not from Tuohey but from Kosic. Rollo gave Robbie a deprecating glance through one eye and took the trouble now to stub out a cigarette. There was no further response out of any of them.

"Judge, you don't get it. It's not me I'm really worried about. It's Mort. Somebody looking at things could get ideas about him."

Mentioning Mort had not been part of the script. It invited considerable difficulties if Tuohey decided to talk to his nephew. But like most of Robbie's vamping it was clever and effective. The Presiding Judge was finally caught short.

"Morton?" he asked.

"You know him. Captain Oblivious. There were a couple of things—I mean, I don't even want to talk to him about this shit. I haven't said a word yet—"

"A good thought, Robbie."

"But Judge, there was a thing with Sherm—"

"No!" said Tuohey suddenly. The rebuke, though not above a whisper, was delivered in the severe tone of a schoolmarm. "No, Robbie. I can't be hearing this. You have to talk to your attorney. That's how this must proceed. Have you someone in mind?"

"Well, Jesus, no, I mean, I wanted to talk to you—"

"Give it some thought, Robbie. This deserves careful thought."

With Tuohey's full attention upon him, Robbie spun through a series of baffled gestures. Finally, as if it was almost plucked from the air, Feaver mentioned my name as a neighbor in the LeSueur Building and an attorney who referred cases to their office. Tuohey lowered his face a bit, almost to the line of the camera, as he dutifully reflected.

"Wonderful lawyer. Saw quite a bit of him when he was Bar President a few years ago."

McManis, beside me, had taken in the unfolding scene with his customary mute resolve. He'd leaned toward the monitor motionlessly, except as things grew particularly tense, when he allowed himself to circle his thumbs. But now he looked over his shoulder, giving altitude to one eyebrow and displaying the lump his tongue made in his cheek, so that I actually felt a bit sheepish. Tuohey's claim of close association with me was mostly blarney. I'd seen him twice in connection with an initiative he'd suggested on mediation. Visiting Brendan's capacious chambers in the Temple, I always found myself thinking about the term 'apartments' as in papal or royal—so many little rooms, so many county employees of such brisk cheer nearby, all of them with unfaltering reverence for the man they referred to as 'the Presiding.' The outer offices were thick with relics of his rule: photos of Tuohey and various Some-bodies; gavels and plaques and framed mementos. The inner chamber, though, where Tuohey worked, was spare, the bookcase decorated only with a scale of justice and a re-alistic portrait of Jesus laying on hands. Given his culti-vated political sense, Tuohey knew that to favor one—anyone—was to exclude others.

"Very careful. Lawyer's lawyer," Brendan now said of me. "But in these circumstances—" Brendan gripped his chin thoughtfully, before delivering the judgment he'd in-tended to render all along. "I don't really think he's the choice I would make."

"Really?" Leaning on an elbow, Robbie looked up at Brendan obediently.

"Stan Sennett's best man." From Feaver's minute jolt, I suspected I'd glossed over this detail. I was amazed at the nuggets Tuohey had laid away. "Second marriage he stood up for him, if I'm not mistaken. Very touchy, be-cause that's the kind of thing that could be helpful, you know. But overall, I'd say too close for comfort."

McManis let his eye roam toward me with one more sidewise ironic twinkle, but I felt lanced by Tuohey's observation. Too close for comfort, I thought. I was entirely powerless to look at Stan, although I doubted he would focus for the present on much besides the artful manner in which Tuohey was dancing further and further away.

"Suit yourself, of course," said Tuohey. "You can never tell. But were I you, I'd be more inclined to someone who's known to give the government no quarter. Do you know Mel Tooley at all? Solid as an oak, Mel. Ask around about him, I suspect you'll like what you hear. Mel in fact was famous for never flipping a client. "If you talk to Mel, he might even want to come by to see me."

With that, Brendan allowed the chromed legs of his chair to ring as he pushed away from the table. The meeting was over. Tuohey sat erect and proud. He knew he'd handled himself with customary deftness, tiptoeing down the chalk lines with the delicacy of Nijinsky. From his feet, with Milacki and Kosic beside him, Brendan laid his dry hand on Robbie's coat collar and delivered one more perfect line.

"I don't feel concerned, Robbie. Not a bit. You're the kind of fellow who can stay the course in hard times." Tuohey reaffirmed that supposed compliment with a solid nod and turned, his two retainers on his heels. Across from me, Sennett began groaning again as soon as Tuohey started moving away. Stan ran his hands over his hair. He rarely allowed emotions to affect his grooming.

"Ugh! What a wienie performance! He should have gone for it. He *had* him."

I started to defend my client, but McManis uncharacteristically interrupted. Jim had given his usual dry eye to Stan's outburst. He allowed his tousled head a single shake.

"Stan, I don't think he was ever close. These guys are in no-man's-land. They know about Evon, but they're not sure about Robbie. They don't want to cut him loose and **give him** a reason to turn on them, but they're gonna be way careful."

The van had left the curb. Another undercover agent, Tex Clevenger, a lean six-footer in his late twenties who posed as McManis's messenger, was at the wheel today so Joe could run his crews from the street. Tex asked if there were instructions for Amari, but Stan, still dying a thousand deaths, ignored him.

"There's a way," he told Jim. He raised a fist, the knuckles white. "There *is* a way."

CHAPTER

34

THEY DID NOT COME FOR HER. NOT THAT
Evon expected it. She never felt in danger. Shirley and she
drove to the office each morning with a cordon of surveillance cars whipping past them. Within a week, both of
them knew all the OGVs, official government vehicles, or
CARs, as human beings put it. While Evon was at work,
a local agent was sitting in the dark in her apartment, using
a flashlight to read magazines. Nothing happened.

McManis finally let her have a gun. There was no point
in sitting there unarmed while she was waiting for the bogeyman. The only weapon he could get her on short notice was one of the S&W 10 millimeters that nobody in
his right mind really wanted. Typical D.C., good idea gone
wrong. After the death of three agents in a shootout in
Miami, the thinking types wanted eleven-inch penetration,
lighter ammo, fast expansion. Smith & Wesson made the
gun to spec, but the thing was the size of a cannon—she'd
need a beach bag, not a purse, to hide it—and the handle

was bad. At home she had an S&W 5904, high-capacity double-action semiautomatic, 9 mm. That was a weapon.

At McManis's urging, she'd spent the Memorial Day weekend following the break-in in Des Moines. She'd wanted to go to Denver to see her sister, but Merrel and Roy and the kids were at their new condo in Vail, fly-fishing, and given the difficulty of booking flights over the holiday weekend, Evon would not have gotten there for much more than twenty-four hours. Instead, she turned the key on the life of DeDe Kurzweil. The house she rented was dark and had a close, unpleasant odor. The mice, she suspected, had had a field day, but the smell was more like what you'd expect in the home of an elderly person locked up with a dog. She made some calls and went to a barbecue with Sal Harney, another agent, who'd used her car while she was gone. Before he drove her home, she made him open up the safe at the resident agency office and she removed her 5904. Sunday, after church, she went to a civilian range and shot for an hour. The proprietor and a couple of his greasy-looking flunkies were watching by the time she was done. She kept the pistol in her purse now, storing it at McManis's when she ran over to the Temple with various filings she was doing for Mort.

Matronly, good-humored, Shirley slept on the sofa. At night, she talked to Evon about her kids and drank a little too much. Shirley wore a white terry-cloth robe that wrapped around her tight as the dressing on a wound, with long hairy fibers dancing down from each sleeve. She had three children, two married; the last, a girl, a junior in college, was thinking about the Secret Service.

Robbie was seldom in the office now. The excuse imagined only a month before, that Rainey's decline would require his full attention, had, like some ill-omened wish, come true. Alf felt there was no way to ensure secure conversations over the phone equipment in Feaver's home, and so twice a day, in the guise of transporting work from the office, Evon appeared there to ferry messages back and forth from McManis. Robbie's capacities for buoyant denial seemed to have failed him entirely in the wake of his mother's death. Often when Evon arrived, she was startled to see that he had not bothered to shave. He explained himself succinctly one morning. "No matter how much you tell yourself you know what's coming," he said, "you don't."

Once a day, Evon went upstairs to greet Rainey. She was weakening quickly. The routine functions of life commanded all her energies. After a meal, she would sleep for at least an hour. Toileting, dressing, massage were exhausting and, as a result, she seldom had the energy to maintain her focus through much of a conversation, except with Robbie. The cuirass, which looked a great deal like a bowl-style vacuum cleaner, was fixed over her chest to aid her breathing in, but it tethered her to the bed. The equipment hissed away with an unnerving sound like a child sucking too hard through a straw. Worse, the doctor had said that Lorraine's carbon dioxide levels made it likely that within the next two weeks she would have to decide on ventilation. The alternative was descent into ALS's final phase, a slow, desperate suffocation. Robbie was sparing with the details, but his demeanor suggested he was losing in his effort to persuade Rainey to go on.

ON TUESDAY, JUNE 8, I chaired the annual fund-raising luncheon of the Kindle County Bar Foundation, an organization I'd started during my term as Bar President. At moments, I wondered if I'd just wanted to leave a small monument to myself—so much of what is supposed to be charity has always been the refuge of ego. On the board, I was often wearied by the frequently politicized squabbles over which of many underfunded legal projects should be stinted. Yet I signed on every year. Doing less good than you'd want doesn't mean you're doing no good at all.

For the event, judges and public officials were 'comped,' as they say in the fund-raising trade, and seated, one for each table, with paying guests, so we could peddle elbow-rubbing and access in the name of charity. By this and other shameless devices, we had managed to gather nearly five hundred people in the enormous Grand Ballroom of the Hotel Gresham. The room was an antique, a Gilded Age leftover. Its gilt-ribbed pilasters and wedding-cake ceiling leafed in gold almost mocked the poverty of the people intended to benefit from the event, who were brought to mind only in the obligatory mid-meal video.

Our keynote address this year came from Supreme Court Justice Manuel Escobedo, who was funny for five minutes before he sank like a weary traveler into the valley of his prepared text. Like most former courtroom lawyers, he was reluctant to leave the podium once he had returned there, and it was nearly 2 p.m. by the time the justice had finished. A dark-suited phalanx, eager to pound the phones and the word processors to pay for lunch, rushed between the majestic marble columns at the back of the ballroom even before the applause had died. Elsewhere, in smaller circles, some of the routine grip and grin that had gone on before the meal was briefly resumed, lawyers passing quick shots and greetings amid the gilt-armed fauteuils turned at all angles by the hasty departures.

I hopped down the stairs of the rickety risers erected to form the dais and cast a parting wave to Cal Taft, this year's Bar President, who mouthed a word of praise for a successful event. When I turned, Brendan Tuohey was directly behind me in the space between tables. He was having a word with a couple of men I did not know, but his eyes crept my way once or twice, so I knew he'd noticed me.

"George!" he cried when he was free. He grabbed my right hand and layered the left over it to add a special measure of sincerity. He said it was grand to see me. "You fellows always do such a marvelous job with this affair. And it's such a fine thing for the bar. It's the Lord's work you folks are doing, George, it makes all of us proud."

I'm afraid my doubts may have reached my expression.

"No, no. Who was it who was talking about you, George, just the other day, as if you had wings comin out of your shoulder blades? Lawyer, I think, sayin such nice things I'd half a mind to blush on your behalf. Who was it?" Tuohey was a formerly handsome man, with regular features. In age, a wizened, pinched look had enshrouded his light eyes, and whiskey or time had been harsh with his skin. There were large rosy patches, feathered with veins, on his cheeks, and when he gestured, the backs of his hands resembled fallen leaves. "Robbie Feaver!" Tuohey shouted and gave his long, dry fingers an impressive snap that sent a shudder southward from my solar plexus.

Robbie, I said, yes, Robbie.

"Thinks you're a wonder, George."

I joked that I should probably ask for more than a third of the fee the next time I sent Feaver a case.

Hail-fellow-well-met, Tuohey allowed a moment of contained laughter. Behind us, the busboys and waiters were already breaking the room down, snatching off the stiff linens to reveal the plywood circles with folding legs that lay beneath. There always seemed a fine irony in the disclosure that everyone had paid $100 a plate to dine on wormy lumber.

"Terrible burden that boy is carrying," Tuohey advised me, growing somber. "Well, 'boy,' now listen to me. But I've known him all his life. A grown man many years, but that's how I think of him. Partners with my nephew, did you know that? I take an avuncular interest. Concerned about him, naturally. I worry that all of it—" Tuohey folded his lips before resuming. "He seemed a bit, I'd say, irregular when I bumped into him last Tuesday. Have you seen him since? Does he appear all right to you?"

I was no match for Brendan. I'd been bred to a reserve that if nothing else generally left me time to think, but I didn't have Tuohey's speed or his guile. His probes, placed with the delicacy of acupuncture needles, could intrude barely noticed. What was coming to me through a process of plodding calculation was known to Tuohey largely by instinct, but I finally realized he was at my side because he'd heard nothing from Mel Tooley.

Mel was a former Assistant United States Attorney, who had gone from being one of Stan's darlings to, more recently, a Satanic outcast. Once he'd left the government, the appetites of private practice had led Mel to begin defending many of the same made members of the Mafia he'd formerly investigated. There had been outrage in the U.S. Attorney's Office and protracted battles, which the government lost, aimed at throwing Mel off the cases. Stan had entertained thoughts of sending Robbie, attired in his sound-wired boots, to visit Mel, as Tuohey had suggested. UCORC, however, found there was no hard evidence of a potential crime and declined to authorize a recording. Stalemated, Sennett had figured that silence might drive Tuohey or his minions to recontact Robbie on their own. Instead, Brendan had clearly concluded that, despite his discouragement, Robbie was seeking legal advice from me.

Tuohey's glance swept over me like a searchlight. I did not know if it was my weakness or my honor that Brendan meant to exploit, but he was sure I would never mislead him, whether as a matter of highminded rectitude or out of knee-knocking reluctance to offend the mighty. Appropriate lawyerly conduct was to let Brendan's lingering question pass with no comment, but I knew that, given his suspicions of me, he would feel he could no longer count on Robbie.

And so in this grand old ballroom, with its velvet-backed chairs and huge mirrors veined in gold, I swung like a spider caught in descent on its own web. I should have moved off with the myth of the waiting conference call, and let Stan clean up the resulting mess. But I stood my ground. I was driven by too many motives to know which was dominant—commitment to my client was part of it; so was what Sennett, with his craft, had long counted on, namely, my anger and disdain over Brendan's private appropriation of the power of the law. Whatever, as I'd always suspected, I was thrilled to tempt the fates. Well knowing where the line lay that I'd long drawn for myself, I marched across it, committed to making the man who in all likelihood would soon run all the Kindle County courts an enemy for life.

I gave Tuohey a look as grave and level as I could muster and said that Robbie Feaver was a tough guy and not the kind to share his woes. He did not understand why anybody would want to make trouble for him, but he was a stoic and would take the weight of whatever came his way.

From the withered depths that gave his light eyes an aspect of privacy, Tuohey's look remained on me as he evaluated the message.

"Ah," said Brendan slowly. "So he's okay?"

I was sure of that, I said with no wavering.

"And you'll let me know if there's any change? I want to help however I can."

Departing, Tuohey shook again with a fierce two-handed grip, pleased with me and himself and my assurance that Robbie was a stand-up guy. He'd given another bravura performance, finding out what he needed without admitting a thing. His remark that Robbie'd seemed 'irregular' might even have loosed a weevil of doubt about the reliability of anything Robbie had let slip to me, although I'd done my best to convey the impression that Feaver had told me nothing.

"You didn't have to do that, George," Robbie said, when I shared the details of my encounter with Brendan. We sat in the parking lot of a McDonald's near his home where I'd stopped on my way from the office that evening. Together we watched the young moms coping with the anguish of dinnertime. Robbie was sharp to the nuances of practice and knew the burden I was taking on if Tuohey escaped.

I reassured him that I'd chosen to do it. But I had one request.

"Anything," he answered.

Let's not tell Sennett, I said.

CHAPTER 35

ON FRIDAY AT NOON, EVON MADE A TRIP to Feaver's, carrying an urgent message. She found him in no state for visitors. He answered the door in tears. Like a child, he wiped his eyes on the sleeve of his polo shirt as she stepped into the marble foyer. Her first thought was to leave, but he took hold of her wrist, clearly craving company.

"We were talking," he said. "About kids. I mean, you understand." His black eyes briefly rose to her as if the look alone betrayed a secret. And it did. Evon, for once, immediately made the connection. Rainey must have indicated that she did not have the same reasons to continue her life she might have if she were a mother.

"I mean, you know—regrets?" he asked. "Millions. But that's number one. Kids." They were on the long white sofa in the living room where Robbie had first faced the IRS agents last fall. She had no place to ask for details, but Robbie, as ever, spoke.

"It was always an issue. I was for kids. I mean, I was afraid of fucking up like my father, but, you know, I wanted the chance to do better. But Lorraine, with that screwy upbringing of hers? It became kind of a *mañana* thing. She had her job, and wow, she made big money. And then, you know, I was trouble. I made trouble. She was always with one foot out the door, and I'd say I'd mend my ways, and I didn't. And then, to teach me a lesson, she did some stuff. But when we got the news, whatever it was, three years ago, I was like, No, wait one minute, we were just about to get this right. I think we would have. I do. Every New Year's, for maybe five years, it was my last loopy thought right before I crashed through into sleep: This year we're pregnant.

"Before she got diagnosed we were talking about it more. We even named this kid we didn't have. I mean, goofy names. Sparky. Flipper. We'd toss around funny things the kid would do. Don't get pizza with olives, she won't eat olives. It was always a girl, I don't know why. And somehow we got to doing that just now." He'd been staring straight into the high pile of the white carpet, but, unexpectedly, a comic thought came to relieve him, impelling a brief laugh.

"We got a great name today. I said, I want a nice Jewish name. We'd just finished this book she really liked, so she looks over there and says, 'Nancy Taylor Rosenberg' So that's who we were going on about, Nancy Taylor Rosenberg. Nancy Taylor Rosenberg needs sunglasses for her big blue eyes. Nancy Taylor Rosenberg has an outie like her mother. Every screwy thing. Nancy Taylor Rosenberg loves chocolate cake and has terrible allergies. We really got rolling. We were both bawling our eyes out, but we kept going for twenty minutes. So," he said in abrupt conclusion and slapped his thighs. "What's up?"

She eyed him, not sure he was ready for business, but he indicated she should proceed. Sig Milacki had called this morning and wanted Robbie to phone. The next move was at hand.

"Sig," he said and considered the message slip. She'd brought the phone trap. The device used to record the call was a tiny earpiece, the size of a good hearing aid. The earplug was miked to pick up both the signal from the telephone handset and Robbie's voice, which was transmitted through the bones of his skull. The lead ran to a portable tape recorder she'd brought in her briefcase. Alf had wanted to do this himself, but, as always now, the fear was he might be tailed.

Listening in on an extension, Evon could hear Milacki approach the phone from a distance, assailing his underlings with gruff wisecracks.

"Feaver!" He proceeded with his standard banter, jibes about attorneys. His daughter, Milacki said, had now finished her first semester in law school. "I'm watching her real careful," he confided, "to see just when it is she grows the second face."

"Fuck you, Sig."

"Be the best piece of ass you ever had." Milacki exploded in raw laughter. He loved that line and repeated it several times. Finally he explained himself. "Sort of wanted to catch a look at your ugly mug. Thought maybe we could have a soda pop. Six okay at that yuppie-duppie joint of yours with the six-dollar brewskis?"

Robbie tried to get a hint what the meeting was about, but Milacki roared as if Robbie had told another joke, and with no more ended the call.

AT FIVE AFTER six, Robbie strolled into Attitude, as he had on many another Friday night. Perhaps it was the familiar atmosphere or his acting skills, but he looked far better than he had in days. He was in an Italian sharkskin suit, his big hair blown dry, his cologne, as always, redolent for yards around.

For Klecker, getting a decent recording amid the shattering ambient noise of a Friday night crowd presented a technician's nightmare. To deal with that, Alf had wired three of Amari's surveillance team members with directional mikes in the hope they could work their way close to Robbie and capture better sound. To augment the problematic audio, both Klecker and Sennett wanted cameras. The jostling in the hurly-burly of the bar made a stable picture unlikely, and in the meeting at McManis's beforehand, Feaver had claimed that he'd dislocate a shoulder if he had to stand there holding the ponderous briefcase-camera for an hour. Ultimately, Klecker had dispatched another member of the surveillance squad with that unit, instructing her to take a table on the loft level where she'd get a good wide-angle image of the entire scene. A second camera was manned downstairs by three agents of Asian descent, two Japanese and one Korean, whom Amari had requisitioned on short notice. The three men were in the middle of the barroom floor. In another of Klecker's inspirations, they played the role of happy tourists, passing what looked to be a video camera back and forth among themselves, as they endeavored to record every moment. Only one of the agents spoke any foreign language, but he crowed at volume and the other two laughed and bowed in a vigorous parody of American expectations.

To conserve the batteries, none of the cameras were switched on until Robbie entered the bar. In the van there was the inevitable Zantac moment waiting to see if the equipment would function. The space here in the rear was extremely confined tonight. It now looked like a TV studio. Klecker had added two video monitors and three additional sound receivers to the pyramided equipment. Tex Clevenger, trained in the Army as a sound tech, worked with Alf, helping spin the dials. Sennett, McManis, and I did not have room to spread our elbows.

In front, Shirley drove. Evon was beside her in the passenger seat. Like the rest of us, she'd been provided with headphones, but she listened through only one side, the other ear being already equipped with the infrared receiver hidden under her hair. Robbie's assignment tonight was direct: try somehow to get another meeting with Brendan. In order to dramatize Feaver's desperate need for further advice from Tuohey, Sennett and McManis had worked out a scenario around Evon. Executing this plan depended on how long Robbie remained inside and what Milacki wanted. On that score, there was still no clue.

From the audio output alone, it was clear Attitude was rocking. The crowd, packed tight from the door, was full of libertine energy. They'd survived another week, had taken the punch, and were ready to make the most of it. Alf flipped between the radio channels sampling the sound, almost all of it a waterfall of unintelligible chatter, while the tape decks turned. One of the miked agents had already i.d.'d Milacki and was drinking next to him. A second had followed Robbie through the door.

A woman whom Robbie knew, a legal secretary who once had worked at Feaver & Dinnerstein, pushed up to greet him as soon as he cleared the tall glass doors. Carla. We could see her on the output from the video cam with which the three agents were posing. She was smoking a cigarette and barely remembered to remove it before kissing Feaver on the lips. She was conventionally pretty, near Robbie's age. She clutched Robbie's arm above the elbow as she asked him about Mort and shared stories of her two sons, both now in the Marines. Her straight blond hair, heavily sprayed and treated, divided like a stream around the rock of her shoulders. She licked the ends absentmindedly as they spoke.

"I'll see you, hon," Robbie said eventually. "I gotta get with a guy."

"That's how it is anymore. Everybody's always running. I'm over by the window by Rick and Kitty."

He blew her a noncommittal kiss and worked his way toward Milacki, who was in the second row of standees near the bar. He had one finger in his ear as he yelled into his cell phone, apparently reaming out somebody who worked for him. When Robbie arrived, Sig pointed at the phone and mouthed an insult about the person on the other end.

In the van, Alf signaled, instructing us to switch our headphones to channel three. The mike in the briefcase of the surveillance agent who was beside Milacki funneled far clearer sound than Robbie's FoxBIte.

"Say, listen," Milacki said, and caught Robbie by the arm, after they had said hello. "We just had a thing at the courthouse. I swear to God, I nearly soiled my skivvies. One of these macaronis with the aluminum-foil hairdo, you know, so they don't get too many of them weirdball radio signals from outer space, one of these wackheads goes right through the metal detector. Holy Tamoli, we got bells and lights like a pinball machine. So the boys pull him over to the wall to frisk him. Here," said Milacki to Robbie, "here, pick up your arms. I gotta show you this."

On the second monitor, we could see Milacki spread his hands, ready to pat Robbie down.

"Oh shit," said McManis. He tried to stand up, forgetting his seat belt, and was jolted back. After popping it free, he crowded closer to the monitor. There was no mistaking Robbie's hesitation either. After a second, McManis pushed Evon's shoulder and told her to get in there. She looked into the side-view to be certain she was clear and jumped out in a rush.

"Whatsa matter?" we heard Milacki ask. "Ticklish?"

"Very."

"Come on, Roberta. I won't pinch. This is a scream." He hitched his head, and still appeared to be smiling. Even in black-and-white, you could see he had high color and a beautiful widow's peak. Years ago, he'd been a dirty blond but his oiled hair was now mostly gray.

Robbie raised his arms vaguely, like a suspect unsure about giving up.

"I paid two grand at Zegna for this suit, Milacki. I oughta make you wash your hands."

"Right, it's very pretty. So they go like this"—he frisked Robbie, starting from the boot tops, while he maintained his patter—"and so help me God, the jamoke has a three-foot salami in there, wrapped in tinfoil." He reached right into Robbie's jacket at that point to feel under the arm. "Can you imagine? We were all laughing so hard, I thought somebody'd bust an artery."

In the van, not a breath was taken in the interval.

"Where is it?" Sennett asked quietly.

Evon had initiated today, but McManis said that since acquiring his new footwear Robbie had made a habit of placing the FoxBIte in a holster in his boot.

"Could he miss the lead?" Sennett asked.

It was taped along Robbie's inseam, McManis said, so it was possible. Indeed, Milacki so far had not dropped a beat. He put his arm on Robbie's shoulder, then patted him up and down the back as he racked with laughter. Robbie, onstage again, showed no further sign of flinching, even when Milacki gave him a cheerful clap on the butt.

Sensing he'd passed, Robbie, as he explained afterwards, figured the only credible reaction was outrage. He grabbed his suit coat by the lapels to settle it on his shoulders and pointed at the cop.

"Why didn't you just bring the fucking metal detector, Sig?"

Milacki didn't bother with pretense. "Better safe than sorry, bunky. Times we live in. Your lady friend's made everybody a little jumpy, maybe it rubs off on you. Couple folks been worrying about you, anyway. Said you seemed a little frayed around the collar." Crowthers and Walter, probably. This wasn't good news, either.

Robbie kept up his front. "Is that right?"

"Yeah, there's talk. It's like what Minnie Mouse told the judge when she asked to divorce Mickey? You heard that? She said she had to get out because he's been fucking Goofy." Milacki, taller than Robbie, could see he was getting nowhere with the efforts at humor, but he pounded Feaver's shoulder anyway as he roared.

"I got a lot at home, Sig."

"Hey, fuck, who loves you, baby?" Milacki took his large ruddy hand and jerked Robbie by the neck, as if trying to shake him into a better mood. "Fellow down the bar would like to see you."

In the van, McManis tapped his heart. In the meanwhile, Sennett leaned toward the top monitor, which displayed a panorama of the entire establishment. Bulling through the happy throng, Robbie seemed to know where he was going.

"Tuohey," Stan whispered. "Make it Tuohey."

"Kosic," Alf said and stood for just a second to touch the top screen. Rollo again was at the extreme end of the bar under the white piano. One of the surveillance agents who'd been tailing Kosic for weeks had spotted him before and turned out to be on the stool beside him. The pianist, a different one than last time, was accompanying himself, crooning in the style of Tony Bennett, and the music piped up loudly on every channel. Alf spun his dials to little avail and griped, saying what everybody knew: these guys were smart.

The trio of Asian agents had apparently kept pace with Robbie crossing the room, as a clear image of Kosic suddenly came into focus on the bottom monitor. Rollo was on his third old-fashioned by now. The glasses were lined up on the bar in front of him, the other two empty except for the maraschino cherries whose stems looked like hands waving for rescue as they sank between the melting cubes. When Feaver arrived and greeted Kosic, the surveillance agent seated beside Rollo abruptly picked up his drink, allowing Feaver to slide onto the brushed-steel stool. Feaver's initial words to Rollo were largely lost by the time the applause died down after "Three Coins in the Fountain," but Robbie could be seen addressing Kosic, looking forward to the mirror in a dead-eyed, humorless fashion. When his voice came through again he was talking indignantly about his encounter with Milacki.

"Yeah, we just had a touchy-feely, Sig and I. The wrong kind. I had the impression he sort of expected my balls to go beep."

Kosic, much as last time, showed no reaction. Dressed in a golf windbreaker, he lifted his hand toward Lutese, the index finger crooked to hide the bad nail as he signaled for another drink. Then he removed a pen from his jacket pocket and began doodling on a cocktail napkin, while Robbie went on.

"You know, I respect you, Rollo. Mama brought me up right. And maybe, okay, maybe my trolley's a little off the tracks these days. I don't need anybody's shoulder, but I got a load now. But I gotta tell you, after all the beer that's flowed from the brewery, I don't think I deserve to be treated like somebody nobody knows." As if he half expected to be poisoned, Kosic raptly watched Lutese shake the bottle of bitters over the new glass and drop in another cherry. "You tell Brendan I said that."

Kosic, who had started to reach for the drink, flinched, reacting as a religious conservative might if Feaver had said 'Jehovah.'

Lutese, who'd remained for Robbie's order, had cut off all her hair. Her dark scalp was gristled with the sandpapery nubbins the clippers had left behind. "Kind of radical," she acknowledged. If anything, she was more striking, nearly six feet, with cascading earrings that looked like the crystals from a chandelier.

Kosic was taking in the usual byplay between Robbie and the bartender when he suddenly turned toward the room. Beneath his chin, where he showed most of his age in the stringy grayish wattles that hung there, his Adam's apple bobbed several times and he finally knocked his elbow on Feaver's.

Evon was three or four feet behind them, holding a glass and yukking it up with the agent who'd just vacated the barstool.

"Oh shit," Robbie said when he faced back. "Figures. She's busting my balls. Hell hath no fury. She's sky-high cause I gave her two weeks' notice."

Kosic spoke for the first time. "Two weeks?"

"Sure. Like I said, I want it to look normal. I told her I'm ramping down cause of Rainey. But she's not going gently. She's breaking real bad on me in the office. And following me around half the time when I leave. I can feel a lawsuit coming on," said Robbie, "the way Grandpa felt bad weather in his lumbago."

Kosic watched Evon in the mirror, his look as unfeeling as some cats', then broke off and returned to his doodle. Now that she'd been noticed in accord with the plan, Evon drifted off to a safer distance, while Robbie continued speaking about his problems with her.

"I mean, Rollo, I'm asking myself, What the fuck am I doing? You know. Maybe it's not that way and I'm turning her into an enemy. Maybe I'm shooting myself in the foot letting her go. Could be the uncle was wrong when he said to fire her. I'd like to go over it with him again.

Explain. I don't wanna piss him off, but maybe we should be thinking about this."

As ever, there was no way to tell if Kosic had even heard Feaver's remark. He doodled again for a minute, then turned toward the room, his eyes drifting over Robbie's shoulder as he apparently took in the tumbling scene, the women and men joshing, tippling, holding their cigarettes overhead to avoid accidental burns to passersby. On the monitor, Rollo looked straight at the three agents and their camera without any change in his unpleasant expression. Watching the tape afterwards, you could see that as he was surveying, he slid the little cocktail napkin he'd been writing on in Robbie's direction. What attracted him, Robbie said subsequently, was that Kosic had unfurled the bad nail and tapped it a couple of times. There was writing amid several geometric shapes, the first two lines slanting off from what was inscribed below them:

FBI FOR SURE.
GET RID—NOW!
DON'T TELL ANYONE ANYTHING. EVEN MASON

On the replay, Rollo could be seen taking the most fleeting glance to be certain that Robbie had the message, then he crushed the napkin within his fist and slid it in his pocket.

"Whoa," Robbie said finally. He'd taken a tight grip on the bar. "Motherfuck. Are you sure?" Kosic looked up toward the piano. "Where the hell does this come from, Rollo? Why me? Does anybody know?"

Kosic took the bad nail and tapped it on his lips a little too precise to be random.

"Rollo, cut the crap. I'm trying not to have a bowel movement in my trousers here, Gimme some help. What's she there for? How do yo know all of this? Listen, what

I'm hearing is that they've been looking at accident swindlers, okay? Guys setting up phony accidents and suing. Fella I saw thinks that's what this is. Okay? Does that match?"

Kosic delivered his lethal glance, then scooped up the four cherries and popped them in his mouth all at once. He ate them after coming to his feet beside his stool. Robbie grabbed Kosic's sleeve between two fingers to keep him from getting away.

"Listen, I'm the one hanging out there, Rollo. Way out there. That's okay, I'm a big boy. But I'll be fucked if I won't be treated with some respect. Anybody's got any more messages for me to take on faith, wanna hear them from the organ-grinder, not the monkey. You tell Brendan I said that, too."

Kosic finished chewing with his face lifted into the smoky air, then leaned Feaver's way before he departed. It looked as if he was going to whisper some final word, but instead he suddenly took hold of Robbie's necktie. Improbably, Feaver jerked back, virtually strangling himself, as he braced his arms on the smooth mahogany curve affixed the leading edge of the granite bar. At the time, it was unclear what was happening. But, looking at the tape later, you could see that as Robbie had first been elevated off the seat by Kosic's grip on his tie, Rollo had reached under the bar with the other hand and grabbed Feaver's genitals. As Robbie reported it, Kosic had one testicle and his penis inside his fist and he squeezed for quite some time, until he finally whispered in his high ladylike voice. What he said was too soft for the FoxBIte pick up in the clamor, but Robbie heard it and took note as well of the sick smile with which the message was delivered.

"I'm the only organ-grinder you know," Kosic had told him.

CHAPTER 36

EVON DID NOT SEE WHAT WAS COMING.

After they left Attitude, she sat in McManis's conference room while Jim went through the debriefings of Feaver and the surveillance agents. They replayed the tapes. On the audio, critical points in the conversations were frequently obscured by the piano and the raucous laughter; occasional odd remarks were sucked in by the directional mikes as unpredictably as coins rattling up in a vacuum. Someone complained bitterly about Clinton's proposed tax increase; another moment revealed the passing of insider information on an upcoming corporate spinoff. The listening took more than an hour and a half.

Including the surveillance agents, the core group was now up to fifteen, far more bodies than there were chairs. They passed around pop and chips, since no one had had dinner, and as ever tried to figure the next move. Sennett was still talking about another shot at Tuohey.

"As long as you can give me a transplant down there,"

Robbie answered. There was a lot of laughter. "Kosic'll pull it off, Stan, the next time I use Brendan's name."

Sennett looked toward McManis for his evaluation. Jim thought there was no chance of getting to Tuohey.

"They're writing notes, for fear of speaking."

"But Robbie passed the frisk. They have to trust him more now."

"Only so much. Stan, these fellows know better than to trust anyone. They told Robbie about Evon because they don't want him to get himself in any deeper. But they know he's radioactive—he's about to get it from the feds and all bets are off then. You can run all the scenarios you want with Tuohey. We'll just stack up the tapes he can play during his defense case. He's never going to step in quicksand with Robbie."

"They all do," Sennett shot back. "If you find the right thing, they *all* do." His eyes flashed over to me. This was a bit of prosecutorial parlor talk probably best not shared in front of a defense lawyer.

Jim's advice was to abandon the frontal assault. The best approach to Brendan was from the flanks. They had to hope that someone turned on him. Someone like Kosic—or Milacki—might be able to catch Tuohey unawares. If they kept pushing with Robbie, they could blow that chance.

The eminent good sense of what Jim was saying seemed to win over everyone else. But Stan was unwilling to say quit. His great scheming intelligence worked in service of the gratification he got from winning in the direct showdown. The triumph he craved was to outduel Brendan, one-on-one.

Near the end of their argument, the two stepped outside. When they returned, McManis waved Evon into his office. She still didn't realize what he was going to say.

"We're pulling you in," he said. "It's over."

She felt like one of those eggs from which, as kids,

they'd blown out the yolk and the white to make Easter decorations. That frail. That hollow.

"Because you're worried about what Kosic meant about getting rid of me?"

"We're not going to wait to find out. But that's not the problem. You're burned and Robbie's supposed to know that. He has to get you out of the office on Monday. There's nothing left for UCA Evon Miller to do."

"What does Sennett think?"

"This isn't Sennett's call. And he recognizes the logic."

"Maybe I can stay in town, though? Maybe they'll make a move."

"No," he said. "I'm done saying I dare you. There's no operational need. After Monday, it's adios."

She felt absolutely desperate. She couldn't go back.

"Go home," he said. "See your family. You've got accumulated leave for months. We'll probably pull you back when we start the flips. You won't miss the grand finale. But for now I want you out of harm's way. Orders," he said. He watched her absorb it, seeing how little good he was doing. "I told you," he said, "this isn't easy. The whole journey. Start to finish. It's rugged."

When Jim opened the door, Sennett was waiting. She hoped he was there to argue with McManis, but instead, he took her hand. He said all the right words. And meant them as near as she could tell. Extraordinary, she heard him say. He said Courage, more than once. He said Patriot.

"The people of this district will never know how much they owe you, DeDe. You're a tremendous pro. Everyone in the Bureau is proud of you. And I'm so honored to have worked with you."

They said that about Stan, that he could scrape bottom and then reach the stars. Whatever bitterness he felt over McManis's decision, he allowed it to have no impact on the way he spoke to her. His dark eyes glistened. At the oddest moments with this guy, you saw what was really important to him. She felt as if she were getting another Olympic medal.

Then the three of them went back to the conference room and announced that Evon was coming in. The fifteen or so people assembled stood and applauded. Klecker popped an empty chip bag and every person in the room hugged her or jostled her shoulders.

It was happening, she realized. Really happening.

She was done.

FOR SEVERAL WEEKS NOW, a large garbage truck, painted in the red and blue colors of County Sanitation, had been periodically touring the alley behind Brendan Tuohey's home, picking up the trash from every house on the block. The truck, with its two-story walrus back and predatory iron maw on the rear, was the property of the DEA, but it was lent freely to the other federal agencies and even had a predetermined route each day, albeit one that frequently covered an area one hundred miles wide. Because no warrant is required to seize property the law views as abandoned, the confiscation of trash has become a standard armament in the war on crime. Tuohey's neighbors' trash was discarded, while the dark green bags from Brendan's cans were delivered to Joe Amari so that he and his crew could go through them with rubber gloves. Interesting tidbits had turned up. Brendan, improbably, had a deep interest in the lives of the saints, and there were several receipts each day for money orders, which the IRS bloodhounds would trace when the investigation surfaced.

Early Monday morning, when Evon arrived at McManis's for a final debriefing before going up to Feaver & Dinnerstein for the last time, Joe Amari placed the cocktail napkin on which Rollo Kosic had written his warning to

Robbie Friday night on the conference table. It was already in a plastic folder and every UCA entered to take a look, as if were a piece of the True Cross. The napkin, sporting Attitude's black-lined logo and the heavy geometric doodles in the corner, had been torn in four, but the pieces fit neatly. It would go out for fingerprinting and handwriting analyses as soon as Feaver identified it.

He arrived at nine-thirty to set the scenario for Evon's curtain call upstairs. After the weekend at home, he again looked a wreck.

"That's it." He smiled as he held the plastic envelope, but it seemed to require a second effort.

Kosic was a lock now. Dead-bang on obstruction and without much room on the conspiracy overall. McManis wanted to start planning an effort to flip him. Rollo was key. There was still no direct evidence against Tuohey, nothing to actually prove he was in league with Kosic and the others.

McManis gave the napkin a second look and asked Robbie about the reference to Mason, which he hadn't mentioned Friday night. Feaver shrugged. Apparently, Brendan figured he'd gone to Mason because he hadn't knocked on Tooley's door.

Robbie went up to his office first. When Evon got there, the receptionist, Phyllida, a lean Australian whom Robbie had employed because he loved her accent, told Evon that he wanted to see her. When she closed the door to Robbie's office, an unexpected swell of melancholy gripped her; she experienced the fine cityscape through the broad windows and the harmony of the spring light and took in yet again that she was leaving. In memory, she'd realized, this experience was going to be similar to hockey—another broad marker in her life, something to live up to, another stream she couldn't step in twice.

"So," he said. His eyes were dead. "Blah, blah, blah, you're fired."

He should have been sticking with the cover. Evon was supposed to yell at him and call him names, which was likely to bring some of the office folks close to the door. The idea was to create the impression of a final lovers' row. But he clearly wasn't ready to begin.

"So do we get together again or is this sayonara?" he asked her.

She was leaving in half an hour. Amari was going to take her to the airport. She told him that McManis said she would be back whenever they began the effort to flip the investigation's leading targets. He sat in his tall black chair and shook his head, smiling at himself.

"You know," he told her, "I always thought one of the greatest things about women was they stuck around." He looked in the direction of the red rug for a while. "Times change," he said.

She smiled sadly at that, and then, on impulse, crossed the room and hugged him, waiting what seemed to be quite some time for him to let her go.

"You better raise your voice now," she told him. "Let them hear 'You're fired,' like you mean it."

"You're fired," he said listlessly and then, staring miserably at her, began to cry. "Don't take it as a compliment. I cry about everything these days." He got out his handkerchief. "You better do the yelling. Now's your chance. Tell them what a lying heap of dung I am."

She settled for slamming the door and, as she emerged, muttering under her breath. Four steps away, she stopped in order to pull back from the precipice of disordering emotions. Bonita, with her raccoon eyes and piles of black hair, brittle as fiberglass, was staring. So was Oretta from the file room. Perfect, Evon thought. Perfect play.

*　　　*　　　*

MIDWEEK, SHE FLEW out to Denver to see Merrel. She arrived Thursday, and on Friday afternoon they drove up to Vail to see the brand-new condo. It had cost three quarters of a million dollars and Evon felt she could put her hand through the walls if she knocked on them too hard, but Merrel and Roy were thrilled, as they always were by their possessions. Together they showed off everything in the place—the patio, the mountain view, the hot tub, the rumpus room furniture, even the stove and microwave. In Roy's view, this was the same thing as Jesus handing them a report card telling them they were doing good. Roy spent five days a week riding on airplanes. Evon had picked up the phone sometimes when she was visiting and heard him say he was in the most ridiculous places, Sumatra or Abu Dhabi. But the longer she knew him, the more she realized he was a lot like her father, clinging to a few simple things and otherwise completely baffled.

Merrel's girls, ages fourteen to three, were wonderful. Grace and Hope, Melody and Rose were all blondes and all their mom's kids, each with painted nails and arguments about how Merrel should do their hair. Evon took especially to Rose, the littlest, who was said to favor her aunt. It wasn't really a compliment. Poor Rose had not been born with the silky, long-legged look of her mother. She was what Merrel called a 'pudge.' Rose was never neat and, at the age of three, already somewhat frantic, incorrigibly committed to screaming whenever she wanted to be heard. But for whatever reason she loved her aunt. She drew Evon into her games and could already throw a ball accurately.

Saturday night, dinner got messed up. Roy was on the patio, getting exercised about the gas grill that wouldn't ignite, and the meat sat out there with him, as the light dwindled and shrank the bulk from the mountains. The smell of cedar rose up from the forest floor as the chill began to drain the little bit of moisture from the air. Merrel, trying to ignore Roy's growing agitation, finally fed the smaller girls noodles, while she and Evon ate half of a wedge of Brie and drank most of a bottle of wine.

Evon tried to entertain the little ones. Rose told her that Momma said she'd be the flower girl when her Aunt DeDe got married.

"Oh, honey," she said, "I don't think your Auntie DeDe is the marrying kind."

Merrel, who was still unpacking boxes in the kitchen, heard this and sang out with a story about a colleague of Roy's, a woman named Karen Bircher, who at the age of forty-one had gone from being a powerhouse career gal to a mom at home in the space of fifteen months.

"It just takes the right guy, De," Merrel told her, crossing into the small dining room carrying a tray of glassware.

Lightly, laughingly, actually strangely happy, Evon said, "Oh, I don't think it's a guy."

Who knows why these things happen? Her sister stood stock-still, her anxious glances divided between the tray of Orrefors, which she plainly feared she might drop, and Evon. Merrel was terrified. No other way to describe the look that evaporated much of her beauty. She literally snatched up Rose, stating that it was time for bed, and ran away with her daughter.

When Merrel returned to the kitchen, she was furious. Evon was stacking plates in the cupboard.

"Please, DeDe," Merrel whispered, "*please* don't ever say anything like that to Roy."

Roy. Evon laughed again. She was instantly afraid it was another of those moments when her reactions were dead-wrong. But she was so happy. And the thought of saying anything to Roy was purely amusing. Simple Roy was just a fellow walking through a tunnel looking for the light.

"Oh, hon," Evon said, "it's been fifteen years before I could even say it to myself." She still felt like a bubble rising in a soft drink. She found her sister's eyes. It took a moment for Merrel to reorganize herself. She was working her way back toward something. Love. Merrel loved her. In their family, they loved each other best. And there was a reason for that, because there was a piece of one another they always carried around, the someone else they might have been.

"Oh, sweetheart, sweetheart," Merrel said and opened her arms to her sister. They stood there in the little pantry laughing and crying both, but for just a moment, because Melody walked in, upset about the ravaged mess Grace had made of the hair of one of her dolls. Knowing nothing else to do, Merrel reached down and hugged her daughter urgently and grabbed at DeDe and took her in as well.

CHAPTER
37

DURING THE WEEK EVON WAS GONE, nothing happened. By Wednesday or Thursday, Stan and McManis had realized that Tuohey and his people were hunkered down, waiting to see what the G was going to do to Feaver.

After Kosic's note to Robbie was presented to her, the Chief Judge had authorized the installation of a fiber-optic camera in Kosic's office to augment the bug Alf had placed in the phone weeks before. She allowed the equipment to remain on throughout business hours, but the results were no more revealing. A couple of phone calls—one from Sherm Crowthers—were suspect, but Kosic, according to the surveillance agents patrolling the courthouse, had gone down to Crowthers' chambers for whatever talk took place there. On Wednesday, Kosic told Milacki, during a long conversation about various unserved summonses, that he'd heard that Feaver's girlfriend had left town. There was no specification how Kosic knew that, although presumably it came from Tuohey, who would have learned the news from

Mort. The Presiding Judge appeared in Kosic's office once or twice, just standing in the doorway, but their exchanges were innocuous. Rollo referred to him as 'Your Honor.' More significant conversations were in all likelihood reserved for home.

By Friday, Sennett had concocted a new scenario, securing McManis's agreement to make one last-ditch effort against Tuohey directly. When Evon returned to Des Moines late on Sunday from Colorado, there was a message on her machine from McManis.

"You're back in business," he told her. She caught the 7 a.m. plane Monday morning and was in Kindle by 8:30.

Amari and McManis picked her up at the airport and drove her into the Center City. At 9:30 a.m., Evon arrived in the reception area of Feaver & Dinnerstein, accompanied by two agents from the local field office of the FBI. She asked for Robbie again. Phyllida knew enough to realize that Evon's appearance was trouble. Over the intercom, Feaver told Phyllida to say he wasn't in, but when she relayed the message Evon removed her FBI credentials from her purse and snapped them open, as if it were a potent magic trick. Phyllida was bright, but she couldn't make any sense of it. She scooted her little castered chair back from the reception desk until she bumped into the wall behind her, placing a narrow hand, with pink polish, near her heart.

Evon swept past her, with the two agents trailing. She threw open Robbie's door and strode to the glass desk, where he was speaking on the phone. He looked miserable, worse than when she left. He was losing weight, she realized. He caught himself, halfway to a smile, as she approached.

"ROBERT FEAVER!" she called in a voice resounding throughout the office. She flashed her creds. "Special Agent DeDe Kurzweil of the Federal Bureau of Investigation.

This is a subpoena *duces tecum* requiring you to appear before the Special June 1993 Grand jury on Friday, June Twenty-fifth, at 10 a.m." She threw it on his desk and turned heel. Robbie, in role, scurried behind her, spewing curses.

By eleven, he was at Rollo Kosic's office. He had no difficulty appearing haggard and frantic. I knew he'd had a horrible weekend. On Friday, Rainey, much earlier than the doctors had predicted, had lost her ability to move her right wrist enough to operate the computer mouse. For forty-eight hours, she had lain there with no ability to communicate except by blinking her eyes or tapping her fingers. By Sunday, a friend from the computer business had attached a new tracking device, laser-controlled through the movement of her eyes. Yet the period Rainey had spent locked in, without voice, had been a peek into an intolerable future. She had resolved to take no further measures to prolong her life. When he appeared on the screen in the surveillance van, where we were all watching, Robbie's anguish seemed as palpable as in Kabuki.

Kosic's office was tiny, formerly reserved for a law clerk. There were bookshelves on three sides, all empty. In Brendan's style, Kosic did not bother with a picture or memento of any kind. The many court papers he dealt with stood on either side of his desk in two neat stacks. With the benefit of hard-wiring through the phone lines, Alf was able to zoom the camera in and out via a handheld remote. Kosic was yawningly impassive when Robbie came through the door and dropped the subpoena on his desk.

But for the dates, it was the same as the document served on Robbie last September by the IRS. It asked for the records of the secret checking account at River National. While Kosic read it, Robbie said, "They know."

As always, Kosic offered no response.

"I need to talk to him, Rollo."

Kosic's eyes rolled upward, the whites prominent.

"Rollo, that's where I get the cash. That account. They know. I have to talk to him."

Kosic seemed to realize he had no choice about speaking. "I don't see the point in that."

"I've got to, Rollo. I haven't told Mason shit. But I have to tell him *some*-thing now. This checking account looks pretty funny, with all the cash flying out of it. We've gotta figure out how I can keep Morty clean. I'm not sure anybody'll believe it if I say he didn't know where the money was going. And some of the things I might say, that wouldn't be so hot for his license anyway. I need to know what Brendan can swing over at BAD."

Rollo had shaken his head metronomically throughout Robbie's remarks.

"Barking up the wrong tree. He can't help you with that."

Feaver feigned fury. He picked the subpoena up again and threw it down. He leaned over Kosic's desk.

"This is my fucking law license. This is God knows how long in the joint with God knows whose joint up my can. I'll handle the weight, but I need help. And I need it right now, Rollo. I gotta say the right thing."

For Kosic, for Tuohey, the dilemma was exactly what McManis had described: they had to keep Robbie on the reservation, but not say or do anything that might lead to further troubles for them down the line, if Feaver didn't stand up. Rollo pondered with a finger on his lips, the bad nail revealed. He said they'd get back to him.

As Robbie neared the door, Kosic finally volunteered something.

"It's too bad your dick ain't a weather vane, Robbie. With all the time you spend waving it around, you would have seen this coming."

There was no further word from them for more than

twenty-four hours, but on Tuesday afternoon, Milacki appeared in Robbie's reception area without warning. Feaver called Alf, hoping to get the FoxBIte upstairs instantly. Instead, Klecker told Robbie just to leave his telephone on speaker. Downstairs, Alf rolled tape and muted his end so there would be no telltale sound from Robbie's phone as it broadcast the conversation. Phyllida then showed Milacki back.

Sig was impressed by the stylish furnishings.

"Is that real client skin you got there on the walls?"

"Just the Polacks. They're the only ones who believe it's a face-lift when I ask them to bend over."

Bonita had brought Sig a Coke and he excused himself after he belched.

"How's your golf game?" he asked.

"About as rusty as my clubs."

"Couple guys thought you'd like to catch an early round before work. Out at Rob Roy?" Brendan's club. "This is on the Q.T., okay? They don't open up for play until eight-thirty, so these guys sneak out to number five." Milacki gave him instructions. Robbie was to park his car at the far end of the club lot, near the maintenance shed, and then walk down a quarter of a mile or so, on a path through the Public Forest. Robbie knew the spot from childhood picnics.

"There's a little lake there?"

"Pond, right," said Milacki. "Tee off at 6 a.m."

Called to the conference room along with Stan, I heard the tape that afternoon. It sounded as if it had been recorded in a canyon.

"How'd he react when you mentioned the lake?" I asked Robbie.

Feaver responded with a faint fatalistic smile. It was a remote setting. We were all thinking the same thing. Even Sennett.

"I want the surveillance tight," Sennett told Amari. "I want guys dressed up as the birds in the trees. Whatever it takes. I don't want Robbie out of sight."

Amari shrunk up his mouth sardonically. "We're on their turf. Literally. I bet you Tuohey can play that golf course in the dark. He knows when a twig is moved. And I gotta get my guys in place in the middle of the night? We'll be damn lucky if one of them doesn't fall in that lake and drown."

"They're setting it up to feel secure," said Sennett. "Tuohey thinks he won't have to look over his shoulder. If you do it right, Robbie, he'll let his hair down. He's got to make sure you'll stand up and take the hit for all of them. You just have to get him to say it out loud."

I cornered McManis before I left. I wanted to know what he would say if I insisted that Robbie wear body armor, a bulletproof Kevlar vest. He might be able to hide it under a jacket. Jim turned over the idea. He skipped what I later realized was the correct response: Up close, it would be a head shot anyway.

"Look, George, I can't tell you it's completely safe. Because it isn't. But we're going to have surveillance all over the area. If anybody shows up we don't like or don't know, anybody the Kindle County agents recognize as hooked up, if it looks like Milacki or Kosic are packing—if anything's wrong, I'm closing down, George. That's my word to you." His light eyes did not leave mine. "But I don't see them writing Robbie secret messages and then disappearing him ten days later. They'd have made a move last week, if they were going to do that. That's the logic, at least." Then he turned his palms up, acknowledging how little any of these efforts at prediction were worth in the end.

CHAPTER 38

WE MET AT THE HICKORY STICK MALL, one of those vast emporia where the immense parking lot, all but empty in the still darkness of 4:30 a.m., bore silent comment on the trivial appetites that would have this place swarming by midday. A large reader board for the multiplex, the only thing illuminated, against a ghostly sky tinctured with the first gray drops of early light, advertised a number of the films I hadn't yet seen. *Last Action Hero. Jurassic Park.* For the moment, I had no need for imaginary adventures.

As cover, we'd agreed to wear fishing attire, posing as a group of Center City yahoos trying to land a crappie or two before work. I'd borrowed a khaki vest with zippers and pockets from Billy, one of my sons. The surveillance van moved around the huge lot picking up each of us, our signal no more subtle than our parking lights.

Robbie and I were together on the north side of the mall. We'd had only a few moments to talk before the gray van came by. Robbie had been up all night with Rainey.

Looking him over, I realized that Robbie Feaver had turned an important corner in his life in the last few weeks; he remained good-looking, but worry and sleeplessness and depression and poor diet had worn on him in a way likely to be permanent. They had stolen some of his glory. Yet he'd maintained the show-must-go-on spirit, and had done his best to look his part. He had on a snappy golf shirt, with a rich firestitch weave, and fancy golf spikes, wing-tip style, with kelties over the laces.

I told him he could still say no to this.

"No I can't," he answered. "I always knew I was gonna get Brendan or die trying." The best news, he said, was that he'd be in the woods, so he wouldn't have to worry about taking a dump in his trousers.

In the van, I asked for a minute with Stan. As we stepped out, McManis handed each of us a pole. Neither Sennett nor I was much of an outdoorsman and McManis briefly called us back, warning us, completely deadpan, to watch out for the hooks. Stan and I stood out among the vacant painted stripes of the parking lot, a hundred yards from various expensive department stores, pretending to test the flex of the rods.

I told Stan that my client seemed fairly concerned he was about to be killed.

"Won't happen," said Sennett. "If I didn't think we could protect him, I wouldn't be going forward. Don't let him back out on me, George."

That wasn't the issue, I said. I just wanted Stan to assure Robbie that he'd virtually sing "The Star-Spangled Banner" every time he mentioned Feaver's name to the sentencing judge.

He did it, but Robbie didn't look much happier. In the van, we reviewed the scenario one more time and Alf readied the equipment. Odds said Milacki wouldn't frisk Robbie again for fear that one more insult might drive him into the government's arms. Even so, with Robbie wearing neither boots nor a suit jacket, hiding the FoxBIte was a challenge. Considering everything, Alf had decided to secrete the units in the crown of a wide-brimmed Australian-style raffia golf hat, concealing them under a sturdy rubberized lining. Klecker made Robbie go through several swings to be certain the headgear would stay on. The one serious problem was that in order to fit the recorder and transmitter within the slender space available, Alf had to use a smaller battery. That meant Robbie couldn't meander through the round with Tuohey waiting for him to get conversational at the nineteenth hole. The FoxBIte would run out of power after an hour and forty minutes.

A staticky squall of radio reports reached the van from the agents positioned in the Public Forest. The communications were easily overheard and sometimes unsettling. The surveillance was not as comprehensive as planned. Amari's guys had erected deer blinds in four of the oaks that bordered the golf course. The process of building them in the middle of the night, with the County Forest Police occasionally sweeping down the neighboring roads, had been both comical and hair-raising. But even with night-vision binoculars, it had been impossible to fully scope out the terrain. As light began to perk up, the agents were reporting that there were a number of spots—especially the deep bunkers of the sand traps—where Robbie would be completely out of sight.

There had been some discussion of putting the portable camera in Robbie's golf bag, but it would have been almost impossible to keep the lens trained in the right direction. Instead, the four surveillance agents in the trees were each equipped with cameras, two standard video cams that would record in color, and two of the 2.4 GHz models that would transmit a picture to the van. A cordon of additional agents would be poised at the perimeter of the course with binoculars, joggers and walkers, out with the first sunlight, were not uncommon, but Sennett for once seemed unconcerned about the risks of detection.

"If we get blown, we get blown," he said. Nobody could get word to Tuohey anyway in the middle of the golf course. Sennett, to his credit, was determined not to lose sight of Robbie.

Finally, at 5:30 a.m., it was time to go. Amari had a unit tailing Tuohey, and they radioed that Brendan and Kosic had just pulled out of the garage of the stone house in Latterly. Two surveillance cars, new Novas that had been fitted over with the rusted bodies of earlier models, swept into the mall lot to follow Robbie to the country club. Evon and McManis and I walked Robbie to the Mercedes.

"Any time you think this is out of control," Jim said, "you say 'Uncle Petros' and we're coming to get you. You don't have to be right. If you're spooked, bring it down. Nobody'll say word one afterwards."

I shook his hand and Evon gave him a half-embrace with an arm quickly raised to his shoulder.

"Big show," she said. "Big star." He liked the thought.

We drove to a predetermined spot in the Public Forest, a small graveled area where bikers and canoers commonly off-loaded their equipment. Alf and Clevenger worked feverishly on the electronics; everything functioned. From the outposts in the trees, the cameras captured an impressive panorama, and, with the benefit of manual operation, could magnify images up to 48 times as they zoomed in. Alf reported that the agent-cameramen were belted to the tree trunks like loggers.

At 5:45 precisely, the Mercedes appeared in the club parking lot. The hot pink of sunrise was almost gone from the eastern sky. Robbie, who had put on a white vest to protect against the morning chill, looked to the woods with a commanding face-aloft expression practiced in the courtroom. Then he threw the heavy white leather golf bag, with a brand name emblazoned on it in gold script, over his shoulder, and set his hat on his head with both hands. To conserve power, the FoxBIte had been turned off after McManis recorded the customary initiating speech. One of the surveillance cars now prowled along the edge of the road and the agent on the driver's side hit the FoxBIte remote. In the van, we heard Robbie state, "This is a test, this is just a test of the emergency warning system." Alf radioed and the agent's auto pulled away.

As Milacki had promised, the maintenance gate was unlocked, and Robbie began trudging through the heavy midwestern woods. This was, for the most part, a first-growth forest, full of the old hardwoods, bur oaks and pin oaks and white oaks and hickories, with ferns and runners growing up in their shade. Primroses and wild raspberries clustered in the marginal patches of sun. Robbie tromped along, preoccupied and unconnected to what was around him, much like the settlers who'd walked the forest a century before. The traders, farmers, and merchants who'd first come to this area were hardscrabble types looking solely for the chance to profit. The land to them was not the home of the spirit but a commodity to exploit. The Public Forests had been saved from despoliation at the end of the nineteenth century through the efforts of a few Eastern-educated architects and city planners, rich men's sons who were indulged because these parcels seemed too remote to be worth quarreling over.

On the audio, as Robbie walked, there was an almost musical background of birds and insects, the rutting calls of squirrels and chipmunks, and the rushing water of little brooks descending from the pond where Robbie was to meet Tuohey. He groaned now and then under the weight of the bag, but skipped the occasional wisecracks that sometimes punctuated the recordings when he was alone.

Eventually, he reached the road through the Public Forest. The parking lot where we were stationed was no more than three or four hundred yards away. He walked down in our direction, then followed a woodland path back toward the golf course. On the screen, we saw him step over the galvanized guard rail at a curve. The ground was soft as he approached the water and, off-balance with the bag, he stumbled at one point, catching himself against the steep bank. Even so, a spot of black mud stained his vest. Habits being what they are, he fussed with it for a time before heading on.

The chain-link fence between the country club and the forest broke at this point for a bridge that crossed the neck of Galler's Pond. The spring waters spread with indifference between rich and poor, over both public and private land. The bridge was divided along its length by a four-foot stockade fence. The rear side, with the cross-braces running between the posts, faced Robbie. He was supposed to dump his clubs over and then use the ties to vault onto the club property. He had just boosted the bag across when, on the screen, he cranked a concerned look over his shoulder.

The agent operating the nearby camera was taken unawares. He'd kept a tight shot on Feaver for fear that he'd lose him among the leaves. Now, as the cameraman attempted to locate what had distracted Robbie, he panned far too quickly and couldn't regain focus as he retreated to a wider shot. By the time he'd readjusted and found Feaver, Robbie was back at the bottom of the bridge talking to a Kindle County police officer. We'd heard Robbie tromping down the span, dispensing a sunny greeting, but it was a shock to see it was a cop who'd accosted him.

"Playing golf, are you, sir?"

"Right. I'm meeting some friends."

The cop was huge, a former jock of some kind, a physical presence in the tight blue uniform. He sized up Feaver.

"The club isn't open now."

"Right, but these guys are members."

"Uh-huh," said the cop. "They've had a problem here recently. People sneaking on and messing things up. It's private property, you know."

Robbie said once again that his friends belonged to the club. When the cop asked who they were, Robbie, with some hesitation, gave Brendan's name. The officer pointed through the fence, noting that nobody was on the fifth tee. Tuohey, Robbie said, would be right along.

"Can I see some i.d.?" the cop asked.

From the overhead view, we could see Robbie nodding agreeably and gesturing in the wide way he employed when he was attempting self-conscious charm. He appeared such a picture of confidence that it was hard not to believe he'd get by. It was another mini-coronary, but we'd survived many by now. Tuohey would be arriving any second to bail Robbie out. We all hunched behind Alf, leaning toward the monitor. Amari was issuing orders over his radio. The second camera could not pick up Robbie, but had found the cruiser parked around a bend in the road. It was a Police Force vehicle, not from the Public Forest Division.

The cop took Robbie's wallet and without returning it asked him to come away from the fence. He traded places with Feaver and with one hand hoisted the golf bag back to their side, then remained behind Robbie as he walked him the thirty or forty feet up to the road. When they reached the black-and-white, the cop said, "Put your hands on the vehicle, sir, and lean against it, with your legs spread."

"God bless you, Alfie," Stan whispered. Klecker, busy with the dials, tossed off a salute. Detected, the FoxBIte, which bore the recorded preamble, would have given away everything, once someone figured out how to play it.

The cop went down Robbie's sides quickly. For one hopeful second it looked certain Robbie had cleared. Then the cop straightened up.

"Now slowly lift your hands to your head," he said "and remove your hat."

"Hey," Robbie answered good-naturedly, "don't you think this has gone far enough?"

"Remove your hat, please."

"Think my brains are gonna fall out? I couldn't have a gun in my hat."

The cop withdrew his baton and told Robbie he was asking him for the last time to take off his hat.

"How about I call my lawyer?"

With that, the copper lifted the baton to shoulder height

"Oh, Lord!" That was Evon. But the cop didn't hit him Instead he flicked the hat off with the end of the nightstick. The hat plummeted to the asphalt with suspicious speed. The FoxBIte emitted a resounding ping and, with that, the frequency hopper went dead. Klecker sprung even closer to the equipment, switching dials and plugs to no avail, barking at Clevenger. It now became a silent movie.

Robbie, with a show of tremendous irritation, grabbed the hat off the asphalt before the cop could reach it. The policeman shook his stick at Robbie twice and Robbie waved his hands around indignantly. He finally put the hat back on his head, looking grumpy and clearly making ready to depart. The cop took another step back, remonstrating further. Finally, he removed his service revolver from his holster.

The sight of the gun coming up had a Zen-like intensity, prefigured as it was by our worries. I was still uncertain about the cop and his intentions, but Sennett had arrived at a far clearer interpretation of events.

"God, no!" he screamed. "No, no. Move!"

McManis already had the handset at his lips. "We're up!" McManis yelled. "All agents in at once. Go! Go!" he shouted.

Before he had finished, Evon was out the door of the van, sprinting down the yellow center line in the narrow forest road. McManis in his blue seersucker suit seemed to have been drafted out behind her and took off in her wake at full canter. He said later he did not think about the fact he was unarmed. Until then, Evon's sporting background had been little more than a curiosity to me, but the speed with which she disappeared into the distance, putting more and more space between McManis and herself, looked almost like a cartoon.

Inside the van, Amari was screaming instructions into two different walkie-talkies. When I looked back, Sennett was crouching, gripping the monitor by its sides, his face close enough to be colored by the gray glow.

Robbie was still alive. He had both hands in the air and he was nodding vigorously to the cop, who had hold of the hat. The policeman shook it several times, while Robbie yammered what, given his nature, was all but certain to be a ludicrous explanation. As it turned out, he had told the officer that the hat was equipped with a biorhythm meter to help promote an even golf swing. The copper appeared to be considering that, but all the same, he put the hat under the arm in which he was holding the gun, and ripped out the lining. He stared for some time into the crown, where the complex electrical equipment was wound tight within a cocoon of colored wires. Then he lifted the weapon straight at Robbie. For the first time the copper looked seriously angry.

"No!" wailed Sennett again. "God no!"

The officer claimed later he'd thought it was a bomb.

*   *   *

BEFORE SHE REACHED THE BEND where the police cruiser was parked, Evon hopped the guardrail and began breaking through the woods, swinging her arms to clear the thorny undergrowth. By the time she reapproached the road, she saw the cop with his arm fully extended and his service revolver two feet from Feaver's head. Her own handgun was over her belly in something called a Gunny Sack, an enlarged fanny pack that could be pulled open, exposing the firearm. She extracted the 5904 that way and assumed position, yelling as loudly as she could.

"FBI! FBI! Drop the gun or I'll shoot."

The cop's head swung a quarter turn. She was about fifty yards from him in the trees and he was obviously uncertain where the voice had come from.

"I am Instructor-Qualified at Quantico. I can put a bullet inside your eardrum fifty times out of fifty from where I am. Drop the gun."

The cop crooked his arm instead, keeping the revolver directed at Robbie, but from a foot farther away. He tucked the FoxBIte under his armpit, and with his left hand squeezed the transmission button on the radio fixed to his shoulder and spoke into it.

She repeated her instruction, but the cop's posture had slackened and she realized for the first time she would not have to fire. She could hear the cavalry rampaging through the leaves and the brush, and an entire posse of agents suddenly poured out of the woods, five or six of them, all screaming "FBI!" Three wore blue plastic parkas with the Bureau initials in huge yellow letters. They surrounded the cop and Robbie, crouching in a semicircle directly behind the policeman. Evon ran up to join them, and McManis arrived right behind her, badly out of breath. He put his hands on his thighs to recover his wind, then came around to where the cop could see him.

"I want to ask everyone to lower their weapons on the count of three," he said.

At three, the cop cheated a look back to make sure the agents had complied, but then directed his gun toward the ground. The FoxBIte remained in his other hand.

McManis told the cop he'd gotten himself in the middle of a Bureau operation.

"So you're saying this guy is yours?" the cop asked about Robbie. Robbie's hands had sunk when the cop lowered his gun, but they were still held at a small distance from his sides as a gesture of compliance. His eyes remained grimly fixed on the officer. At one point, he caught sight of Evon to the rear and winked, but under the circumstances, he'd been unable to manage a smile.

McManis avoided the cop's question. What he wanted was the FoxBIte. Drawing on the military heritage of many of its agents, the Bureau lived by a code which said that the next worst thing to losing a body to the bad guys was losing your equipment. Even if they couldn't salvage Robbie's cover, they needed the FoxBIte back to maintain the security of future operations. Besides, the unit was cutting-edge, borrowed by Klecker from the Bureau's black-world spooks who worked foreign counterintelligence. Evon knew it was in capital letters this time: Don't Embarrass The Bureau.

The standoff was still ongoing when Sennett jogged up. I was about one hundred yards behind, Stan having outrun me as usual. He had just approached the cop when I got there.

"I'm the U.S. Attorney." From his blue suit coat, Stan withdrew his own federal credentials. "I'll take that, please." He reached out for the FoxBIte.

The cop pulled the unit farther away, but he looked down to what he held and for the first time put his revolver back in the holster. He watched TV like everyone else and recognized Sennett from the news. He was finally convinced these were really the feds.

Sennett took a step closer and asked for the equipment again. He was almost a foot smaller than the cop, but he gave no quarter and appeared hard enough to seem threatening.

"You want it, call my C.O.," said the cop.

"Which is who?"

"Brenner, Area 6."

"Six?" said one of the agents standing in the narrow semicircle to the rear. "What the hell are you doing out here? You're fifteen miles from the North End."

"I live out here. He told me to look into this on my way in for roll call."

From the distance, I could hear sirens keening. In less than a minute, another black-and-white made a squealing halt at the roadside. Two other Force cars shortly appeared from the other direction. The six cops trooped down together and stood beside the officer who'd been surrounded.

Everyone held their places for some time. The sun had broken through an early morning haze and shone pleasantly. Eventually, several cops, including the first one, removed their caps. There was not much joviality, even though a couple of the local agents who'd been working for Amari were vaguely acquainted with a few of the policemen. It was the usual thing, Evon figured, the Bureau and the locals. The agents frequently viewed cops—less educated, more intuitive, and lower paid—as slugs, often embittered ones, because many had failed the Bureau's qualifying tests. The cops tended to see the Bureau types as pansies who knew more about filling out paperwork than dealing with real crime.

Amari suddenly came trotting up the road, waving. He had one of the large walkie-talkies in his hand and two other agents were behind him. McManis met them on the shoulder. After he heard them out, he gathered a number of us, including Stan and Evon and me, about fifteen yards farther up the pavement.

The unit tailing Tuohey had reported that about fifteen minutes ago he had abruptly changed course. Brendan had just arrived at St. Mary's, an hour late for his usual Mass. Amari had sent an agent into the clubhouse. The locker room attendant, who'd just come in, said Tuohey hadn't been out here for two weeks because of bursitis.

Jim looked at us, his graying forelocks lifted from his brow on a breeze.

"We have a city cop sitting out here just waiting for him? And no Brendan? And Robbie ends up completely blown? We just fell through Tuohey's trapdoor." He looked away, trying to cope with the bitterness of getting beaten this way.

"Christ, this guy is smart," Stan said. He screwed up his face to absorb his own distress, then said something I'd never heard in the more than twenty-five years of our acquaintance. "This guy," he said, "is smarter than me."

CHAPTER 39

AT THE DOOR TO BARNETT SKOLNICK'S modest house in suburban Chelsea, Sennett and his party, which included Evon, were greeted by a stout older woman. She wore an inexpensive housecoat, her nightdress trailing below with an uneven hem. Her old face, spotted and wrinkled, glistened with Vaseline or moisturizer. In her free hand she held a half-eaten chocolate bar.

Sennett introduced himself as the U.S. Attorney and pointed to the people behind him—Evon, Robbie, McManis, and Clevenger.

"We'd like to speak to Judge Skolnick."

"This is something to do with court?" she asked.

"Exactly," said Sennett. "It's official business."

She shrugged as she opened the screen.

"Bar-*nett*!" she yelled. "Barney. You got friends here!" She was, apparently, not unacquainted with nighttime visits by lawyers. Skolnick was the kind to leave the bench promptly at five. If lawyers wanted more of his time, they could come to him, and lawyers, being who they were, oc-

casionally did on emergency matters. No doubt there were
also visits for less savory purposes now and then.

Skolnick's voice rose from a distance with the same
phlegmy cheerfulness heard in his courtroom. He asked his
wife to send them down. Behind Sennett, Evon and the
others descended a narrow stairwell. A few steps from the
bottom, Sennett waggled a finger at Robbie to stay put.
Feaver would be a surprise, Sennett's own jack-in-the-box.

It was well past 10 p.m. by now and they had been
scrambling all day. With the assistance of a late-arriving
sergeant from Community Relations, the impasse at the
roadside in the Public Forest had been resolved with a deal
to deliver the FoxBIte to Linden Seilor, Chief Deputy P.A.,
who was a former trial partner of Stan's. Sennett recovered the recorder personally. Linden had heard Tuohey's
name in the subsequent accounts and was determined to
ask no questions. However, he vouched for the cop, who
was named Beasley. Beasley's lieutenant had directed him
to stake out the bridge by 5:45 and to stop whoever went
over. The lieutenant warned that the groundskeeper had
chased somebody away last week, ceasing pursuit when
the fellow actually turned on him with a gun. A thorough
pat-down was therefore in order. If the cop found anything,
he'd been instructed to give a shout over the police radio.
Seilor had already had a word with the lieutenant about
where his information and instructions came from, but it
trailed off to smoke up the chain in McGrath Hall, police
headquarters. As usual, there were several layers between
Tuohey and whomever it was on the Force he'd reached
out to for this favor.

Yet it was certain that the cop's story of seven FBI
agents drawing on him would soon be departmental legend, along with the inevitable deduction that Robbie Feaver
was a Bureau informant. Tuohey had almost certainly
learned that this morning, but his people would spread the

word slowly for fear that anybody they spoke to might be wired. Nonetheless, given the panic that would grip everyone Robbie had dealt with, the Presiding Judge and his circle would need to make stealthy efforts to hold them in line. Despite the dwindling odds, Stan maintained one last hope that in the fraught atmosphere, Tuohey might blunder. If Sennett could quickly turn someone whom Brendan was unlikely to suspect, or whom he had no choice about talking to, there might yet be an opportunity tonight, or early tomorrow.

For this effort, the FBI had put the entire Kindle County Field Office at the Project's disposal. Sennett had fielded a full squad of Assistant U.S. Attorneys who were grinding out subpoenas to banks and currency exchanges and the courthouse, which would be served tomorrow to prevent records from going astray. In the meantime, several 'flip teams' had been organized. Klecker and Stan's First Assistant, Moses Appleby, were sent after Judith and Milacki. Another group would go to the homes of various clerks—Walter; Pincus Lebovic; Crowthers' clerk, Joey Kwan. Sennett reserved the top targets for himself.

Amari's people had staked out Kosic all day. The idea was to catch Rollo alone so that Sennett could confront him with the array of incriminating evidence the government had developed and offer Kosic the deal of a lifetime to turn on Tuohey. But Rollo never left Brendan's side, although this, more likely, was for protection and counsel in a moment of crisis, rather than to foil Stan's plans. Once surveillance put the two back inside Tuohey's house in Latterly, Sennett decided to go after the others, leaving Rollo for the next morning.

At the bottom of the stairs, they found Skolnick huddled on a new tartan sofa—a colonial piece with dark maple arms—watching the Trappers game on TV. He was dressed in green pajamas with black piping, and a velvet bathrobe, adorned at the pocket with the crest of a family to which he surely did not belong. The room was clad in lacquered knotty pine and newly carpeted. The astringent factory odor of the rug did not quite obscure a lingering smell of mold. Along the paneled walls, built-in pine shelves were filled with family memorabilia, snapshots of children and grandchildren, trophies earned by Skolnick's kids in long-forgotten athletic triumphs, and a few photos from Skolnick's official life, including one 8 x 10 from his induction as a judge more than a quarter of a century ago. In it, he stood flanked by a large group, including Tuohey and the dear departed Mayor Bolcarro, as well as Knuckles, Skolnick's connected brother. By now Evon recognized all the faces, which appeared so much more appealing in youth that she had to suppress an impulse to laugh. Looking around, she realized the basement had been refinished recently. She made a note to get the IRS guys Sennett had in the background to go through Skolnick's financials for evidence of how he'd paid for the renovation. Nine would get you ten there'd be no credit card records or checks. Barney, almost certainly, had been a cash customer.

Skolnick jumped up to welcome them. "So come in, come in."

Sennett introduced himself as Skolnick was pulling the wooden barrel chairs from his leather-topped poker table into a circle, a task with which Tex Clevenger rendered wordless assistance.

"I know you, I know you," said Skolnick. He mentioned a moot-court function at Blackstone where they'd met. He resumed his seat on his sofa, pulling his robe closed to assume whatever dignity he could under the circumstances. He cast a final shameless glance at the game and then used the remote to darken the set. "So, fellas," he said, "what have we got here?"

He always proved as dim as Robbie's initial portrayal.

Every now and then, given the peculiarities of certain statutes, the United States was forced to appear in the Common Law Claims Division, and Skolnick seemed to believe that Sennett and his coterie had arrived for that reason. An emergency motion of some kind.

"Judge, I'm not here as an attorney, at least not one appearing before you. I need to ask you a few questions. On behalf of the government of the United States."

"At eleven at night? This can't wait till the morning?" Confusion swarmed over Skolnick's large pink face, and he glanced to the others as if they might explain. When his eyes lit on Evon, the only female, he smiled very slightly and she found herself mildly surprised by the impulse to respond in kind. It was like being nice to an infant or puppy.

"There's a case I'm concerned about, Your Honor." Stan named it. "Involving a painter who fell off a scaffolding? A widower? There was a motion for a judgment on the pleadings. Do you recall that?"

Slowly, very slowly, Skolnick was beginning to realize there was some gravity in this situation.

"Mr. Sennett," he said. "I can call you Stan? Stan, there are hundreds of motions before me. Thousands. Thousands, actually. You should come and sit in my courtroom one day. It's not like the federal court, you know. I know a lot of the fellas sit on the federal bench—Larren Lyttle I know for years and years—and it's not the same. We still give argument now and then. We don't have full-time law clerks. It's a terrible backlog. And one motion, you know, it can look just like another. Now, if you had the papers, the documents, I'm sure I'd remember."

Sennett nodded and from her briefcase Evon withdrew Robbie's motion and McManis's response. Sennett let them drop on the new colonial coffee table, which matched the sofa arms.

"So I'm supposed to start reading this stuff at eleven at

night?" He murmured in Yiddish under his breath. "You know what that means? A horse should have such luck. Wait. Where are my glasses?" He found the spectacles in his pocket. "All right, all right," he said. He tossed his head back and forth as if he were reading a score, mumbling a few of the phrases aloud. There was no indication he was really taking them in. "Yeah, so okay, so there's a problem here?"

In his perpetual blue suit, Sennett was implacable. He turned his face for one second to scratch at his cheek.

"Judge, do you know a lawyer named Robbie Feaver?"

Skolnick sat back. Sennett finally had his full attention.

"Feaver?" Skolnick's tongue, like some furtive animal, appeared briefly and circled his lips. "I know Feaver. I know thousands of lawyers.

"Judge, did you have any private meetings with Feaver while you were presiding over this case?"

"Talk to him, sure. He's a likable fella. You tell him a joke, he tells you a joke. Did I see him on the street? In the courthouse somewhere? Of course. You should pardon me, Mr. Sennett, Stan, but that's not exactly a federal case."

"No, Judge, I'm asking if you ever met privately with Feaver to discuss the merits of this lawsuit and the outcome?"

"You mean without— Who's on the other side of this thing?" He thumbed through the papers. "This guy, McManis?" Skolnick paused, his heavy face slowly gravitating through the motions of thought. Was that his problem? This new guy, McManis? Was he beefing? Recognition suddenly flooded his expression. He pointed at Jim, finally drawing the intended impression, albeit far later than anyone might have predicted. "That's you! I see, I *see*! So you ran to the U.S. Attorney without even a how-do-you-do to me? I'm a reasonable fella. Tell me what's on your mind. You think we need this in the middle of the night?"

Sennett asked again if Skolnick met privately with Feaver during the case and Skolnick did an unacceptable version of what was meant to be a hearty laugh. His breath got caught up and he could not manage the kind of heaving exhalation he'd intended. His color, too, was rising.

"Well, I certainly don't remember anything like that."

"You'd remember that, wouldn't you, Judge? Discussing privately with a lawyer how you're going to rule on his motion?"

"Well, you know, lawyers can say most anything, Stan. They're not timid creatures. The *baytzim*, balls, on some guys, frankly. Sometimes I leave court, I say to myself, Barnett, you're too nice, you should have held that young fellow in contempt. But I don't." His bovine form rose and fell with his shrug, as if he himself were baffled by his benign nature.

"Judge, didn't you meet with Feaver on March 5 in your automobile?"

"Oh!" said Skolnick suddenly. He was happy as a child. He remembered now: Feaver had a flat and Skolnick picked him up while Robbie was flagging a taxi. He laughed as he gestured toward Jim. "So you saw that and got the wrong idea? Silliness," said Skolnick. "Stan, my friend, may I make a suggestion? Just be plain, Stan. Tell me who said what and I'll give an honest answer. As best I can. To the best of my recollection."

Sennett asked again if Skolnick had talked to Robbie about the outcome of the painter's case on March 5 in his Lincoln. Skolnick finally denied it.

"Did you meet with him in your car again on April 12?"

"This is a crazy discussion. We're playing ring around the rosy. If Feaver was there—and I said 'if'—then he was there for a good reason. That's all I know. That's all I can say."

"And giving you two bribes—$10,000 on March 5 and

$8,000 on April 12—wouldn't be good reasons, would they, Judge?"

Skolnick took quite a bit of time, apparently weighing the correct response, and then forced himself through the motions of outrage. After a slight quaver to start, he became quite convincing.

"You come here, in my home, and say such things to me? I took a bribe? Me? Barnett Skolnick? After twenty-six years on the bench? Me, who could have retired with a full pension four years ago? I don't need this *tsouris*, Stan."

"You're saying those things didn't happen, correct, Judge? You never met with Robbie Feaver to discuss the painter's case? You didn't receive a $10,000 payoff from him in March, or $8,000 in April because you'd forced McManis to settle before he was able to conduct any discovery? Is that what you're saying?"

"You're darn tootin that's what I'm saying. You're darn tootin. Nobody gives Barnett Skolnick money. That I would throw a case?" His face appeared on the verge of crumbling; a lip wiggled and his eyes watered at the ugly insinuation. He pointed again at McManis. "You go to hell," Skolnick said to him. "Go ask Feaver, for crying out loud. This is a complete *bubbie meize*, a wives' tale. He'll tell you that."

Stan nodded to McManis, the faintest foreshadowing of a smile apparent. Evon figured he had stifled a naughty impulse to simply lean back and call, "Come a-w-w-n down."

Robbie's tread was deliberate. He arrived looking quite drawn, ducking his head to avoid a soffit where the acoustical tile ceiling dropped to box out a heating duct. Evon gave Robbie credit. He looked straight at Skolnick and he did it with no smugness, no anger or pride. He wouldn't play it Sennett's way. He was unhappy to be here. Then, when Sennett lifted a finger, Robbie opened the button of his suit coat, undid his shirt, and displayed the FoxBIte, which had been positioned for show just under his heart. Even though she knew what was coming, the moment had the piercing effect of one of those sci-fi movies where a totally appealing character is revealed as a robot or some other creation with a mechanical brain and no blood, rather than a person.

Even as Feaver continued to face Skolnick, there was a certain vacancy to Robbie's expression. After six months of skipping along the government's tightrope, he was starting to lose his balance. Of course, he'd had a day to remember, starting at 6 a.m. with a revolver pointed at his forehead in a serious way. He'd told all of them in the van afterwards that, given what had happened at Evon's place, he'd realized as soon as he saw the cop that Tuohey had sent him. He saw it for what it was, a clever pretext for a frisk, one he couldn't complain about. He was still thinking Tuohey would show up, when the revolver was drawn.

'I heard the snap on the holster, and I was like, Well, okay, so this is how it's going to be. And I was actually all right with it, and then I thought, Oh my God, Rainey, how can I do this to Rainey?'

He cried at that point. McManis, Sennett, Evon, and I were all in the van with him, and I took the tears as a sign of the overwhelming terror he'd endured. I'm sure only Evon understood the full implications. Sennett, who'd remained visibly upset by the way things had gone awry, dispatched Robbie for home. He would be under twenty-four-hour guard now and there was a tap on his phone. Were it not for Rainey's condition, McManis would have preferred to move both of them.

As Robbie had disrobed, Skolnick had actually stood up from his seat on the family sofa. He issued a tiny, stifled outcry, ticking his head in disbelief. Barnett Skolnick, however, was not entirely without resources.

"You crummy son of a bitch," Skolnick said to Robbie. He seemed momentarily surprised by his own show of gumption. He coughed then and grabbed at his chest and, finally, in pure frustration began to weep. The extraordinary pile of creamy white hair resembled the topping on a soda fountain creation, almost luminescent against the sanguine hue that rose through his brow.

As Skolnick continued crying, Sennett directed Tex to play back some of the recorded output from the Lincoln. Tex turned on the TV Skolnick had been watching and found the VCR. He replayed the section in which Skolnick acknowledged the envelope Robbie had buried in the seat, saying to Feaver, '*Genug.* We're friends, Robbie. We've done a lot together.' Skolnick rocked on the sofa with his eyes closed, weeping and murmuring, "Oh God, oh God, *oy vay,* oh God." He could not have seen much of it. But he'd already gotten the point.

"I'll never live through this," he told Sennett when it was over. "Never. I'm a dead man. I'm totally a dead man."

"You'll survive, Judge. It's up to you to decide how hard this goes for you."

Skolnick issued a tiny disgusted sound. Even he wasn't stupid enough not to recognize the pitch.

"Sure." He pointed to Robbie. "I should be a *schtoonk* like him. Right? That's what you want to tell me, right? That's why you're in my house in the middle of the night."

Sennett remained himself, calm and unrelenting. The Angel of Death. Skolnick was exactly where he wanted him. Already broken.

"You can help yourself. You can help yourself a great deal. A *great* deal. You have a lot to tell us. But I can't offer you the same opportunity later. Right now, tonight, you have to tell us everything and agree to help with the people we should be concerned about. We don't think you're the mastermind." Again, for the fleetest instant, a nasty grin played at the corners of Stan's mouth. "We know somebody put you in that courtroom. We know that not every dollar you receive remains with you. There's one name especially." Sennett sat down on Skolnick's new coffee table and, virtually knee to knee with the man, spoke in a low, intense tone.

"Judge," he said, "what can you tell us about Brendan Tuohey?"

Skolnick's mouth flapped around. "Tuohey?" he asked weakly.

"Judge, have you ever had occasion to deliver money to Brendan Tuohey personally or received instructions from him of any kind—explicit or implicit—about how he wanted you to deal with a lawyer or a case?"

"*Per*-sonally?" He seemed astonished, even flattered by the notion. "I barely talk to the man. My brother, Maurice, you know, Knuckles, he talked to Tuohey. Me? I talk to his schmuck. Whatchamacallit. Kosic. I talk to Kosic."

"But you do talk to Brendan Tuohey, you say, from time to time. You could have a conversation with him? You could try, for example, to ask his advice about how to deal with us, what to say?"

Skolnick's reddened eyes enlarged as he got the picture.

"With a jimjick on my stomach like him?" He pointed at Robbie. "Oh, sure," Skolnick moaned. "Sure. I'd be dead for sure. I'll have a bullet through my brain."

"This is the government of the United States," said Sennett. "No one's killing anybody here."

"Oh, right, hotshots. What, am I going to live with bodyguards and a nose job and a new name?"

"You'll be safe where you are. And afterwards your security can also be assured."

Afterwards. Skolnick's mouth fell open when he real-

ized that Sennett was speaking about the penitentiary. He
had not even considered that. He had been thinking about
shame and scandal. Ugly gossip. About losing his judge-
ship and his pension. Now another intense spasm constricted
his face. With a humbled moan, he fell again to uncon-
trollable tears.

"I think you should consider some other people," Sennett said. He pointed to the display shelves with the family photos.

"Ach!" remarked Skolnick in apparent rejection of Sennett's suggestions. He started to stand up, and it was only
as his hand suddenly shot to his throat that Evon could see
he was in trouble. His left leg came out from under him
and he canted backwards at an oblique angle, lingering an
instant, like a leaf in an updraft. Then gravity took hold
and he tumbled heavily to the floor, his shoulder striking
the arm of his new sofa and his hip flipping over the coffee table on which the court documents rested.

Everyone rushed toward him. He was conscious when
they eased him to his side. He seemed able to respond, but
for the fact that he was again overcome by weeping. He
cried in great waves.

"Should we call 911?" Clevenger asked. It was only then
that Skolnick spoke, getting to his knees and weakly waving a hand.

"Angina," he said in a wee voice. "I get light-headed.
I'll take a pill. I just need some time. I need some time
with this thing." McManis had him by an arm now and
pulled him back up to the sofa. They all stood in a circle
around him while the old man held his face in his hands
and poured out tears.

Eventually McManis motioned to Sennett and Evon, and
Tex came as well. They stood like the infielders around a
manager and the pitcher at a tense spot in the late innings.
The only one not part of the circle was Robbie, who'd

taken a seat on the bottom tread of the stairwell, appearing far too blown out to absorb much.

"Stan," said McManis quietly, "if we keep this up, we'll croak this guy."

"For Godsake!" responded Sennett. Tomorrow, tonight, while the bad guys were all scrambling like ants after their nest was flattened, something might slip. Once they were organized, layered off by lawyers who'd share information and forbid the government to contact their clients, nothing of value would happen. "Give him a few minutes. He'll calm down." He asked Clevenger to get Skolnick water, but McManis detained Tex.

"Stan," said McManis slowly, "Stan, this is not our guy. He can't do Brendan. Not face-to-face. He *never* talks to him. Tuohey will see hin coming a million miles away. He'll do the three monkeys, the same way he did with Robbie. And this guy won't be one-tenth as good as Feaver. It could be the *Titanic*. By the time Tuohey's done with him he'll have Skolnick swearing Brendan didn't know anything."

Sennett stared bitterly into a corner of the room.

"Stan," said McManis quietly, "this guy can testify. We can make him a witness. Let's preserve that possibility. Let's not kill him tonight."

"Shit," said Sennett. He thought another moment, then gave in with one of his unpredictably ugly remarks. "I suppose that's not the first headline we want to make."

Skolnick in the meantime seemed to have made up his own mind. He was wandering drunkenly toward the narrow, paneled stairwell.

"I can't do this. Not now." He wobbled and braced himself, applying both hands to the walls. His wedding band glistened under the basement track lights and seemed to attract his attention. "Oh God, Molly," he said. He took the first step and wavered again, clearly on the brink of collapse. Robbie, who was nearest him, reached Skolnick before he could go down. He threw an arm around the old man and, once the judge was righted, helped him up the first stair.

"One at a time, Barney," Robbie said. "One at a time. Let's just take it slow." With their arms entwined, they slowly made their way up together.

CHAPTER 40

SHERM CROWTHERS LIVED IN ASSEMBLY
Point, a spit of land jutting into the Kindle River which
had been the site of a French fortress in the pre-Colonial
days and of various tanning facilities when the city was
first settled. By the 1930s, as barge traffic diminished, it
had become the most prominent enclave of Kindle County's
small black middle class. After the Second World War, some
pioneering residents who were not afraid to mix—or to
bear what inevitably went with it—moved to University
Park, one of the first integrated neighborhoods in the United
States. Later, there was some exodus to other areas of the
city which had become more welcoming. Recently, a
strange transformation had started in Assembly Point, with
younger white and Asian families buying houses here,
prompting outcries from some long-term residents that the
Point was losing its 'unique character.'

For African Americans, however, Assembly Point retained a special significance. Many had been raised within
earshot of envious conversations about the Point, the bet-

ter life lived there, and the events—the country club golf, the debutante balls—that were otherwise alien to African-American life. A large number of black folks of means still refused to consider residing anywhere else.

Sherm Crowthers was one of them. His house on Broadberry was a mammoth redbrick Georgian, replete with white columns that supported a portico three stories above the circular drive. When Evon and the rest of Sennett's company arrived, it was only a few minutes shy of midnight, but Stan and McManis had agreed to proceed. Not only timing, but tactics, compelled them. They wanted these men at home unaware and literally undressed, in the bosom of their families, close to the comforts from which they would be exiled in the penitentiary. This was one of many hardball maneuvers Stan had learned while he was at the Justice Department in D.C., supervising prosecutors around the country. After indictment, Stan loved to swoop down on white-collar defendants—presumed innocent by law—and lead them off in handcuffs before waiting cameras. He called it a deterrent. Despite the howls of protests arising from the defense bar—me included—the Court of Appeals continued to tolerate these harsh techniques as if they were wartime necessities.

Robbie had been directed to the remote shadows of the front lawn, while the remainder of the party continued to Sherman's front door. The Crowthers household was thrown into an uproar as soon as Sennett touched the doorbell. A dog bayed and lights filled several windows. Finally, the porch's overhead lamp snapped on and a voice boomed through the heavy oak door, demanding to know who was there.

"It's Stan Sennett, Judge Crowthers. The United States Attorney for this district. I need to speak with you. It's urgent."

"Stan Sennett?"

"The U.S. Attorney."

"What kind of emergency is this?"

"Judge, why don't you open the door so I can discuss this with you without waking your neighbors. I'm standing right under the light and you've got a security eye in that door. I know you can see it's me."

"And who-all is that with you?"

"They're FBI agents, Judge Crowthers. Please open the door. No one here will hurt you."

At that, the latches and bolts were quickly slapped back. Looking no smaller to Evon than he did on the bench, Sherm Crowthers loomed barefoot on his threshold. Behind the front screen, he had a chromed pistol in his right hand. He wore boxer shorts, decorated with small red emblems, and a sleeveless undervest taut over the vast hummock of his midsection. His eyes were somewhat watery, so that it appeared he might have been drinking. At the sight of the gun, Evon had changed her position. Beside her, Clevenger opened his coat and put a hand on the holster over his hip.

"You think I'm scared of *you*?" Crowthers asked Stan, clearly inflated by rage. "That what you imagine, Constantine? I'll have tits 'fore I'm scared of you." Sennett, assessing the situation—and mindful perhaps of the pistol—chose not to answer. "Now what kind of damn emergency is this, six minutes of midnight?"

"Judge, you know, I'd feel just a little more comfortable if you would put down that firearm. Would you mind doing that?"

"Hell, no, I'm not doin that. I'm standin in my own home. It's six minutes to midnight. You a bunch of damn intruders, whether you're the U.S. Attorney or not, and I got a permit and registration and a constitutional right to this pistol and you can go head and check that. Now speak your piece and get."

Evon had gradually crept up close behind Sennett to look at the gun. Crowthers was waving it around, but eventually she recognized it, a Beretta 92 SBC double-action semiautomatic. He'd dropped it to his side after telling off Sennett and she could finally see what she'd wanted to: the extractor was flush with the slide and no red was showing, meaning a round was not chambered. She whispered to Stan that the gun wasn't ready to fire, reminding him it might yet be loaded. Sennett made fishlike circles with his mouth while he thought things over, then pointed to her briefcase for a document.

"Judge," he said when he had it, "this is a federal grand jury subpoena which requires your appearance tomorrow morning downtown."

Sennett held the white sheet right up to the screen so Crowthers could read it. He'd calculated correctly that this would alter the momentum somewhat.

"Gimme that here," said Crowthers and reached outside. He snapped the paper from Sennett and rang the screen shut, locking it before he bothered to study what he'd been given. He took only a second to do that, and opened the screen again, tossing the subpoena, which he'd grabbed into a tight ball, outside the cone of light on the front porch. It landed somewhere in the row of low yews that fronted the perimeter of his brick home. "Ain't no subpoena served after midnight gone require somebody to be somewhere at 10 a.m. You know that and I know that. So now you done your business, go on." He pointed again with the Beretta and stood back to close the door.

Sennett stepped forward to grab the screen's handle but, considering the pistol, resisted the impulse to pull the door open.

"Judge, if you have an objection to a subpoena, then you better take it up with Chief Judge Winchell in federal court in the morning. You and I both know *that*. And frankly,

Your Honor, when you go on trial, I don't think the jury is going to think very highly of a sitting judge treating a lawfully issued subpoena as a piece of rubbish." At the words 'trial' and 'jury,' Sherm had briefly allowed his head to fall back, revealing the full bushy depths of his gray mustache. "Judge, you're about to be indicted for racketeering, extortion, bribery, and mail fraud. By my calculations, the sentencing guidelines will keep you in the penitentiary for about eight years. And we came here because I wanted to talk to you before it happens. Now may we come in the house?"

"I hear you fine where you are, Constantine." Somewhat more subdued, Sherm eyed everyone else on the porch. At a signal from McManis, Clevenger had stepped into the bushes. Equipped with a rubber glove, he was placing the balled subpoena in a plastic evidence envelope. "I don't know a damn thing about any kind of racketeering or bribes. Or whatever else you say."

"Would you like to refresh your memory, Judge? We can play you a recording? It's right here."

He waved at that point, and Robbie, with his hands sunk deep in his pockets, emerged into the light. He looked only a little less unhappy than he had at Skolnick's. He did not come all the way to the porch. He'd undoubtedly seen the pistol and had had his fill of guns for one day. He stood about twenty feet from the stoop, just close enough that Crowthers could tell who he was. And then, as he had at Skolnick's, he opened his jacket and his shirt.

Crowthers said nothing at first. And then his craggy, smoke-stained teeth made a brief appearance as he bitterly smiled. Sennett again offered to play the tape.

"I don't need to hear nothin, Constantine. I knew exactly what that lowlife was up to." He looked toward Robbie through the night, assailing him with savage eyes. "Goddamn fool that I was," Sherm quietly added.

"Judge, that's your option. There are a lot of things we want to ask you. But the most important is to know where the money goes after it gets to you. Because we're very certain all of it doesn't remain in your hands. And if you're willing to cooperate with us, right now, right here—"

Crowthers gave his big head a single solemn shake.

"You'll hear from my attorney in the morning. There idn't nothin else to say now."

"Judge, I can't make you the same deal tomorrow. You have to do it now. You'll pay a high price for protecting your friends—"

Crowthers, facing all of this—the grand jury, trial, the penitentiary—laughed out loud. He even put the pistol down on a side table near the door.

"Listen, I don't have friends, Constantine. Never have. I got a wife and a sister and a dog and that's it. I don't owe nothin to anybody else and I don't expect anything from them either. That's how it is."

"Then help *yourself*," Sennett implored, raising his voice for the first time.

Crowthers laughed again. He appeared sincerely amused.

"Is that what you call it? 'Helpin' myself? You know where I was raised up, Constantine? Down in Dejune, Georgia? I used to pick walnuts for two and a half hours, before I walked to some shabby single-room school they'd set aside for the nigger-folk, and most days I didn't have very much to eat, virtually nothin except those nuts, which my momma naturally enough was always beggin me to leave alone. And then after—" He stopped himself, suddenly drawing up both large hands, the pale palms exposed.

"No," he said emphatically, "no, I'm not goin on like that. You've heard all these stories. Everybody's heard em now. Any black bastard over the age of fifty in a pool hall can tell you these stories, Only I'm not just woofin. This here happened to me. And to my sister. My mommy and granddaddy. And I'm not tellin you this to break your heart, Constantine. I know better'n that, and wouldn't care to have your damn sympathy anyway. No, I just want you to know one goddamn thing: you never gone do worse to me than I've already had done. And I haven't come all this way—from Georgia and totin those bags of nuts bigger than I was, and bein so hungry I sometime ate beetles I found in the road—I ain't come from there to have some posse of white men—and you ain no better," he added to Clevenger, who was black, "I ain come from there to have you-all tell me what I gotta do 'fore you do something awful to me. You do what you're gone do. But there is no one in this world can stand on my doorstep tellin me, 'You gotta.' And surely not some pissant, stick-up-his-ass Greek-town greaseball who can't even look in the mirror and re-member that's all he really is."

Crowthers glowered briefly, then reached to his side and took hold of the slide on the pistol. The sharp click of him jacking a round into the Beretta was weirdly distinct in the midnight silence of the quiet neighborhood. Everyone on the porch reacted at once. McManis yelled, "Gun!" and more or less smothered Sennett, flying with him toward the bushes. Clevenger hit the sidewalk and rolled to his belly, scrambling to get hold of his weapon as he whirled around on the concrete. Behind her, Evon could hear the change and the keys in Robbie's pockets jangling as he fled. The best trained, she had simply stepped out of the light and dropped to her haunches, leveling her weapon with both hands. She had a clear line on Crowthers, brightly backlit by the handsome slate foyer of his home, but she saw at once there would be no need to shoot. Crowthers had bent his face close to the screen with a broad mirth-ful expression as he surveyed the chaos he'd created. Once he'd taken sufficient enjoyment, he slammed the front door so hard that the brass knocker raffled back and forth. From inside, as he snapped all the latches and chains and bolts in place, they could hear him laughing, a sound that went on for quite some time, even after he'd shut off all the lights and left them there in the dark.

CHAPTER 41

THEY WERE BACK IN THE CENTER CITY AT
about 12:30 a.m. and went up to McManis's conference
room to talk over where they were. Sennett was unexpectedly paged. It turned out to be the City Desk at the
Tribune. They had the story: government mole in the courthouse. Tuohey had figured a way to spread the word to his
cohorts without risk. Stan had about ten minutes before the
1 a.m. deadline on the late edition to decide how to respond. He settled on no comment, hoping the paper didn't
have enough confirmed information to run the story. If so,
the Petros investigators would get one last day to operate
with the advantage of surprise.

At 1:10, the reporter, Stew Dubinsky, called back. They
were going with their story. Stan had known Dubinsky for
years and concluded this wasn't a ploy. After talking it over
with McManis, Stan went on background with Stew. Sennett's goal was to make it sound as if Petros was already
a staggering success. Thousands of hours of tape, he said.
Dozens of undercover encounters with an enormous array

of courthouse personnel. No comment on how high it went, but judges, plural, were sure to be indicted.

The group—Stan, McManis, Evon, Robbie, Tex, and Amari—sat around the conference table skulling things out until nearly two. There would be calls tomorrow from defense lawyers feeling around. If somebody out there was frightened enough, he might make an anonymous proffer hoping for immunity. Things could break from any direction.

By now it made no sense to go home. Robbie called again to check on Rainey, then went up to his office to sleep a few hours on his sofa, something he had often done during trials. For almost everybody on the team, it was the second straight night with little or no sleep, but Evon was still running on adrenaline. Twice within twenty-four hours, she'd had a gun in her hand, ready to fire. You didn't come down from that fast. She volunteered to go upstairs with Robbie to stand guard. She was ready to talk, but he waved to her from the couch and with that fell backward, appearing to succumb to sleep in descent.

At 4:15 she made coffee in the office kitchen and brought a cup back for each of them. It seemed unimaginable that she'd lived six months without caffeine, while she'd been playing Mormon. Robbie was awake, just setting down the phone when she opened his door.

"Rainey?" she asked.

"Mort. I wanted to talk to him before he read the papers." He hadn't put on his shoes yet and took an instant to study his toes. She asked how Morty had taken it.

"Shock? Disbelief? I told him to hire a lawyer, you know, cause he can have some trouble with his license, but he seemed more worried about me." He was by himself momentarily, smiling contentedly at the thought of Mort. "He knows he'll be okay anyway, if the story is coming from me." He looked up at Evon after he'd said that, but she was too tired to probe.

Everyone assembled again at 4:45. Driven by Amari, the surveillance van swept into the garage beneath the LeSueur, and Sennett, Evon, McManis, and Robbie jumped in. They'd just parked across the street from St. Mary's when Tuohey and Kosic arrived at the foot of the three tiers of cathedral stairs. Rollo looked down the street, a cigarette hanging from his lips, while Tuohey headed upward deliberately, his pace and posture suggesting he would pray with special determination today. Several vehicles from Joe's surveillance crew circled on the avenues.

Summer had not yet arrived and even spring was frittering. It had been less than forty overnight and the smoke of the furnaces kicking in wisped away above the roofs, carried off against the livid hues of first light. The large redbrick church was narrowly imposed on a triangular piece of land. The adjoining streets, largely untrafficked, angled off beside St. Mary's, the big buildings set back from the pavement and all but vacant at this hour. An arid beauty arose from the quiet avenues in these last few moments of repose. This was the city, thousands of souls nearby in slumber. The race, the journey would begin again soon.

Rollo walked alone. He was cold. He jammed his hands in the pockets of his windbreaker, striding briskly toward Paddywacks, where Milacki would meet him as Plato opened the doors.

As soon as Kosic was clear of the church, McManis gave the signal and the first car pulled up abruptly at the curb beside him. The agents surrounded Rollo, pointing back to the van. The idea was to get him inside, where they'd planned an elaborate show-and-tell. But Kosic just threw his hand at them and resumed walking.

The van followed him along the curb, but he refused to look over. Finally, Sennett disembarked. Stan had to hustle to catch up with him. Evon watched through the bubbled window. Kosic wouldn't stop as Sennett spoke to him. Finally McManis alighted and trotted up to the pair. He touched Rollo's sleeve, and although Kosic shirked him off violently, he halted when McManis spoke. He seemed to recognize Jim somehow and finally appeared taken aback. Apparently, they hadn't yet realized the intricacy of the government's deceptions.

McManis had left the van with the torn note Rollo had written at Attitude and with some of the bills on which his prints had turned up. They were all stored in clear plastic envelopes, edged in tape that said EVIDENCE in red. Jim was careful not to let Kosic touch any of this. Instead, he stood a few feet away and displayed each item, holding it by its upper corners, looking like a streetside vendor outside a shrine. Sennett was talking all the time. Evon could not read his lips but she knew the pitch anyway. Rollo was dead. Deader than dead. There were stiffs in the graveyard who were lively by comparison. They had taps on his phone. Surveillance. Rollo had just a few minutes to make a decision that would control the rest of his life.

Finally, as the coup de grâce, Sennett motioned to the van and both Robbie and Evon stepped out to the curb. Feaver, this time, seemed robust. He winked at Rollo and threw up one palm in greeting.

Kosic's eyes, as always, were daggers of malice. He said one thing to Sennett.

"Suck my dick," he told the U.S. Attorney and resumed walking, bucking his arms like chicken wings to warm himself. Sennett called threats down the street. He was going to convict Kosic, then immunize him. He'd jail him for perjury or contempt if he lied or remained mute. Kosic would do time, then more time. Rollo had two choices: a lifetime in the can or putting it on Tuohey. His number was up.

Thirty feet on, Kosic finally wheeled. But he directed nothing to Sennett. It was Robbie on whom he focused, his dry face wrenched by anger. Kosic pointed the black nail, then threw out his hand at groin level, twisting his wrist violently in the air. It was not clear if this was a wish about what he'd done the last time he saw Robbie at Attitude, or a threat for the future, but it was certain he did not mean well.

MY PHONE RANG at six-thirty that morning. I picked it up in the kitchen, rushing to grab it before it wakened Patrice, who'd just returned again from Bangkok. It was Sennett. I'd already seen the headline on the *Tribune* on my doorstep. GOVERNMENT MOLE NABS JUDGES.

Stan received my congratulations with little enthusiasm. The atmosphere of manic secrecy had finally lapsed; there were no code words or subverted tones. Stan sat in the United States Attorney's Office after an exhausting evening and gave me the lowdown on what had transpired last night in a weary but forthcoming fashion.

Despite Sennett's failures with the biggest targets, the prosecutors had still had some success. Judith had 'pancaked'—flattened and flipped—when Moses Appleby explained that the government would be able to forfeit her restaurant, once she was convicted of racketeering. Milacki had sent Moses away, but without acrimony; Sig appeared to be considering his options. Another team, led by Assistant U.S. Attorney Sonia Klonsky and Shirley Nagle, had also had mixed results. Walter Wunsch had shown no inclination to meet his maker with a clean conscience. He'd listened to Robbie's recordings in his living room. His wife, in her curlers, had more or less bullied her way in and, once she had the picture, berated Walter about his brains and character, a barrage Walter'd absorbed like a stone. When Klonsky's pitch was over, Walter referred to Malatesta as 'a cluck' and stated that he "never gave Silvio shit.' Aside from that, he'd refused comment, except to note that he now had two reasons to be glad he'd be dead soon. He did not elaborate on either, but he was glowering at his missus when they left.

After that, things for Klonsky and Shirley's team had improved. Two clerks, Joey Kwan and Pincus Lebovic, had turned, without any promises, and had been debriefed through much of the night. Both had named several lawyers for whom they had carried money; Kwan gave up three judges who were now sitting in the Felony Division. Both Pincus and Joey were on the phone in the federal building at this very moment, the tape recorder reels turning behind them as they called every lawyer and judge they'd implicated, telling them about Robbie, and trying, supposedly, to cook up stories that would explain various odd-looking financial transactions when the Bureau knocked on the door. Rousted from bed at three or four in the morning, many of the subjects had been too frightened to be guarded and the results were notable already. Petros, like an ink spill, was already spreading darkly.

For the moment, Sennett was wondering whether to let TV cameras into McManis's law office. He'd have to clear it with UCORC, but the elaborate cover, the equipment, the expense and care of the government's efforts would be intimidating to the bad guys and might shake a few of them loose. The news that the FBI had been operating a law office right out of the LeSueur Building was bound to break soon anyway. Stan seemed to be seeking an opinion from me, but I expressed none. Now that the veil had been lifted, we'd all have to resume our standard roles.

In relating all of this, Stan's tone had been somewhat listless. I assumed he was exhausted, or perhaps taking it easy on me, guessing correctly that I felt a considerable pang that I hadn't been there to witness the concluding scenes in the drama. But it turned out that despite the government's advances, the same bone was still stuck in his throat.

"I can't believe we won't get Tuohey. I can't believe it."

He had a solid case on Kosic, but nothing beyond that. No matter how obvious it was as a matter of common sense that Rollo could not have been freelancing, there was no evidence, circumstantial or direct, that tied Tuohey to either the money Rollo accepted or the directives that Kosic occasionally issued. As Robbie had always insisted, Tuohey had seen far ahead and planned accordingly. Kosic stood between Brendan and trouble like a castle moat.

Stan had sent Robbie home to sleep, with several agents to guard him, but there was a problem with Feaver that had prompted Stan's call. Robbie insisted on paying a personal visit to Magda Medzyk, in order to explain face-to-face. He knew he'd never get through the buzzer at her apartment, so he intended to make a trip today to the courthouse. Stan was worried about the reactions Feaver's presence there might excite. My assignment was to convince my client not to go.

When I arrived at Robbie's house, there were two agents in the driveway. I had a little trouble with them, until Klecker appeared and walked me inside. Evon was taking a sleeping shift in an empty bedroom upstairs. Robbie was also out cold, and I decided I'd let him sleep a while longer.

I'd brought a stack of the newspapers for all of them, and Alf and I talked it over—he'd gotten his own reports on the flip teams and he was, as usual, jolly. Joey Kwan, in his haphazard way, had already made two great tapes on felony court judges. He'd played dumbbell, the language-hampered Chinaman who needed everything repeated and explained several times. The perps had barfed all over themselves.

Robbie wandered down. He'd gotten up to check on Rainey, who was unchanged. I'd heard the quiet whoosh of the inhalation equipment without realizing what it was. Shallowly, desperately, she breathed, drowning, as it were, in her own bed.

"Finally a star," Robbie said, when he caught sight of the papers. "Christ, where'd they get that picture? It's worse than my driver's license." It was an archive photo of Robbie coming out of the courthouse, an off-angle hurried shot, taken as he was emerging in the thrall of a big win. He sported a vulpine smile, which would send exactly the message Stan desired.

Eventually, Robbie and I drifted back to the family room, a huge space, which descended a few steps off the kitchen. Like the rest of the house it had been glamorously decorated in an overstated contemporary fashion, with raw silk wallcoverings and bowl-shaped furniture. Because it fell to another level, the room had been virtually abandoned during the course of Rainey's disease. The giant projection TV formerly housed here had been moved to their bedroom, while the various machines that had aided Rainey in earlier stages of her illness were now warehoused in rows: the motorized wheelchair, lifts, trapezes, an elevated bed she had given up. It was like sitting in a hospital supply room.

Robbie literally gave Stan's request the back of his hand.

"I'm not really asking, George, I'm telling. They can help me or not. I gotta see Magda. They can bring me there in the Popemobile, but I'm going."

I made a desultory effort to change his mind, then let it go. He told me I should be braced for a call from Mort's lawyer, whoever it might turn out to be.

It was approaching nine as I drove back into town. I already had eight messages from attorneys and one from Barnett Skolnick. I asked my secretary to contact each caller and explain that if they'd phoned concerning the FBI's investigation at the courthouse—and, as it turned out, they all had—a conflict would prevent me from holding any conversation. The local news stations, when I flipped on the radio, were all Petros, all the time. I told myself not to gloat, it was none of my business. But my hair stood on end when I heard an anonymous lawyer who'd been pulled aside on the street remark that practicing law in Kindle County would be better from this day forward.

Nonetheless, a good 80 percent of what was reported was wrong, some of it almost comically in error. Every station, for example, claimed authoritatively that Robert Feaver was actually an FBI agent. As a result, I wasn't sure how to take the flash item that ran around nine-thirty, as I was approaching Center City. Despite the heavy traffic, I pulled over in a no-parking zone to be certain I didn't run anyone down as I punched between stations. The same story was repeated everywhere: within the last hour, a high-ranking court official in the Common Law Claims Division named Rollo Kosic had entered the men's sauna at a downtown health club and shot himself through the head with a police-issue revolver. There was speculation, presently unconfirmed, that Kosic's death was related to the widespread FBI investigation of courthouse corruption, code-named Project Petros.

CHAPTER 42

AROUND TWO THAT SAME DAY, A DELE-
gation comprised of Evon, Amari, Klecker, and Robbie arrived at the Temple in the surveillance van. Judge Winchell
had signed an order authorizing the FBI to seize Barnett
Skolnick's Lincoln and to remove the taping system from
it. Skolnick had hired Raymond Horgan, Sennett's old boss
in the Prosecuting Attorney's Office, to represent him, and
Raymond had turned contentious when he was served with
the seizure notice. He'd forced a brief hearing in front of
Judge Winchell at noontime, but he'd ultimately surrendered the key, rather than require the car to be towed. While
Raymond was almost certainly posturing for purposes of
negotiation, Moses Appleby had directed Klecker to make
an elaborate video for the benefit of a future jury, not only
depicting the removal of the equipment but also demonstrating how the taping of Skolnick had taken place. When
that was done, Sennett and McManis had agreed that Robbie, with an FBI escort, could pay a short visit to the chambers of Magda Medzyk.

In the wake of the news about Kosic, everyone seemed off-kilter. Evon herself did not know what to make of it. They'd spent so many months telling themselves there were mortal dangers to what they were doing that a fatality could hardly be called unexpected. But she'd never envisioned it might be one of the bad guys. No one was collecting for a wreath, but even Sennett had wondered out loud if he'd overdone it this morning. Rollo apparently believed him when Stan told him he had no way out.

Rollo'd had his revenge anyway, since he'd taken with him the last hope of prosecuting Tuohey. Brendan's defense was now patent: blame Rollo, say he was the mastermind. Clothed with the authority of the Presiding Judge, Kosic had collected money, made assignments, given orders, all without Brendan's knowledge, much as the government's own evidence would show had occurred with Walter and Malatesta. The bastard had misled poor, trusting Tuohey and then taken his life rather than confront the boss and friend he'd betrayed. That would sell with the public, even some segments of the bar. Kosic had saved Tuohey not only from indictment but also from ridicule.

In the Temple garage, an agent operated a standard video cam as Klecker showed how he'd punctured Skolnick's tires. Then the Lincoln was repositioned out in front of the courthouse. For the camera, Robbie briefly stood on the spot where he'd met Skolnick, then he entered the Lincoln and turned the key to power the system. Standing outside the surveillance van, Klecker used the remote to turn the camera on and off a couple of times; then the van was driven down the block to demonstrate the range of transmission. Once everything had been acted out for the jury, Feaver killed the ignition.

With the Lincoln parked right in front of the courthouse, they decided it was best to take Robbie in from here now and to remove the equipment later. Amari remained behind in the surveillance van down the block to watch over everything. Klecker had brought a bulletproof vest for Robbie, but Robbie refused it and turned petulant when Evon attempted to persuade him to put it on.

"A lot of people in there want to kick my ass, but nobody's gonna shoot me in broad daylight." He hiked off alone, forcing Klecker and Evon to catch up.

Robbie was in and out of Judge Medzyk's chambers in ten minutes. He said he'd spent most of the time waiting for her to get off the bench. Magda had made her law clerk stand in the room as a witness, which had proved a mistake, because she had been unable to keep herself from crying near the end.

"She's pretty Catholic," said Robbie to Evon on the way out. "She turned herself in to the Supreme Court Judicial Disciplinary Committee." He had suggested nails through the palms might have saved her time, which was when she'd asked him to leave.

They emerged from the courthouse with Klecker a few steps ahead. Evon was supposed to cover Robbie from the rear, but he was still smarting from the visit. What he felt worst about, he said, was that Magda had seemed resigned to the world of locked closets and prim restraints where she'd been cloistered when they'd first taken up. "She's at less than zero now" was how he put it. Whatever he'd given her had been jettisoned as she'd yielded again to the *in terrorem* lectures she'd practiced on herself over a lifetime.

Evon heard him out, unexpectedly pricked by sympathy for both Robbie and the judge. Then she let him take off a few steps ahead of her as she surveyed the broad plaza around the courthouse for signs of danger. There was nothing notable, attorneys with briefcases, messengers, clerks, citizens all moving briskly. The spring chill had persisted and the wind, a winter remnant, snapped the flags overhead, ringing the halyard of one of them against the steel pole. A few passersby cast looks at Robbie, who had suddenly grown recognizable thanks to the morning press, but they made no movement toward him.

Reaching the center of the plaza, he skirted the large modern fountain where the water was now running again, cascading over the stepped planes of travertine. Circling the perimeter, Robbie stopped in his tracks. Evon dashed two or three steps, until she saw the problem.

Brendan Tuohey was no more than ten feet away, hurrying back to the courthouse with a heavy briefcase. The weight of the satchel and the fact that he was uncharacteristically alone left Evon with an intuition that he'd been cleaning out safe-deposit boxes he'd shared with Kosic. Whatever the accuracy of that conjecture, the Presiding Judge, a man long practiced in concealing his troubles, appeared grayer and grimmer today. He was deep in thought and did not notice Robbie at first, even as Feaver stared at him. But when he finally glanced up, the fury that shot through his expression exposed him to the core: anger lay at the heart of Brendan Tuohey like fire in a forge. His long face, with its uneven complexion, settled into a harsh smirk, a poor attempt at his customary effort to evince feelings that had no connection to what was actually taking place within.

Klecker by now had looked behind and seen Robbie stopped, but hadn't yet realized why. Evon circled a finger at her side so that Alf would double back, but he was never going to get close enough. Instead she crept as near as she dared, and took a seat on the fountain's low basin, only a few feet from Robbie. She was fairly certain Tuohey wouldn't recognize her. She tried not to stare at either man, affecting the perplexed expression of the average citizen seeking a respite after receiving the usual scuffing from the law. Tuohey's words were blown to her in the wind, wavering as it rose and fell.

"Speak of the *divil*," he said. "Quite a bit of talk about you today, Robbie. Many good folks seem quite vexed. Must say, I'm a bit surprised to see you about in these parts."

Feaver said he'd had a little unfinished business.

"I'd quite imagine," said Tuohey. From the corner of her eye, Evon caught the older man creeping closer. "It's always been my lot to reassure folks about you. 'Known Robbie his entire life. Always trusted the boy. No need to doubt him.' That's what I've been saying. But now I read the papers, Robbie."

"You can cut the crap, Brendan. My life's over. My prize for flipping on you is a trip to the pokey."

Klecker by now had reached the other side of the fountain, but the two men remained far closer to Evon. Robbie seemed to be aware where she was and had edged a step or two her way. She remained directly downwind in the cool breeze and still within earshot. Tuohey was taking no chances, however.

"Can't imagine a truthful word you'd say about me that would be the least concern. But the penitentiary'll be a good place for you, Robbie. Give you time to contemplate your sins. You've been up to some terrible mischief over these years, if what the papers are saying is true."

"Brendan, you're not impressing me with this routine. I'm not wearing my electronic underwear anymore. Some big boy stole my toy." With that, Robbie stepped over the side of the fountain and into the low retaining pool. It was only knee-deep, but, looking in Tuohey's direction, he flopped down for a second into the frothing basin, then spun up like a dog, shaking off water in long silvery spangles. Feaver extended both arms laterally to demonstrate the lack of telltale bulges in his clinging garments. The temperature still hadn't reached much over fifty and Feaver eventually drew his arms back, encircling himself in the chill. His designer sweater now hung to his thighs and he still hadn't left the pool.

Tuohey watched him with his mouth pulled to the side, puzzling it through.

"You're a dramatic fellow, Robbie. I'll give you that. Master of the scene. I remember you, six years old and singing show tunes like your front stoop was Broadway. Only it wasn't, was it?"

"No, Brendan, I'm not in a Broadway musical. But neither are you. It seems kind of shitty that only one of us is going to the can."

Tuohey took his time, assessing this bitter reassurance and the mood in which it had been offered. Robbie was doing a great job of punching his buttons, and in the whirlwind of feelings, Tuohey had drifted a few steps but was unable to make himself simply walk away.

"You've always lacked perspective, Robbie. You've had blood in your eye whenever you heard my name since you were nine years old, lad. You never much cared for the way I'd take your Mame out on that sleeping porch in your apartment and give her a recreational screw on Sunday night. But you know, Robbie, mother or not, the woman had her needs. I've always realized what the burr was under your saddle when it came to me. And been good to you a hundred times over, ever since. For her sake. And yours. Not that it made an acorn of difference to you." The rage, so rarely near the surface with him, boiled over again as he pondered Robbie, still up to his knees in the turning water. "Just a mercy fuck now and then for a horny divorcee, and look what it's come to. Can you imagine? And a dead fuck, at that."

Having driven the nail in as far as he could, Tuohey turned in the direction where Evon was seated and swept by her and Feaver, without a glance at either of them. Robbie hopped out of the fountain. He was tightly bound in his arms and bent nearly double in the cold, but he wasn't finished. He called Tuohey by his first name.

The judge paused to deliberate, but remained unable to resist the contest and turned halfway.

"Pity about Rollo," Robbie said. Across the short distance that separated the two men on the plaza, Evon half expected the sizzle of a high-voltage arc. It was even now. They'd each trampled on the other's grave, but Robbie had one more shot, purely for vengeance. Apparently, he was well past the point of calculation. "You just remember, Brendan, while you're out in the free air, that the big difference between you and me is that I looked after my best friend."

He'd struck Tuohey dumb with that, much as intended. A victor of kinds, Feaver sprinted the twenty or so yards to Skolnick's Lincoln in a metered space at the curb. Klecker had not recovered the key from him, and Robbie slid inside. He was not thinking about much, he told me later, besides getting out of the cold and turning on the heater full blast.

Evon approached Klecker on the other side of the fountain. "Whoa," Alf suddenly said. Wheeling, she caught sight of Tuohey, hiking rapidly back toward Robbie and the Lincoln. She began running, but Tuohey was already motioning for Robbie to roll down the window. If Tuohey went to the briefcase, she realized she'd have to draw on him, but instead the judge set the case on the curbside and briefly poked his gray head inside the car. He reached in with one arm. When he turned back to the courthouse, there was a discernible spring in his walk.

Whatever Tuohey had said, it had troubled Feaver. He shook his head dumbly when she asked for an account. In the meantime, Amari, in his cowboy boots and his sportcoat, had come dashing across the avenue to the car. Joe, who was far more intense than McManis but generally as contained, was rattling both hands in the air.

"You're the greatest c.i. I ever worked with," Amari cried. He grabbed Feaver by both shoulders through the lowered window. "The sharpest. The best. Definitely the best." After a moment, she understood. Once Robbie had jumped in the Lincoln and turned the ignition, the camera had revived. Amari had been able to start the taping system, capturing the interlude when Tuohey leaned into the auto. "If I saw what I think," said Amari, "you just bagged this guy."

All four of them rushed back down the block to the surveillance van. Alf cued the tape, and the image of Robbie in his wet clothes resolved out of the jumble between scenes. He had one arm around himself as he rocked back and forth on the red leather of Skolnick's auto. He was fiddling with the heater controls when he suddenly started in response to Tuohey's motions offscreen. Robbie groped for a second before he found the chrome button to lower the automatic window. From the way he drew back, it was clear that Tuohey had leaned in, but he wasn't fully visible. Only the top of his gray head and his gnarly hand appeared within the frame. Out of the wind, though, his voice was clear as he pointed.

"Speaking of your best pal, Robbie," he said, "when Morton came to warn me on Tuesday about what you were up to, I left him with a message for you. Mind now, Robbie. So many tongues are wagging about you, you might get confused. So I want you to remember, when you get this, that it came from me." On the screen beside Feaver, Tuohey rotated the hand with which he'd been pointing. His thumb suddenly came up. With the extended index finger it had the form of the imaginary pistol little boys forever point at each other. And then, to remove any ambiguity,

Brendan, in a bare second, let his long thumb fall like a firing hammer and his hand jump in recoil.

"He's threatening you," said Meeker. "My God, we have him on tape threatening a federal witness!"

"I'm telling you," said Amari. "It's a dead-bang obstruction."

Amari and Klecker cuffed each other, then Alf shook Evon. Klecker started for Robbie, but Feaver had already gotten up to rewind. He wanted to see it again. He replayed the tape, standing right near the screen so he could listen, and then rewound and replayed it once more. By the third time, it was clear which line of Tuohey's he was recuing. 'When Morton came to warn me on Tuesday about what you were up to . . .' She was baffled herself about what it meant.

Alf hailed her up front so they could all call McManis together.

"Off the skyscraper, through the window, off the scoreboard, nothing but net," said Jim. He permitted himself a single giddy laugh.

They had yet to remove the camera from the Lincoln's roof. They drove both vehicles to the federal building, where the entire company, save Robbie, left the van and worked with two evidence techs to extract the equipment without any permanent damage to the auto. Then they returned to the LeSueur, where, they'd been told, a substantial audience was already gathering to watch the tape.

Robbie was too cold to come along, preferring to get into a change of clothes he kept in the office. For his protection, Evon accompanied him up. This morning, there had been frantic calls from the office about TV crews parked in reception, but building security had routed them by now. Two rent-a-cops were guarding the door.

This was the first look any of his employees had gotten of Robbie since the news broke, and he strolled through the overdecorated corridors of his own office to a remarkable silence, deepened both by his bedraggled appearance and by the presence of Evon, who seemed to vacillate between friend and foe on an hourly basis. Outside his door, Bonita, looking a bit bleary, shook her dark tresses.

"You don't want none of these messages," she told him.

Evon made Robbie promise not to leave the office without calling; then she returned to McManis's, where they'd held off the viewing until everyone was together. McManis and all the other UCAs, as well as the local agents from the surveillance squad, were elbowed into the conference room. Sennett came huffing in last and delayed one second further to call me, but my office reported I was with a client.

Alf slid the cassette into the recorder and worked the controls.

The screen filled with snow.

Alf rewound and fast-forwarded. He fiddled with the connections. Eventually he realized the tape was blank. He went back to the van to search and returned only with an empty box. It was quite some time before they started looking for Robbie, and that was long after he'd brought the tape they wanted down to me.

ROBBIE HAD BEEN A SIGHT in my reception area. His clothing was still wet, and for warmth he'd put on a heavy overcoat, a spare he kept in his office. His hair was clinging to his face, looking, without its blow-dried buoyancy, like the plumage of a crow that had been jumped by a cat. He asked to see me alone. I was in a meeting, but he promised to be only a minute. In the little reading room beside my office, he handed me the cassette and told me what was on it.

Ostensibly, he wanted legal advice about whether he had

any grounds to retain the tape. We both knew that was dubious, but Robbie was shopping for time. He had visions of Sennett making a nighttime visit to Mort's home. The tape would be the feature presentation on Mort's big-screen TV, while Stan banged away, trying to find out what Tuohey had meant when he said it was Dinnerstein who'd warned him what Robbie was up to. Robbie wanted to get the answer to that one himself, and, more important, ensure that Mort knew he had no more time before hiring an attorney. Sennett's terror tactics, especially his threats of prison, would turn Morty to pudding.

I asked Robbie if he'd told Mort he was working for the government. I'd long suspected that Robbie had informed Dinnerstein months ago, but Feaver insisted he'd kept his partner in the dark, not out of any commitment to Sennett, but because he had realized that telling Mort would place Dinnerstein in an impossible position. Sheilah Dinnerstein would never have forgiven her son if she knew he'd done nothing when he had a chance to save his Uncle Brendan. Even on Monday, after Evon's melodramatic appearance at the office, when she'd identified herself as FBI Special Agent DeDe Kurzweil and served that subpoena, Robbie had told Mort only that he had the situation 'completely covered.'

"He must have scoped it out on his own," Robbie said. "I don't know how. But I figure Brendan was up his alimentary canal with a router the past couple weeks. You know, 'What's the story with Robbie, why's he so strange?' I still can't believe Morty told him what he figured. I mean, it's *Brendan*, for Godsake. What'd he think his uncle would do, throw me a tea party?" Robbie was abject, unable even to face me, which was just as well, since I could not think of an appropriate consolation. Blood thicker than water? I realized Robbie had been protecting himself from just this moment when he'd chosen not to tell Mort in the first place.

He headed back up to see Dinnerstein, promising to call me as soon as they were done. By six, I'd heard nothing. I'd had several urgent messages from Stan Sennett by then which I'd failed to return. I was sure, though, that agents had fanned out seeking Feaver, and I expected McManis or Stan at my door any moment. My inside line rang at that point. It was Robbie on his car phone. He'd just been driving around, he said. He told me I should call Mort's lawyer, Sandy Stern. Feaver was about to hang up and I shouted to him to wait.

Had Mort explained, I asked. Had he said how he came to tell Tuohey.

"Yeah," said Robbie. For a moment he seemed determined to say no more. Then he gathered himself to the task and added, "He said Stan Sennett asked him to do it."

CHAPTER 43

ALTHOUGH HE IS ONLY A FEW YEARS older than I am, Sandy Stern has always been something of my hero. I met him immediately after law school. We were two Easton graduates practicing as defense lawyers in the inferno of the North End courthouse, and I was instructed by Stern's example. He showed me that no matter what the crime or the client, an advocate could remain an emblem of dignity. He is not much to look at, portly, bald, dark, with a face whose small features are engrossed by too much flesh. But his presence is imposing. He is Argentine by birth, his family the wandering Jews of the saying. A muted Hispanic lilt sings its own rhythm in his careful speech, in which the central cadence is always one of a precisely balanced intelligence. Much like me, he can be remote and chary of feeling. Our friendship has its tidy boundaries that are never crossed. But I came of age here thinking of him as the best lawyer I knew, and for that reason I'd never resented the fact that, in informed minds, he remained, more than me, Kindle County's lawyer of

choice in delicate criminal matters. Besides, whatever the
wounds to my pride, they were salved by his generous referrals. I was the first outlet for the overflow.

Sitting that evening in a corner, amid the precise Chip-
pendale surroundings of Stern's club atop the Morgan Towers, he told me a disturbing story. One night last June, Stan
Sennett and three agents of the Internal Revenue Service
had appeared at Mort's home. Sennett claimed to have reliable information—from Moreland's records, as it turned
out—that Dinnerstein had a pattern of remarkable success
in the Common Law Claims Division, over which his uncle,
Brendan Tuohey, presided. Sennett was going to find out
why, one way or the other. Here and now, Mr. Dinnerstein
could receive complete immunity and speak with total candor. The alternative was to watch the government wreak
havoc in his life, issuing grand jury subpoenas to his bank,
his accountant, his clients, his employees, even his neighbors. When Stan found what he expected, Mr. Dinnerstein
would be sitting in a federal penitentiary long after both
his children had finished college, assuming they'd received
scholarships, since Sennett would use the racketeering
statute to forfeit every penny Mort had made practicing
law.

Dinnerstein begged time to speak to an attorney, who
turned out to be Stern. Fully briefed by his client, Sandy
knew two things with reasonable confidence. The first was
that Sennett had nothing concrete at the moment; immunity wouldn't have been offered otherwise. The second was
that as soon as Stan reached Mort and Robbie's secret
checking account at River National, he'd have a good
foothold on proving what Mort had acknowledged to Sandy,
namely, that under his uncle's guidance, Dinnerstein and
his partner, Robbie Feaver, had been paying off judges of
the Common Law Claims Division for years.

What Stern offered, therefore, and what Sennett ultimately accepted, was that Dinnerstein would become a true confidential informant, and only that. Dinnerstein would fully and truthfully answer any questions Sennett asked. None of the information he gave, and nothing that came from it, could ever be used in any way against Dinnerstein, and he would never be called to the witness stand. His identity as an informant would be revealed only if Dinnerstein chose, an unlikely event given the tumult the news that he'd turned on his uncle would cause in his family.

In the best case, if Sennett's investigation foundered, Dinnerstein would suffer no disadvantage at all. In the worst, if the full truth about him emerged from other sources, Dinnerstein would resign his law license and attribute escaping prosecution to his attorney's sly manipulations of various legal technicalities arising from the fact that Mort had never actually had the stomach to deliver any money.

And my client? I asked. On his own?

Stern allowed his eyes to slowly close, then open.

"Just so," he said. "It was quite painful."

Quite, I thought, reflecting almost against my will on the lies Robbie had blithely told to save Mort.

The only consolation Stern had offered Mort was that Feaver was likely to negotiate an arrangement to guarantee his freedom. Since Robbie alone had had the fortitude to actually make the drops, he was an indispensable witness for Sennett. Stern suspected that Feaver's deal might include an undercover role, but they knew nothing for certain until mid-April. At that point, Sennett had been forced to tell them because of Dinnerstein's relentless pursuit of the settlement money due poor Peter Petros—and his lawyers—for Peter's fall from the stadium balcony. To keep Feaver in the dark, Mort had agreed to a ruse in which he, like Robbie, immediately recycled his portion of the settlement check which the government briefly advanced.

"Our agreement with the government," said Stern, "is quite clear that Dinnerstein need only answer questions, not volunteer information. But Sennett is a treacherous fellow and I warned my client from the start that sooner or later the U.S. Attorney would utilize even the most paltry inaccuracy so he could renegotiate. And, naturally, that came to pass." Stern eyed me across the top of his drink, scotch neat in a short tumbler etched with the club's crest. "Your client's phantom law license," he said.

As I'd surmised last month, Mort had known about that since law school. A few months ago the IRS agents who'd remained Mort's keepers, much in the way the FBI Special Agents worked with Feaver, had noticed something in the financial information Mort gave the firm's CPA every year. He listed only his own annual dues to Bar Admissions and Discipline as a deductible partnership expense, never Feaver's. By then, Morton had referred a hundred times to Robbie as an attorney, to having practiced law together. Sennett regarded this as a critical deception rather than a figure of speech.

"You can imagine the back-and-forth. But it gave Sennett the opening he wanted. On Monday of this week, three days ago, he informed me that all could be forgiven if my client agreed to play a speaking part in the elaborate drama in which your client was involved. There was again quite a bit of to'ing and fro'ing. But it was less, frankly, than my worst fears. He simply wanted Morton to tell his uncle that Feaver was going to join hands with the government and turn on all of them. I took this as some complicated strategic gambit, part of an endgame. At some point in the future, we'll have a number of brandies and you'll tell me how it fit in. I was puzzled, and had some dark thoughts. But I have never really followed the tortuous path traveled by Sennett's mind."

Several years ago, I was one of the lawyers who assisted Stern when Stan Sennett was threatening to jail him for contempt. Despite my all-night work on a friend-of-the-court brief in support of Sandy, his formal manner prevented me from ever learning—or even asking—precisely how the matter was resolved. Stern was free but somber in the aftermath and more inclined to speak kindly of vermin than Sennett. I usually tried to avoid any mention of Stan in conversation.

A waiter in a green frogged coat approached and fulsomely inquired whether either gentleman wished another cocktail. Another unemployed thespian, he was heavily committed to his role as a servant and actually backed off three steps before turning about.

Sennett had wanted recording devices and testimony about Mort's encounter with his uncle, all of which Stern stoutly refused. Dinnerstein had bargained to remain forever in the background; he would be a messenger and no more. Proof was Sennett's concern. But Sennett was resourceful. After years of surveillance, the government knew a great deal about the cast of characters at Paddywacks. On Monday evening, the Immigration and Naturalization Service paid a visit to one of the busboys, who held a counterfeit green card. At five o'clock on Tuesday morning, a local IRS agent named Ramos presented himself at the back door of the restaurant to fill in for his cousin, the busboy, who'd purportedly taken ill. An hour later, Mort joined his uncle for breakfast.

Mort had been instructed to withhold his revelation about Robbie until the agent playing the busboy was close enough to overhear it. Dinnerstein had barely been able to keep his eyes off the fellow as he circled the tables in his checked pants and white tunic. Finally, when Ramos began swabbing the adjoining four-top, Mort blurted out his news to his uncle and his cronies. Not long after Evon had stormed into the office on Monday, announcing she was an FBI agent, Feaver's secretary had supposedly approached Dinnerstein, mortified by a phone conversation she'd overheard: Robbie had just called a lawyer and told him to cut a deal with the government under which Feaver would turn and testify against everyone—the judges, Kosic, Tuohey, even Mort.

It seemed at first that the agent would have no more to report. Tuohey said absolutely nothing. Milacki uttered a variety of curse words, but Brendan had reached immediately for Sig's hand to still him. Instead the three men watched as Tuohey deliberated. They were drinking coffee out of the heavy, crash-proof crockery at Paddywacks, and Brendan picked one of the plastic stirrers up off the table and fiddled with it at length, occupying himself. Then Brendan Tuohey, Presiding Judge of the Common Law Claims Division, had held up the brown stirrer by the very end and Mort had seen what his uncle had fashioned: a noose. Brendan had tied a noose. He twirled it for just a second between his fingers so that Kosic and Milacki could view it, then let it fall to the table. Special Agent Ramos picked it up as he cleared the breakfast dishes, dropping the stirrer in his pocket.

A noose? I asked.

"In the eyes of a prosecutor. Or a best friend. Sennett appeared ebullient. But perhaps it was the letter 'b.' Or 'R,' for Robbie. Or simply a nervous gesture. A matter of opinion, no? And at any rate, it might be passed off as table talk, an impulse. Without some subsequent act to make the meaning more specific, it's worth very little as evidence. No?" Stern swirled down the last of his scotch and held it in his mouth a moment to enrich the descent.

"Those are the major details. My client instructed me to report them, for whatever they might be worth. Your discretion, as always, George, is depended upon and appreciated." He took my hand then and squared himself to seek my eyes. "There is deep feeling between these men," he said. "Your client has already heard this directly from Dinnerstein, amid a predictable flurry of tears."

And how had Robbie reacted? I preferred not to touch tissue so raw with my client. But these were the imperial moments of the criminal lawyer's life. What did humanity say and do in extremis, when a death sentence was pronounced, when a jury set a guilty man free, when a fellow found that the dearest friend of a lifetime had betrayed him? How could the impoverished gestures of daily existence accommodate such a momentous change in understanding? Stern needed no explanation why I wanted to know. Instead, he let his eyes go to the oak beams crossing the ceiling, sharpening his recall of the answer to the question he, too, had asked.

"I am told," he said, "that Feaver said, 'What else could you do? With the kids? With Joan? What else could you do?'" Stern brought his small alert eyes back to mine. "Interesting fellow," he added.

CHAPTER 44

"SO WHAT ELSE COULD HE DO, RIGHT?" Robbie asked Evon. She'd had a moment of terror when it turned out Feaver had left the office unaccompanied, but he turned up in the first place she'd looked, here at home. There were two Glen Ayre cops in front, reminding several camera operators from local TV stations exactly where the Feavers' property line fell. The officers said they had been running up and down the block for a while, shooting through the windows. There'd been a few more who'd left after getting several seconds of Robbie in the Mercedes as he came up the driveway. One jerk rushed in front of the car and Robbie had rolled him right off the hood. The coppers were still laughing about it.

She approached the door in a brusque mood, but Robbie looked like hell and he'd told her straightaway about Mort. Feaver wept, describing how Mort, too, had bawled like a baby as he admitted that he'd given up Robbie to the government to save his own skin. He didn't put a prettier face on it. But he still wanted to be forgiven. And Robbie forgave him. Mort had the kids and Joan. Mort was Mort and he was Robbie. There was stuff each of them could do the other couldn't, they'd always known that, and Mort couldn't handle pen time, no way was it possible. So what else could he do?

In the paralyzed stillness that followed, she attempted to let her feelings go to him, but they became caught up instead in shock for her own sake. There were a million details to sort through, months of events that she knew intuitively had an entirely different shape than what she thought she'd seen. What the hell had she been doing here? Why an undercover agent in the office, if Mort was already reporting to Stan? But that was obvious after a while. She was a beard for Mort, to keep Robbie unsuspecting about who was really informing on him, as happened, for example, with Magda. And without recognizing she was doing it, she in turn was watching Mort for Sennett. All of them secretly spying on somebody and Sennett the only one to know the truth. He must have felt like God on a bad day, laughing at all His creatures.

Embarrassed, Evon nevertheless told Robbie at last what she was supposed to: Sennett wanted the tape.

"Well, I don't have it. Not now. And George told me not to say anything else."

She tipped a hand. She wasn't going to quarrel. She called McManis to tell him Feaver was okay.

"Glad there's one of us." McManis had just learned about Mort from Sennett, who had been forced to explain what Tuohey meant on the tape. Jim had spent about ten minutes alone, then raised D.C. and asked them to start scouting around for a replacement, somebody to run the Project as it moved into its next phase. Thirty days was the best he could give them. The personalities here, he said, were just too rugged.

Jim had already said goodbye to her before he remembered to ask about the videotape. For the moment, he didn't sound as if he cared much more than she did. Thinking about it, as she cradled the phone, she realized what must have been getting to McManis. Not just Sennett. But UCORC. They'd agreed from the start that Jim wouldn't get the skinny about Mort. Some of that was understandable. Agencies rarely shared snitches. The IRS had Mort and kept him to themselves. Need-to-know, after all. But Jim had been sent out here to do all the heavy lifting, risk the life and limb of his people on the understanding he was in charge. The truth was he was just another marionette, and one who'd worked for months away from home on a case where the IRS, which had developed the critical information, would get most of the credit.

She found Robbie in the kitchen, a gigantic space, where one side was given over to floor-length sliding windows, another wall to a series of restaurant appliances which Rainey'd had privately enameled in the brightest white known to humanity. Robbie took a half-eaten chicken out of the refrigerator. They sat together at the small breakfast bar and picked at the meat while they each drank a beer. They said very little at first, then, unexpectedly, he began talking about Mort.

"You know, I didn't like Morty at first. When I was a kid?"

"Really?" She tried to make her curiosity sound more remote than it was, but the pang which remained seemed to constrict the word.

"Well, I'm six years old. That's when my father ditched us and my ma parked me next door with Sheilah Dinnerstein so she could go to work. Now, naturally, I feel like I've been given the greatest screwing since Jehovah called time and adiosed everybody from the garden. I'm all alone and I'm stuck with this geek with a leg brace, this strange, sickly momma's boy, who can't run, who's got this drippy nose and this weird hair, who spent a summer in an iron lung, which made him as frightening to me as the Mummy. Not to mention that his mother's a goy in a neighborhood with thirteen synagogues in eight square blocks."

Robbie had begun solemnly, but by now he'd taken on some of the brightness that inevitably reflected from him as he told his stories.

"So for a good six months solid I was ragging on Morty and slapping him around. And one day I give him a belt as usual for the pure pleasure of watching him cry, and something in his eyes— It came through like a rocket, this is the moment of my life. I said to myself, almost out loud: Morty feels just as bad as I do. I'm six, seven years old now, so I mean this is basically $E=mc^2$ for somebody at that age—and I don't know, that young, you have to say it was only a feeling, but I knew then everybody's got this, what I felt, this hurt, everybody has it somewhere in their heart. And I knew that I'd never really get away from it, and neither would anyone else. And life bears that out, doesn't it? It's being poor, or being alone, or being sick, it's not being loved enough or not loving the way you want to, it's feeling you're the doormat to the world, or a mean crud, or just not quite as good as the people you want to be like or be with. But it's always something, and it's devouring, for most people, this parasite always eating a hole in their hearts.

"And I wondered, I wondered and wondered why. Why did God make a world where everybody's heart is in pain? And hanging with Morty, looking at him, you know what I figured out? The answer. I mean, I think I did. You know why it's like that? So we need each other. So we don't just each take our guitars and go off one by one to the jungle and eat the breadfruit that falls off the trees. It's so we stick with each other, do for each other, and build up the world. Because misery does love company, and another soul's comfort is the only balm for the wounds.

"And how would you say it? How do they put it in the Bible? 'The shadow of God came over him.' I looked at Mort and knew all of that. And Mort knew that, too. And from then on, we just sort of held on to each other for dear life."

She did not know exactly what this meant now, and neither did he. Perhaps he was saying again that he forgave Mort, or was explaining why he would have to. Or perhaps he was telling her that Mort had violated the fundamental assumptions of their relationship. He twirled the chicken's wishbone in his fingers and considered it in the kitchen's nuclear glow, resuming his silence.

Talking to McManis, she'd volunteered to stand guard over Robbie again tonight. There were several agents who'd be arriving shortly to cover the house, but this, after all, had been her assignment to start, to keep an eye on Feaver. Right now she had no other place to stay, anyway. There were reporters encamped in the lobby of her building, hoping to get a look at Secret Special Agent Evon Miller.

Elba called down that Rainey's eyes had opened and Robbie was gone for quite some time. Rainey had seen something about him on TV during the day. He was going to tell her the story, he said, in about three sentences and skip prison. She was too weak to summon much by now, even occasionally too weary to wear the laser contraption that's looked like a miner's light which she'd been using to control the computer and the voice device.

While he was gone, Evon settled herself again in the spare room or the second floor. It was done up with elaborate yellow frills on the window treatments and the coverlet, a dayroom of kinds. She still could not accommodate herself to this life where money was spent just to be spending money. Looking for a pillowcase, she wandered into the would-be nursery for Nancy Taylor Rosenberg next to the Feavers' bedroom. A sofa bed was made up. Both Elba and Robbie took spell sleeping in here, while the other was looking over Rainey, massaging, applying lotion, checking the oxygen and the color of her fingernails Through the wall, she could hear the clanking from the cuirass as it finished its cycle of compression. Over it, intermittently, Robbie's voice was audible, cresting in the plaintive timbre of some disagreement. The speech synthesizer carried clearly through the plaster, but Rainey lacked the energy to employ it very often. Evon, however, heard one phrase that sent a shock straight to the marrow.

"You Promised," the robot declared.

Robbie emerged a few minutes later, as Evon was going back down the corridor, and he motioned her once more into the nursery. He was blowing his nose.

"She wants to talk to you later. Now that she knows you're FBI, she thinks you'll make me keep my word." He smiled faintly, but she felt a pulse, colder and more desperate, of what had traveled through her a moment before. She and Robbie had never spoken about this. Rainey must have just told him that she'd confided in her. Discovered in unexpected possession of a secret so intimate, Evon felt a brief impulse to double over in shame.

She said softly, "You don't have to do that, Robbie."

"Yes I do. I can't say I was lying. Not this time. I promised if she took it a day at a time, she'd always be in control. You'd do it, too, Evon. If you'd promised. If it was someone you loved."

Would she? The horror of the prospect sank through her. It was easy to say no, never, she'd learned right from wrong in church and in school, but those lessons took the living as healthy hopeful creatures, not the poor suffering soul who lay next door already most of the way to passing. The doctor visited every day now. He had told Robbie that he'd had one ALS patient who'd chosen ventilation at the ultimate moment, and remained alive for several more years. For days, Robbie had awaited that change of heart. But Rainey had seemingly made the other choice. As a trapped moth beats its wings, she breathed now, with famished urgency, requiring too much effort to allow normal slumber. The deprivation of oxygen and sleep would soon produce a hallucinatory state. While some clarity remained, Rainey was determined to go.

"Tomorrow," he said, "maybe Saturday. There are a few people she has to see. I don't know what to do about Morty and Joan right now. And I want to get past this fucking grand jury thing." Sennett had called the first session of the Petros grand jury for the next day. Robbie raked his fingers back through his hair and took a seat on the sofa bed. "It's not like you're thinking anyway. It's just letting nature take its course."

"I'm not judging, Robbie. Nobody has that right."

He accepted the reassurance, but, as ever, he talked. The doctor and he had tiptoed around this subject pretty carefully, he said. There were vials of leftover sleeping pills lined up on the bookshelf near her bed. Just a normal dose, the same amount she'd been taking a month ago, would be enough to plunge her into a slumber that would persist when he disconnected the cuirass. That was all. She would go on her own, in ten to twenty minutes, in peace. He was entirely still, imagining the event, the reality of being there with her at the moment she went from the present to the past. He took as much of it as he could stand, then his mind, predictably, jumped.

"So what exactly did you girls do that day when you were alone?"

She was vague. Read, she said. Talked sometimes.

"About?"

"You two," she said. "Love."

"Yeah, love," he answered and shook his head over the largeness of life. Then he angled his face in curiosity. "What about you?" he asked "Ever been in love? Along the way? Like I told you about Rainey? You know: Boom. She's right. She fits. She gets me and I get her."

"You mean do lesbians fall in love?"

He reared back. "Fine, you don't want to talk about it, fine."

She suffered herself a second, then apologized, battling back the reflex not to answer him, or herself. Had she been in love? Tina Criant, if that had happened, that might have been love. But it hadn't and she wasn't going to pretend.

No, she told him, she couldn't say she'd been in love.

"That's too bad," he answered. "You missed a lot of fun." He gave her a level look. "There isn't a bonus round, you know." To soften that he took her hand for a second. Then he seemed to come back to his own troubles.

"Jesus," he said. "Talk about the week from hell." He keeled over on the sofa bed and lay immobile a second, his arms thrown wide. "So would it like violate the FBI Code of Honor if I ask you to sit here for a little, while I sleep?"

"Nope."

"I mean—"

"Hey," she said.

He did not bother undressing or pulling the coverlet back. She went down and got a magazine to read by the hall light. His eyes popped open when she returned.

"So can I say I slept with you now?"

She reached over to bat his foot with the copy of *People*.

"Straight up," he said, "have you ever thought about that?"

"What?"

"Sleeping with me."

Good Lord! She shot her eyes toward the wall behind which his wife lay dying.

"I mean, I understand that I'm not the main attraction," he said. "And I'm not even hinting about anything real. But I just wondered, if just for a second—"

"People think a lot of things for just a second, Robbie. Most of the world's inside your head, right? But that's not my play."

"No, I know," he told her quickly. He was pleased nonetheless.

She looked at him with the feeling of something as large as a monument moving within her. How in the world could you ever explain this? They said some sculptors often saw form, beauty in the flaws within stone.

"Go to sleep," she said.

He did. His mouth at moments moved involuntarily like a baby's, smacking his lips.

Once the silence settled in, she felt something returning that she'd shunted away. Then Pandora's trunk swung wide open and she heard him again: No bonus round.

She crept down the hall to one of the bathrooms, needing to contend with that in privacy. She knew. Oh, she knew. There were moments when she felt she would melt with sheer yearning. But she didn't want what some other people settled for, what Merrel had with her husband, a love inseparable from the riches the world showered on him, or even what Rainey had put up with, loved, but as a captive, humiliated and paralyzed long before her body had deserted her. She needed something better than either woman had. So she just had to hope, like so many other people in the world, who went to bed each night and prayed, God, God, please send me love. She prayed. It was probably going to be a woman, almost for certain. She'd gotten herself that far. But today, examining herself in a mirror again under harsh light, she believed for the first time in her life that she'd actually recognize love and be willing to accept it when it came along. She'd missed her chances in the past, she knew that. But she believed—oh, truly believed as you did when the feeling of the holy entered your heart—she believed she was ready. She turned on a faucet and briefly bathed her face, then let her eyes rise so she could see herself as she dared even to think it.

She was someone else.

CHAPTER 45

WHEN OUR LAW SCHOOL FRIEND CLIFTON
Bering was prosecuted for the bribe he'd accepted in that
hotel room, Stan not only withdrew from Clifton's case but
appeared as a witness in his behalf at his sentencing. It
was a dramatic gesture, fond and forgiving, and I always
admired Stan for it. But it also burnished the patina on his
statue. It was important to Stan, the racially sensitive Re-
publican, to be seen as Clifton's friend. The same, I realized, could not be said about me.

Sennett was sitting on the hood of my car when I got
back to the garage under the LeSueur after my meeting
with Stern. As I subsequently learned, agents had been out
looking for me. When one of them had noticed me trudging down Marshall Avenue, Sennett had been called and
he'd relieved the G-man who'd been staked out on my
BMW. There was another agent at the door to my office
and a third waiting a discreet distance down the block from
my home.

'I greeted Stan by telling him to get off the car. He didn't move.

"I want the tape," he said.

I had spent quite a bit of time by myself in Stern's club, sorting things out. It's said that a lawyer who litigates against a friend is likely to end up one friend short. I'd always known that. And I'd never had illusions about Stan's nature when he was on the job. As had once been joked at the Bar Show, Stan was the true Hobbesian man: nasty, brutish, and short. I didn't mind that he'd kept Mort's secret; he was obliged to, having promised him complete confidentiality. And he'd warned me from the start that Robbie was lying, and was thus at his own peril for saying that Mort knew nothing of the payoffs. All of that was rightfully as it should have been. But I knew our friendship was over, nevertheless.

I clicked the remote to open my car. At this hour, close to 9 p.m., the garage was nearly empty. The light was murky from the naked sixty-watt bulbs hanging intermittently from porcelain collars in the concrete abutments overhead. The air was unpleasant with exhaust fumes and the lingering smoke of the tobacco exiles who snuck down here on break.

"Don't pretend you don't know what I'm talking about, George. It's grand jury day tomorrow, remember? Everybody's been served. And when Robbie gets in there, I'm asking the jackpot question: Where's the tape? And don't think I won't land on him with both feet if he perjures himself."

Moving toward the car door, I told Stan I was sick of his threats.

"It's not a threat, George. I'm advising you of consequences. There's a difference."

I had a consequence or two of my own to acquaint him with, I said. Raise the issue of that tape before the grand jury and I'd go straight to the Chief Judge, Moira Winchell, with a motion to suppress.

He sneered. "You can't make a suppression motion in front of a grand jury."

But he was wrong about that. There's a single exception in federal law in the case of an unlawful electronic interception of private communications.

"There was nothing illegal about making that tape."

No? I asked. Show me the consent form. Show me where Robbie provided the authorization the government needed before it could overhear his conversation with Brendan Tuohey. There was surely no warrant, as there had been with Skolnick.

It was always an odd moment when I outsmarted Stan Sennett. It happened rarely, but he appeared so flummoxed and defenseless at those instants it was hard not to feel sorry for him. But not tonight. Tonight, I had a good time watching him sputter.

"It's implied. His consent is implied. He turned on the car."

Only for heat, I answered.

"He had a deal and a duty to cooperate, George. Given all the circumstances, Moira's going to find his consent was implicit."

I wasn't worried about that anymore, I told him. No court would ever find that Robbie's consent was fully informed—or that he had any further duties under his deal. Not after the U.S. Attorney had engaged in attempted homicide.

"*Hom*-icide!"

Attempted manslaughter, at least I said. He had sent Robbie out to the Public Forest believing to a moral certainty someone was going to try to kill him on Brendan Tuohey's behalf.

Something in Sennett went into retreat. Seated on the

hood, he became a narrow, smallish man, unable to still a faint nervous flaring of his nostrils.

"He was completely covered. The surveillance, the protective detail couldn't have been tighter. And he knew he was at risk, George. He knew what he was getting himself into."

On the contrary, I answered. The setting was frightening. But as McManis had explained, logic—based on what the rest of us knew—said Tuohey and Kosic wouldn't share secrets with Robbie at Attitude, only to kill him a week and a half later.

But watching Rollo on Monday, when Robbie displayed the subpoena Evon had served, Stan had finally accepted that Feaver was not going to get close to Tuohey again. And so he'd decided he would have to nab Brendan another way. On Tuesday he'd sent Mort to betray Robbie to Brendan, carrying a message calculated to lead Tuohey to but one conclusion: they had to kill Feaver before he started to talk. And Brendan obliged Stan. Sitting at the table, Tuohey had tied a noose. And then Stan let Robbie go to the Forest to make sure the government had an ironclad case— for conspiracy to murder a federal witness. He might as well have painted a target on Robbie's back. And Stan had told no one any of that. Not because of need-to-know or his promise to Dinnerstein or any similarly flimsy rationale for manipulation. He'd kept silent because he realized that if anyone else understood his plan, it could falter. Robbie almost certainly wouldn't have gone out there. Nor would McManis have let him.

"I made judgments," said Stan. "On the fly. Under pressure. I see how you're looking at this, George, but these are evil people. Truly evil. They have messed with this city far too long."

In many respects, I still regard Stan Sennett as a great man. A great public man. He believed in the right things.

And if improving the world is the measure of a human's ultimate worth, he will forever be deemed a better person than I am. His commitment to vanquish wrong and restore justice was as powerful as Superman's. Yet military strategists will tell you about replication, an inviolate principle which says that organizations which oppose each other tend, over time, to become alike. In that light, it was no surprise that fighting evil, as Stan put it, tempted him to evil. But if self-respect couldn't restrain his crudest appetites, his zeal and his ambition, when they led him into darkness, why, I asked, didn't he at least feel some obligation to me? It was a sad conclusion after a couple of decades to find he lacked even a minimal desire to preserve our friendship, especially when it might have preserved his decency as well.

"Georgie, for Godsake. Don't be histrionic. We've had a tough day, you and I. We've had them before. Life will go on."

No, I said. No.

Still on the hood, Stan pondered me over his shoulder in the grimy light. A floor above, tires squealed on the rubberized paint applied to the ramps.

"Revenge, George, personal spite, that's not a good reason to let someone like Brendan Tuohey walk away. It isn't and you know it isn't. What do either one of you get out of that? You or your client?"

I had always yielded to Stan. That was our history. Not that I ever sold a client short or failed to challenge Sennett's positions in court. Yet I'd long let all matters resolve on the basis that he held the high ground of moral conviction; I swam, as defense lawyers do, in the brackish waters of compromise. I'd decided to represent Robbie Feaver to find out if there were absolutes I could cling to with the same tenacity as Stan, hoping that would provide me some comfort. And it did. At the moment.

I told Stan that whether or not he got that tape had nothing to do with me. Were it my call, I'd probably throw it in the river Kindle. But the decision was Robbie Feaver's.

You'll have to ask him for it, I said. You'll have to ask him, knowing he's got every legal right to say it should never see the light of day. You'll have to appeal to him, Stan. Maybe beg him. And I'm glad that's going to happen. Because it will remind you of something you've completely forgotten: what it feels like to be at another person's mercy.

I got in and started the engine. He scooted off the hood quickly enough to reflect some concern I might damn well drive away with him still on it. I'm not sure Stan had ever been frightened of me before. Needless to mention, the moment provided me with no small measure of satisfaction.

CHAPTER 46

THE GRAND JURY ROOM WAS SITUATED IN
the new federal building, a floor above the United States
Attorney's Office. The Chief Judge, whose ostensible duty
it was to restrain prosecutorial abuse, was a block away,
across Federal Square, in the grand old courthouse to which
the District Court judges all returned once the new building proved nearly uninhabitable. Built in Augie Bolcarro's
heyday, with subcontracts sprinkled down upon his henchmen like sugar from a baker's hands, the new building had
heat and air-conditioning systems that were eternally on
the blink. The windows, until each one was replaced, frequently popped out in high winds, terrifying pedestrians on
several blocks. For years it was commonplace to find a
herd of attorneys standing twenty or thirty abreast in half
a dozen federal courtrooms, bickering about one of the
pieces of complex litigation the new construction had
spawned.

The grand jury room's reception area looked as if it
might be attached to a homeless shelter or a cheap motel.

The low-grade plasterboard was marred and gouged, and the likes of the foam furniture, soft forms without armrests or separate cushions, had not been seen since the height of the sixties. The pieces had apparently been discovered in the recesses of some government warehouse and offered to various federal agencies at a price they couldn't refuse in the former Reagan era of suffocating budgetary restraint. Looking at the furnishings, you could just about imagine hippies in beads dropping acid and holding on to their headbands. Instead, for more than a decade, the witnesses awaiting their appearances had perched there, dejectedly hunched like molting birds.

Today there was an extraordinary assemblage. As always, Sennett had acted with cunning and subpoenaed everyone whom Robbie had recorded to any effect at all. Several obscure court clerks and deputies were here, as well as persons far more prominent. Sherm Crowthers sat like a lump of stone beside his lawyer, Jackson Aires, a skillful and obstinate government foe whose analysis of any case, much like Sherman's, reliably started and ended with race. Jackson had brought a colleague, a cat's-paw to represent the ravaged-looking Judith McQueevey, who by now had recanted her confession of two evenings before. There were thirteen or fourteen persons subpoenaed in all, and some obvious absences, Pincus Lebovic and Kwan, and, most notably, Barnett Skolnick, all of whom by now had folded and turned. Everyone else who stood in peril of indictment was present, even Walter Wunsch, whose pancreatic cancer left him unlikely to live until even the speediest trial.

The point of this exercise was relatively clear to me and not particularly pretty. To force an appearance, each of the prospective defendants had been served with a subpoena *duces tecum*, demanding the production of documents or physical objects in their personal possession. Datebooks seemed to be the chief item required, although two of the clerks had been summoned to bring merchandise Robbie had presented as 'tips.' Gretchen Souvalek, Gillian Sullivan's clerk, clutched a Tiffany box containing a set of earrings Robbie had provided for general ingratiation. Walter Wunsch, seated with his attorney, Mel Tooley—who represented a number of those present—had brought not only various court volumes but also the set of expensive graphite-shafted irons which Robbie had presented to him several weeks ago. Walter held the clubs, complete with a snappy black leather carry bag, against his knee, manifesting a state of glum agitation which made it look as if he'd discovered only after arriving here that he had not been invited to play. Following Robbie's testimony, each person would be called before the grand jury by Sennett or one of the phalanx of Assistant U.S. Attorneys assisting him, and, after various legal gymnastics aimed at skirting the Fifth Amendment, forced to surrender what they'd brought.

This exercise, however, would be largely pageantry. Stan had other motives in dragging his targets down here. He wanted them to confront Feaver, to see for themselves that his cooperation was not simply half-baked media speculation. He wanted them to face each other, familiar figures, silent conspirators, now brought low. Yet even this was ancillary to Stan's principal purpose. The morning papers had announced that the Petros grand jury was convening today, a result no doubt of one of Sennett's well-timed leaks. TV crews were downstairs, just outside the building's doors, and print reporters were stalking the hallways. They could not attend the grand jury sessions, which were secret by law, but they would report who had come and gone from the courthouse. As a result, each of the persons who could not find a comfortable spot on the uncomfortable furniture would be vilified by the end of the day. Still shots and video clips of them would appear in all the media organs. It was no less than a naked march through the streets, during which their presumptive criminality would be displayed like waffles and belly fat to the amusement or horror of every person they knew. That was Sennett's real aim—to crush them, to deal the first of many hard blows to be borne as the cost of refusing to cooperate, and to show them that most of the esteem they'd held in the eyes of others was already gone. Looking around the room, seeing everyone else similarly devastated, they would know that sooner or later one of them, probably many more, would do the only sensible thing—capitulate, snitch, do time, and move on.

Most of these persons didn't know me. When I emerged after escorting Robbie to the attorney/witness room down the hall where Evon and McManis were now keeping him company, only one or two of the future defendants cast spiteful looks in my direction. Sherm Crowthers, who sat clutching his sister's hand, clearly wished me dead. But the enmity that I felt broil me like microwaves came from another source: the lawyers. As the persons charged with protecting their clients from just the kind of savaging Sennett had delivered, the attorneys here—Tooley, Ned Halsey, Jackson Aires, several others—were in a nasty mood.

Tooley came to pal around first. With his silly toupee, like the coat of a shaggy poodle, and his tight Continental tailoring, ill suited to his hogshead physique, Mel was a vision of disingenuousness.

"I'd like to talk to your guy. Down the road, you know. Possible?"

Unlikely.

"Will you get me the answer to a question or two?"

That was more in the realm.

"I'll call you," said Mel. "You know," he said, turning back, "the one with titanium testicles is you. Your guy got squeezed. But nobody was forcing you to help him, George. I hope I don't have the co-defendant the next time you're in state court."

It was advocacy of a kind, the underhanded variety in which Mel specialized. He was suggesting I'd better quickly disassociate myself from the prosecution and help out the defendants if I wanted my practice to survive.

I had already turned heel without comment when, at the stroke of ten, Stan appeared. He was tight as a bowstring and in the happy clutch of the intense precision that sustained him. It had not all worked out as he hoped, but it was still a bright moment for him. He stood among the despised as the man who had vanquished them. He said good morning only to the grand jury clerk. Then, as he reached the door of the grand jury room, he faced me.

"Give me a second," he said, "to tell the jurors what this is all about."

"*I'll* tell them!" yelled Walter Wunsch. He was closest to the door. "I'll tell them plenty. American citizens! I fought for this goddamned country and now it's like Red China with spooks and bugs. Lemme in there." Walter had risen to his feet, a somewhat pathetic exercise, because he was already wasting. His flesh hung just enough to leave the impression that in the degenerative processes of the cancer his skin was attempting to slough itself from the muscle and bone. Tooley advanced from my side and made his client sit down.

"He's just tellin it like it is," said Sherm Crowthers wearily from across the room.

Stan took this in with an indulgent smile. At other moments he would have hated the disorder, but now he knew he'd caused it. He suggested I get Robbie ready.

I returned to the small attorney/witness room down one of the interior corridors. The space was often used for coffee breaks and quick lunches by the court reporter and the clerk. Arriving earlier, I'd nearly reeled from the driving odor of the white onions arising from a half-eaten sandwich that had remained overnight in the drab metal trash bin. Although I'd removed the can, the odor was still strong.

Except for questions about the tape, Robbie's testimony was predictable. Once he entered the small windowless room where the twenty-three grand jurors waited like the audience in a small theater, a desultory exercise would take place. He would identify his initials on the dozens of reel-to-reel tapes and computer magazines, and say, 'Yes, that's accurate,' when Evon's 302s describing various critical events were read to him. When that was over, come what may, Robbie could not change his account of what had happened without risking a conviction for perjury. There was even some chance this would be the last time he testified. Understandably, Stan had never wanted to stake his prosecutions on Robbie's credibility, and he'd constructed the evidence, especially the recordings, so he could prove his cases without putting Feaver on the stand. If he called him at all it would only be as a show of openhandedness for the juries.

We had brought Robbie in through the back corridor and secreted him in the witness room, but there was only one door to the grand jury room. As Stan had planned it, Robbie would have to run a gauntlet of more than a dozen persons who felt their trust in him had been primitively violated. But the notion that they were all out there seemed to amuse him.

"Curtain call," he said. His mood was somewhat dislocated. He was clearly too exhausted to be going through this today, but because of his refusal to surrender the tape, I had no ability to appeal to Sennett. At that point, Moses knocked and beckoned us.

"Ready?" I asked.

Feaver wanted one second and motioned for Evon to follow him the other way down the corridor.

"When Stan asks me for that tape," he said to her, "if I tell him to go scratch, where does that leave me with you?" The cassette was in my briefcase, but I still had no idea what Robbie would do. I didn't expect Stan to try to coerce Robbie into surrendering the tape before the grand jury, because I had the upper hand on the law. If Sennett forced me to go to Chief Judge Winchell, he stood a good chance of losing the right ever to use the tape against Tuohey. Instead, I anticipated a personal appeal at some point, an apology to Robbie, and a request he give up the tape and sign a form acknowledging, somewhat fictitiously, that he'd consented to the recording. I thought in the end it would come down to whom Robbie hated more, Brendan or Stan, although shame was also a factor: in a way, the tape memorialized Mort's betrayal. In arriving at a decision, however, Robbie was worried about something else.

"If you feel like I'm screwing you over by not letting him have it," he told Evon, "then I'll give it to him."

She weaseled at first, said it was his decision, not hers, but he wouldn't let her off that way.

"You know me," she said. "It's black-and-white. That's why I have such a damn hard time with myself. Two wrongs don't make a right. That's where I come out. Personally. But I'll stand up for you either way, bub. You tell him to go spit, I'm right here behind you." She stiffened her chin and nodded. Her only hesitation was McManis. She cared about what he would say, the same way Robbie cared about her, and she told Feaver that. They returned to the conference room and Robbie put the same question to Jim. Would he feel personally messed over if Sennett didn't get the tape? Would he feel like he'd wasted his time?

Jim adjusted the large frames on his nose. His demeanor

betrayed some of the intense calculation going on within, but his tone was placid.

"I think we did a lot of good work here. I'll always be proud of it. I'd like to get Tuohey. He's a bad guy. But I've lived twenty-two years on this job convinced that the government comes out the loser if you get a bad guy a bad way. So I'll handle whatever you decide. Personally, I'd say take some time. Sort it out."

Feaver nodded and looked at the three of us.

"I can't give it to him," he said. "Not today."

We all lingered there, perhaps waiting to see if hearing him say it changed anything, but it didn't seem to. Evon was as good as her word and patted his arm.

"Show time," Robbie said then, and opened the door himself.

"I think I'll come along just to keep you company," said Evon. "Just to make sure nobody gets disorderly."

Robbie reminded her that there were metal detectors at the entrance of the courthouse. The firearms and switchblades had presumably been left behind. But he seemed content to go forward with his honor guard, Evon leading and Jim covering him from behind and me at his shoulder. Robbie emerged from the shadowed corridor with his eyes fast and his stride certain. He looked handsome and heroic, fitting snugly once again into his role. His life as a lawyer was behind him and he had celebrated by appearing in a black shirt, beneath his suit, and no tie.

"Judas Iscariot!" cried Walter as soon as Robbie had stepped around the corner. The news that he was dying had filled Walter with abandon and rage. Evon immediately fronted between Robbie and Wunsch, and Tooley returned from one of his other clients to take hold again of Walter's arm. He was not easily stilled. "Fucking Judas Iscariot!" cried Walter. "You're just another loudmouth, stinking sell-out."

Robbie's wits remained in order.

"Right, Walter," he said, "and you're the Messiah."

His delivery was perfect and the acid rain of humiliating laughter drizzled down on Walter, even from a number of his confreres. Despite his condition, malice had revitalized Walter and it took a considerable effort from Tooley to push Wunsch back down into his seat next to his golf clubs.

At the door to the grand jury room, Sennett stood, his hands folded primly.

"Mr. Feaver," he said with imposing formality. He wanted Robbie to know he was prepared for anything. "How are you this morning?"

"Sick and tired," said Robbie, "especially of you."

Stan didn't flinch. God knows what he thought he deserved. Without a word, he opened the door to the grand jury room and extended a hand to show Robbie in.

I told Robbie I would be just outside and reminded him he had the right to stop Sennett at any time to consult me. Robbie smiled generously. He shook my hand and, as he often did, thanked me for everything I'd done, before he advanced to the threshold.

The sequence of events after that has always remained jumbled. In the ensuing moments, my reactions remained a step behind; I was still attempting to make sense of the first sensation by the time I was hit with the next one. Initially, I heard a sudden crescendo of voices, culminating in a drilling female scream. As it turned out, it was Judith, but for some reason I thought it was Evon and swung in her direction as something flew past me, stunning the air. A bird was my first impression, a pigeon, some silvery form. I jumped back in panic, and at the same time heard a flat sound, vaguely like the noise I knew as a boy when for mean sport we'd smash melons on the hot tar of the road. I realized, though, that something was broken. A small hard pellet ricocheted off my face and I was spattered with what I took first for mud. There was an animal smell from somewhere, sudden heat, then the low, guttural sound that Robbie Feaver made as he slumped against me.

I caught him and his completely inert weight pulled me to the floor with him. The back of his suit and the arm I had around him were warmed with what I improbably took first for soup, then realized was blood. There was enormous turmoil now, people yelling for the phone and for doctors, screams from inside the grand jury room, and Walter Wunsch hollering to leave him be, as Jim and Evon and three or four other persons subdued and disarmed him. In the process, they broke two of his fingers, but they pried from his fist the number two iron whose blade Walter had driven straight through Robbie's skull.

I saw the wound then, which looked wildly out of place, a welling gash distinct in spite of the gobs of thickened blood that already matted Robbie's crown. Somehow it resembled an open mouth, almost that wide, with red matter that might have been skin crushed inward and a single protrusion, white and ghastly, which I knew was a piece of Robbie's cranium. I had no idea what to do. For the moment everything in the universe seemed open to doubt. Realizing there was absolutely no point to it, I applied my handkerchief to the wound, watching the spreading blood-stain creep over the cloth. Evon had reached us by then and I told her quietly what I'd sensed from the first instant he'd fallen against me: I was afraid Robbie was dead.

Evon grabbed his wrist for a pulse, then tried his neck, and finally brought her face to his lips to feel for breath.

"Turn him over!" she screamed. Several of us helped her. She pounded his chest three times, then she grabbed his nose, from which a thick line of blood had already emerged, and, after a tremendous inhalation, applied her mouth to his. She went on with this for at least a minute as every person in the room, even those scurrying about at the periphery, watched. A phone rang repeatedly and no one picked it up.

A moment later, two Secret Service agents with paramedical training bolted in. They'd been summoned by one of the Assistant U.S. Attorneys who'd gone screaming for help. In another minute, an M.D. who had been testifying down the hall as an expert witness crashed through the door and took over. He placed his fingertips on the carotids, then got on his hands and knees and lifted Robbie's head gently to examine the wound.

"Jesus Christ," he said. "Somebody say it was a golf club? It looks like a hatchet."

The club, brown from the shaft to the toe, was still in McManis's hand. Walter, confronting what he'd done and the phenomenon of death that would soon claim him, sat in the same foam chair. His head looked almost unstrung from his body, leaning against the metal doorframe of the grand jury room. He held his broken hand rigidly in the air. A private security guard had appeared from somewhere and stood over him.

The 911 paramedics arrived then. They were wheeling oxygen tanks and they fastened the mask over Robbie's mouth and strapped him to the cart.

"No, I don't want to pronounce him," the M.D. said.

Evon sat on the floor with her back against the wall. Her hand, blood-painted up to the knuckles, was over her mouth and she stared out unseeing. Sennett, who had run for help, dashed back into the room. When he saw me, he averted his eyes. He addressed McManis and asked how the hell it could have happened. Jim did not bother to reply.

I stood and helped Evon to her feet. I realized we should go to the hospital.

As we headed out, Mel Tooley, who had dug his hands

in his trouser pockets, passed a remark to the man guarding Walter.

"I don't think this is going to do much for his handicap."

AFTERWARDS

TODAY I SIT AS A JUDGE OF THE APPEL-
late Court. As the stink of scandal spread through the Kindle County courts, the Democratic Farmers & Union Party
grew desperate to recruit judicial candidates whose independence was not open to doubt. In another example of
life's ability to elude expectations, my role in Petros had
come to be widely viewed as an emblem of my fortitude.
I was just the person they needed. I was elected to a ten-
year term and took the oath of office with my father's Bible
in my hand.

In all, six judges, nine lawyers, and a dozen sheriff's
deputies and court clerks were convicted in connection with
Project Petros. The ricochet effect that Stan had hoped for
from the start—the first cooperator implicating a second
who turned on a third—more or less occurred. Skolnick
and Gillian Sullivan and a judge who had moved on to the
Felony Division all pled guilty and talked. Sherman
Crowthers baffled the government bravely through trial,
only to succumb after two years in the penitentiary. In his

orange jumpsuit, forty pounds thinner and unable to shake the cough left by one of several bouts of pneumonia, Sherm made a sad sight. He barely raised his eyes above the rail on the witness stand as he implicated two of the judges from the Felony Division to whom he'd passed money years before. He seemed most humiliated by the sheer collapse of his own bravado.

Despite these successes, Stan returned to San Diego. He was following his own advice, having shot at the king and missed. Brendan Tuohey was never convicted, nor even implicated in any public testimony. Despite a few murmured cavils, he succeeded old Judge Mumphrey as Chief of the Kindle County Superior Court a few months after Robbie was killed, inheriting administrative power over every other judge and courtroom. He retired a little more than a year ago. His home in Palm Beach was big enough to cause him to remark often on his extraordinary success in the bull market, but he died in his first month there, as the result of a drunken boating accident in which he crashed headlong into a pier at night.

The week after Robbie was killed, Stan Sennett had come to see me. He wanted to know what Robbie had done with the tape. He pleaded for almost an hour. He did not understand how I could allow Robbie's death to remain unpunished, or how I could willfully leave a monster like Tuohey at large. Robbie's killing was grisly and inflammatory enough that, with the videotape, Stan might yet have been able to convince a jury to convict Brendan Tuohey for conspiracy to murder a federal witness. Whether there was a factual basis to the charge was another matter. It's possible that Tuohey, by way of his usual sinister indirection, incited Walter to what he did. But Wunsch, who died at the Federal Penitentiary Hospital in Rochester, Minnesota, long before any case could come to trial, maintained he'd been acting on behalf of no one but himself.

McManis, who interviewed him several times, told me that to the end Walter remained acid and unrepentant.

After lengthy consultations with Stern in his role as attorney for Robbie's executor, Morton Dinnerstein, we turned the cassette over to Judge Winchell. Notified by the court, Mel Tooley appeared for Tuohey and, as I'd predicted, prevailed on a motion to suppress the tape. The best truth the law could make of the murky circumstances was that Robbie had never consented to the recording, which was, accordingly, unlawful.

Mort has survived the years with his role in all of this untold, but his grief, the most visible of anyone's at the extraordinary double funeral the following Sunday, seemed to break him irreparably. He left both the practice of law and, in time, Kindle County, after his younger son, Max, graduated from high school.

There were happier trails. McManis finished twenty-five years with the FBI and moved to San Jose, California. He passed the bar there and, inspired in part by his experiences in Petros, began trying lawsuits at the age of fifty-two. I hear from mutual acquaintances that juries find his even demeanor soothing.

Evon remained for several years in Kindle County, testifying in half a dozen of the Petros cases, and eventually becoming supervisor of the surveillance squad. Two years ago, she moved back to the West with a friend, a woman, who couldn't forgo a glorious job opportunity. By then Evon and I had revisited the events reported here over many evenings. She never discussed investigative details safeguarded by Bureau regulations, but her candor about herself was remarkable, and I have always felt it was offered in some fashion as a memorial to Robbie.

Despite her willingness to reprise remarkably intimate matters with me, Evon has never shared precisely what occurred after we left the hospital the day Robbie was murdered. Yet I've imagined it in the same detail as so much else I've described but never witnessed. Those were probably the most disoriented hours of my life. I felt as if nature had been reversed, as if my lungs and heart and nerves hung outside my body. What had happened was not unimaginable but, in fact, something that seemed confined only to the realm of the imaginary. Confronting it, I lost all sense of boundaries.

But Evon, who'd always experienced a special clarity in urgent moments, was sure about the tasks at hand. She must have returned to Robbie's, since for the time being she had no other place to stay, and showered very quickly, before she dismissed Elba so she could speak to Rainey alone. She applied the laser mount over Rainey's eye in order to allow Lorraine to operate the voice synthesizer, but Rainey, with no small effort, requested it be removed. With the pace of her breathing, she could not focus or move the cursor reliably, and she preferred to see who was talking to her.

In the Feavers' bedroom there was a mortar and pestle, used to grind up Rainey's medications so they could be ingested, and in plain sight of Lorraine, Evon retrieved the tablets Robbie had mentioned last night and began pulverizing them. She chatted to Rainey all the while, telling her several endearing stories about Robbie: the way he joshed with Leo, his blind cousin, in the courthouse, or cried when he first met his clients.

"Quite a boy," she told Rainey. "Quite a boy." She mixed the powder in water, as Robbie'd said he'd do, and then, after using an alligator clip to clamp the line to the feeding tube in Rainey's stomach, Evon poured the solution into the clear plastic bag on top of the IV stand.

"Now, Rainey," she went on, "you see what I'm fixin here. And you might wonder why it's me, but in the end, it turns out Robbie can't do this himself. You have to forgive him. You've forgiven him a lot of things in this life and you'll have to forgive him this one, too. There's a whole lot of weakness in the man, you just can't get around that, you have to take the hide with the fur, but that's the fella. And he is just never gonna be able to do this, Rainey. Not this part. That's the bald unchanging truth. So I'm here. Rather not be, naturally. But I'm here. And I'm easy with it. You know how it is with him, Lorraine. Sometimes you're even glad to be able to do what he needs.

"But once you get on your way, he'll be right here with you. I promise you that. He's gonna come right in and take hold of your hand as you're falling asleep. He's gonna be tellin a hundred funny stories about some of the great things you've done together and sayin a few prayers. You're gonna feel him right with you. Right here." Evon directed herself to Rainey's remarkable amethyst-colored eyes, where her soul still shone unimpaired. She felt Robbie himself could not have lied more convincingly; indeed, she felt, as he'd feel, that she was not lying at all. Evon had pulled up a chair beside the bed and stroked Rainey's hand, bruised from the injections and infiltrating IVs, the muscles so wasted they felt almost liquid within the skin. She went on with what she had to say, as Lorraine struggled for breath under the fogged plastic of the oxygen mask.

"Now this, me being here and everything, this may be a little quick. And if it is, I can come back tomorrow. Or the day after. Or whenever. Or never. Because maybe right now, as you, you know, as you face it, I guess, maybe you might very well feel that, after all, this isn't what you want to do. Everybody will still be here for you. We'll have that doc here, we'll have that vent going in no time, no time at all. Now, if you're ready, then I'm here with you, and if you're not, that's just fine, I'm here with you, too. But I need you to tell me. If you're ready, if this is what you want, then you have to tell me. I'm gonna count to three.

And after I get to three I want you to blink your eyes very slowly, if you want this to go ahead, if this is your time. Squeeze em shut for a three count, you know, one-one-thousand, two-one-thousand, three-one-thousand, and then open them again, and that means for me to go on. Unless you do that, nothin's gonna happen except me gettin Elba in here to set up a new IV. But otherwise, you have to blink. Blink to say this is what you want. All right? You ready now? I'm going to start."

She blinked.

AUTHOR'S NOTE

courage, honesty, and eloquence of their responses. Of them all—Martin Blank, now deceased, of Mundelein, Illinois; Arturo Bolivar of San Juan, Puerto Rico; Jim Compton of Bethany, Oklahoma; Tom Ellestad of Santa Rosa, California; Ted Heine of Waverly, Iowa; David Jayne of Circle Rex, Georgia; Eugene Schlebecker of Indianapolis; Philip B. Simmons of Center Sandwich, New Hampshire; and Judy Wilson of Stamford, Connecticut—I will remain forever in awe. That is doubly so of my faithful correspondent Dale S. O'Reilly of Philadelphia, an articulate advocate and a spirited example of the vitality, wit, and imagination that survive this disease.

I have had such openhearted support and encouragement from those affected by ALS that it would sadden me enormously if any part of this novel, especially its conclusion, were regarded as disrespectful of them. More than 90 percent of end-stage ALS patients choose not to accept ventilation, but I cannot imagine a decision more personal or one which, no matter how resolved, requires greater bravery. To the very end, ALS deserves its grim nickname as the Cruelest Disease.

Again and again, I was told that ALS obeys no rules. Nonetheless, I am sure there are inaccuracies in my portrayal, just as there are likely to be in other parts of the book that depend on technical information. For all such errors I bear sole responsibility.

—S.T.

Jersey; Professor Lanny J. Haverkamp, Ph.D., of the Department of Neurology at Baylor College of Medicine in Houston; and Lewis Rowland, M.D., of the Neurological Institute of Columbia-Presbyterian Medical Center in New York. Lisa Krivickas, M.D., daughter of an ALS patient and a member of the Department of Physical Medicine and Rehabilitation at Spaulding Rehabilitation Hospital, Boston, and Harvard Medical School; Simon Whitney, M.D., of Stanford University; and Matti Jokelainen, M.D., of Central Hospital Lahti, Finland, also provided generous responses to questions.

Two speech pathologists, Kirsti Peak-Oliveira of Children's Hospital in Boston and Iris Fishman, Executive Director of CINI (Communication Independence for the Neurologically Impaired), helped me learn about voice augmentation devices. If I have incorrectly attributed later innovations to 1993, that is the result of a novelist's liberties and not any misinformation from them.

Three professionals with experience in nursing those with ALS—Peary Brown, R.N., of Jonesboro, Maine; Meraida Polak, R.N., Neuromuscular Nurse Clinician at the Department of Neurology at Emory University; and Ovid Jones—shared poignant reflections.

Alisa Brownlee of the ALS Association's Greater Philadelphia Chapter and Claire Owen, Patient Service Coordinator of Les Turner ALS Foundation near Chicago, both helped guide me to sources of information about the disease.

Nothing, however, was more moving to me or of greater importance than the communications I received from those who live with ALS. Family members—Kathy Arnette of Fenton, Missouri; Linda Saran of Lake Zurich, Illinois; and Sherry Stampler of Weston, Florida—offered loving and unflinching accounts of the daily accommodations ALS requires. Those afflicted simply broke my heart with the must also acknowledge the characteristically incisive suggestions of my agents, Gail Hochman and Marianne Merola, and the impeccable guidance of my editor, Jon Galassi, as well as several other persons at Farrar, Straus—Bailey Foster, Elaine Chubb, and Lorin Stein—who made important contributions to the editing process. And of course I have relied at every point, as I have for nearly thirty years now, on the wisdom and judgment of my foremost sounding board, Annette Turow.

For technical expertise about firearms, I went to the ultimate informed source, my former trial partner, and blood brother for life, Jeremy Margolis, Commander of the World Police. Two friends in the FBI, Kevin Deery of Charlotte, N.C., and Gayle H. Jacobs of the Los Angeles Division, helped with details of Bureau life.

I would also like to thank Al Smith, a Mercedes salesman in Northbrook, Illinois, who continued providing information to me about the 1993 Mercedes S-class sedans, long after it became clear I was never going to buy one.

Finally, I owe my greatest debt to the community of persons afflicted with and concerned about ALS. The cruelty of this disease cannot be overstated, but the intense support that PALS, their families, their doctors, and other caregivers provide to one another is inspirational. An ALS patient, Doug Jacobson, maintains a remarkably informative Web site (which I reached through www.phoenix.net/~jacobson) where I began my research. Patients, physicians, nurses, family members, speech pathologists, and social workers were extraordinarily frank in responding to my inquiries, no matter how ill informed or prying my questions were. Three neurological experts answered repeated queries and directed me to resource material: Jerry Belsh, M.D., Director of the Neuromuscular and ALS Center at the Robert Wood Johnson Medical School of the University of Medicine and Dentistry in New

I TOOK ADVANTAGE OF THE PATIENCE AND knowledge of many persons in writing this book. I am indebted to all of them.

Several Chicago tort lawyers—none of them bearing the remotest resemblance to Robbie—took the time to reflect with me about their practices. Mike Mullen provided an initial primer. Jordan Margolis spent hours with me; his humor and candor were of immense help. I was greatly informed, too, by the reflections and stories of Howard Rigsby, who also read and commented on a draft of this manuscript, a kindness also generously provided by Julian Solotorovsky.

There were several other persons I depended upon for frank comments about earlier drafts—Jennifer Arra, Mark Barry, Arnold Kanter, Carol Kanter, and James McManus (the wonderful novelist and poet, unrelated, even in jest, to the similarly named character) all went over the manuscript scrupulously. Rachel Turow not only read but doubled for several weeks as a premier research assistant. I